JOSS *and* GOLD

JOSS *and* GOLD

Shirley Geok-lin Lim

Afterword by Leong Liew Geok

THE FEMINIST PRESS
AT THE CITY UNIVERSITY OF NEW YORK

Published by The Feminist Press at The City University of New York
365 Fifth Avenue, New York, New York 10016
feministpress.org

Library of Congress Cataloging-in-Publication Data

Lim, Shirley.
   Joss and gold / Shirley Geok-lin Lim.
      p. cm.
      ISBN: 978-1-55861-401-7
      1. Americans—Malaysia—Fiction. 2. Chinese—Malaysia—Fiction.
      3. Women—Malaysia—Fiction. I. 4. Kuala Lumpur (Malaysia)—Fiction.
      Title.

    PS3562.I459 J6 2001
    813'.54—dc21   00-069145
                                              CIP

This publication is made possible, in part, with public funds from the
National Endowment for the Arts and the New York State Council
on the Arts, a State Agency. The Feminist Press would also like to thank
Mariam K. Chamberlain, Helene D. Goldfarb, Florence Howe,
Joanne Markell, and Genevieve Vaughan for their generosity in sup-
porting this publication.

Text design and composition by Dayna Navaro.

Printed on acid-free paper by Transcontinental Printing in Canada.

06 05 04 03 02 01   6 5 4 3 2 1

NATIONAL
ENDOWMENT
FOR THE ARTS   NYSCA

To Charles Bazerman, as always, with gratitude

ACKNOWLEDGMENTS

~

My thanks to Florence Howe, Jean Casella, Amanda Hamlin, Dayna Navaro, and Lisa London of The Feminist Press, to Shirley Hew and Karen Kwek of TimesMedia, and to Leong Liew Geok, Jenny Wang, Abdul Majid, and my colleagues at the University of California, Santa Barbara, and at the University of Hong Kong for their love and support.

CONTENTS

~

Book One

CROSSING

~

KUALA LUMPUR/PETALING JAYA

1968–1969

One

Li An was rushing to get to her second class on time. A new tutor, she was timid with her students, arts freshies just arrived at the university in June. The big dark Ceylonese student, Gomez, had looked at her during the first meeting as if to say he didn't believe she understood Keats's "Ode on Melancholy" as well as he did. His superior stare had made her doubt her decision to begin the year with the poem, considering there were easier passages in the practical criticism collection every first-year student had to read. She had selected the "Ode on Melancholy" on impulse, although she had presented it to the class with an air that suggested she had carefully planned to teach it. That was her first mistake, and being late now was her second.

Henry had taken the car early. He was always up early and in his biology lab by 7 A.M. She had insisted on keeping her motorbike after they married. The 125 cc Honda couldn't keep up with the Norton and Suzuki motorbikes and speeding taxis on the Federal Highway, but it carried her fast enough, with lots of wind in her face.

Six students were waiting for her in the tiny seminar room—four girls, Gomez, and a pale Chinese boy who had made the wrong selection in courses. Wong, inarticulate, giggled nervously when he didn't understand something, but when she spoke to him about changing to a different subject, he refused. He had heard the geography lecturers were notorious for failing their students, and he hoped she would be easier on him.

It wasn't more than a few minutes after the hour, but the students looked at her reproachfully, as if she had stolen something from them. This morning she had prepared a prose passage from D. H. Lawrence's *Sons and Lovers*, and she read it aloud, relishing the overflow of sibilants like spiced chickpeas in her mouth. When the students ventured no comments, she spoke with increasing recklessness, ignoring the giggles from the corner and Gomez's glare: "You see, Lawrence suggests that physical attraction, sex, is a powerful force."

The Chinese girls lowered their eyelids. Pretty Eurasian Sally listened intently, and Mina, the Malay student whose father worked in the Ministry of Agriculture, who said she wanted to be an actress, and who Li An knew admired her, remained silent, seemingly unconvinced.

When the hour was over, Li An sat in the empty room, unable to move. Was this struggle of English words against unyielding minds what she wanted?

Only last year she had been cramming for the exams and couldn't have enough of English literature. The library was crowded with students—a hundred seemed to be waiting on line at the reserved books counter—and so cold with air-conditioning that everyone wore sweaters and cardigans. She sat upstairs, reading old copies of *Scrutiny* and copying fine phrases by F. R. Leavis, occasionally tearing off her sweater and running outside in the blazing sun to the back of the faculty lounge, where she bought sizzling flaky curry puffs and smoked two cigarettes in a row. All the English lecturers seemed glamorous and witty, even portly ones like Mr. Mason, and Jane Austen's novels dazzled her with social comedy that unfailingly ended in civilized marriage.

Henry was very kind to her that year. One afternoon in the library she fainted from lack of sleep and food and too much reading, and he offered her a ride back to the residential hall in his car. That evening he visited her with jars of Brand's Essence of Chicken in their distinctive green boxes and a bottle of eau de cologne. He was a chemistry graduate student whose father owned rubber estates, a brick factory in Segamat, a lorry transport company, and blocks of housing estates in various towns, including a few in Petaling Jaya. Henry, the eldest son, was living with his father's second wife in Kuala Lumpur while he was studying at the university.

"You can't be serious!" Gina said, when Li An began seeing Henry. "He's such a China-type! What can see in him, lah?"

"Plenty of money, man," Ellen mocked. "Now no more hawker food, only air-con coffee shops."

"Henry, oh Henry, buy me diamond ring, big like pigeon egg," Gina yodeled unbelievingly.

They pummeled each other, hooting and laughing.

Of course Li An wasn't serious! She was wild, smoked a pack of cigarettes a day, spent the rest of her small scholarship funds on petrol for her secondhand Honda, and hardly ever washed her three pairs of Levi's.

She brooded on Henry's love in between studying for finals. It was like being on two different planets.

In the library there was her body's silence—a silence that was filled by the conversation she was listening to intently, in a world of insidiously overpowering words. To be an English student was the most enviable position in the world! Everyone should be jealous of me, she thought.

Outside the library she swung her dirty blue-jeaned leg over the Honda and turned the throttle till it roared, grinning at her Indian friends, Raja, Maniam, and Paroo. A swaggering teddy boy, she rode her bike bent over the handlebars. The Indian students made a space for her in the lecture halls whenever she rushed in late, having sped her motorbike all over Kuala Lumpur and Petaling Jaya.

But later, in Henry's white Mercedes, on her way to dinner at his second mother's house, she thought of his father with fear. Mr. Yeh, a short thick man in his late forties, spoke Hokkien with a loud brutal voice. He wore sleeveless undershirts and transparent tetralyne shirts that didn't conceal the powerful rolls of muscle in his chest. His hair was cropped short like a Hailam butcher, and if you didn't know who he was, you could easily mistake him for one. She had seen butchers just like him, standing behind blood-splattered wooden

5

trestles in the wet markets, hair bristling under their bloodied singlets, cleavers in massive hands, looking as meaty as the unskinned haunches of pork hanging on giant hooks beside them. A rich odor surrounded them, the fragrance of lard cakes, and she imagined them like impassive murderers before their execution.

Second Mrs. Yeh was dressed in an expensive lace blouse and London-imported skirt. She studied Li An carefully.

"Hello, Auntie," Li An said. She wriggled her toes in the worn Bata sandals and hoped the stain from the afternoon's curry puff wouldn't show on her jeans.

Second Mrs. Yeh, she suspected, could probably see right through her cotton T-shirt to the discolored bra straps. Auntie had those peculiar women's eyes that could detect immediately where a fingernail had cracked and not been filed. Whenever she looked at Li An, her glance stayed on the frayed thread, on the loose button.

Auntie was very different from Li An's mother. Li An's father had died when she was three, and her mother had remarried a year later. Then, beset by baby after baby, she had never had time, it seemed to Li An, to look at her. Li An's stepfather, Han Si-Chun, a rubber trader who spent many weeks each year traveling to plantations in the interior, had commanded every atom of her mother's body ever since—in childbearing, housecare, cooking, and dutifulness to his family, his loud bossy sisters and infirm yet ever-present parents. No one ever talked about her father, whom, Li An concluded, was supposed never to have lived if her mother was to prove a good wife to her second husband. Her older brother escaped to Sarawak when he was seventeen and seldom wrote. In her turn, with a scholarship to the university in Kuala Lumpur, she had fled Penang and a home more pathetic than an orphanage, she told herself. In an orphanage at least one could feel sorry for one's life. Her mother had asked for no pity, and all Li An's British children's books forbade self-pity and imagined adventure instead—flight, exploration, conquest. She could find no sentiment in her childhood.

So it surprised her that she found Auntie's judgment important, indeed, longed for her approval. Auntie, who

held her queenly head high, seemed quite pleased that Henry
had found a common modern college girl like her.

People like Second Mrs. Yeh, she thought, didn't need books.
Their lives were straightforwardly one-way. All their moments
were filled, but they never had to rush, for they had already
arrived. For them, life was settled and smooth.

Such women saw details. Details were important for them.
Auntie told Li An how she had shopped for blankets with exactly the correct peach shade to match her sheets and bedroom curtains and walls. She showed her the blankets while
they were still in their clear plastic covers.

"How lovely!" Li An patted the plastic, hiding her impatience.

Pleased, Auntie showed off the reddish brown jadeite
carving of the goddess of mercy, Kuan Yin, that she had
bought in Hong Kong last month. "Very good bargain," she
said in her pleasant slow voice, stroking the stony flow of hair
on the Kuan Yin.

Li An tried to memorize the jadeite's translucent veins, its
gold color pouring through polished brown and red streaks like
running fire. One day, she thought, when she became an older,
confident woman like Second Mrs. Yeh, she might be examined on how much she knew of the world of stones and
things, and this was her first lesson.

They ate giant black mushrooms steeped in wine, cold
abalone, paper-wrapped chicken, bok choy fried with prawns,
curried pork. Li An took small helpings, but still her jeans
grew uncomfortably tight. Did Henry eat like this every
evening? The food was delicious, but too much of it and
it became hateful, the tastes clashing in an indigestible
mass.

Auntie gave orders to the servants who carried the dishes in, Mr. Yeh silently ate several large servings of meat and
vegetables, and Henry talked about Professor Forster's experiments with mimosas.

"You know, whenever you touch them, the leaves close up?
Forster is studying where the sense of touch is located
in the cells and measuring the degree of sensitivity—why
the mimosa doesn't close when the wind blows on it but

reacts to human breath. If there's a trigger threshold, where the trigger is encoded genetically."

Henry spoke with concentration, paying no attention to the food and eating whatever Auntie put on his plate.

"I'm thinking of switching to biochemistry. Forster is a geneticist, and he wants me to make the move."

"Why, it's almost like poetry," Li An said. "That's the touch-me-not, isn't it? I prefer the name to mimosa. Mimosa sounds like a European flower, alien. We played with touch-me-nots for hours when we were kids." She remembered the delicate branching foliage with its pink-purple globular flowers. Common weeds, they grew thick with painful prickly thorns over the wasteland by her home in Penang.

"I'm not sure what poetry is." Henry smiled with a slight embarrassment. "But Forster's work is exciting. Biogenetics is the real science of life. All the exciting discoveries are waiting to be made there."

He didn't understand the fuss Li An made over words. "Words are more a bother than anything else," he explained. "They create problems for people like me who can't use them very well, and they make problems for people like you who use them too well."

He didn't tell her he knew most people found him boring because he was shy and couldn't express his feelings, and they thought her wild because she was always expressing her feelings. He thought he understood her very well. She was a shy girl who used words to cover up her insecurity in the way he used silence to disguise his shyness.

When he had picked her up off the library floor where she had fainted, she had seemed an undernourished parcel of fragile bones. But when he came by the residential hall that evening, she had recovered and become brash and talkative. Full of ideas, spilling long sentences, she dazzled him. He suspected she was putting on an act, but she entertained him even if he didn't take her talk seriously.

She was being entertaining again tonight, talking on the similarities between their two courses of study. "The real science of life! That's exactly how I see literature!"

Henry marveled that Li An was so enthusiastic, running after every little bit of excitement.

"What literature does is connect things, even the most un-likely things. Like Donne and the Metaphysical poets. He con-nected sex with a flea bite, love with a compass. That's what we have to do in our lives, connect with others."

Henry glanced at his father. Although Ah Pah generally spoke only Hokkien and Malay, he understood English and could speak it if necessary. Henry wasn't sure what Ah Pah would make of her patter, but he wished she hadn't mentioned sex. Old-fashioned Chinese couldn't be expected to under-stand that kind of talk.

"Do you want some fruit?" Second Mother interrupted. "We have Australian plums."

He looked at his Second Mother to observe her expression. She was absorbed in moving the dishes to the side of the table.

Li An shook her head. "No, thank you, Auntie, I'm full already. It was a very nice dinner."

Relieved, Henry returned to his mushrooms. Ah Pah, he knew, never bothered with family affairs. People expected his father to demand certain responsibilities of him, the eldest son, but that had never been the case. He had done well in school, and Ah Pah had allowed him to proceed in his stud-ies without once talking to him about his plans for the future. His brothers were still in high school, and Mark, who appeared to like business, was expected to work in one of his father's companies.

Henry was interested only in science. From an early age he had been fascinated by the properties of materials, how mat-ter changed properties when combined with other elements, how reactions could be measured and predicted so that the entire world might be seen as a matter of measurements and reactions. One needed only to observe phenomena careful-ly to understand and predict how nature worked. Second Mother's calm self-absorption predicted that Ah Pah would find Li An acceptable.

None of his friends talked to him about Li An. They were all pushing to finish their master's and win a fellowship to some university in Europe or America. Many were plan-ning to marry before continuing; it would be too difficult being alone in a strange country, they confided. Their girlfriends were nurses or elementary school teachers who cooked well and smiled a lot.

He had not been interested in a girl before. He had been too shy, and the kinds of girls who went out with the science students were shy plain ducks also, so he had never tried. Li An, however, was different. She talked too much and too fast, which embarrassed him. She liked roaming on her motorbike like a boy. Her tight jeans showed her thighs and calves, and her smoking made her conspicuous in a crowd. Men picked her out immediately as someone they could tease. She was like a Western girl—bold, loud, and unconcerned about her reputation.

He liked her bright round face that buzzed with ideas, but he wanted to marry her because her body drove him crazy. In the evenings when he kissed her good night, with her breath in his mouth, he wanted to swallow her. In her men's cloth-ing, she was still soft and curved. He trembled each time he held her, the longing was so bad.

That night he drove to Lake Gardens and parked under the tall African tulip trees. He switched off the car lights, and they were silent in the fuzzy darkness for a long time, breathing the moist cool air.

Backed up in her corner, Li An looked out of the car window as the shadows slowly yielded to her sight. The faint glow from a sky seeded with stars and a quarter moon showed neatly scythed fields and tall reeds concealing dim puddles.

He felt a painful pressure in his upper chest and twisted his body to evade it. He resented that she could sit so near and seem indifferent, her profile hidden in a reflectiveness that he suspected didn't include him.

This must be what a man feels when he is in love, he thought, this jealous stab in the chest, this desire to take, to penetrate the other and leave her no space for anything but himself. His voice quivered as he spoke. "What will you do after the exams?"

Li An laughed. "Do?" She seemed to be mocking him. "It depends on the results. If I do well, I'll get a scholarship and go to America."

"America? Why America?" He choked as he repeated the

word. He had not thought she would leave—leave Kuala Lumpur, leave the university, leave him. But then, they had never talked about her plans.

"Why not America? Isn't that where everything is happening? It's so boring here. Nothing ever changes. No one is doing anything, no one is writing poetry, no one is painting, no one is singing, no one is going anywhere. So why not go to America?"

"You're like a child!" He was glad that the anger filling him was easing the pain in his chest. Yes, she was childish, playing at dressing up like a boy when she was already a woman, whining about boredom and roving on a motorbike as if she could chase it away.

"All kinds of things are happening here. This is the time for us to assert ourselves. We are going to be the most important people in the country because we are the people with brains. Malaysia has just become a nation. It's only eleven years since independence, so how can you expect there to be poetry or art yet? It's like science. You have to work every day with your experiments, and then someday you will discover that truth which no one else has found. Malaysia is like an experiment. Going to America is a selfish way of acting."

She had never thought of her life as something belonging to a group, rather than to herself. It was the first time she'd seen Henry angry. He was usually objective and tolerant, like a kind teacher.

"You really believe something is happening here?"

"Happening? Why are you always asking for something to happen? Perhaps when it does you may not like it after all!"

"But nothing ever changes here!" she cried out. "Everybody seems so dull. The girls only talk about boys and worry about their hair and clothes, and the lecturers drone on and on. I don't want to spend my life teaching in some small town, like Mrs. Devi in sixth form, teaching the same history year after year, growing old and stuck in a rut."

"Am I so dull?" He could no longer bear it. His anger had disappeared, leaving his arms weak. He could not raise them to touch her.

He knew he was dull. Short and pallid with unremarkable

eyes, he was pitifully unobtrusive. Although he was successful at work, girls like Li An paid no attention to men like him.

"Please forgive me, Henry."

She put her arms around him and squeezed him as if to comfort a child. He liked the strong way she tightened the pressure around his arms.

Putting her head on his chest, she rubbed it against him. He found the gesture unnerving.

"I don't mean you. You aren't dull at all. The work you're doing on genetics is wonderful! I envy you because you have work that is important. You know where you're going and where you belong. I wish I were a man and a scientist. Then there would be a place for me here. I could be a doctor and learn to cure tropical diseases. Or I could work with tropical plants like you are doing. But all I know is English. The only thing I can do with English in Malaysia is to teach."

He couldn't think with her face so close to him. "Marry me," he said, his cheek against hers. "Marry me, and stay with me. You won't have to teach. I'll pay off your government bond, and you won't be forced to go back to your town. You don't have to work if you don't want to."

His body was shaking as if he was hurting. He closed his eyes as her breath, a warm breeze, went by his ear. His lungs grew congested with fear, and he felt in such danger he could hardly speak.

He had not meant to say it. They had known each other for only three months, since September, and he didn't approve of her. She had a reputation—not a bad one like a loose woman, but a reputation all the same—for being bold and free.

"Oh, no, Henry, you don't know how poor I am." She didn't move away from him. "I have nothing in my life. My father's dead, my mother's remarried someone who doesn't want me in his house, my brother in Sarawak has a child and no time for me. All I will have is my degree."

She dropped her arms and moved away, pressing her back to the far corner of her seat. Her voice was strong and mocking again.

He was confused. Was she saying yes or no? "I don't care. I have money." He stopped. Did it sound as if he were trying to impress her? "My grandmother left me an inheritance."

He felt ashamed even as he spoke. That wasn't what he wanted to tell her. He didn't want her to marry him for his money. "You could write, Li An. I'll let you write. You say it's time for Malaysians to write about themselves. You can't write about Malaysia in America."

He wanted to tell her he loved her, but he was too shy.

She wished he hadn't spoken. She had been having a good time looking at the curved bow of the moon and the black drooping branches, thinking that trees were more often black than green to animals that came out at night, when he had begun questioning her.

She thought she understood what Henry wanted when his body trembled, and if he insisted she might be willing. She was curious, and he would be grateful; he wouldn't hurt her.

But then he put his arms around her and put his head on her hair. He was like a little boy silently demanding her attention.

The sliced moon remained unmoving, a stationary section of an illuminated body, unreachable in space.

Like me, she thought. No one can reach me. She was terrified by the power of her isolation. Pity for herself overcame her, and she turned her head up to kiss him.

They married in March, before Li An was offered the position as tutor in the English department. Henry didn't have to pay off her government bond after all. She was still going to teach, but here at the university.

Two

Relieved Li An was marrying well, Mrs. Han made no suggestions to delay the wedding. She came to Singapore for the ceremony without her children or her husband, who had long ago stopped acknowledging his stepdaughter's existence except as an unwelcome intruder from his wife's intemperate youth. Henry's mother had decided on the festivities, a combination of traditional and modern; the most important ritual, the tea ceremony, was held in her home.

Outside the large rambling bungalow off Tanglin Road, pink oleander bushes bloomed by the entrance and a tall casuarina trailed long-needled branches along the side of the circular drive. Li An was given Henry's old bedroom, and Henry slept in his brother Mark's room. Mrs. Yeh, showing utmost respect, put Li An's mother in the large bedroom in which Mrs. Yeh's mother-in-law had once slept. After the wedding Mrs. Han was taking the train alone home to Penang, and Li An and Henry would stay at the Shangri-La Hotel for a few days before returning to their new house, which Mr. Yeh had bought for them, in Petaling Jaya near the university.

Li An was struck by how different Henry's mother was from Li An's own mother or from Second Mrs. Yeh. Although Chinese, Mrs. Yeh wore a sarong and kebaya, and chattered in Malay. Unlike Second Mrs. Yeh, she did not speak English. Her buxom body, unconstrained in a cotton chemise, gave the impression of an overstuffed pillow, while Auntie held her trim body as if it were on a tight leash. Li An's mother, belted and dowdy in a Western dress, kept to the outside of the Yeh family circle, smiling and silent.

Mrs. Yeh appeared to be looking at ten things all at the same time, as if the world were a vague blur of objects and people, and she depended on her amah for everything. Throughout the day she could be heard calling, "Amah, amah! Where's my purse? Amah, did you call for the dumplings? Have you cleaned Henry's suit? Bring me some chrysanthemum tea— I'm so tired I feel ill."

Yet she did no work that Li An could see, except to talk at the same time to everyone around her, stopping only to address someone new who might have walked into the room. Li An's mother seemed pleased to offer Mrs. Yeh an acquiescent ear, agreeing to all her suggestions in soothing sounds that could have been in any language.

The house was full of visiting aunts and cousins. Mr. Yeh, however, stayed with Auntie in a friend's house nearby. Li An was surprised to see how well First Mrs. Yeh got along with Auntie. "Sister," they greeted each other in Hokkien, and Mrs. Yeh insisted on serving drinks herself to her husband and his second wife when they came into the house.

It must be very strange, Li An thought, to have your husband a distant visitor, and to welcome his mistress—even though the Chinese called her a second wife—to your home. She studied Mrs. Yeh, expecting to find hidden jealousy and resentment, but Mrs. Yeh was offering jolly comments about the wedding to Auntie, smiling her shortsighted smile, and seeming really pleased to have everyone, including Auntie and Li An's mother, with her.

The morning of the wedding, Mrs. Yeh and her husband sat on two heavy rosewood chairs in the living room. Li An, wearing a short clinging red dress that she had found in a boutique on Orchard Road, poured tea into small porcelain cups, knelt, and served them to her new in-laws. Mr. Yeh was impassive. Only when Henry knelt and gave him the cup with two hands did he blink and nod his head.

The night before, Li An's mother had whispered to her that as she had come without her husband she did not wish to have tea served to her. But when Mrs. Yeh led her by the hand to her chair and made her sit down as Henry's new mother-in-law, she sipped the tea that Henry and Li An offered, smiling and giggling even as she protested at the respect shown. While Mrs. Yeh smiled and smiled at Li An, Henry, Mark, and Jing, her youngest son, Li An noticed Auntie standing behind the gathered guests, head erect on her squared shoulders, frowning moodily at the scene.

When the wedding party drove in Mercedes sedans to the downtown office for the civil ceremony, Li An wore the white lace gown with puffed sleeves and the tiara of white satin flowers and tulle, like a flirty veil, that Auntie had picked for her at Robinsons in Kuala Lumpur. She had taken Li An to the fitting, and had carried the gown with her to Singapore.

At the civil ceremony, Auntie stood by Mr. Yeh's side while the two younger sons accompanied Mrs. Yeh. For a moment Li An felt Second Mrs. Yeh was standing in for her mother, who had stayed behind with the guests in the confusion of hurrying to make the appointment on time. "Go, go," her mother had urged when Li An lingered to persuade her to join the Yehs for the drive to City Hall. "Go with your husband and your family."

When Li An said "I do," the strange phrase fell out of her mouth with an unexpected pang, as if she were surrendering something precious or had accepted responsibility for some lifelong task she didn't want.

Henry gave her a big grin, but she put her head down and stared at the fancy lace that gleamed like white metal in the fluorescent lighting. The gown made her look like the brides in photographs that photo studios plastered on their walls to advertise their business. The tulle tickled her forehead, and she had to restrain herself from scratching. The gown fit so tightly that the long zipper pressed against her spine like a hard rod and forced her to hold herself stiffly even when she wanted to droop and sigh.

But the mood passed. The wedding dinner, shark's fin soup, crab rolls, roast squab, and what seemed like twenty other dishes, also passed.

Li An sat with the six Yehs, herself now a Yeh, and poked at the squab that still looked like a pigeon, its delicate soy-stained wings folded under a puffed chest. The white-clothed table was littered with fragile wing bones. She couldn't make herself eat. Noisy gnashing and chewing from the forty tables, each with ten guests, shattered against her ears. She imagined she could hear a brittle crunch of teeth against the frail tendons of lovely blue-brown birds in flight.

She was wearing her straight red dress again. Gently, under the tablecloth, she rubbed her stomach to ease her nausea.

She had wanted to sit with Ellen and Gina, but of course that was impossible. A wedding was a family affair. She moved her head unobtrusively, trying to spot them.

They had been called the Three Musketeers at the university, for they had done almost everything together. When she wasn't alone, she was with Ellen and Gina. They had rooms on the same floor, called each other in the mornings for breakfast, showered in the evenings at the same time, walked at night to the library together, holding hands and joking. They separated when they had lectures, for Ellen was studying economics and Gina history. Then Henry came along.

After she told Ellen and Gina she was marrying Henry, they stopped making fun of him. A barrier had come up between them. Gina began walking back to the residence hall with Paroo, who was smitten with her. He carried her books, ignoring the university men who passed them on motor-bikes yelling, "Ho, Paroo."

For the last few months of their final year, Paroo waited in the television room each evening until Gina came downstairs. "Oh, it's you again!" she'd say. "What, you want to walk with me to the library, yah?"

Paroo, almost six feet tall, a fair-skinned Hindu Punjabi, wore a crushed look around Gina, who was only five feet tall, and he responded in the gentlest voice to her abusive humor.

"Hey, why you never talk, lah?" she demanded of him whenever Li An joined them. "Your mother make you scared of woman. You one big baby."

Among them, Gina's family was the most traditional. Her father was the principal of a Chinese school in Johore. Her mother had been active in the Kuomintang movement in China before she had come to Malaya in an arranged marriage, and Gina was the only one in her family to have an English education. All her brothers and sisters had been educated in their father's school, but to mark their new British citizenship in the Federated States, her parents had sent Gina, the youngest child, to an English-language school.

Gina had a Chinese name, Wei-hua, but called herself Gina after Gina Lollobrigida, whose movies she loved.

"I hate everything Chinese," she declared, "including tight-fitting cheongsams, greasy dim sum, kung fu movies from Hong Kong, and boring Chinese boys!"

For a time she made friends with the Malay students. "Everyone should marry Malay, because that's the future of the country," she repeated to whoever would listen.

But the Malay boys didn't care for her. She was too talkative and playful. The Malay girls shunned her, and the boys began to talk about her, which someone or other was sure to report back.

With Li An and Ellen, she showed a superior Chinese side. "We Chinese," she said. "We Chinese are brainy people. We Chinese know how to make money. We Chinese know how to respect the past. We Chinese have the oldest history in the world. We Chinese are the people making this country run."

At the same time she disliked the Chinese she met. Walking out of a shop, she fumed, "Chinese are so money-minded. It's not the British who are a country of shopkeepers; Chinese also got shopkeeper mentality."

Once, passing by a table crowded with Chinese students in the silent library, she whispered loudly, "Aiyo! China-types only good for mugging. Everything must learn by heart. Got no brains otherwise." The students stared at her, then returned to their books, not having seen her at all.

She thought their flat cheeks and noses the ugliest faces on earth, called their straight hair oily, and was repulsed by their slender build. "Chinese men got no sex appeal," she declared. "All like tapeworms. I like Technicolor men with backbone."

When Li An met Gina's father at the beginning of their second year, she found him stern and strict. "Wei-hua, carry your bags, ah!" he ordered Gina as he stood by the car with her bags still in the trunk, and then looked Li An up and down as if to check on her qualifications to be Gina's friend. "He's like a king cobra, ready to strike," she told Ellen.

After the exams Gina returned to Johore, where her father had arranged a teaching position for her at the local high school, and Paroo returned to his family in Ipoh. He had not come with Gina to Singapore, although Li An had invited him to the wedding.

Li An and Ellen couldn't see Gina living with her Chinese family in a small town full of Chinese-educated families. She had enjoyed too much freedom during the three years of university studies.

Ellen was even more Westernized than Gina. It was because Ellen was always talking of America that Li An had first begun to think she would like to go there also. "But, of course, you can afford to go," Li An said enviously. "You're rich!"

Ellen's father owned a successful stationery store and a bookshop in Kuala Lumpur, and she was the only daughter in a family of three. Much spoiled, she received a Hillman Minx in her first year at the university so she could drive the short distance home for visits during the weekends.

She had grown up reading all the comics and Western magazines that her father's bookshop carried, beginning with *Superman* and moving on to *Teen*, *Seventeen*, *True Confessions*, *Time*, and *Life*. The bookshop attracted tourists and expatriate shoppers, and Ellen spoke English with an exaggerated American accent, imitating the white people she met there.

She sometimes spoke English with what she thought was a French accent. A Frenchman had come by the bookshop a few times, trying to persuade her father to carry French newspapers like *Le Monde*. He had taught her some French phrases, and she sprinkled her jokes with these phrases whenever she was in a good mood.

"Parlez-vous français? Oui. Je t'aime toujours." Ellen ran these words through, varying the sequence every so often, like a clever parrot rewarded for showing off her words.

The Frenchman left Kuala Lumpur after a few weeks, but Ellen never forgot him. He was a hero to her, with his romantic language full of rolling consonants and seductive vowels.

But she didn't like any of the boys she met at the university, although they liked her. Big boned, with full pointy breasts, she looked more like Gina Lollobrigida than Gina did. Men usually stared at her with watering mouths. Her hips were unusually curved for a Chinese, and in jeans and an expensive American sweater she attracted even the white teachers, who usually acted as if students were a faraway mirage to whom they airmailed their lectures. Mr. Pound, who had come out of England just two years earlier, had asked a male student about Ellen, and the gossip soon went around that she could have Mr. Pound any time she wanted.

Ellen, however, preferred being with Li An and Gina. "Humph!" she'd sniff. "All these men want only one thing. They all have dirty minds."

She was not happy when Li An took up with Henry, and she became depressed when Gina and Paroo began dating.

It was Gina to whom Ellen was really close. In the first two years at the university Ellen had roomed with Gina. When Li An visited them, Ellen taught them nonsense songs she had learned from the Western tourists at the bookshop. They sang their favorite again and again, beginning softly and ending at the top of their lungs with boisterous laughter.

> Everybody hates me,
> Nobody loves me,
> Guess I'll go eat worms.
> Big fat ones and skinny little ones,
> Oh how they wriggle and squirm.
> I'll bite off their heads
> and suck out their juice
> and throw their skins away.
> Nobody knows how I can thrive
> on worms three times a day.

Each time they finished singing the song, they tickled each other under the arms and ended up wrestling on the bed.

Li An knew Ellen missed the good times, when they were three together. What, she wondered, was ahead for them now, separately?

Auntie, sitting next to her, nudged her with her elbow. "You should eat a little from each dish," she urged softly. "The family will think you don't like the dinner or that you are proud."

The waiter had already removed the squab and was slicing fillets from the large steamed snapper. Li An looked at the snapper's huge eye, turned gelatinous in the ginger wine.

Celebrating a wedding with slaughtered birds and fish is not a good omen for anyone's future, she thought rebelliously. We should have driven north to the Cameron Highlands and been married by an Anglican pastor, with only a gardener and a cook for witness. We would have had cucumber sandwiches by ourselves in front of a fire, and I would have drunk Darjeeling tea with real cream. I would have brought my copy of Wordsworth's poems and read the "Intimations" ode to Henry.

She was certain Henry had never read the poem. But would he have understood what Wordsworth meant by "splendour in the grass" and "glory in the flower"?

She remembered the actress Natalie Wood in a movie with the title *Splendor in the Grass*, which was about young love, heartbreak, and death. At her wedding the only dead things were birds and fish. She knew Henry, who found her hand on her stomach and led her up to each of the thirty-nine tables to wish their guests yam-seng, would never break her heart.

Ellen and Gina, sitting together, giggled like old times. They had paired off naturally, having traveled together in Ellen's Minx, and were sharing a room at a small hotel.

"Yam-seng, yam-seng! Drink up!" Henry's relatives, his father's associates, friends and their wives, all kinds of strangers drank to their good health and happiness.

Gina said above the shouts, "Samseng, samseng!" and Ellen waved her glass of Hennessy brandy tipsily to Gina's heretic cry of "Hooligan, hooligan!"

Three months after the wedding, Ellen called and suggested they meet for lunch to discuss how they could help Gina and Paroo.

Gina was still teaching history at the Chun Hsien High School and came up to Kuala Lumpur only during school holidays. Then she met Paroo, who would come down from Ipoh.

Gina and Paroo had become a despairing couple. Over rounds of Tiger Beer at various pubs, they complained endlessly of their families' disapproval, usually to Ellen, who lent them her flat and went to live with her parents whenever Gina came into town.

They were an unlikely romantic pair. Li An couldn't imagine what they talked about when they were alone together, except their despair. They were like a pair of lapsed believers, hating their Chinese and Punjabi communities, and clinging to each other to make up for everything they'd lost.

The Bistro was dark and frosty with air-conditioning. Li An couldn't see anyone's face at the tables, and everyone whispered like spies. The smell of fatty lamb chops and stale mustard circulated in the blowing air, providing a foreign excitement indoors, away from the afternoon's humidity and glare.

"Hss, hss, I'm here," Ellen whispered, as Li An walked between the tables and banquettes, peering at the diners while trying to avoid appearing nosy. She was already drinking a beer, and the waitress was waiting at the table before Li An could slide into her seat.

"Two San Miguels," Ellen ordered. "You want lamb chops or spring chicken?"

"They've got fried mee?"

"No fried mee," the waitress interrupted. "Only Western food here."

"Two lamb chops." Ellen didn't wait for Li An to choose. "Bring mustard."

"You shouldn't have ordered the beer for me. I'm riding the Honda today, and one beer goes right to my head."

"Don't worry, man. You don't have to finish it."

Li An knew Ellen meant she would drink her own second beer and then finish Li An's also. After graduating with a Second Lower in economics, Ellen had worked for the Federal Bank, hated the bureaucracy, joined the Overseas Chinese Bank, hated the managers—all swollen-headed men, she said—quit, was looking for another job, only not teaching, and thinking of applying to do a master's at an American university. Her father paid her bills and gave her an allowance while she was making up her mind about her future. Each time Li An met Ellen, they drank beer. Ellen would have three in a row. The beers loosened her tongue, and she talked for hours in a drawling half-American accent.

"What are we going to do about Gina and Paroo?"

"Do? What can we do?" Li An sipped the San Miguel cautiously. The waitress had left a large head of suds in the glass.

"They should either marry or separate."

"Looks like they want to get married. I can't understand why they don't just run away and do it. After all, they don't need anyone's permission."

"You know Gina is scared of her father."

"So what? Who isn't scared of her father? But this is the twentieth century. We are all Malaysians. What is this nonsense about cannot marry Indian, cannot marry Chinese? Even Malays and Chinese are marrying each other now."

The lamb chops arrived, slippery and tough. Li An struggled with her dull knife and sawed at the gray undercooked meat. Thin blood oozed under the blade.

"You've never understood Gina!" Ellen swallowed the last bit in her glass and reached for the second. "Gina's putting on an act. Actually she's insecure underneath. That's why she gets along so well with Paroo. They're both fakes and cowards. People think Paroo is tough because he's six feet tall and a Punjabi. You know, like the Punjabi guards at the Overseas Chinese Bank? But he's a softie inside. Gina tells me he cries more than she does."

Li An reached with her napkin and wiped the foam mustache off Ellen's upper lip.

"Thanks. Well, if we don't take charge of their lives, they are really going to be ruined."

"I don't see how they are being ruined. Besides, no one can take charge of anyone else's life."

"Li An, you are one of the most selfish people I've ever met." Ellen chewed a piece of lamb fat. "Just because you are happily married to a rich husband you've forgotten your friends. Now you're an important English tutor, going to be an important English professor, all your old girlfriends are out of the window."

Ellen had said this so often Li An didn't mind her.

"Look, why don't we arrange a civil wedding for them the next time they come to Kuala Lumpur? Then their families can't interfere anymore. Paroo and Gina can find jobs teaching here, and you can take care of them as much as you wish."

In the semi-darkness she could see Ellen grin.

"You are so naive," she said, drawing out the last word. "First, they have to sign to request the marriage. Second, they are bonded and can't just leave their jobs. And third, they are afraid their families will reject them."

"Oh, I can't stand this weakness!" Li An thrust her arms out so violently that she spilled some beer. "Who cares about families? If they love each other, what does it matter what the parents say? Sometimes I think Gina enjoys making a fuss. She wouldn't marry Paroo even if she could. He's an excuse for her not to make a decision about her life. He's a spineless jellyfish, and she's using him for her own crazy reasons. She's determined to make her life miserable, and she's having a good time crying and carrying on with him."

She knew she was talking too loudly. Even as she spoke she was sorry for speaking as she did.

The last time Gina and Paroo had come to Kuala Lumpur for a weekend, they had spent more time with Ellen and Li An than alone.

"My mother, she cries every day. She says she is already arranging a marriage for me with a young college lady from New Delhi, her uncle's friend's daughter. She is every day showing me her picture, although she says I shouldn't look because it's like taking the young lady's virtue away. Quite pretty girl. But how to marry a stranger?" Paroo crossed his ankles, appearing like the man of the house in bare feet and lounging on Ellen's new rattan rocker.

"Hell, stranger!" Gina sat cross-legged on the floor beside him. "Your mother thinks she's Indian, so cannot be stranger. Not like me, Chinese girl. How to make me part of her family, eh?"

Listening, Li An could see how someone might consider it ludicrous for Gina and Paroo to marry. She saw Paroo at home with a pretty dark Hindu wife in a green-and-red sari carrying a solemn-eyed child in her arms. The house would smell of turmeric and sandalwood, and Ganesha would be smiling by an altar in the corner of a neat living room, elephant's trunk upraised for Deepavali visitors. This should be Paroo's future, Li An thought.

And Gina? Gina should never marry. She was too difficult, too unhappy, too confused.

No clear picture of Gina's future came to Li An, only rooms visited, like Ellen's, with fashionable glass-topped coffee tables and beer glasses leaving wet rings on them. No vision of a Chinese marriage came with Gina, only single women joshing each other, walking through shops and restaurants in large cities, heads together companionably like flocks of blue and gray pigeons pecking at life together.

Perhaps this was because she couldn't imagine Gina as other than what she had been when they were a trio. She knew it was unfair to dismiss Paroo so lightly. After all, she had married Henry, and she had changed. Paroo must have changed Gina in some way also.

•

"Ho, so you agree that Paroo is useless?"

What was Ellen smiling at, Li An wondered resentfully.

"That's two of us," Ellen continued. "But Gina thinks she can't live without him. She writes these miserable letters, ten pages long, about how she loves his Punjabi soul, how he is so pure, how he even smells different from Chinese men, like a manly flower. Can you imagine that, a manly flower?"

For a moment they hooted as in the old days, but the feeling of abysmal hilarity quickly vanished.

"She doesn't know how her letters hurt me." Ellen coughed to clear her throat. "Every day, ten long bloody pages, going on and on about her misery and Paroo's pure love."

"Why don't you just not read them?"

"Oh no, there may be something else in them. Sometimes she remembers me—and you—and then she does tell me a bit about herself in Johore."

Li An felt hopeless. It all seemed rather boring—Ellen's intense interest in Gina, Gina's unhappy affair with Paroo. It reminded her of her tutorials, her intense unhappy interest in language, and the discussions that went on and on, saying the same thing in different ways while the secret of it all, the mystery of the life behind the words, was never talked about. "Well, then, what do you suggest?"

"Gina should marry Paroo. Then she can decide whether that's what she really wants." Ellen finished the second beer.

Li An looked at her watch. She had promised herself she would do some reading at the library in the afternoon. Besides, she wanted Ellen to leave before she could order another beer. "Here, have mine," she said, pushing her half-filled glass over. "You know that's not the way to do things. You decide whether you want to marry first, before you marry."

"But you didn't do that," Ellen said, her face in the glass. "You married without deciding."

"Oh, shut up!" She thought for the thousandth time that Ellen should have taken English. Ellen's fascination with European accents, her admiration for everything Western, and her quickness of mind would have made her as good an English student as herself.

"I made the right choice, didn't I? Even if I didn't make it. Henry's a wonderful husband. What do you know about men, anyway? You don't even like them. I bet you'll remain a virgin all your life."

"Since when does losing your virginity make you a bigger expert on men? Does making a hole in the earth make you a farmer?"

Li An laughed. It was impossible to hide anything from Ellen. Ellen saw with a witch's eye. Li An didn't mind marriage, it was only the boredom she minded—but Ellen insisted on seeing that Henry was the reason for her boredom.

If it wasn't for Henry, Li An didn't know what she would do. Probably drink like Ellen, or get messed up in some miserable affair like Gina. It was only the first month of tutoring at the university, and already she was tired of the routine.

Threading...

The next tutorial meeting was better. She had picked a
George Herbert poem.

> Sweet day, so cool, so calm, so bright,
> The bridall of the earth and skie,
> The dew shall weep thy fall tonight,
> For thou must die, . . .

This time every student approved of her choice. Something
about death appealed to Sally, Gomez, Mina, the Chinese girls,
and Wong. They were all enthusiastic about the sentiment
of making something spiritual out of death, something
stronger than wood or sweets, something that lasted longer
than a human life. She left the seminar room thinking perhaps it wasn't so terrible to be an English teacher if she
could get everyone to agree on one beautiful poem.

Ellen was trying a new job as an assistant manager at the
Cold Storage supermarket and had not called her in five days.
It was good to be by herself for a while, Li An thought,
smiling as she entered the faculty lounge to buy a pack of cigarettes. She noticed the tall American because he was also
looking for cigarettes.

"You teach here?" he asked. "Can you ask him if he has any
filters?"

She gave Ratnam an amused smile. "Ratnam understands

English. He's just too embarrassed to speak it to you. Dia nak rokok filter," she said to Ratnam, who never minded her bad Malay.

Ratnam ducked his head under the counter to check his cigarette store.

"I'm American," the stranger said, as if it explained his ignorance. "Chester Brookfield." He stuck out his hand.

It was hairy and sweaty. She was sure it wasn't clean.

She shook it delicately, still reticent around white people—unlike Ellen, who had seen them steal books and cheat on bills. The only white people Li An had met were British teachers and lecturers, and she associated whites chiefly with governors and other colonial officials, and with the great Romantic poets and novelists about whom F. R. Leavis wrote. Every white person in the university seemed to be superior and aloof, and she avoided the lecturers when she could.

Chester was different, she supposed, because he was American. For one thing, he didn't have an important job. He was teaching woodworking at the Petaling Jaya Vocational High School.

Woodworking, he explained, was carpentry as an art. You made dowels, fitted joints and pegs, and didn't use screws, nails, or glues. Instead, you planed wood to make joints so tight and smooth that water would not leak out of a wooden pail, and a dresser drawer would pull in and out as if on grease.

Like poetry, she thought, but she didn't dare say it in case he disagreed.

"Lee Ann?" he said, his voice making a melodious upturn below his long pinched nose.

"No, Li An," she corrected him, beating out the syllables in a spondee.

But he couldn't get it right. "Lee Ann, okay?"

His voice seemed naturally lazy, his words slid one into the other like a smooth ride, and she relaxed and smiled, "Okay."

Chester was taking Malay lessons at the university after teaching his morning woodworking classes. His classes at the Vocational High School had not been going well. In fact, only three students had registered for them. No one wanted to be an artisan-carpenter in Malaysia, he said exasperatedly. The three students came because they wanted to hear about America, and they spent the entire morning asking questions. "How big is America? Is it bigger than Malaysia? England?" "Where you live? What? Con-ne-ti-ket? Oh, New England? New England has Hollywood?" "How rich is America?" "Why you keep your hair long? All Americans keep long hair?"

The Malay language lessons were just beginning. He knew how to say "good morning," "thank you," and "how are you?" and he used these words as often and charmingly as he could. She saw that Chester badly wanted people to like him. He didn't have time for other Westerners, because he spent as much time as he could with Malaysians.

But he didn't keep to one group. He had Chinese friends, who soon included Henry and herself, and Indian friends like Dorisammy and Gopi, and Malay friends like his roommates, Abdullah and Samad.

Being in the Peace Corps, he didn't have much money, but that only made him seem more likable. Not that he borrowed money or asked for anything. When he and Li An started meeting for lunch, he insisted on paying for her. But he wouldn't buy newspapers or shop at stores like Robinsons because, he said, he didn't have the money.

Henry liked Chester. She had invited Chester home for dinner that afternoon after they had spent the lunch hour talking about woodworking and Malaysian attitudes toward manual labor.

"People don't build their own furniture," she told him, puzzled by his classes. "We don't repair anything. If something goes wrong with the roof? Why, Henry gets a laborer to repair it. If the door gets loose? I don't know. I suppose Henry will get a carpenter to fix it. If I need a bookcase and don't have the money to buy it? That doesn't happen. If I'm the type that needs a bookcase, I'll have the money to buy one. Otherwise I won't be reading books."

He looked at her incredulously. "Do you mean only rich people read books here?"

She thought of Second Mrs. Yeh. Rich people she had met didn't read books at all. "I mean the middle class," she replied smugly. *Middle class* sounded academic; she felt she was claiming the status of a university lecturer by saying it.

He laughed. "You can't fool me. I've been here for only four weeks, but there's no way you can convince me that the shopkeepers and restaurant managers and bank cashiers read books. That's your middle class."

She was humiliated. Listening to him she felt ignorant of her own society.

When he came for dinner, she asked Letchmi to make a Malay meal, the most Malaysian food she could serve the American newly arrived from New England. While she was checking the food in the kitchen, Chester and Henry talked about the discovery of the structure of DNA. Chester told Henry about experiments that a biochemist at Princeton was doing with protein nuclei, and Henry asked polite questions about cellular structures.

She was glad she had asked him home. She was determined to adopt him and show him that Malaysia was a modern country, not backward as he had been told during his Peace Corps training.

"What kind of literature do you teach?" Chester asked after he had stuffed himself with rendang and chili kang-kong and rice. She was surprised at how he could eat the spicy food in huge gulps without any complaints. "Perhaps I was a Malay in another life," he laughed when Henry commented on this ability. "Actually I've been eating Malay food with my roommates, and I've grown accustomed to the heat."

She showed him the practical criticism text, a mimeographed stapled collection of typed poems and passages from the sixteenth century to contemporary times. She was familiar with every piece, for she had written on all the selections when she was a student.

Chester turned the pages and began to laugh. He laughed so hard he fell off the armchair and the yellow sunflower cushion fell with him.

"I don't see what's so funny," she said, picking the cushion off the floor and pretending to dust it.

"This is too rich! I can't believe you are teaching this stuff here. Why, there's nothing here but English poetry and excerpts from British novels. What can your students learn from this?"

She wanted to push the cushion into his face. "This is a collection of the best in English literature. There's Donne, and Keats, and A. E. Housman, Lawrence, George Eliot, Dickens, even the most contemporary like Hopkins . . ."

He laughed harder, thumbing the pages like a gambler rifling through a stack of cards. "Hopkins? Gerard Manley?" He began reading aloud from the page, "'I caught this morning morning's minion,'" then asked, "What's he got to do with Malaysia? And Housman? I'm not sure I've heard of him."

She snatched the textbook from him, glad to find him ignorant on one thing. "There," she said, finding the page and returning the book to him.

He read the poem aloud while Henry listened with a sympathetic smile.

> Into my heart an air that kills
> From yon far country blows:
> What are those blue remembered hills,
> What spires, what farms are those?
> That is the land of lost content,
> I see it shining plain,
> The happy highways where I went
> And cannot come again.

He chanted the words, exaggerating the rhythm and lifting his eyebrows at the images.

She knew he was making fun of the poem, declaiming the words *spires* and *farms* with mock relish. But at the same time she couldn't help appreciating the music of the English words. The killing air came out of the words and echoed in her body even as Chester and Henry were smiling at the absurdity of the ideas. Her body went quite still. How beautiful! she thought, and felt the poem making her a different person.

Then Henry began to laugh loudly.

"Give that back to me!" she cried, reaching for the text.

The two men were immediately silent.

"Don't get so mad! It's not a sacred book, like the Bible.

Look, I don't mean to be rude, but it's no good teaching these kinds of poems any more. This is all British culture, get it? British. We had a revolution and threw them out with the tea bags, so I know what I'm talking about. You've got your own culture. That's what you should be teaching." Chester offered her the text with two hands as if in a peace offering.

"But it's not culture I'm teaching. It's literature. It's language, words, images, feelings . . ."

"The English language, you mean. English literature, English words, English images."

"Well, aren't you speaking the English language, too? Did you throw it out with your tea bags? How come you don't have your own American language? What would it be? American Indian? Eskimo?" She took the text gently, as if he had battered it, and like a mother she were going to heal its wounds.

"Li An can win any argument," Henry said proudly.

"You should be in politics then, not English literature." Chester stressed *English* as if it were a dubious term.

"I'm in literature," she corrected him, "except the literature is written in the English language. I've read American literature too, you know, and a lot of American literature is as English as Housman. Like Pound and Eliot and Henry James. What do you think of them, going off to Britain and living outside of the United States most of their lives? Yet Professor Sanders included them in the American literature course. They were some of the most important American writers we studied."

Chester shrugged. "I majored in anthropology. I think artifacts are important, things people make for their daily lives. I haven't studied too much literature, especially the kind that gets taught. I don't think I can learn as much about people from books as from the things they make and use every day. Like pots and pans, and clothes, and sleeping materials, and statues for worship."

Boring! she thought, but she was too polite to say it. Instead she asked, "So, have you learned anything from your classes?"

"Not from my woodworking students. Except that working with your hands is not valued here. No, I've learned more from my roommates and from the Malay lessons. You know, Malay is the only real culture in this country."

"What do you mean?" Henry wanted to know.

"It's the original thing. People are still living it, not like Hopkins and what's his name, Housman—poetry that comes from somewhere else."

"And the Chinese?" Henry asked.

Chester pushed his long brown hair off his face, a woman's gesture that shocked Li An. She noticed that his hair grew in a clear pointed widow's peak in the middle of his high forehead. It had reddish tints like Auntie's jadeite Kuan Yin, and glittered like a live animal.

"The Chinese aren't really Malaysian, are they?" he answered. "They're here for the money. They speak Chinese and live among themselves. They could as easily be in Hong Kong or even in New York's Chinatown."

Henry's cheeks were spotted with red, and his eyes were yelling louder than his words. "What does that make Li An and me? My family? My friends? We don't want to be in Hong Kong or what you call Chinatown. Our traditions are Chinese, but that doesn't make us less Malaysians. What makes Malay a real culture and Chinese not real? Are you not real here in Kuala Lumpur and only real in America?" Under his breath he muttered in Hokkien, "Red-haired ghost."

She was grateful for Henry's uncharacteristic rudeness. She felt they formed a united pair in their outrage.

"You better watch out, Chester," she said in a sisterly tone, holding Henry's hand. "Saying things like that could get you killed. Oh, I'm joking," she continued as Chester sat up, alarmed. "You wouldn't know that recently people here have been having the fiercest arguments about what is a Malaysian. You sound just like the ultra-Malay politicians who want to kick the Chinese out of the country. My mother's family has been in this country for five or six generations, and some of the Malays are really immigrants who have just arrived from Indonesia in the last few years. You can't make any judgments based on who or what is 'original.' Sure, the Chinese traditions came from China, but Islam came from Saudi Arabia, didn't it? And no one says it's not original. Everything in Malaysia is champor-champor, mixed, rojak. A little Malay, a little Chinese, a little Indian, a little

English. Malaysian means rojak, and if mixed right, it will be delicious."

"Rojak? That hot salad with mango and bean curd and peanuts?"

"And lots more. You see, what you are saying is quite wrong. Chinese and Indians are also Malaysians here. What matters is what you know you are, inside." She put her hands to her chest. "Give us a few more years and we'll be a totally new nation. No more Malay, Chinese, Indian, but all one people."

"Hey, Lee Ann," Chester said, beaming, "you almost sound like an American."

Five

Chester looked glum the next time Li An saw him. She had been going to the lounge every afternoon, hoping to meet him there, but it was more than a week before she saw him coming in to buy cigarettes from Ratnam.

"Whatever you have must be catching," he said. "The headmaster has switched me from woodworking to teaching English. The Peace Corps told him it would have to be woodworking and he agreed, but now he says he really needs another English teacher, not a carpenter."

She laughed maliciously. "You'll be teaching Donne and Shakespeare and Hopkins?"

"Worse. He caught me singing folksongs to my students. You know," Chester sang a line, "'To everything, turn, turn, turn.'" He grimaced as Li An applauded. "They wanted to learn American songs. But based on that he thinks I can teach the 'General Paper'—writing essays and answers to comprehension questions. Now the students expect me to write essays for them to copy and memorize for exams. I don't understand why everyone wants to learn English. It's not going to do them any good. No one seems to understand that the British are gone."

"But you're not British. You're American, and you're here."

"Well, you people sure are going to have some problems."

She bit her nails, annoyed. "I don't see any problems. Why is a language a problem?"

He stared at her through the cigarette smoke and pushed his hair back nervously. "My roommates have been telling me things. They don't like it that I'm teaching English. They call it the language of the bastards."

"In English?" She made her voice sarcastic.

"You don't understand. I'm just visiting. I don't live here. Hell, I don't want to be responsible for anything here. In the Peace Corps we're not supposed to interfere with a country's politics. You know, Lee Ann, you should be doing something else."

Her good humor at seeing him again was gone. "Why do you worry about me? I was going to offer to bring you to Pusat Besar, the new Malay bazaar, but you're so whiny, better forget about it, lah!"

"Now you're talking like my roommates," he said, smiling.

"Okay. We go, lah."

It was strange having Chester behind her on the seat. She thought everyone stared at them as the Honda roared down Batu Road. He was heavy, and the bike couldn't move as fast, but she liked the way his hand rested lightly on her shoulder. He was so much taller that as he spoke she couldn't hear him above the wind, and he had to bend to talk into her ear.

The new Malay bazaar had opened just last week. Strings of ceremonial palm and decorative paper flowers still hung between the stalls, but there were few shoppers. The stalls were crowded with carved wood statues, krises, serving spoons of buffalo horn, the distinctive black and white of Kelantan silver, and all kinds of batik cloths—folded in sarong lengths, laid out as tablecloths and napkins, and swaying from poles in long tunics and skirts. Each stall displayed the same goods.

The shopkeepers sat on chairs by their stalls, sullen and ill-at-ease, as if they would rather be somewhere else. Everything smelled new and artificial. Business was not good.

She didn't want to buy anything. The Malay bazaar was for tourists, but Chester was the only tourist in sight. "So many things to sell, and no one to buy!" she said lightly, although she felt oppressed by the sight. "You'll have to buy something."

Finally he picked out two pieces of checked sarong cloth

for himself. Abdullah and Samad wore sarongs like these around the house, and he wanted to surprise them with his own.

"Wait," he said when they got back to the Honda. He took the key from Li An, gave her his package, and straddled the machine. "Get on."

She liked to feel the air speeding by with her eyes closed. He was not as reckless as she was, and his tall trunk sheltered her from the stink of afternoon traffic. The railway station with its arabesque of Ali Baba minarets passed in a flash. The motorbike wove in between the packed lines of cars leaving the city, then Chester stopped by an open shack near Brickfields, an area so crowded with immigrant Indians that she had never dared visit it.

"My favorite tea place," he said. "Come on."

They squatted on low rickety stools. Flies buzzed over the tables and tin plates of lentil cakes covered with wire meshing that lined the counter. The Indian cook, chubby and bare-chested with a stained white dhoti carelessly wrapped over his round stomach, poured the beige-colored tea in long streamers from one metal container to another, stretching the liquid into a shape.

The tea was hot and sweet. Sweat immediately sprang up on her cheeks and the nape of her neck. She felt hopelessly out of place, but Chester was munching a slice of fruitcake with every sign of satisfaction.

"I come here every day. Best tea in town."

She stared at the unwashed concrete as black as a dirt floor. Clusters of flies were dipping their proboscises in puddles of what must have been orange squash. She was glad the tea was burning hot.

"Where did you learn to ride a motorbike?" she asked, turning away from the flies to look at his flushed face with its sharp lines, so unlike Henry's face.

"Bermuda. We used to go to Bermuda for winter vacations."

Bermuda. The word struck her like a cymbal. Chester had ridden a motorbike in Bermuda. He had been everywhere—America, Bermuda, now Kuala Lumpur. He seemed to her rich in experience, a prince passing through, while she was a frog sitting in a well.

"I don't have a license. Samad says the police will never stop me because I'm white, orang puteh."

It was almost five. Henry would be home soon. Without looking at him, she said, "I have a license. And I have to be back before six."

He got off the Honda at a bus station near the university and she rode home alone, arriving in time for a shower before Henry returned from the lab.

Ellen knew at once that something was happening.

"Nothing's happened, stupid!" she protested. "Henry likes him. He's a friend."

"Where can you hide?" Ellen said, her eyes watchful. "When a woman has the itch, the whole world can see it."

"Oh, rubbish!" Li An had not wanted to meet Ellen for lunch. She had been going to the lounge every afternoon hoping to meet Chester there. They had run into each other this way several times, and he had taken her on her Honda each time to some sight or other in Kuala Lumpur. They had even ridden to the Batu Caves.

She climbed the more than one hundred steps in the silent sizzling afternoon humidity gladly. They were the only people at the caves. No one went up those steps in the afternoon, when the equatorial sun was at its cruelest. At the top, inside the cool dark cave smelling pungently of bat droppings and of the marigold garlands that wreathed the stumps swelling out of the earth—lingams, Chester told her, representing the Hindu concept of male godhead and potency—she had almost fainted, and had to sit on the earthen floor with her head below her knees.

He was apologetic. "You're so small, I forget you don't have the same energy I do. No, stay there and keep your head down. The blood has to circulate. That's what causes the blackout, when there isn't enough blood circulating."

She wondered if her cream-colored jeans would be horribly dirty when she stood up. The earth was cool beneath her, dry and firm. She put her head further down and cocked her knees high to keep her balance. The strong smell of the marigolds mixed with the smell of her body coming up between her legs and with the sweet brown smell of the earth.

She breathed slowly and deeply as he had advised her. The dizziness was gradually slowing. Her head ached, but a stable center expanded and her stomach righted itself. She concentrated on blood, which she saw circulating through the millions of veins in her brain, but all the time she was conscious of Chester squatting beside her and patting her on the back. Pat, pat. His hand was large and determined. She wished he would stroke gently instead.

They didn't stay long at the Batu Caves. It was a distance from her house, and he knew she had to be home each day before six. This afternoon she barely had time to get into the shower before Henry arrived home early.

At first she had wanted to tell Henry about the sightseeing trips with Chester. After all, he knew she met Chester occasionally in the afternoons.

Henry approved of the Peace Corps. He knew the Peace Corps was doing good work in some villages with irrigation and improved rice seed. They both admired Chester for volunteering two years of his life to teach in a low-ranking school when he had a degree from Princeton and could be studying at another prestigious university. It was the kind of idealism they had never felt. Only America, they said, could produce such idealistic people.

But she never told Henry. She knew he wouldn't approve of her wasting time.

He himself worked hard every day, going to the lab on Saturdays and Sundays to check on his experiments. His work did not stop on weekends. Plants grew and reacted every day; cells multiplied and died whether one was watching them or not, and he had observations to make, tests to do, notes and reports to write, measurements to calibrate, new tests to carry out, new observations to make, and so on.

Henry had no time to waste, and when she did mention Chester he was relieved she had someone to talk to and didn't complain as much about being bored.

But Ellen knew something was different when she talked about Chester.

"So America has come to you," she joked. "What are you

going to do when you run out of interesting places to see? You'll have to make a decision then." And again, "You'd better not see any sights at night. At night all colors look the same."

Today Ellen didn't talk about Li An and Chester. Gina and Paroo were coming to Kuala Lumpur for the school holidays, and she was trying to arrange something for them.

Gina was being most uncooperative, Ellen complained. She wanted to be with Paroo, but she wouldn't consider marriage, not with Paroo's mother against it and her own family ignorant of his existence.

Ellen had finally written to Paroo, to his school in Ipoh in case his mother opened his mail, suggesting that he request a civil wedding in Kuala Lumpur and present it as a possibility to Gina when they were next together.

Perhaps his flowery manliness would overcome Gina's hesitations, Ellen said cynically.

"I'll talk to Gina," Li An offered reluctantly, "although you are closer to her. You're right. There's no reason they shouldn't marry if that's what they want. She shouldn't be miserable because he is of a different race."

She thought she now could imagine Gina as Paroo's wife. As teachers, Gina and Paroo would serve as models of a new kind of Malaysian. Gina would wear a sari occasionally to prove her adoption of Indian culture. She would tie her long hair back in a neat bun and wear the bindhi, the red mark of the married woman, on her forehead, but otherwise she would be the same Gina, loud and brash, for that was what Paroo loved about her, the spirit that rudely scolded herself and everybody else with laughter. Once Gina was married, whatever drove her crazy about life would quiet down. She would have light-brown children who would look both and neither Indian and Chinese, the new Malaysians.

Chester had told her the problem was the same all over the world. He told her about Martin Luther King, Jr. "People should be judged 'not by the color of their skin, but by the content of their character,' the man said! Of course, Paroo and Gina would both be seen as non-whites in America. But it's the same problem all over the world." Yes, Li An thought, the dream seemed the same for Gina as for Americans.

Six

When she heard that Paroo had requested and received a date for the civil wedding, Gina screamed so loudly that Li An ducked.

"Bloody nosy idiots!" she screamed. "You all think life is so easy, just go get married, everything comes out right. My father will disown me if I marry a keling-kwei, a Tamil devil. He cannot even tell the difference between Tamil and Punjabi! How can I live with Paroo? I am Chinese. How to hold my head up? My brothers and sisters will jeer at me. All my friends in town, I'll be dead to them. You and Ellen have your own lives to live, you can't take care of me all the time. What am I going to do without my family?"

Paroo sat beside her, his elbows on Ellen's dining table and tears sticking to his lashes.

"Oh, never mind," Gina said, kissing his shoulder. "I know Ellen and Li An put you up to this. They're my best friends, but they don't know our problems. We'll think of something, I promise you."

"Maybe if you come to my house and my mother meets you she will like you," Paroo said in a forlorn voice. "My mother is usually a nice woman, she is very nice to our relatives. She will not treat you badly."

"You don't know my father! He would kick me out of the house if I brought you home. He's already a Confucian, daughters are no good anyway, and if I bring home a Punjabi, forget it! I'm disowned!"

Paroo must have heard this argument many times before, for he hid his face in his hands and wouldn't say a word. Finally Li An left, indignant at their cowardice. She would tell Ellen her interference had done no good. She was washing her hands of the two; they could do whatever they wished as far as she was concerned.

But it was Ellen who called her the next morning. "Oh God," she said. Li An had never heard Ellen distraught. "Gina and Paroo. They took sleeping pills. In my flat. The police just called me. I'm going over to the police station. Oh God!"

"What happened to them?"

Ellen's sobs seemed to shake the receiver. "Gina's dead," she wailed. "She's dead. She killed herself."

That fool! Li An thought angrily. Into the mouthpiece she said, "Do you want me to come over? I'll wait for you at your parents' house. You're not going back to your flat now, are you?"

It's strange, she thought. I should be crying, like Ellen. Instead she felt strangulated, as if Gina had placed an invisible bag over her head and she was choking.

Ellen didn't know how long the police questioning would take. Her father was insisting she talk to a lawyer first in case there were problems with the families suing her. She didn't know what was going to happen in the next few days, and would call when they could meet.

Li An had no tutorials to give that day. The morning stretched on as she found herself wandering between the library and the lounge.

The library was crowded with students, although it was still months before the final exams. Groups of young men stationed themselves at the entrances to the different buildings, staring at the young women as they walked to their lectures.

She was safe from these public intrusions. Less than a year separated her from the senior students, but she was a tutor, had passed into the forbidding company of teachers, and had taken on their properties of privacy and power.

How alone she was! There was no one she could share her feelings with, no one to talk to about Gina and Paroo. Ellen had forgotten to tell her what happened to Paroo. Was he dead?

Didn't he take the sleeping pills as well? Where were their bodies? Who was going to tell their parents, Gina's large family clustered in the Chinese school in Johore, and Paroo's nice mother probably grinding her curry paste this morning? Would they be buried together? That was unlikely. Each family would blame the other's child. If my son hadn't met your cheap dishonorable daughter. If my daughter had not met your murderous seducing son.

She found a grassy bank with young nipa palms between two buildings, away from students' lecture routes and the groups of young men buzzing by, and sat in the frugal shade to think out why Gina would have chosen to die rather than to live. But there was something artificial in her solitude. The bright tropical morning, the open campus with its neatly mown grass and carefully planted trees and bushes, in the distance young people moving gracefully, books in arms—none of this corresponded to the confusion in her mind.

She could see Gina's and Paroo's bodies sprawled casually over Ellen's bed, more casual together dead than alive. How was she to make sense of their despair and stupidity, of the apparently numberless and nameless family members they feared?

No breeze stirred on the grounds. The undergrown nipa palm fronds hung still as if etched in the blue sky.

She stood up impatiently. She was only playing with her thoughts. The feeling that was clear to her was this constricted anger, not guilt. If Gina had survived, she would have shaken her for playing the fool.

Then she thought, but Gina isn't in this world anymore. The entire blue sky and the hot still air contained Gina nowhere. Her tears came slowly and reluctantly.

She drank the fresh lime juice she loved and hoped Chester would come by the lounge. She smoked one cigarette after another, thinking, he'll come before this cigarette is down to its stub.

She had finished half a pack before he came in with Abdullah.

Abdullah had completed a degree in history the same year she'd graduated and was a journalist at the new paper. She seldom read the new paper; it was too political, and it published daily editorials demanding special rights for Malays. Reading it made her feel she was in danger of attack in an alien country, and she refused to buy it. If enough Malaysians refused to buy the new paper, she hoped, it would simply stop publishing. At first it had made her uncomfortable that Chester and Abdullah were roommates, but then she had spoken to Abdullah on several occasions and found him funny and gentle. She liked talking to him, although his conversation was always about politics. His position was quite clear, but he argued with her subtly, like a good partner observing the patterns and courtesies of an elaborate dance. She didn't feel threatened when he explained the need for Malay special rights intelligently and elegantly; he made it seem fair and just, a readjustment to the fundamental design of the dance. She liked the idea of the Malaysian future as this gentle weaving readjustment and had asked Abdullah why his paper did not present its position in that light. He answered that it did, she was simply not reading it correctly. Now, however, she wished Chester had come alone.

"She's your friend, yah?" Abdullah asked. "The one who kill herself? I call Chester at school soon as I hear. My paper is covering the story, you know, and I recognize her name. She part of your gang, yah?" He gave her a sympathetic glance as he took the seat beside her.

She had sat at the table furthest in the corner, and the ashtray was a mound of stubs.

"Is there anything we can do?" Chester took the other seat, on her left.

She felt comforted. It was a small world after all; one kept running into people one knew or had met in a previous life. Even Gina and Paroo had not been so alone, if only they had taken advantage of their friends.

She looked more keenly at Abdullah. Of course she would rather Chester had come without him, but it was he who had brought Chester here.

"Were you one of the Malay boys Gina flirted with in her second year?"

"Yah, she flirt with everyone. It was Samad she like best— she like the cowboy look."

Li An remembered Samad as the one who wore a hat when he stood with his group outside the library. "Like Shane, lah!" Gina had exclaimed, and teased him shamelessly for minutes in front of all the boys. But Samad had never taken her up on her teasing; he had merely grinned and remained with his friends. The Malay boys never visited the girls at their residential hall.

"The Indian boy didn't die," Abdullah said, in reply to Li An's question. "Not enough sleeping pills, so when he woke up, he try to slash his wrists, but he make so much noise that the landlord come up and find them."

"Jeezus," Chester said as if hearing it for the first time. "You people sure take things hard."

She found herself crying. The thought of Paroo, his wrists wrapped in bandages, in a hospital ward, thinking of Gina dead, was more than she could bear.

Abdullah gave her a paper napkin from the stack on the table, but the tears kept rolling from her eyes. She was aware the two men had shifted their chairs a little away from her; she was embarrassing them, so she swallowed hard and licked the salt from her lips.

"Very difficult, this interracial affair," Abdullah said to Chester. "Better that like stay with like. Indian and Chinese cannot mix, too many differences—food, custom, language. To be husband and wife must share same religion, same race, same history. Malay and Chinese also cannot mix, like oil and water. Malays have many adat, Islam also have shariat. All teach good action. Chinese have no adat, they eat pork, they like gamble, make money." He stopped, then said to Li An, "Of course Chinese also have their own religion. But they must become like Malay if they want to marry Malay."

She wasn't listening. The pink napkin crumpled to wet shreds as she blew her nose, and she picked up another one. The napkins were edged with prints of red phoenixes. Only last month Auntie had given her a red sateen jacket stitched with red phoenixes just like these. "Phoenix is very strong good luck charm," she'd explained, one long finger tracing the upraised wings, red silk thread melded onto red fabric. "Best for long

life, new life. Best for young married woman." Remembering,
Li An picked nervously at the napkin's edges.

Abdullah must have understood her silence, for he said he
had to return to the office and left.

She put a cigarette to her mouth with damp fingers.

"Don't cry," Chester said as he struck a match.

Through her tears and the smoke she saw his frank brown
eyes and the high long nose. She wished he would kiss her,
but then there was Henry, and it was nothing like that
between Chester and herself.

"Why didn't you call me at the lab?" Henry asked when she
told him about Gina that evening. "You know you can disturb me any time. How could you have stood it alone all day?"

She didn't tell him she had spent the afternoon with
Chester.

Chester had taken her to his favorite tea shack. She was
so pleased to be away from the university that she loved the
dirty floor stained with the same old sticky orange squash puddles, the crinkly cellophane-wrapped fruitcake slices, even the
fat Indian cook reknotting his dhoti unselfconsciously in front
of her.

She had told Chester about Gina and Paroo, lowering her
voice in case the cook was listening when she narrated
Paroo's description of his mother's obstinate rejection of
Gina. After all, it was disloyal of Paroo to complain about his
mother, and any Indian might be offended by the story.

Chester had said Gina probably had a father problem. It
wasn't just Chinese, but a universal psychological problem.
Gina really wanted to marry her father, and her relationship
with Paroo was never a serious thing with her.

Li An was shocked, but she didn't want to show him how
much she disapproved of what he was saying. That Gina might
have loved her father in that way! Even to consider it was
painting a sin on her memory. And who would dare tell
Paroo that Gina wasn't serious about him! She had killed herself out of love for him. This thing Chester called an Electra
complex was all right for American girls, she thought, they
had a perverted sexual culture, but Gina was not a pervert.

47

But she didn't argue with Chester. There was so little time before she had to return home, and she loved listening to his deep authoritative voice, even if he didn't understand the kinds of race barriers that Gina had faced.

Henry understood all too well. "Gina was too Chinese," he said. "It's all her fault. Poor Paroo! She didn't have enough guts to change herself, so she took the easy way out. He isn't so lucky."

Gina had always struck Li An as terribly bold. It wasn't courage she lacked, she thought, but imagination. She hadn't been able to imagine what kind of life she could have without being Chinese. History taught no lessons about changing one's race. It only taught about war and violence between people, even people of the same color and blood. Gina hadn't been clever enough to rise above history.

She didn't attend Gina's funeral in Johore. Her family had not informed Ellen of the arrangements, and Ellen, on her lawyer's advice, had distanced herself from the tragedy. She was simply an old college friend who had loaned her flat to Gina and had known nothing of the affair with Paroo.

"You don't know how difficult it was to lie to them," she said passionately to Li An, who had come to help her move out of the flat.

Ellen had paid for movers to pack her furniture and possessions. She couldn't bear to be in the flat for long.

The police had removed all Gina's and Paroo's things—Ellen had pointed them out. There were a few articles of clothing, a couple of small suitcases, some makeup.

Ellen had lied and kept Gina's hairbrush for herself. It was a small bristle brush with a wooden handle, and when Ellen showed it to Li An some of Gina's short coarse hair was still tangled in the spikes.

But they couldn't cry anymore, and handled the brush tenderly as if it had been a part of Gina's body, a piece that wouldn't be buried with her.

Ellen was drinking a Tiger beer, although it was only eleven in the morning. Despite her parents' pleas she was moving to a bungalow, alone.

"Cannot live with them. This cannot do, that cannot do. I have an interview with Weston Allen. Good pay. I won't need my father's bloody money."

She did not talk about leaving for America again.

When the moving van arrived, Ellen wouldn't do anything. She stood by the bedroom window morosely looking out at the rows of small yards below. Every yard was fenced with a high iron gate and hurricane steel mesh. Half of each yard was covered with concrete; the other half-yards were a curious mix—overgrown with crab grass or thick thrusting lallang, crowded with pots of yellow and purple flowering orchids on trestles, or littered with broken bricks and overturned plastic pails.

Li An stood by Ellen for a moment. Did Gina and Paroo gaze out at this scene of shabby litter before they lay on the bed with their pills and glasses of water? The living room and kitchen at the back looked out on to the more scabrous sight of sheets, towels, and underwear drying to a tough texture in the burning sun.

The movers were yelling at each other as they maneuvered the rocker down the stairs. Ellen was leaving the bed and mattress behind. The landlord, who had never met Gina, was happy to have it for his next tenant.

"Would you ever throw yourself out of a window?" Ellen asked. The steel-framed window panels were opened wide, and she pressed lightly on the sill, her rounded breasts and trunk leaning slightly over the edge.

"Oh no!" Li An said, without thinking. "Never."

"Me too." Ellen turned away. "These workmen are so slow, they take all day to move. Let's go to the Bistro after they've finished."

"But you have to direct the movers to your new flat and wait for them to unpack," Li An reminded her. "One always moves to some place else! You can't just pack and leave, you also have to unpack and settle in."

Ellen was slower these days. She wasn't so quick with her comments. Something had turned in her, and her affection wasn't as free. She had a grudge against the world, and was concentrating only on the possibility of the new position at Weston Allen.

Li An felt she could leave Ellen alone, but Ellen still called, sometimes every day. Even after she began the new position, which meant six weeks of intensive training, she called every night. Sometimes they talked about Paroo, whom Li An had visited at the hospital. Ellen wouldn't visit him although she said she had nothing against him; it wasn't his fault that Gina died and he lived.

Li An took Chester with her to the hospital. At their first visit Paroo had wept the entire time. It was as if she had carried in the vision of Gina dead beside him as he sawed at his wrists with the shining blue Gillette blade that he had brought from Ipoh for shaving. His cries that had sent the landlord upstairs were less from the pain, although the cuts had hurt sharply, than from the discovery that he was still alive while Gina was cold. She was no longer breathing, she would never come back. That was what made him cry aloud, and also what made him less urgent with the blade. He had realized that even in death she wouldn't be there for him.

Paroo cried without dignity, sobbing so hard the nurse came running in and told them they had to leave, they were upsetting him.

Li An called before going the second time. Paroo came to the phone and said yes, he was leaving the hospital in a few days. He was returning to Ipoh, although his principal had written a letter terminating his post, and yes, he would like to see her to say good-bye.

"I don't think I should go with you," Chester said. "After all, I don't know the guy and he may want to see you alone."

"No, no!" She could not visit Paroo alone. She was afraid of him after what he had been through. He had been so close to death that he seemed to her like a ghost or a murderer. She needed someone to protect her.

Dressed in a short-sleeved shirt and the striped blue pajama pants of the hospital, Paroo was able to smile this time.

"Peace Corps volunteer?" he queried in almost his old hearty tone. "What trouble you Americans doing here, ha? All Peace Corps fellows in India belong to the CIA. My good friend Pushpa tells me this."

Chester talked to him about teaching the General Paper. They could almost have been conversing in a coffee shop. "But, you know, my headmaster, he's not an understanding fellow. He reads the papers and thinks I am a bad man. Now I don't have a job in Ipoh." Paroo smiled as he gave this dismal news. "Hey, maybe I can get something for you at my school!" Chester was excited. He liked making things happen, fixing up problems, fitting pieces together. "I'll speak to my headmaster. He's also Indian, Mr. Govinand, M.A." He laughed at his own joke. "He's very keen on that title. We all have to address him as Mr. Govinand, M.A., especially if we want anything out of him. I'm sure he'll help you out. The school is short of English teachers. The students are complaining that I am the only trained English teacher they have, and I am not even an English major. The kids who aren't in my classes are constantly getting their parents to complain. Mr. Govinand will jump at the chance to have you teach in his school."

Paroo beamed. His face filled out and lost its shadowy contours. What a good friend Chester was, and he didn't even know him. Would Mr. Govinand really offer him a job? How wonderful if he could teach in the same school with this very nice Chester! Was there a place for him after all he had been through? Would everyone let him forget what had happened? His eyes filled, pity for himself and fearful hope all mixed up with the tears.

Seven

Taking one direct glance at Li An's slatternly Indian wrap skirt and T-shirt, the seam under the right armpit fraying, Auntie said to Henry, "When are you going to have your baby?"

Li An, who had barely slid her slippers off by the accordion gates, stubbed her toes sharply against the raised floor. Did Auntie see something in her she had missed? She had been fitted for the diaphragm and used it every time. Henry was planning to continue his biochemistry studies in West Germany. Professor Forster had nominated him for an impressive doctoral fellowship at Baden-Baden, and he was taking German classes at the Goethe Institute every Saturday.

The professor had invited Henry and Li An for dinner last month—a compliment to Henry, as Forster was not gregarious—and had told her she could easily teach Chinese there. Germans were enthusiastic about everything oriental. He was surprised when she said she couldn't read and write Chinese and spoke only Hokkien. He didn't believe the Germans would accept her as an English teacher: they were meticulous about the correct accent, he said, and while it was good she was doing a master's degree in English literature, it didn't—he paused here—it might not do her much good in Baden-Baden.

Later that night, Henry said she would always find something to do, she was so self-reliant. She would make friends, study German literature, learn to cook German meals. She could write poems about their travels. Having a baby was not in their plans.

Second Mrs. Yeh had said "your baby" as if there were already one present. Li An closed her eyes and hoped it wasn't true. Henry seated himself on the La-Z-Boy lounger near the air conditioner and opened the pages of the *New Straits Times*.

"You must have a baby soon," Second Mrs. Yeh said directly to Li An.

Relieved, Li An walked on the shining terrazzo floor, polished and cool beneath her bare soles. "In another few years," she replied, stroking her favorite blue ceramic vase by the carved rosewood coffee table. Everything in the house was expensive.

She liked coming to visit when Mr. Yeh wasn't home. This time he was in Kuala Kangsar checking on the lorries at his new transport branch. She called him "Ah Pah" now, but they didn't speak to each other.

He spoke occasionally in Hokkien to Henry about his studies. "Are you working? Good. What kind of work? The same kind as last time? Why always the same kind? Scientists work like that? Good, good."

But usually he was silent, almost somnambulant, when they came for dinner on Sundays. Li An told Chester it was amusing that important Chinese towkays in real life were just tired old men.

"I could not have a child," Auntie continued, "although I prayed to Kuan Yin and gave money to the Peng Ho Temple. Such is my fate. But you have a healthy body. Use it while you're young."

Her eyes penetrated through Li An's crumpled clothes. Li An felt her body unused, like a sealed jar. Auntie probably knew all about her diaphragm.

She watched as Li An walked restlessly on the smooth stone, sank on the pillowed sofa, and tapped one bare foot before her.

"A woman marries for children. She cannot be safe otherwise." Turning to Henry, Auntie said softly, "We are always changing. You must let her change with you."

"After Germany," Henry said with a pleasant smile.

Li An thought again how good he was. She would have screamed with frustration at Auntie's bossiness. Henry always spoke gently, as if addressing his laboratory touch-me-nots.

He explained things clearly, specifically, and with Li An, in such a pleading tone that it left her abashed.

With him, she felt all her brassy prickly ways withdrawing, closing, as if she were going to sleep. She was a sleepwalker in Henry's life, and she trusted him implicitly to decide their future.

Still, she didn't understand why she did not tell him about her meetings with Chester. Perhaps because he didn't seem to mind whenever Chester came over or perhaps because he liked Chester and she didn't wish to suggest something about their relationship that would get in the way of the friendship.

Henry hadn't been upset when Chester brought Abdullah and Samad one evening for a visit. He had just come home and Li An was coming out of the shower when the car honked out on the road. "Must be Ellen," she called from the bedroom, hurriedly toweling her hair dry.

"Chester brought some friends," Henry warned from the front door, and she took the time to comb out the knots in her damp hair.

She did remember Samad, the boy who had smoked with the cigarette dangling from his lower lip, one hip hitched out and a cowboy hat shadowing his handsome face in front of the library entrance most afternoons. He was almost as tall as Chester but didn't have Chester's ease.

"Nice house," he said, lighting a cigarette and crouching on the Danish armchair Auntie had picked for them. His eyes slid over her quickly to look at Henry. Handsome as he was, he was more comfortable with men. "Your own?"

"My father's," Henry hesitated. "Drinks?"

Li An wondered if they would ask for beer.

"You have rose syrup?" Chester answered. "That's my roommates' favorite drink." He was a teetotaler, he explained, like Abdullah and Samad, and he also had a sweet tooth and liked very sweet drinks.

Chester is right, she thought, he could have been Malay in another life.

Instead they drank Coca-Cola, Chester making a fuss about how he had come to Malaysia to get away from the States, and here he was with Samad, the cowboy, drinking Cokes. Abdullah and Samad kept looking at Henry with reflective eyes. "Science types and arts types never mix, lah," they explained to Chester. "That's why Henry stay away from people like us. But Li An so pretty he cannot stay away."

She laughed at their flattery.

Samad was doing radio work, writing reports. Soon, he said, he would be put in charge of a new program, "The World We Live In." He was planning to interview farmers, fishermen, tradesmen like hawkers and stall-keepers, and religious teachers.

She gathered he would interview only Malays. The program was going to be in Malay. Again she felt uncomfortable. Samad had done his degree in geography—surely his program was intended to bring in the entire world?

"That's just great!" Chester had finished his drink while the others had only sipped at theirs. "Abdullah in the papers and Samad in broadcasting—between them they will conquer Malaysia!"

"Of course, there will always be place for English," Abdullah said, smiling at Li An, "and for scientists."

The smell and sizzle of fish frying in the kitchen made Samad jump up. "Must go and leave you to your makan."

They wouldn't have dinner with them; besides, Li An wasn't sure if pork was being served. Abdullah and Samad, she knew, would be mortally insulted if pork were on the table. She let Letchmi cook whatever she wished and was thankful she didn't have to do the shopping for meals.

She brought out peanuts and potato chips instead and pressed them to stay a little longer.

"The politics today is not good." Abdullah crunched on a handful of peanuts. "The Chinese not like the government so much, but they make big mistake. It is this government that protect them. The Malays are very very patient. We don't say Chinese no good. All people good. Our religion teach us this. But why Chinese say Malay no good, government no good, want to change government?" He looked at Henry to gauge his response.

Henry said, "I see your point."

"Like English," Abdullah said. "Don't want you to feel bad, yah, Li An, but English is bastard language. In Malaysia we must all speak national language."

For a moment everyone stared at each other.

Could they really do it, she wondered? What would happen if they all suddenly switched to Malay right now? How would she express herself? Like a halting six-year-old, groping for light in a darkened world? Her world was lit by language. The English ingested through years of reading and talking now formed the delicate web of tissues in her brain. Giving up her language would be like undergoing a crippling operation on her brain. Of course, she would be able to move and sleep and eat, her outward appearance would not change. But without her language she would be as handicapped as any armless and legless beggar in the street.

"For us Malays, yah, we have to speak English everywhere—in school, office. We not so good in English. But why must we speak English? That not our national language." Abdullah's voice was gentle; he spoke in the same manner Henry did, like a teacher explaining a difficult lesson to a favorite child.

Of course, she thought, it must be just as bad for Abdullah to express himself in English instead of Malay. He must feel like the blinded six-year-old groping around in his mind for the objects of his thoughts. He must have been made mute at the university by the loss of his language.

But how well he explained himself, even with his simple slow English! She felt an admiration for him.

"But what will happen when you go overseas?" Henry shook his crossed leg a little impatiently. "I'm learning German now, so I understand how difficult it is to study in a foreign language. But I have no choice. If I want to continue my studies in Germany I have to know German."

"That is less than one percent of the people," Samad replied. Unlike Abdullah, he refused to eat anything. "For the one percent, of course they must learn English. This one percent will be top government people. Everybody else like taxi driver, even teacher, why need English? Malay is good enough for this country."

"But who will choose the one percent? What about Malaysians

who may want to strive to join that one percent? What if they don't want to be taxi drivers but want to be scientists? What if they believe they need English as well as Malay?" As soon as Li An stopped her rush of questions, she saw she had done something wrong. Samad had hooded his eyes in a blank expression, Abdullah was frowning, and even Henry was biting his lip.

Chester stood up, stretching his arms above his head. His arms were so long they almost touched the ceiling. He scratched his sharp peaked hair. "Got to go," he said. "Dinner time. Must makan, lah."

She stood by the wrought iron gate sadly to wave good-bye. Abdullah was driving a new Fiat. They were laughing as they drove away, as if they had already forgotten the conversation.

Henry came up to her while she continued to stand indecisively. The sun had set and it was dark, although the heat still rose from the asphalt road.

"What did I say wrong?" She was desperate.

"It is rude to contradict people."

"But I wasn't contradicting, I was only pointing out . . ."

"You see," he interrupted, "you're doing it again." He sighed. "You have become too Westernized. First, you must accept what people say. If you cannot agree, you must still be quiet. Men get upset when women contradict them."

"But you're not like that, Henry. You let me say what I feel. I know you couldn't agree with Samad's position, he's . . ." She couldn't find what she meant.

"It is better not to disagree." His voice, while gentle, was cold.

She burst into angry tears. "You're like everyone else in Malaysia, Chinese, Malay, even Chester. A woman has no right to a mind of her own. She should only listen and echo what men say."

Surprised, he put his arm around her shoulder. "I don't believe that. Of course I'm proud you're so intelligent. But you must use your intelligence for agreement, not for arguing. That's the Chinese way. Even the men follow that rule."

She shook his arm off. "Oooh!" she ground out from the back of her throat. "But I'm not Chinese. I'm Malaysian!"

Eight

Ellen and Chester liked each other immediately.

"So, this is the secret boyfriend," she said, poking him playfully in the ribs. "Why she's hiding you? So husband no see?"

Chester laughed. "Husband see, husband don't mind. I'm just a harmless guy from the United States of America." He lifted his arms to show he had nothing to hide.

She poked him again, but he wasn't ticklish. "Ha!" She poked him some more. "When men sniff around, they want only one thing."

Li An was painfully embarrassed. "Ellen doesn't think women and men can be friends without some hanky-panky."

"That's never been my experience either." Chester bowed to Ellen, who laughed loudly and pressed a hand to her side as if she were having a stitch. "At last," he said, "a Malaysian with a sense of humor!"

Ellen wasn't pleased Paroo was to begin teaching in Petaling Jaya in January. "You'll see," she warned moodily, "he's a troublemaker. Better watch out, Chester. Some people bring trouble wherever they go."

"That's not fair!" Li An remembered Paroo's face all slack with unresisting tears at Chester's offer. "Why, Paroo is the one who suffers from other people's troubles. He is all soft. He couldn't make trouble if he tried."

"That's exactly what I'm saying." Ellen moved a chair vigorously from one side of the room to the other. She glared and shook her head when Chester offered to help. "What do you think I am, soft like Paroo?"

Ellen had found a two-story house in old Petaling Jaya, where fast-growing softwood trees kept the front yard in deep shade and a constant litter of rotting leaves. Overgrown bushes bloomed with blood-red ixora. The house had an appearance of utter neglect, and the gray-green ivy trailing over the hurricane fence—an original sight in an area of pampered flowering hedges—added to its air of desolation. The rent was exorbitant, but Ellen preferred living alone, and her parents helped with expenses.

Her job at Weston Allen was so-so, she said. It didn't pay as well as it should because it had three levels of pay for the same work: a high salary for the British brought over on two-year contracts, a lower salary for the Malaysian men, who were all scrambling for promotion, and the lowest pay for women like Ellen, who were hoping the company would change its policy soon.

Dragging the rocker closer to the coffee table, she placed her bare feet on the glass top with a bang. "You know, Paroo's a jinx. He's empty inside. That's the kind that attracts trouble. Nature abhors a vacuum."

Li An thought Henry would have approved of Ellen's words. Newton had said that. Or was it Einstein?

"We know Gina was the trouble, but she would have survived if it wasn't for the vacuum." Ellen kicked at the tabletop viciously with her heel. "You'll see, he's a parasite. He needs to suck on someone, and you'll be the one, Chester."

But then, one could say that Paroo would have been all right if Gina hadn't come along, Li An thought. Remembering what Henry had said about her arguing, she kept silent instead.

"Isn't it true?" Ellen appealed to Li An. "Gina was just like us. We all have problems. That's life. Of course," she smiled maliciously, "Li An doesn't know yet she has problems, but we know, right, Chester?"

"So why should Gina have killed herself?" Ellen's voice spun upwards. "We're strong. Gina was a strong person. It's Paroo's fault she's dead."

She caught herself on the up spin of hysteria and laughed. "If only you men would leave us women alone, we'd be all right." Li An picked up the beer mug from the coffee table as Ellen's foot swept close to it. Chester leaned back on his chair as far as he could.

It was Saturday afternoon and Henry was at the Goethe Institute studying German with Mrs. Schneider. He was already able to read some elementary passages.

Li An had refused to take the course with him. "It will give me something to do when I'm in Germany," she said. "Besides, after listening to Abdullah and Samad, I'd be better off studying Malay literature." She was half serious about it. Chester could read Malay better than she did, and he had been studying it for only six months.

Now whenever she looked at the wretched mimeographed practical criticism poems she disliked them. She felt like a fraud after every tutorial. Did she ever believe these were her poems, speaking from her body as much as from the poets'?

Her body felt stranger and stranger each day. Her nerve ends vibrated on a strangely immediate and vivid plane, but everything else was distant. When she talked about the poems to her students, there was no longer a singing connection between the language and her body. Instead, there was talk, slow and difficult, the students unable to grasp the thick leaden ropes she threw to them. Then there was her new body, singing to itself, without any form or language. She could not reach it with her mind.

When Henry kissed her, when he penetrated her mouth, she could not reach her new body even then. The resonating sensation, she thought, was like a golden honey piling in combs in the hive of her body, sweetening somewhere else beyond her mind and beyond Henry.

She spent less time with Chester now. When they were together there was a numbness in her, as if she were waiting for a disaster. Instead of heading off on adventures, they spent most of their time together talking. Rather, he talked and she listened.

Listening nervously to Ellen now, Li An wondered if she was also turning into a vacuum, like Paroo.

Chester was explaining to Ellen that Paroo had asked to room with him, but with three bedrooms in the house, Abdullah and Samad were adamantly against the idea. "Not to worry," he added. "My friends Zuni and Bala say they are looking for someone to share their apartment."

"Flat," Ellen said. "Why you Americans use big words like *apartment* and *elevator* instead of *flat* and *lift*? Aiyoh, everything about America must be so big, lah. Even your words are all so long." Ellen gave a wicked smile.

Li An saw that Ellen amused Chester. He looked appreciatively at her bold lounging body, her legs propped on the low table and her large breasts stuck out in the air. Ellen rested her head on the back of the rocker. Her whole stance was insolent and carefree.

She also appreciated Ellen's stance. Her own body was like a tuning fork that had been struck. She could not sprawl like Ellen did and be self-contained—she would be quivering and pained. She tensed her shoulders and clenched her hands instead, even as Ellen looked knowingly at her, and she knew that Ellen knew.

"Do you like her?" she asked Chester jealously. She had wanted them not to like each other. She wanted them each, separately, for herself, the way she had Henry and Ellen. Ellen was barely polite to Henry, who disliked her but wouldn't admit to it.

She kept the bike engine running as he answered. He had gotten off by the shop corner near his flat.

"Sure," he spoke loudly above the engine. "I've met lots of women like her at Princeton. They make the best friends for guys sometimes." But he looked uncomfortable even as he said this and rumpled her hair good-bye.

She wondered what he meant, and also what he meant in touching her hair. It was the first time he had touched her so intimately. But he had spoken in such a way that she knew she didn't have to be jealous of Ellen.

To Ellen she said, "Be careful, he's going to fall for you!"

Ellen only said, "Naw, he's a dope. He's not going to fall for anyone but himself."

But she knew Ellen liked Chester. Ellen asked each time they met, "Where's your boyfriend, ah?" When Chester came along for visits, she drank more avidly, always Tigers, and the two argued endlessly about American politics. She was as com-fortable with Chester as she was with Li An. In her everyday jeans—she wore only tailored suits for work—she sat with legs wide apart or flung over furniture.

Sometimes Henry came along. He and Ellen negotiated con-versation around Chester and Li An. It was almost a foursome, except Chester still went out some afternoons with her, to the tea shack at Brickfields or around Kuala Lumpur; then she felt it was just Chester and herself.

"No use hiding behind me," Ellen said one afternoon over lunch. "You're as bad as Gina. You want or you don't want? Your Henry is really blind. Everyone else can see what's happening."

"I don't see why you're always suggesting there's something between Chester and myself." Li An was petulant. "We don't meet each other as often anymore. In fact, he usually has Abdullah with him when we meet at the lounge. If Henry doesn't think I'm doing something wrong, I don't see why you should."

"Don't see, don't see," Ellen mimicked her. "Your Henry doesn't want to see. Why women so crazy, I'll never know! I bet Abdullah can see what's happening. You don't have to lie to me. I see the way you look at him. You never look at Henry that way. That Chester, I can kill him!"

It was true Abdullah had said just the other week as Chester was in the washroom, "My good friend Li An, you must be careful. These Peace Corps people, they leave us and go back to America. They are not our people."

She pretended she didn't understand him. "But Abdullah, you tell me I'm not your people either! Soon Henry and I will go to Baden-Baden. Where am I ever going to find my people?"

Abdullah had kind dark eyes. "You must find your way, Li An. If you a Malay girl, I can help you. Sometimes I think too bad you are born Chinese. Chester, he's very nice man, yah, but, you know, he also inside orang puteh. He try to be Malaysian, but it's only playing. He's not serious, you know?"

It was hopeless. No one understood why she liked Chester. They all believed she was having an affair. Except Henry. And Chester. Chester respected her. He treated her with friendly restraint, as a guide to Malaysia.

He was someone who was at loose ends, like she was. Bobbing in the busy directed lives of other people, they were unmoored and uncaptained. They had bumped into each other accidentally, and now sometimes found themselves drifting together down the same stream.

She was always rushing, late for somewhere, but actually, her life was an aimless spinning sensation, passive and pushed about by all sorts of people. Like Abdullah, whose newspaper she now read every day. It frightened her more and more. She couldn't understand how gentle, understanding, kind Abdullah was connected to those articles, which preached that there was only one kind of people that counted, that anyone who disagreed should be imprisoned or sent back to China or India.

"Would China want me?" she wondered. She had been born in Malaysia. What did China have to do with her? But she had learned her lesson. She never argued with Abdullah. She made herself grateful that he was kind to her.

When she was with Henry she was moored to his life. Professor Forster was arranging for Henry to begin his fellowship in Baden-Baden in June 1970, after he finished his doctorate. She could never get so far on her own, she knew, and she was pleased to be towed beside Henry.

Auntie had stopped nagging them for a baby and was teaching her how to dress properly for a colder climate. To please her, Li An gave up wearing jeans when she went to her house for dinner, and she spent afternoons shopping with Auntie for fitted dresses and elegant skirts. She gave up her attempt to write poems and instead, to satisfy her department head, read about seventeenth-century English poetry in her library cubicle.

Chester complained that he didn't want to continue teaching at the Vocational High School. He had been there for less than a year, but he was beginning to dislike Mr. Govinand and his officiousness. Paroo was always waiting for him after classes and during breaks. He wished Paroo would find another girlfriend—he didn't want to listen to him talk about Gina again. He'd never even met Gina!

The longer he stayed with Abdullah and Samad, he said broodingly, the more he realized how different he was from them. He was tired of drinking rose syrup and of having chilies in his food. When he ate with Li An, he ordered pork chops and poured thick ketchup on the meat defiantly; he wasn't a Muslim, he repeated, and pork had fewer calories t han fatty beef.

He liked her company, he said, because she alone didn't expect him to behave in any one way. He was teaching her about the United States, and she was interested in the constant news from Washington, the demonstrations against the Vietnam War, what was happening on the American campuses. He took her to the United States Information Service library, where she chose books by William Carlos Williams, Wallace Stevens, Robert Penn Warren, and John Dos Passos.

"You can't write poems based on those Shakespearean sonnets, Lee Ann," he said. "The world's changed. If you'll read modern writers, you'll see what I mean." America seemed so far away, he complained; he hadn't realized how much he missed home till then.

They were like two homeless orphans when they were together, Li An thought. Out for a good time. They talked about her desire to write, and how difficult it was for her to write in English, and he told her about how the United States was a melting pot. Everyone melted into the American middle class. In his junior year he had taken a course on American literature, and he had been impressed by how writers like Walt Whitman spoke for a democratic American vista.

"Of course, black people in America face a lot of discrimination," he said, "because of their color. You Chinese Malaysians will never have the same problem of social discrimination. There are too many of you here. The only thing is, you'll have a problem writing in English. English has left with the British. You should really emigrate to the States."

She felt her boat whirling in the current of his talk. China, Baden-Baden, America. She felt at home only with him and with Ellen.

Nine

It's not that I suspect you," Henry said, swallowing hard. "But Chester is a man. Perhaps I've been too busy. I should have done more things with you. You are so lively, I always knew you would need more attention than other women."

Forster had told him that he should have a few days off and perhaps take Li An away for a holiday. "Ah, it's not to alarm you," Forster had mumbled, "but women, um, don't like to be neglected. You, um, you've been working very hard. You have a great future in front of you. But a young scientist, he's got, he's got to take care of his family too."

Perhaps he'd seen Li An with Chester more than once at the USIS library or riding on the Honda to some coffee shop. "Those Americans," he'd added dryly, "they're new to Malaysia. They don't observe the rules like we do."

"But nothing's happened!" she protested. "You see him as often as I do." It wasn't true, but she refused to be shamed by her lie.

Henry was miserable. He had never felt such burning misery—it made him want to turn his face away, shut his eyes so he wouldn't have to see her. No, he didn't suspect her. Wouldn't a man know if his wife had been with another man? Wouldn't he feel her skin, her inner flesh, as tainted? He would have felt the difference in her.

But he did suspect. He suspected her tomorrows. Forster had closed off the possibility of trust. What could he tell of what Li An might do the next day, or next year, with Chester or with any other man? He suspected the future in her.

"Let's go to Bangkok for two weeks," he pleaded. "It's April. You don't have any tutorials, and I can miss my German classes. We've never had a holiday together."

Just last month they had celebrated their anniversary. Or rather, Auntie had reminded them to.

Auntie liked the Western custom of romantic anniversaries and holidays, and made occasions out of Christmas and Boxing Day, the English New Year, Easter, St. Valentine's Day, and personal birthdays. She kept a calendar that marked British holidays—the Queen Mother's birthday, Queen Elizabeth's birthday, Whitsunday, Bank Holidays, Poppy Day—but she celebrated only the holidays that the expensive department stores observed. Although she wasn't a Christian, she bought colorful chocolate eggs for Easter that no one ate, and decorated the house with palms blessed in the Anglican Church. Unlike Mrs. Yeh, out of the Chinese religious festivals she celebrated only the Chinese New Year. His mother, Henry told Li An, had prepared elaborate food and invited monks to the house for Vesak Day, Ching Ming or All Souls' Day, and the anniversaries of his grandparents' deaths. She had observed special feast days to request blessings for important family events, such as when Mr. Yeh's new cement factory was opened or when Henry was sitting for his final examinations.

He and Li An didn't take holidays seriously. Christmas had been merely an interruption in his lab work; in fact, he had been so anxious about an experiment that he had gone to the lab on Christmas day.

They refused the banquet Auntie wished to throw for their anniversary. Instead, she gave a dinner at her house, and Preofessor Forster and his wife, Mrs. Schneider and her husband, and Ellen had come.

Li An didn't ask Chester because Abdullah and Samad would have to be invited as well, and that would have made the dinner difficult as Auntie would have had to avoid serving pork in the meal. Samad especially had become very strict about exposure to anything haram, like pork, that was a spiritual pollution.

Henry saw now he had been unwise to encourage Li An to amuse herself however she pleased. "Yes, Bangkok," he repeated. "We'll stay at the Oriental, it's supposed to be very romantic. And you can buy as much Thai silk as you wish."

She sat subdued beside Henry in the small Fokker Friendship plane, relieved that he was making all the decisions. The stewardess wore a tightly wrapped printed skirt and moved down the aisle modestly, her swaying buttocks a focus for the passengers' eyes. She handed them cold towels sprinkled with cologne. Li An hated the sticky scent, and she despised the purple spotted orchid on her plastic meal tray.

Over the isthmus, the plane hit an air pocket and the trays went bouncing off the retractable tables. The woman behind her screamed. Li An clutched Henry's warm hand and thought that she wouldn't mind dying now. Her mind was so distant from her body, she couldn't tell which was further away— both were receding from her, as she spun down a stream in the bucking plane. Then the airstream turned smooth and they landed safely.

The airport was breathlessly humid and noisy. On the broad road from the airport, she looked out at the pleasant flat fields and wide drains—they could have been narrow canals—with thick clusters of large-leafed plants and white and pink lotus flowers floating on them. In the city, the taxi honked and honked as pedicabs darted and blocked its way. Masses of pedestrians stepped off crowded curbs and pushed against the taxi even as the light turned green. The air was distinctly brown and clouds of carbon monoxide puffed out of the backs of buses and lorries into the taxi's open windows. She closed her window although the taxi wasn't air-conditioned: the press of traffic and people and the sour air made her nauseous.

In the Oriental's red and gold lobby scattered with brocade-covered chairs, Li An pretended not to notice the porter's rude handling of their two small bags. "He probably thinks we won't tip him," she thought miserably, and in their cool carpeted room she could only stand in suspense until Henry handed over a handful of coins.

In the mornings Henry accompanied her as she wandered through the boutiques in expensive hotels. She fingered the heavy texture of silks shimmering with unlikely colors—the sheen of fuchsia, oleander pink, tart lemon yellow, and pale cream like the first squeeze of coconut. She studied the flowered cottons. Their huge blossoms seemed obscene—hungry mouths that would fix on her body if she wore them.

She didn't like anything in the shops, although obediently she chose three lengths of silk and obediently stood still as the saleswoman passed the measuring tape around her chest, neck, and arms. She was being bound in duty to Henry, who was pleased she was having the silks tailored into loose tunics. They would be sensational in Baden-Baden.

In the hot afternoons they visited the temples. She walked in a torpor through the Temple of the Emerald Buddha. When they emerged from the dark interior, the stone court-yard burned under her bare feet as she scrambled to put on her shoes. Friezes of bodhisattvas, demon kings, and royal personages blurred as she moved slowly before them. At the sixth or seventh temple, she stared at the giant reclining Buddha and wanted to sink down with it and swell with emptiness. She could not see the figure whole. It was too vast. She could only observe as separate parts its enormous head, then the glazed eyes as large as empty dinner plates, the panoramic trunk parallel to the ground, a river of flowing robes frozen in gold. The great feet were sculpted horizontally inert, their toes perfectly formed—not like her small ones, permanently crooked.

The worst time of the day was the evening, when she had nothing to say to Henry. They had tea at the Oriental and she ordered cucumber sandwiches that were exactly as she fancied the British must have enjoyed them, thin sliced white bread and translucent wafers of cucumber between, and the butter to stick them together.

They ate in hotel restaurants. She could have Thai specialties, continental cuisine, Shanghai delicacies, Mughal curries, even Australian carpetbagger steaks stuffed with oysters. She chewed her food and felt it stick her mouth shut.

She wasn't homesick. She didn't think at all of their house in Petaling Jaya with the real Danish modern furniture, the open living room, and the young banana trees Letchmi had planted in the backyard. She was struck down by a vast emptiness that swirled in her like the brown water of the Chao Phraya River swirling lazily past the garden of the Oriental.

Even Henry knew the holiday was not a success. The last night at the hotel he held her close in bed. "You don't like Bangkok," he said, wrapping her in his arms, she lying still like a bird in a covered hand. He didn't want her moving restlessly, gazing restlessly, never concentrating on one sight, always on the verge of moving away from his side.

"I do, I do," she assured him. "Only it's too large. I feel like a fly on a wall. I'm not sure what to do here, the whole city is a blank wall to me."

"But we've visited temples and stores. We took the boat down the river."

"I do like it." She kept her face hidden on his chest and muffled her voice. "Thank you, Henry. It's the grandest holiday I've had." She licked his ear and caressed him carefully, yielding obediently as his passion silenced them.

He was jubilant the next day. He loved returning to their home. Letchmi didn't like being alone for two weeks and fussed over them. "Missy want a lime drink? I iron all master's shirt."

Letchmi had come to them from an unhappy childless marriage to a tapper on a rubber plantation. One day her husband had knocked at the door and threatened to drag her away, and Henry had called the police. Her husband never came back, and she doted on Henry.

They had bought a brass Nataraja in the Bangkok Sunday flea market for Letchmi, and she hurriedly kissed it and carried it to her room, afraid they might change their minds about the gift. Now she unpacked their bags and was busy arranging piles of clothes for the wash.

Li An picked up a book, a study of seventeenth-century Puritanism in the American colonies, and lay on the uncomfortable Danish sofa to read it. Chester had found it for her in the USIS library. It would help round off her readings in English seventeenth-century poetry, he said; there was more to Western history than British history. She hoped Henry would leave for the lab. It was Sunday, and perhaps Chester would be at home. She knew she wouldn't see him, not after Henry had disapproved, but they could talk on the phone.

But Henry stayed home all day catching up on the papers, which were full of stories of the upcoming elections.

"Look," he said, "your friend Abdullah is doing it again." It was an editorial in Abdullah's paper.

"How can they expect us to take this quietly?" He smacked the page and it tore.

She smoothed the page and pieced the torn parts together. It was the usual call for unity against a common enemy. The elections must change nothing, the editorial said, unless it was for the benefit of the real people, the ra'ayat. The ra'ayat must assert their power in whatever way necessary. Let the enemy beware of pushing the people too far. The conflict would be deadly.

The black print squiggled before her tired eyes like little worms.

Suddenly she was reminded of Gina, dead, it seemed to her, for the longest time. She fancied these were the same worms that had crawled over Gina's flesh, breeding millions of other black worms, and now they had escaped the steamy earth and were crawling on hundreds of thousands of Sunday papers.

She was afraid of what she read, for the warning rang true. She remembered Abdullah's gentle patient voice explaining his vision of a single people. For separation to be nurtured, there couldn't be the possibility of love. Love broke down the purity of a vision of singleness. Hatred, then, was preferable to the breaking of the single self, to the possibility of a tearing down of race.

Ten

A new Henry waited for her each morning and drove her to the university. He picked her up promptly at noon for lunch, and even followed her in the evenings to visit Ellen. In Henry's watchful company, Ellen sat in front of the television glumly most of the time instead of joking around as she usually did with Li An.

Professor Forster had shamed Henry into recognizing his duty to Li An. He had accepted a one-year position as a lecturer in the biology department, and then they would leave for the sophisticated freedom of Baden-Baden, where she would not feel so confined. In the meantime, it was his duty to lessen the constraints of a narrow academic life, to entertain her and occupy her hours.

Besides, he was writing up the results of his experiments. He did not enjoy writing, and could only write in his office for a limited time. He tired easily when he had to fumble with words to shape them into sentences. They fell into awkward masses that he had to worry over and reform. "I wish you could do the writing for me," he said, jokingly.

She had begun to write again, but in a desultory manner. She tried to begin a daily journal.

1 May
Read Cranshaw. Am getting more interested in Puritan literature. Jane Austen novels too much fiction, worse than True

Romances. No happy-ever-after except perhaps in next life. Very hot today. Lunch with Henry at Maxim's. Papers still full of bad news.

2 May

Tired of English literature. Puritan ideal of new kingdom of God on Plymouth Rock something to think about. Is this what Abdullah means by country for Islam? Ironic history—difference between city on a hill and America after Watts riots, King assassination. Malaysia too tolerant for American-style violence. Visited Auntie with Henry. She's expecting Ah Pah back next week.

3 May

A writer's journal is supposed to be more interesting than this. Can't be a writer when life is so boring. Still very hot today. It's always very hot in Kuala Lumpur, why am I making a note of it? I don't even have weather to write about. Mornings clear, increasing heat and humidity through the day, thundershowers in the late afternoon, clearing by evening, clear skies at night. A daily journal. More interesting reading in the newspapers. Lots of political reporting. Everyone wants his piece of the cake. Problem is it's the same piece of cake; someone's got to lose. Or so the papers say. Is this true of life? My life? What's my piece of cake? Am I winning or losing?

5 May

Have to take the journal more seriously. Haven't written in almost two days. Surely there must be something to write about! Hard to take anything seriously when it's so hot. Stayed in bedroom all day with air-conditioning going full blast. Something's wrong with me—I'm not depressed am I? USIS books overdue, haven't read two of them. Tried to write a poem following Williams's variable foot. Chester's suggestion to read American poetry. Doesn't sound like me. But nothing I've written sounds like me—whiny, petty, dissatisfied. Poetry already too grand, fine attitudes. How to write a good whiny poem? Maybe I should be a journalist like Abdullah. Poetry is for people who know something. No wonder I'm depressed.

6 May
Returned books to USIS. Don't like riding in KL anymore.
It's crowded and dangerous, buses smoking carbon monoxide
in huge clouds, taxis pushing you into the drains, pedestrians jumping at you from hidden corners. Wonder if it'll
become as bad as Bangkok? I'd run away. Strange to be in USIS
library without Chester. First time. Place looked deserted, drea-
ry. His loud voice makes everything cheerful. The library is
dull, feel of heavy novels, *Time*, *Newsweek*, reference books.
Strange, it has Malaysian staff dealing with the public. The
Americans stay to themselves—I can see them in the offices
behind the glass doors. So unlike Chester. I think I see him
everywhere. It's the Peace Corps mentality, he tells me, to be
out with the local people.

7 May
It's Thursday. Ran into him in the lounge. He wanted to know
what happened. I think he misses me. Told him I was working on my writing—he thinks it's my thesis on seventeenth-
century religious poetry. If only he knew this journal is it! Had
lunch with Henry at Bistro. I hate the Bistro. Told Henry I
should spend some time alone with Ellen. After all, our
friendship goes further back than Henry. He's being very kind.
Papers going on about elections. Everyone's talking about it.
Even the department head made some comment in passing,
something about having to be sensitive to everyone's point
of view. Of course, he's so high up he can see everyone's point
of view clearly. I'm confused. Are the Chinese not true
Malaysians? Is the problem that we are not Malays? Maybe
Gina was right after all. Maybe everyone should marry Malay.
Then we'll all be one people. But I can't imagine Henry mar-
ried to a Malay girl, he's such a China-type!

8 May
Friday. Chester called the department, wants to know why I'm
avoiding him. I'm so impatient with him. I don't think he sees
me as a woman. I told him I'm married and Henry doesn't like
me going out with other men. Perhaps that will shock him into

some understanding. Peace Corps men are like modern-day monks, poverty and no idea of women. Henry is right, he's always right. I have to be careful around Chester, otherwise something stupid will happen. Chester wants to talk about us. I know Henry won't like my meeting him. Maybe we can talk in Ellen's house. In front of Ellen. She'll keep things straight.

12 May
Exciting Tuesday. Elections today. Looks like some victory for our side. Our side? Here I am, didn't vote, but I have a side, know which is my piece of cake. Henry wants to go to a party tomorrow to celebrate with his biology friends. Why is he so political suddenly? Seems to me that everyone is so political suddenly, everyone's talking about this right and that right, everyone in the lounge and along the corridor. Buzz, buzz, like red ants, very excited, marching around with rumors. Too much is happening. I haven't been reading for a week, except the newspapers. Even Auntie started talking to Ah Pah about politics on Sunday. All this talk about Chinese rights makes me sick too. Malay rights, Chinese rights. No one talks about Malaysian rights. I am a Malaysian. I don't exist.

"You go to the party by yourself," Li An said. "Ellen wants to talk to me about switching jobs again."

She was only half lying. She had run into Chester in the lounge. This time he appeared to have been waiting for her.

She knew she shouldn't have accepted his invitation, but it was as if the hysteria of the elections had touched her. Chester also seemed more nervous than usual. He kept pulling his long hair off his face and twisting it at the back into a knot that immediately unraveled.

"Couldn't we just talk? Abdullah and Samad are up to their necks with the election news, and I'm getting homesick. Maybe it's just the one-year mark. I've been warned about it. After the first year the Peace Corps gets a whole lot of dropouts. Like your system can't take all that foreignness anymore. I'm even dreaming of my old high school, like I miss it! I'm in bad shape." His laugh was nervous.

She called Ellen at work from the lounge.

"Now you want me to entertain your lover boy? All right. I'll be home by five-thirty. You want a chaperon, but the harm is already done."

Why did Ellen always have to be so brusque, she wondered. She wished she could confide in a caring mother, someone like Second Mrs. Yeh, not like her own mother, all wrapped up in her stepfather and second family.

For months she had thought of Ellen and Chester as her best friends, but now she had too many secrets from them. Secrets about her feelings.

Feelings separated people from each other, even when—or especially when—they were about the other person. Ellen with her witch's eyes had seen her feelings for Chester even before she was aware of them, but she still had to pretend with Ellen. She wasn't like Gina, who had shared her feelings with Ellen. Ellen would like her to do that, but it would be like being unfaithful to Chester. Or was it to Henry?

Li An didn't want to leave the house before Henry did. She was afraid he would follow her to Ellen's house, even though she knew he would never stoop so low. His party began at six, and she had told Chester she would meet him at Ellen's at five-thirty.

At five-fifteen she was ready to leave, but she waited for Henry to get into the shower before riding off. He was touched by her waiting and kept talking to her. Finally she reminded him, "It's 5:35. You'll be late for your party."

Chester was sitting on the cement steps by the gate when she arrived. It was almost six, but Ellen's car wasn't there and the gate was padlocked. The ixora bushes that grew over the fence drooped over his head, and his feet were in a pile of large brown acacia leaves that the wind had blown neatly into the corner.

"I'm sorry," she apologized. "Ellen said she'd be here by five-thirty, and she's never late."

He was gloomy and good-natured at the same time. "That's all right. I'm accustomed to being left alone." He looked at her as if expecting her to do something about it.

"What shall we do?" She pushed the Honda stand down and stared into the dark garden behind the locked gate.

If only she had the key to Ellen's house! She could not ask Chester home—Letchmi might say something to Henry, and what if Henry was still at the house? He would suspect she had planned to bring Chester home as soon as he was gone. "We'll give her another ten minutes. Perhaps her car had a flat tire." His voice was mildly reasonable, while she felt a terrible fury against Ellen. Ellen, she was sure, had deliberately forgotten about them. Ellen was punishing her for liking Chester, just as she had wanted to punish Gina for liking Paroo. Ellen was drinking at some pub in Kuala Lumpur and had ordered another beer instead of leaving.

A large green leaf fell from the overhanging acacia branch and landed at her feet.

Chester did not rise from the steps. He reached for the leaf and fingered it, turning it back and forth in a relaxed manner.

"Have you really been working on your writing?" His eyes were on the leaf.

She couldn't lie to him.

"I have to make a decision, whether to stay on in Kuala Lumpur," he said when she didn't reply. "Perhaps I'm not cut out for the Peace Corps. I know some volunteers who ask for a second two-year term. I met this couple at training camp who'd been to Lahore, a desert village. They were thin and burned brown. You'd think they were victims of a famine. But they were going back for a second term. They couldn't wait to go back to their village. She was teaching school, all ages, from kindergarten to grandmothers. He was helping the farmers find wells. Been digging for two years and found only a few wells. I thought I would be like them, teach and dig wells at the same time. That's why I volunteered for woodworking. You're doing something useful with your hands. Who knew no one would be interested in woodworking here?"

He'd forgotten about waiting for Ellen. Li An saw he wanted someone to talk to. He needed a listener, and the steps before a locked gate, out in the night air, was as good a place for him as any.

"I don't belong in this country." His voice was slowing down, as if he was running out of things to say.

"Oh, go back to America!" She made herself sound hard and uncaring. Chester didn't seem to be listening. She searched the dark road for a sign of Ellen's car. There was no one in sight. The other houses were lit, but all their gates were closed. A television squawked from the next house. They could have been in a foreign country.

He kept talking about having to decide soon. It got dark suddenly, and she couldn't see his face although he was only a few feet away. The scent of cooling leaves and ixora mixed with the night, forming a warm circle around her. She sat beside him on the steps. They were so narrow her head touched his shoulder.

"Come on," he said. "Give me your keys. I'll give you some coffee at my place."

All the way to his bungalow, she wondered if Abdullah and Samad would be home. The corner coffee shop was deserted, and the roads were dark and empty. She didn't stop to ask why. The desertion was like something she was imagining.

Samad was home. He unlocked the iron gates and pulled them in hurriedly. "Why are you on the road? Are you crazy?" His face was unsmiling. "Don't you know there's a curfew? Lucky nothing happen to you."

He looked at her with dislike. "What's she doing here?" He would talk only to Chester.

"I brought her for some coffee." Chester put his arm around her shoulder lightly as if to excuse her.

"What curfew?" She saw again the empty roads and locked gates.

Samad wouldn't answer.

"It's the elections, isn't it?" Chester asked.

"Yah, those people threw pork in our people's backyards and started a lot of trouble."

From the way Samad's eyes refused to meet hers she knew it was also her trouble.

"She has to stay here for the night," Samad said to Chester. He sounded bitter. "But she cannot sleep in Abdullah's room."

"What will I tell Henry? He'll be worrying about me!"

Samad started up the stairs. "I'm going to my room," he said over his shoulder. "There's nothing I can do."

She heard his door shut.

Only Letchmi was home when she called. "Oh, Missy," she babbled, "you be careful! Master already call, say cannot come home. He also worry about you. I pray to Nataraja keep you safe."

Chester remained cheerful. "The bed isn't too clean," he said as he brought her upstairs. "I never was good at laundry." And indeed the bed was unmade, the sheet had been pushed to the foot and was trailing on the floor.

A saucer of cigarette stubs was on the floor, and a pile of paperbacks balanced by the crumpled pillow.

"I'm going on the roof to check if anything can be seen."

She followed him as he stood on a chair and pushed up through a small door in the ceiling and hoisted his body through. He clasped her hand and heaved her up like a sack of rice, and she lay with her arms and trunk on the flat roof, taking in the cool night air before scrambling to her feet.

The roof was flat and without any railings. Although she was standing in the middle of its expanse, she was immediately swept by vertigo. She kept her eyes shut for a time. The air was cool but smoky.

"Look," he said, his hand on her shoulder, "there's a glow over there. And I can see smoke."

When she opened her eyes she saw that one side of the night sky was touched with orange. In the orange light tiny dark lines rose like drifting spider webs. They could hear nothing. The entire area of closely built row houses was silent. It seemed as if there was a blackout as well as a curfew. Everyone seemed to have turned off their lights, to have shut their doors like Samad, and disappeared.

Chester was exhilarated. "It's a historic moment," he repeated. "Do you realize that? May thirteenth. We're seeing history before our eyes."

All she saw was the black silent area of Petaling Jaya, the dim fire on the skyline, and webs of feathery smoke.

Later she lay on his bed and wondered what she was feeling. The riots were the trouble predicted for after the elections. People like Abdullah had been expecting it. The Chinese could not win without trouble starting up, he had said.

She hadn't expected anything. Perhaps, stubbornly, she had hoped that Abdullah was wrong, that elections could be won or lost without race, religion, language, the whole divisiveness of the country going off like strings of firecrackers. That smoke did not come from fireworks, she knew.

Chester had given her a sarong to sleep in. She knotted it more securely around her chest, thinking, this is Chester's sarong.

She couldn't keep the trouble in her mind. Her heart was beating very fast right under the sarong knot, and her body was vibrating quietly. The vibrations, she recognized, were a natural motion of her body. Every body was constantly vibrating. The breath, pulse, heartbeat, set up a ceaseless motion, a tension of desire that was life.

The reading lamp was still on downstairs. He looked up as she walked down the steps. He had been reading a paperback. He wore a sarong around his waist. His chest was broad and flat, and reddish hair grew thickly on the front. His nipples were small and rosy. She could hardly take in his nakedness. "I'm frightened," she said, and meant it.

Before he reached for her, he turned off the light. It was only then that she knew he loved her after all.

Eleven

She was still asleep when Abdullah knocked and pushed the door open. Above the whirring of the standing fan and her own gummy drowsiness she heard him say, "Eh, Li An! You must go now. Get up quick! The curfew lift for only one hour so people can get home. Quick, lah!"

Nervously, she sat up. The checked sarong was still knotted around her. She had fallen asleep without tidying Chester's bed and the stack of paperbacks strewn beside the pillow. Her face had lain on one and its spine had left a painful crease on her cheek.

Abdullah stood by the door. "You get change quick. I take you home."

Her clothes didn't seem to fit that morning. She felt hollowed out and overflowing with a sweet energy. She wished she could take a bath before dressing, but Abdullah was tapping at the door again.

"Better I drive you," he said. Chester was nowhere in sight. She remembered he had walked her upstairs, his arm around her waist, and had kissed her at the door. She had heard him falling into Abdullah's bed before the strongest lassitude swept over her, and then Abdullah had knocked.

The front door was open and the garden gate as well. Abdullah must have just come home, she saw. Her Honda was still outside the gate.

"We bring your Honda another day. Safer you go in my car."

The cool quiet morning air woke her finally. Every gate was shut, every door unopened. They were the only people out on the road.

She looked shyly at Abdullah as he drove through the empty roads. His face, brown with square-cut cheeks and chin, was set and determined. Through puffy eyes he stared at the road ahead. She noticed his white shirt was rumpled as if he had slept in it.

"What happened?"

"A riot in Kuala Lumpur."

"What happened?" she asked again.

"I told you the Chinese cannot push us too far. This is our country. If they ask for trouble, they get it."

She had known, and she hadn't known. Abdullah, she knew now, was telling her his truth. We/Our country. They/No country.

His truth was wrong; she was sure it was wrong. You cannot be born and live in a place all your life without that place belonging to you. How could you not grow roots, invisible filaments of attachment that tied you down to a ground, a source of water? If a tree were pushed off the earth it stood on, deprived of its water, it would die.

But this was not the time to argue with Abdullah. Perhaps after today she and Abdullah would never be able to argue again.

Letchmi was unlocking the gate before Abdullah could honk. She must have been waiting by the window all morning. Henry was on the phone, and Abdullah drove off immediately, without saying good-bye. Henry put down the receiver as soon as she came in, with Letchmi hurriedly locking the gate and door behind them.

"I can't get through to Ah Pah! No one's picking up the phone!" He rubbed her shoulder distractedly.

All she could think of was her shower. She needed to wash Chester's touch off her body; she was afraid Henry would be able to feel where she had felt Chester. Her face, her breasts, her thighs, her fingers, she was sure, must smell of Chester's mouth and sweat. And Letchmi with her woman's sense would surely know she had been with another man.

"I have a nervous stomach," she said, hurrying to the bathroom, where she stripped and stayed under the hot stinging shower for long minutes. Carefully she powdered her whole body, shaking the talc generously as if to cover over the fingerprints.

Henry was still trying the phone when she came downstairs, clean in fresh shirt and pants. "All Ah Pah's businesses are closed because of the curfew. I don't want to call Mark in Singapore. They may become frightened."

He was obviously alarmed. He kept picking up the receiver and dialing the number and counting the beeps before putting down the receiver.

By afternoon Henry was positive something had happened to Ah Pah. Li An had never seen him in this state. He withdrew to the armchair by the phone and in silence sat all day, staring with a frown at the wall. After he had refused her urgings to drink some coffee, have some breakfast, eat some lunch, call again, she sat on the sofa near him and pretended to read.

She tried the radio several times, but aside from the brief news announcement of the curfew hours and reports that the army and police had everything under control, there were only the usual pop songs.

Like his touch-me-nots, Henry sat in closed silence, his usual reasonable cheerfulness and purposeful activity contracted into a suffering suspense. When the call came, he was not surprised.

It was the doctor who called, not the police. Auntie was suffering from shock and minor bruises—she had hidden herself in a cupboard full of Ah Pah's shirts and pants, neatly ironed and hanging from expensive wood hangers. Somehow she had contracted her body, pulled the cupboard door shut, and remained in a folded, contorted position, neck almost disjointed among the entangled hangers, without a cry of pain to give away her presence. She had remained so until the police finally arrived, then banged her head against the door, and so they had discovered her. Mr. Yeh, who had not managed to conceal himself, was dragged into the living room and killed.

The doctors were overworked, with the numbers of reported casualties mounting. Auntie did not have to remain in the
hospital, and she had asked to go to Henry and Li An.

The police would not release Mr. Yeh's body. The family
could make funeral arrangements, but the body could not be
viewed for fear of further public disorder.

Auntie would not leave their house for the next few weeks.
"Don't go," she begged whenever Li An tried to leave for the
university. She didn't like being alone with Letchmi, whom
she distrusted. "She'll open the door to them," she warned.
"You cannot trust other people, only your own kind."

Henry could not help. He was too busy talking to lawyers
and to Ah Pah's business associates and the managers of
various companies and factories.

Their house was filled with wreaths and bouquets of flowers. Ah Pah had been buried quickly, without the customary
public wake, but word had gotten around the community.
Enormous circles of frangipani, daisies, chrysanthemums,
and tall spikes of dahlias and arum lilies that would have been
sent to the wake came to the house instead.

Li An refused to have them in the house. Their heavy scent
reminded her of Ah Pah's corpse rotting in the cheaply constructed coffin the hospital had ordered, one of hundreds of
the same type used for all those killed and sent to the morgue
that Wednesday. But she did not throw the flowers out.
Instead they were placed outdoors, propped on bamboo
stakes and falling over vases, jars, bottles, anything that
would serve to hold them as they wilted and browned in the
stifling May heat.

Even with the wreaths left outdoors, the thick scent of hundreds of full blossoms decaying together filled the house. Without a breeze, the musty air drifted in through the windows and
filled her nostrils with remorse. She had never felt at ease with
Ah Pah. He who to her had appeared brutal had been brutalized
himself, and now her body was slow with aches and regrets.

One morning when she went out to open the gate for Henry
as he went to meet directors of a company in which his father
had been the major shareholder, she saw her Honda parked

outside. She looked for a note attached to the handlebars, but there was only the machine with its worn red plastic seat and the round steel womb of its fuel tank gleaming in the sunshine.

Henry did not notice the Honda as he backed the car out. He had become preoccupied after Ah Pah's death, and he now seemed to have taken on his father's sunken silence.

She wheeled the Honda into the front yard and stood it among the leaning wreaths and over-toppling lilies like another memorial.

She waited for Chester to call.

By the middle of June, Auntie had found a house in Petaling Jaya near them, and Henry put the Kuala Lumpur house up for sale. Much of the lovely rosewood furniture had been broken. Nothing had been stolen, but a furious orgy of destruction had smashed, battered, slashed, torn, ripped, and scattered the possessions in the house. All the blue-and-white porcelain vases, plates, cups, and ginger-jars that Auntie had collected over the years from Taiwan, Hong Kong, Indonesia, and Singapore had been smashed. The delicately colored pastel fabrics that covered the chairs and beds had been ripped. The red-gold jadeite Kuan Yin lay beside Mr. Yeh's body. Someone had used it as a club.

Auntie said she had cried most when she saw the Kuan Yin beside her husband. It was she who should have laid beside him, but she had been so terrified that she had hidden herself, and survived instead.

Even after she moved into her new house, Auntie insisted on Li An's company.

A new group of students began at the university, and again Li An taught Herbert's poem. This time she felt a new awkwardness talking about death. "All must die," Herbert had written. Gina had died, and Ah Pah, and hundreds more in the riots since she had last read the poem aloud.

The students seemed many years younger than herself. "Only a sweet and virtuous soul," Herbert wrote, lived after death. The students, quieter than those the year before, and less critical, listened with neither questions nor conviction. Unbelievingly, she heard herself talk about the quest for meaning in the face of death and the affirmation of absolute virtue in the face of universal corruption.

Every day Auntie tried to recover her settled vision. She would say in the morning, "I'm going shopping for curtains. This house is so dusty, the windows cannot be opened. I have to keep the air-conditioning on all the time. Maybe heavy curtains will keep the dust out."

But in the afternoons she was still waiting for Li An to come home. "It's too soon," she explained. "The shops aren't in a safe area. I don't know what kind of taxi driver I'll find. I may get someone dangerous."

Her sight had cracked and was now crossed with lines of fear. Henry drove Auntie home each evening, where she was met by a Chinese amah, hired to keep her company through the night.

Each day as she waited for Chester to appear at the faculty lounge Li An refused to allow herself to be afraid. She knew he was planning something for them, something wonderful. No man could touch a woman as he had her without love, and love had inevitable consequences. She repeated the consequences in her mind as she drank lime juice and smoked another cigarette. She would not go to Baden-Baden. Chester would explain everything to Henry. Beyond that she could not imagine anything else.

By July she was afraid she had only imagined everything.

When she finally saw him walking through the door, his tall figure coming in from the bright sunshine into the dim lounge, a horrible pain went through her. Chester went to the counter for cigarettes, and it was Abdullah who came up to her first.

"I heard about your father. Very sorry."

"My father-in-law." She felt foolish almost immediately. It didn't matter that Ah Pah was her father-in-law; Abdullah's condolence was the same.

"Terrible," he continued, not seeming to notice her correction. "We must make sure this thing never happen again. The country must change. A terrible thing happen, but it is not so bad if it teach us a lesson. In Malaysia, rights of the ra'ayat must come first, like in the French Revolution and American Revolution. If rights of people not first, then surely more killing and all kinds of problems. This is what history teach us. Some people must suffer; history show some must be sacrifice for majority good. But we all Malaysians, yah, even those who must sacrifice."

Her eyes filled. The admiration she felt for him spilled into her eyes. But she didn't believe him. Mr. Yeh would not have understood Abdullah's nobility on his account. Auntie would have been outraged to see her sitting with him in such a friendly manner. Even Henry, she suspected, would have disagreed with him.

But she wanted to believe Abdullah. He gave a meaning to the senseless slaughter, the unspeakable fears of the last month. Silent, she pressed his hand. He was uncomfortable and moved it away as soon as he could.

Chester joined them with an opened Coca-Cola bottle in his hand. He tipped his head and drank straight from it. "Has Abdullah told you I'm leaving next month?" He noticed her tears and put the bottle down.

"Li An is crying about her father-in-law."

"I'm sorry. We heard about it only last week. It's been a tough few weeks. I had to make a report to the U.S. Embassy. Our parents were after the embassy people to make sure we were safe, and we were warned not to get involved with the local trouble. I was told to stay home as much as possible. If it wasn't for Samad and Abdullah I'd have starved to death. I didn't even get to the market." Chester stopped and drank from the bottle again, for she was crying hard now. "Do you want us to leave?"

When she shook her head, Abdullah said, "I must see Encik Hamid for an interview. I come back and get you later, okay, Chester?"

Li An wiped her eyes with the crumpled paper napkin. "When are you leaving?"

"Umm," Chester lit a cigarette and inhaled for a moment, "about the third week of August. My mother is really pleased I'm coming home. The Kuala Lumpur director doesn't seem to mind that I'm leaving before my term is up. The Peace Corps is concerned about its volunteers in Malaysia, and is urging us to consider our options. It isn't good for Americans to get in the middle of foreign national politics."

She listened hard. Was he explaining something to her that she was missing? "And then?"

"And then?" He sounded surprised. "I don't know. Probably graduate school, if I can find one to take me so late. I don't want to work yet. Teaching here has shown me I'm not ready for the working world—it's a grind."

You don't remember a thing, she thought. Didn't you lie down beside me, didn't you swallow me up? Even as she questioned him silently her feelings closed against him. Her eyes had dried, and without any effort she lit a cigarette, shaking her head at his offer of a light.

"Isn't it strange," she said mockingly, "how people who don't know what they want end up at university?"

Twelve

She could not be cheerful at the farewell party Samad and Abdullah gave for Chester.

Henry had forgotten about Professor Forster's warnings when he heard Chester was leaving. Besides, Li An was constantly with Auntie, while Chester was spending his last few weeks in Malaysia traveling around the country and seeing as much of it as he could.

He went up to Kedah to stay with Samad's family in their village, and to Johore, where Abdullah's father was a retired civil servant. He took off with some Peace Corps friends to the Penang beaches, and spent a day in Malacca among the ruins of Portuguese and Dutch fortresses and tombs.

At the party he described a revelation he had under a flame-of-the-forest tree in Malacca, by the fifteenth-century Portuguese gatehouse, the A Famosa.

"Looking up at those crimson flowers—you know how beautiful they are, with long tassels and so bright against the blue sky—I thought how futile the Portuguese were in coming to Malacca. What I have learned this year is that white people have no place in the East. The East is like the flame-of-the-forest. It's going to remain beautiful no matter what happens. But everything the Portuguese did, their cannons and forts and churches, it's all dead history, out of place . . ."

"Stoned out of your mind!" Robert interrupted.

Robert had been Chester's traveling companion. He was

staying for the second year in Malaysia, and he was enjoying the pathos of good-byes surrounding Chester's departure.

"Would you believe it? First time he's been stoned. What a sight! He's lying under this tree, looking at the flowers as they're falling down, and mumbling. Hey, real Cheng Mai Gold!"

Ellen snorted. "What gold? You Americans are a terrible influence. Marijuana, R and R, Vietnam GIs. Suddenly got prostitutes everywhere. Where Malaysia like this before?"

Everyone looked uncomfortable.

The room was full of different people who didn't know each other: Peace Corps Americans with slim Malay and Chinese girls, Malay journalists and broadcast staffers from Samad's and Abdullah's offices, Indian and Chinese teachers from the Vocational High School, friends Chester had made at Malay classes at the university. He seemed to know everyone.

Paroo was somewhere in the crowd. He had tried talking to Li An, but the noise was too loud and the bodies pressing on them pushed them apart.

Above the confusion Ellen's question was heard by many. She had been drinking but her speech wasn't slurred.

"You're right." Chester was as relaxed as Ellen was sharp. "That's why I'm getting out. Americans don't belong here. We're hurting the place. Like Malacca. It was just an old fishing village until those gunboats came along."

"No, it was never just an old fishing village," Robert interrupted, laughing. "Isabella Bird called the country 'The Golden Chersonese,' way before there was Cheng Mai Gold. That's the fancy Victorian way of saying 'peninsula,' get it? She was on to something. Chester's problem," he added, addressing the circle around them, "is he'd rather be in America. He can't see himself here, even stoned."

Li An hated Chester then. She had visited Malacca with Henry months before she met Chester, and had loved its ruins and air of melancholic decay. Even its rundown shadows breathed of adventures and encounters, and she had pointed out to Henry these possibilities in the moldering colonial, Chinese, and Malay structures that crowded the town. History, she insisted, was living in Malacca, visible in the gorgeous Eurasian children and the Latin mass they heard that

Sunday at St. Francis Church. The tropical breezes from the Straits blew reminders of generations of strangers and exiles from distant places. The rustle in the heavy leaves of the sea almond trees on St. Paul's Hill, by the roofless church and sagging stone walls, carried stories that Li An could still imagine, stories written in the Latin script on the sarcophagi rising from the lallang-covered hillsides, the Chinese calligraphy carved above the ornate doors of merchants' homes, and the cursive Jawi lettering proliferating by the Malay mosques.

Listening to the laughter that followed, she was glad Chester was leaving. How could she have thought she loved him, she wondered, when he was so shallow and ugly in his thinking?

Yet she was afraid all the time. Although she had washed her body thoroughly the next morning, Chester, she feared, had marked her forever.

If Henry hadn't been so preoccupied with his grief, with the legal and business problems arising from Ah Pah's death, with the demands placed on him by his mother, brothers, and Auntie, with his neglect of his lab work and teaching duties, he would surely have noticed the changes in her body. In the mornings she dragged herself out of bed, the early nausea already rising in her mouth.

At first she thought it was because she was miserable over Chester's leaving. But now her nipples were sore. They tingled all by themselves, without touch or thought. Her body had a life of its own—it hurt and was sick. Through the heat and noise she wondered if she should tell Chester. He was flying to London the next day, and then home to New York. But there were too many people at his party.

It was hardly three months since Mr. Yeh's death, since the arson and the riots. Henry and Li An had stopped wearing black after the first month because it made them too conspicuous, mourners of a public execution. There was grief enough everywhere. She saw it in the tight faces of pedestrians, the whispers of once bold debaters in the faculty lounge, the uneasy glances over the shoulders in restaurants as diners lowered their voices.

No one knew what to believe. Was it prophesied in the stars or was it retribution for arrogant Chinese overreaching of goals?

Some excused the killings as a simple matter of spontaneous outrage against economic oppressors; others thought them calculated murderous revenge, manipulated mob hysteria. Someone called the violence a disease of the blood, striking, as the historians noted, every thirty years, like malarial fever that ravaged and then lay dormant before running its course again. How many had been struck? No one dared to ask.

Like a victim, Li An wondered about her past behavior. What had she done to contribute to Ah Pah's death? Perhaps if the brainy Chinese like Henry and herself confessed to their arrogance, gave up their selfish interests in their own well-being, submitted themselves to the will of the Malay ra'ay-at, the killings might not have occurred.

She didn't believe that, just as she didn't believe that if she forgot what happened that night, her body would stop hurting. But she couldn't go on thinking of Ah Pah's death or her body's tenderness all the time. With the other guests at Chester's party, she was tired of grief and fear.

Only a few months after the riots, they were desperate for a good time. Their voices rose in a frenzied babble. Grabbing beers and orange squashes, roasted chickpeas and peanuts, they lit cigarettes and moved restlessly from corner to corner.

A stranger stepped on her foot and didn't notice her wince. Henry was talking to another stranger near the kitchen. A tall, thin American was saying enthusiastically, over Li An's head to someone she couldn't see, "Out at Genting the epiphytes grow to tremendous sizes. Ooah!"

Suddenly the lights went off, music blared, and men of all sizes were clutching women and pushing them around and around the little space in the middle of the room. Li An found herself backed into a corner by bodies gyrating to the scratchy twang and bang of electric guitars and drums.

At the front door Chester, with Paroo by his elbow, was welcoming latecomers. Someone had lit an incense stick and the scent of patchouli overwhelmed the malty sting of Tiger and Anchor beers.

Li An wondered what would happen if she were to push her way to Chester's side and say—she would have to shout to be heard—"I'm pregnant." Would everyone stop dancing?

Would the horrible music be turned off? Would the lights go on, and Henry and Abdullah come running to hold her hand? Would Paroo congratulate her?

But she imagined Chester's face falling, as ignorant of what it meant for her to be pregnant as he was ignorant of what it had meant that night when she—her body—could not be sorry for the riots, when she forgot, never knew, she was Malaysian and Chester was American.

"So your heart is broken?"

Li An's breath caught. Had she been talking aloud? It was only Ellen, who smiled wickedly.

"No, not broken." Li An tried smiling back. "I'm pregnant."

The words were shaped before she could stop herself. No one would hear her. She had merely moved her lips. The guitars twanged more ferociously; the women threw their bodies with greater abandon.

"You bloody fool!" Ellen scowled. "With an American." She scowled in Chester's direction. "You didn't tell him."

Ellen knew everything about her, Li An thought. How did she get so close?

Li An shook her head. A wildly spinning dancer bumped into her, then spun away without a word. The drums pounded in her head.

"What are you going to do?"

Before she could think of an answer, Henry was behind Ellen, pointing to the door. Ellen's nails dug into her wrist, but she pulled away, relieved.

At the door Chester was talking to Robert's girlfriend, an Indian in a transparent sari whose cinnamon skin gleamed like a moth under the door light. She had just arrived, late, and was already waiting for Robert to take her home.

Li An was conscious that she would never see Chester again; she did not plan to say good-bye to him at the airport. She bit her lip, afraid her mouth would shape the words that would change her life.

"Lee Ann, you come and visit me someday."

The dusky goddess was waiting for them to leave—she hadn't finished telling Chester about Robert's bad behavior at her parents' home last night.

"You too, Henry."

Awkwardly Chester hugged her.

As she moved out of his arms she saw his face, young, shy, confused. How could she have expected him to take charge of her life? He was as lost as she was.

She couldn't cry.

She sat in the white Mercedes as Henry drove home, and the satellite streets of Petaling Jaya were as bleak as the silence in her mind when she pondered her future.

Book Two

CIRCLING

WESTCHESTER COUNTY, NEW YORK

1980

One

Jason Kingston's voice had once been a bow touched to a string that drew out taut resonances and made his listeners mentally lean out. Now, like the gut flapping above his belt and falling ever lower toward the earth, his voice flapped at the back of his throat. The string had loosened, and Chester sometimes found himself in danger of dozing off after an hour of listening to Jason talk.

Still, Chester was aware of how his old teacher continued to dominate the room, but now with his formidable bulk, the substance of his life turning to flesh without apology. Even in the auditorium, performing with six other musicians in the amateur gamelan troupe, Jason posed a genial mastery. Holding his weight in restrained yogic balance, he brushed the brass gongs with brief delicate motions while Andrea gave a series of bing-bongs and Chester thumped the skins of his drums to a crescendo.

The audience clapped with some enthusiasm, but already a number of women had risen and were pushing their arms through their coat sleeves. John Gorham, the conductor of the Columbia Gamelan Ensemble, bowed, and the embroidered panels hanging from his loose coat skewered round him in a crazy patchwork of colors.

A woman in the second row raised her hand. "What does your costume mean?"

"'Mean'?"

"Well, it looks exotic, but I don't know what to make of it; it doesn't make any sense."

"'Sense'?"

A ripple of laughter passed through the audience, and the women pushing their way through rows of metal folding chairs stopped and turned to listen. Women by the door drifted back and stood in the aisle.

"I want to know if there is a special significance to your costume."

Meryl always stands up for her rights and her right to her questions, Chester thought admiringly. It was another of the many things that he envied about her and that explained why he was happy married to her.

"Well, the Balinese don't go around dressed like this. The women wear sarongs similar to the one Andrea has on, and the men also, only they wrap them differently. This costume is worn only for the plays. As you can see, it is heavy and very hot, not entirely appropriate clothing for Bali, where temperatures are routinely above ninety degrees. This particular outfit is what the Balinese take to be the military garb of the Majapahit Empire of the thirteenth century. If there is a special meaning in the costume, it is to remind the spectators that the action takes place in an actual historical past."

It was a long speech, and most of the audience had left by the end of it.

Meryl shook her head up and down, up and down, as if agreeing with Gorham's statements. It was a trait Chester had found charming years ago. Now he sometimes thought it expressed her sharp, skeptical confrontation with the speaker. Up and down, yes, if she chose to believe him. And she held her head straight up, eyes cast down, shading her lips politely with her palm if she found him a fool.

Meryl didn't stay to talk with Jason and the other performers. She was waiting for Chester by the car in the parking lot, and he hurried there to meet her, leaving John to pack the instruments.

It was four in the afternoon, and Trisha and Jack Standish were coming to dinner at six. The dinner was for Jack. His

Washington contacts had first brought him to Meryl's attention, and he had just agreed to serve on the community
development board she was setting up for the Parks Department.
Deathly afraid of being bored at her own party, Meryl had also
invited Paul and Lucy Dodd, who lived up the street, arguing that two boring couples would be more amusing than one.
Chester hadn't wanted either couple over, especially for a
whole evening beginning at six on a Saturday. "Damn what
we owe them!" He put his head on his arms and moaned.

"But we had a good time at Jack's Christmas reception, and
New Year's would have been sad without the Dodds' house party."

"I was sad because of them."

Chester didn't expect to win this argument with Meryl. He
was play-fighting because he enjoyed rousing her. After six
years of marriage he still liked to see her bristle, planting her
pragmatic feet squarely on the ground and lifting that Irish
chin up and up as if daring him to land an uppercut there. He
played at irritating her, whining and complaining—"fussing"
she called it—until in her reasonable bristling voice a real rage
had built up and he almost expected a sharp whack on the shoulders from that stubborn temper she kept restrained.

He liked that temper, although she was deeply ashamed of
it. When she had started analysis with Dr. Jenkins, he had hoped
that more of it would show. Instead, it seemed to have
petered out. Her voice grew smoother, she began shopping for
silk blouses and Evan Picone herringbone tweed suits, and she
had taken to knotting scarves around her neck in big drooping swaths that made her warm-colored face fade into
respectability.

Chester didn't care that Meryl was playing grown-up.
"It's damn unintelligent to be grown up in America," he
said, trying to insult the easy confident woman in her, the person who knew so well what she wanted in life and who
believed she would find it.

But she was already rifling through the Rolodex to invite
their guests for next week.

He went to the living room, turned on the television set,
and pretended he was not interested in her conversation. All
the time he concentrated on hearing everything she was

saying and imagining what was being said on the other end. Yet, truthfully, her chatter bored him. He decided he knew Meryl too well. But he could not stop listening in on her conversations, even when they were boring.

"Tricksie Trisha," Dan Swiggart said, when she called to invite him to dinner and told him who was coming. Dan had also worked at the Parks Department before leaving a year ago to begin his own landscaping consultancy.

"Dear Swiggie! You can always be counted upon to say something nasty."

"What? Are you defending a woman like that? Why put up with her mouth?"

"The whole point, Swiggie, is that Tricksie—that is, Trisha—has a brain."

"A better brain than her husband's?"

"That's the point, isn't it? God knows she is a more interesting person."

"Damn it, Meryl," Chester said when she reported Dan's observations to him later that evening, "there's more to life than interesting people."

But she didn't agree.

At one time, she had seemed to want something more. That had been when he was completing his doctorate at Columbia and teaching courses at a community college in the Bronx to pay the rent, and she was a Barnard senior living with Doris and Kate on the West Side.

"I want more than my mother had," she had said passionately, in one of her long confessional talks early in their relationship, when he had been merely curious about who she was. "I don't know what yet, but I don't want her sad story!" Being an Irish Catholic, getting pregnant and hurrying into an unhappy marriage was part of that sad story.

Later, this had explained why she so easily agreed that having a baby then was wrong for them. But, at the same time, it seemed she could not bring herself to go to the clinic.

Her equivocation was puzzling. He didn't participate in her debate over whether to end the pregnancy, which lasted for almost a month after the positive results came in. It was a debate she did not share with her mother, long ago divorced and newly relocated to Salt Lake City. The discussion featured chiefly her roommates, Doris and Kate, while he sat out on the sidelines in the Butler Library, writing up his Bali field notes. Everyone said having a baby was impossible.

"But what if we did?" she asked on the phone the morning Doris was to take her to the clinic.

Chester did not answer. He had been offered a sociology course to teach three days into the semester, and the first class was to begin in an hour. The last time he had studied a sociology text was in his second year at Princeton, so he had desperately crammed himself with the required readings the night before the class. Meryl's question seemed to him more academic than real.

Having a baby was impossible. Even his being with her during the procedure was impossible. He could not miss the first day of his course. Besides, as both Kate and Doris had pointed out, Doris would be a better companion; she had herself been to the clinic last year.

Meryl hung up on his silence.

So it was that they never discussed what happened that day. When Chester, on a few involuntary occasions, recalled her question, it never failed to strike him as odd and out of character.

Now Meryl collected people like playing cards that she dealt out at parties to amuse herself and others. Chester imagined she played solitaire with her packs of interesting people. Once he had come across a list of men's names on her desk. There had been about thirty names on the list and it included his name as well as some names he recognized. When he asked her about it, she had laughed and said she was thinking about a donor list for her Parks youth project.

On Saturday, as she and Chester were shredding romaine lettuce together, Meryl filled Chester in on her conversation with Dan. "Trisha has problems, and perhaps Jack is one of them. He obviously used all kinds of subtle pressure to stop her from finishing graduate school."

"Think Jack is capable of anything subtle?"

"Of course Trisha plays up to him. It's safer for her to stay home; she hasn't got to be afraid of failing. Gardening, dance classes, yoga, and making quiches—I wouldn't mind a life like hers."

"You'd hate her life." Chester wiped his hands on his pants, moved to the living room, and placed a record on the turntable.

Meryl came out to the living room when the record was over. "Hey," she whispered in his ear as he sat on the floor picking through the records in the cabinet, "are you considering the operation?"

"What?"

"You know, the article in the *Times* I showed you."

"Oh, the vasectomy."

"Did you think about it?"

"No."

"Oh Chester!" Meryl straightened up and banged her fist on the coffee table where she had set the salad plates, so that the plates jumped and the knives and forks grew crooked. "It's the easiest thing in the world. An appointment with the doctor, and I won't have to worry. It's not fair that I have been taking all the risks. After all, we've decided we're not having any children and I shouldn't be responsible for the whole decision."

"Have we decided we're not going to have kids?"

She lowered her chin and looked down at him, suddenly calm and self-possessed. "We've looked at our priorities over and over again. I'm coming up for the deputy commissioner's position next year, and if the federal grant comes through, I'll have my own project in New York City Parks to administer. Dan said I could be commissioner in a few years, the first woman commissioner in the history of the Parks Department. You said yourself that there's no way we can have a baby and be fair to everyone."

"Sure," he muttered.

"Don't you care that those pills could kill me?" Her voice was contemptuous now.

Chester turned pale. "Jeez, Meryl, don't hide your knives behind questions." He began to take the records off the floor and carelessly pushed them back on the shelves. The record player slid down its shelf towards him. "Damn. Nothing in this house is stable."

"Well, don't you care that two out of a hundred women on the pill do become pregnant each year? I don't want to go through that ordeal again. And the *Times* just reported that Harvard Medical School is doing a study on increased heart attacks and strokes in nurses on the pill, and the FDA is concerned about breast and cervical cancer risk in women over forty who take . . ."

"On the pill, off the pill. No—why should I care? Anyway, you'll never be forty to me."

The music washed over him. "Do you believe in magic . . . in magic . . . in magic." Feeling exhausted, Chester sat back on the sofa. Not thinking, he stroked his thighs, his fingers patting a tempo. He was going to have a bad evening.

"You're hopeless, Chester. Did you know that?"

"Yes, you've told me often enough." He turned to grab her as she stood in front of him. Her anger made her voice harsh and gritty. That's the sound of the fishwife Mother warned me about, Chester thought.

She stepped back, her brown eyes turning pink and tired.

"Don't cry, Meryl. I'll have the operation. You can keep your heart safe from an attack."

She stayed away, not believing him.

He placed his two hands cupped like a shield before his crotch. "I'll protect you from this. It won't be more than a water pistol."

"You don't mean it," she said in a softer, accusing tone, yielding to his hands and sitting on his lap. "Don't." She twisted her body as his hands moved to her breasts.

He brought them down to her waist and she nuzzled her head under his chin. "That's better."

Chester let her sit there. The large sliding glass doors were bright with late sunshine. He looked at the streaks that remained from last autumn, when they had washed the glass outside and he had forgotten to dry it thoroughly. Small jagged edges of dandelion leaves poked out among the bricks on the patio. The sunshine looked warm but he knew it was cold outdoors, for it wasn't yet April. He still felt cold when she rose from his lap to open the door to their dinner guests.

Paul and Lucy had brought an unexpected companion, Roy Kumar, who had just joined Paul's company in February. "I hope you don't mind," Lucy said to Meryl, embarrassed. "He turned up at our door about half an hour ago. That's the kind of thing Indians do, he says, drop in for a chat without calling." Roy's wife, still in New Delhi, would be joining him in a few months, as soon as her visa could be cleared, Lucy explained. The company was able to rush through Roy's visa by arguing national security urgency, but the wife was a different matter, and the State Department seemed less interested in making an exception for her. "He's lost without her when he's not at the lab, and Paul's keeping an eye to make sure he doesn't decide to go back to India." Lucy shrugged her shoulders at Meryl's questioning eyebrows.

Roy, dark-hued in a cable-knit navy blue pullover and immediately friendly, had left them to talk to the men. "So, you have a farming business?" he said to Dan, who was trying to explain to Trisha how to control aphid infestations on dahlias with a new nontoxic powder.

"I guess you could call me a farmer."

Trisha giggled. "He's a very educated farmer."

"Oh yes, in America, everyone is highly educated. Very different from India, where all the farmers are unschooled." Roy shook his head approvingly. "America and India are like David and Goliath. We have many more people, many many children, but Americans have lots of education, many many universities. Poor Goliath cannot win."

"And what do you do?" Dan asked rudely.

"Kumar is a top researcher in cryptographic ciphers," Paul interrupted. "He's superb with encryption algorithms, especially in asymmetric encryption. My company considers him one of the world's leaders on this. We had to negotiate hard to get him to leave his university in New Delhi, but we expect him to be a key player in getting us a contract with the Defense Department."

Roy beamed. "Ah, yes, your president is very very nice to me. Already next month he is allowing me to spend two weeks at MIT to look at its microsystems labs. I am very happy to be here. America is very very nice to me."

Looking less happy, Dan moved away to join Trisha, who was talking to Chester.

"What a lovely house!"

Chester waved a hand, dismissing her statement.

"What are these marvelous looking things? I just love your swords and hangings!" She stood below an Indonesian ikat cloth and gazed earnestly at the objects on the mantel.

"Umm, that's a kris, a kind of ceremonial dagger."

"And this wonderful statue," she said, not listening. She reached up for the carved piece and handled it curiously. "What can this be?" The knobs and curves turned in a meaningless whirl between her long white fingers.

"Careful!"

Dan laughed, and Chester realized he'd spoken too sharply. He took the carving away from her and held it upright so it faced her.

"It's a dream demon."

The two men saw that she could finally see it—two tails interlocking, the tumescent penis, a pointed tongue sticking out of a fanged mouth, and the smooth black contours of rump, knees, barrel chest, elbows—a figure all lumps, humping itself on air.

Her face was surprised, but she only said, "Oh, how funny," and turned away.

Sorry for her, Chester placed the carving out of sight behind the framed photograph of a Minangkabau house.

Trisha was asking Dan about how to make Christmas cactus bloom all year round. Chester was exasperated now, knowing she blamed him for what had happened.

"Is there anything to drink besides white wine? I hate that putrid stuff." Dan looked at Trisha, then smiled at Chester as if to sympathize.

"Sorry. I left the whiskey in the kitchen."

Dan followed him, plucked a wet glass from the drying rack, and took the bottle of Black and White whiskey from him.

"I didn't know Paul was muck-a-muck with Pentagon types. What do you make of having foreigners involved in our defense system? I don't like it, I tell you."

"Are you talking about Roy Kumar? He doesn't look like a mercenary soldier."

Dan scowled. "Nah. It's all this technology stuff that the Feds don't want us ordinary Americans to know about."

"Edward Teller was not exactly born an American, you know." Chester took the bottle away from Dan and placed it on the counter. "The nuclear bombs that are supposed to defend us, lots of what you call 'foreigners' created them. Who do you think Enrico Fermi was? And Hans Bethe? Of course, many of the first generation of rocket scientists came from the Third Reich."

"That's different." Dan retrieved the bottle and poured a second glassful. "They were all from our part of the world. But tell me, what d'you think of Trisha?"

Chester eyed Dan's glass balefully. "Better Trisha than Roy? They both talk too much."

"One of these wimpy bitches. She's never going to find a job. Like my ex-wife. Got some poor slob to work for her. Meryl is more my kind of woman." He winked at Chester as if they were talking of someone Chester didn't know. "She'd play hardball with anyone, and beat them, too. None of these types with baby formula and baby puke."

"How many kids have you got, Dan?" Chester wondered again why Meryl had asked Dan over for dinner. For him, she had replied when he asked, because he had so hated the idea of eating with the Standishes and Dodds.

"What the hell does that have to do with what I'm saying? You know, anyway."

"Three?"

"Right."

"How old?"

"What's this, a computer dating service? Twelve, ten, and four." Dan, Chester had said to Meryl, had the habit of objecting to anything that seemed to invade his privacy, together with a neurotic compulsion to admit everything. She'd agreed that he was like a Catholic fugitive from a life of crime, looking for a father confessor.

"Don't you miss them? How about the weekends? Didn't you ever want them?"

"Hell, I don't have to take this shit." He carried the bottle of whiskey away with him.

Meryl came in, the furrow between her eyebrows a warning to Chester. "What have you done to Swiggie? He's crying in the bathroom."

"He's probably gone there to finish his bottle."

"Swiggie is harmless, if only you wouldn't provoke him. Or give him whiskey. I thought you knew that."

"I have no idea what I am supposed to know, especially with these pathetic types you collect. At least Kate breaks the mold for you. What can you possibly have in common with Dan?"

Ignoring him, Meryl picked up the extra plate of taco shells from the kitchen table. "Aren't you coming out to talk to our guests?" she asked, walking away.

"Our guests." Chester hated the phrase. It reminded him of all the prissy resort hotels in Bermuda where his parents used to drag him every summer. It especially reminded him of his mother, who slaved in the kitchen every time they had people over. "Oh, no," she would say, picking up another tray, "there's nothing for you to do in the kitchen. After all, you're our guests." The guests would sit politely on the overstuffed velveteen settee and club chair. Father would swivel the three-tiered lazy Susan service set so they could help themselves to the salted almonds, apricot crescents, stuffed prunes, candy chews, and other assorted goodies that Mother served.

Dinner was ready and two of them were missing, Dan and Trisha.

"They're out on the patio looking for the grape hyacinths," Jack offered. He had been talking to Paul about the threatened baseball strike for the last fifteen minutes, while Paul explained the rules of the game to Roy, who appeared fascinated by the game's counting system.

Lucy helped Meryl arrange the dishes. It was a buffet, although there were only eight of them. Meryl had decided against a sit-down dinner because she thought the conversation would be dull and because the dishes didn't quite go together.

They were having cold hacked chicken, chili, warmed taco shells, cheese bread, and a giant salad with blue cheese dressing. When they were first living together, Meryl had announced that Chester would have no consultation rights on meals until he learned to cook. But he never did, and he knew never to complain about Meryl's dinner party combinations. She worked from some kind of food system, learned in elementary school, which told her what formed a balanced meal.

Chester didn't feel like eating. "I'll look for them," he said and slid the glass doors open.

A cloud of steam from the chili pursued him onto the patio.

The garden in the back was bleak. When they had bought the house it was July, and the backyard had been buried in vegetation. Strands of lilac bushes choked its edges. The heart-shaped leaves were mottled with greasy black from some fungus. Blackberry brambles formed an impassable hedge at the far end. The previous owners had told them that the garden was full of different flowers, herbs, and bushes. But everything looked the same: straggly, bushy, fat. Some plants had thin narrow leaves, others had dark serrated ones as large as bowls. Some looked healthy, twining in all corners with tendrils threatening to take over the world.

"I'll do the garden," Chester had said, and while Meryl cooked the dinner each night, he hacked, pruned, chopped, pulled, and gathered bags of branches, twigs, dead leaves, grasses, reeds, and moldy, smelly underbrush.

When Meryl finally came out to see what he was doing he had destroyed the garden, laid it flat and bare. Everything was gone except for the grass and the stumps of some lilacs. They had hoped the lilac bushes would come back, but they never did; the pruning had been too severe, Dan told Meryl, although Chester swore it was the fungus that had killed them off.

Only the small spring perennials, whose leaves had already withered by the summer and whose bulbs lay hidden in the earth so they couldn't be rooted out, survived. And in March they sprang up all over the bare garden, purple scylla and blue hyacinths, green-white snowdrops and piercingly perfumed lilies of the valley.

Neither Chester nor Meryl had much interest in maintaining a garden. Dan had offered to landscape the yard for them while he was still working in the Parks nursery, but as they seldom had time to venture into the yard, they resigned themselves to their spring survivors, and for the rest of the year to the dandelions and the blank lawn covered in snow.

Chester found Dan and Trisha behind the garage. He had surprised them; he saw Dan wiping his mouth with the back of his hand and knew they had been kissing. "Tricksie Trisha," he whispered to Dan, as Dan was loading his plate with food. But Dan was angry and sat beside Paul and Lucy to eat. Meryl was busy slicing the bread and refilling the salad bowl. Chester thought Dan was holding him responsible for catching him out with Trisha. He sat in the corner by the Dayak spear at the south window and tried to eat his taco, hoping no one would talk to him.

Chester remembered a period of many years when he had intensely hated his name. That was the time of pitching ball alone in the yard, the time glued to the television for the Saturday games, trying to make the cries of the crowd sound like a two-syllable war cry—"Chester, Chester"—and not quite making it.

All the guys in school had names that could be shortened to one explosive sound: Bob, Bill, Mike. Even Frenchy Louis Lefester was called Lou. Like the good hard thwack of wood on flying ball, the names had gone flying through the Saturday afternoons on the bench and in camps up in Lake Rocky Mountain. Hey, Mark! Hey, Pete! Hey, Rich!

But Chester still smarted at the memory. Chestnut, Cheshire, Chesty. The two-syllable sound echoing through a distance—Chessst-errr—was girlish. It was on a line with Mary, Lizzy, Dinah, Sharon. Then, on top of that, to have a family name like Brookfield!

The first time he felt good about his name was when he began to sing with the glee club at Princeton, and they sang "America the Beautiful." It became a name he could see having. Brookfield. He could see the brook running somewhere in the middle of the country, right in the center of that vast area from sea to shining sea, running toward the Great Lakes, slate-cold smack in the midst of the amber waves of grain. He could feel his chest expanding with the lakes and rolling prairies. Standing up with the glee club made up for all the years sitting in the bleachers.

The girls there even liked his hair, which ever since he could get away with it he had kept long and falling over his eyes. It was all right then not to have short hair, not like when he was six or sixteen and his hairline grew down in what his mother had long ago told him was a widow's peak.

"It runs in our family, dear." She had fondly traced the dip of carrot-red hair like a scar or an arrow to just above the middle of his eyebrows. A widow's peak. He never told any of his friends what it was called, but it made him look like a convict or an alien from outer space.

When they played, he always had to be an Indian. Luckily the kids never got around to analyzing why he looked weird; he tried so hard for a long time to be just like everyone else.

That was when he first tried wearing his hair long, like bangs that made him look more girlish. Then, in the mid-sixties, especially once he wore it really long at Princeton, nobody thought it girlish anymore. He thought he finally looked like his own person, five feet eleven and a half inches, green eyes, red brown hair, scrubbed clean behind the ears, behind all that long hair, just like his mother had taught him. He had cut his hair short after college, but he had let it grow again as soon as he was accepted into the Peace Corps.

It made Chester uneasy to think of his Peace Corps year again. He supposed it was Roy's presence that unsettled him. He had been avoiding Roy. Short and pudgy, Roy looked nothing like Paroo, but there was something in the rhythm of his voice that called up Paroo.

It had been almost eleven years since Chester left Kuala Lumpur, cutting short his contract to return home to Connecticut, but lately he had been thinking more and more about his year there. Usually it was a sensation that brought him to the past—a sensation he felt when he found himself alone, in between strangers, or finishing a chore and looking for another piece of work.

It was a kind of panic, like the panic he felt when he saw the black smoke the night of the riots in Kuala Lumpur, a sensation of falling through space not knowing that there would be a landing. The same panic he felt when he read Paroo's letter about Li An's baby, and counted the dates and found that they matched.

He had suppressed the panic each time and come through. After all, neither the riots nor Li An's baby had been his business. He could leave and did. Li An had never written to him, and although he already suspected what Paroo would later write—that Henry had left her and that the baby was a scandal—he had been saved by geography and the distance of cultures. He had replied to Paroo, taking care not to mention Li An, and Paroo's letters never raised the topic again.

Funny that he hadn't thought it was important enough to tell Meryl when he married her. He had felt so lucky at meeting her in his first year of graduate school at Columbia. Ambitious, talented Meryl, with her enormous energy and her admiration of his Peace Corps past, his study of Balinese culture, his circle of anthropologists and their endless talk of tribal rituals and magic-inspired lore. Like the dandelions on the lawn, his life with Meryl blossomed in the sun of her energy.

But lately they weren't getting on so well. He hadn't changed, he knew, so it was Meryl who was different. He didn't know if it was because she had grown too serious or not serious enough.

"Chester." Trisha balanced her plate above him. She knelt down beside him like a votary making an offering of wet salad leaves. He moved his foot as her knee nudged against it. "You look very scholarly. Rodin's *Thinker?*"

"Not as neatly assembled, I assure you."

"Oh, much more handsome. You have the body of a swimmer."

He felt himself flush. It was years since he had touched a woman other than Meryl, and Trisha's dark sleek cap of hair, her bold active body and rushes of speech, had never attracted him. He noticed for the first time how trimly compact she was. She was wearing a thin beige knit that showed round unfashionable flesh. He was overcome by an urge to touch her breasts and instead picked up his taco.

"What is it like being married to Jack?" He was astonished by his own question, but she wasn't offended.

"What is it like being married to Meryl?"

They looked at each other.

"Are you talking about me?"

Relieved, Chester pulled Meryl down on his lap and stroked her mass of auburn hair. "I was about to tell Trisha what a wonderful wife you are."

Meryl made a face and got up immediately. "Wife?" She knelt beside Trisha and gave a little laugh. "That's an outdated notion of a woman's place." She turned away from him and he knew she was thinking about their argument that evening. "Don't you think a woman is more than a wife?"

"With two kids I often feel a woman is only a mother." Trisha sat on her haunches and brushed Chester's knee with her body.

Chester felt himself rise to her touch, although he was taut with anger. "What's a woman, then, Meryl?" he asked.

She was defiant. Bending her body away from him, she talked only to Trisha. "A woman should have rights just like a man, don't you think? She should have freedom of choice over her body and her life. Women shouldn't fit one mold, especially a mold made by men."

"What about biology?" Jack had joined them, and Chester was annoyed by Jack's skepticism as much as he was annoyed by Meryl's rejection.

"So what? A different distribution of body fat has nothing to do with intelligence or capability."

"It's not fat but holes I'm thinking of."

Trisha tittered and Jack added hurriedly, "I mean the womb. A woman has the babies and that's a fundamental difference."

"Haven't you heard of contraception, Jack? A woman doesn't have to have babies." Meryl's temper was up. "Of course, if she accepts the condition of a baby-making machine, she deserves to have a man tell her what to do with her life."

Chester got up and left Meryl and Jack still arguing.

Trisha followed him to the kitchen and watched him scrape the food on his plate into the kitchen disposal.

"Sorry about that, Trisha."

"Do you think I should be angry with Meryl?" Trisha pulled her mouth down mockingly.

"Are you?" He washed his hands at the sink.

"Oh no. I'll admit I've gotten myself into that position often." She laughed. "I like it."

Chester wanted to kiss her. Her belly made a little shadowy mound under the knit, and her neck and breasts formed a landscape that dipped and rose in invitation. They were alone in the kitchen, but his hands were wet. He wiped them on his pants and she laughed again. He heard Dan's deep rumble outside, thought better of it, and handed her the carrot cake to bring out.

Holding it in one hand she swiped some icing on her finger and offered it to Chester.

He put her finger in his mouth and sucked on it. The sugar dissolved and the warm salty finger caressed his tongue. "Hmmm," he said and again he felt himself rise.

She looked at her finger in his mouth with a wide smile. "See you for lunch some day," she said and walked away.

Chester wasn't sure if he was exhilarated or depressed. His excitement was forced. It reminded him of the only time he had watched a pornographic movie, in a hot stuffy hotel room in Malacca years ago. As he watched the two Scandinavian figures rehearse in gloomy silence one position after another he had momentarily lost his sense of time. The couple appeared to be slowly climaxing in an eternity of boredom created by the tedium of sexual arousal.

He didn't know if he couldn't accept his good luck or if he was dismayed that Trisha had picked on him to practice her wiles. He avoided talking intimately to either Trisha or Dan for the rest of the evening. Instead he forced himself to listen to Roy explaining how to build machines that could think intuitively, the way humans do, rather than logically, which, according to Paul, was a process fairly easy to assemble. Chester watched Paul's deference to Roy. It had something gentle and unspoken about it, like a respect that came without thought, as if sprung from affection. He was reminded of the way Li An had sometimes spoken to him. Roy's Indianness had called up this memory, he thought, and he was relieved when the party broke up.

•

Watching Meryl plump her pillow, he said carefully, "Trisha is a great flirt."

"She's only playing the feminine game." Meryl pushed her hair off the back of her neck and snuggled into his shoulder. She added sleepily, "Trisha's not a happy person," and fell asleep.

He stayed awake quietly, thinking about how he was going to make his appointment with the medical center for the vasectomy. At least, he thought, he would show Meryl he could be responsible, even if, so long ago, Li An's small, unhappy countenance at another party had shown him his failure.

Two

Chester taught in the social sciences department at Seven Graces College, an exclusive all-girls institution with gray stone and red brick buildings above almost twenty acres of lawn overlooking the Hudson River. He taught sociology and one course of anthropology, although his real interest was anthropology.

At first, he had been surprised that his young female students showed almost no curiosity about actual foreign countries. They traveled to Europe as a matter of course in the summers, but most of them, he complained, thought of Asia and Africa as primitive and unbearably savage. Mead's paean to adolescent freedom in Samoa and the photographs of bare-breasted women, which had fascinated him when he was a boy and which his eyes had fixed on not so much in lust as in the discovery of the freakishness of nature, did not interest them. After all, they stalked the beaches in strings of fabric, exposing their breasts to sun and public scrutiny as a matter of course.

Chester described them to Meryl as handsome and intimidating. He did not tell her that their solid materiality repulsed him. He could not understand their emotional pain—confided in moments of weepy academic failure—or their glossy appetite, which could be quieted by secret feasts of Mallomars and Oreos, parental bribes of Corvettes and Hawaiian vacations, and the bodies of men as handsome as themselves. He did not always like them, but he could not help admiring their concentration on their lives, their fixedness on the pursuit of pleasures.

He had been teaching at Seven Graces College for as long as he had been married to Meryl, and sometimes he suffered a sense that he was lost in an intensely pagan country. He believed some of his students approached a Baskin-Robbins ice cream with more voluptuousness than he was capable of feeling for anything, and he saw them enlarging into the future while he continued to drift among the shallows of his ever-lengthening present life.

This morning, in particular, he found his students' purposeful rush unsettling. For the first time he admitted to himself that they reminded him of his wife: her resolute eagerness and determined grasping of the future, even her stocky tensility of shape, and her sharp sorrows that could be salved by a Bavarian torte.

Standing by his office window on the top floor of the three-storied Higginsworth Hall, he studied the bunches of students as they crossed Bottom's Green to their eleven o'clock classes. He had never fantasized about his students—the kind of fantasies that Vitazelli and McMahon, both sociologists, had relished narrating. In the late March sunshine the young women were walking with swinging strides, their winter coats unfastened, chests swelling in the pastel sweaters they were all affecting this year like crocuses budding under his gaze. Strangely he saw them today as vulnerable, easily crushed under his heavy Frye boots, but this vision neither roused nor gladdened him; instead, he felt tired and sleepy.

Rubbing his fingers on the side of his forehead—an action he had unconsciously repeated in the last two months, ever since he discovered his hairline receding perceptibly—he turned from the tall frame of blue sky and called the Holygrove Medical Center. He worried about how he was going to explain the reason for his call, but the cool female voice at the end of the line merely said, "Dr. Shelley? How about Friday at ten?"

Suddenly he wanted to express his anxiety, and stammered into the phone that he wished to make an appointment for a vasectomy. The voice repeated, "A vasectomy.

Dr. Shelley, Friday at ten," and the line went dead. Feeling foolish, he yawned in embarrassment. His anxiety seemed to have no place in the luxuriously ordered universe, and again the uneasiness he had felt on Saturday night, like a memory of smoke, nudged at him.

He went for his one o'clock lecture exhausted, and spent the hour clowning. It was a general all-purpose sociology course, Man and Society. The hour was slotted for a talk on kinship systems, and he had prepared his usual materials on changes in the American family based on recent census figures. Instead he spoke about substitute and ersatz kinship structures, including feelings for soap opera and movie stars, relationships with pets, sentiment over cars, houses, and other possessions. By the end of the hour he had portrayed a society riddled with superstitious practices, magical rites, and totemic figures, and had puzzled his students, who found his litany of familiar social behavior funny but wondered what all his criticism was about.

Dr. Shelley was Chester's first family doctor—that is, the first to treat him as head of a household instead of as a child. Chester was reluctant to change physicians, although Dr. Shelley had never struck him as a good one. His pediatrician, who had been his family doctor until just before he left for college, had always given him meticulously thorough checkups where he would examine even the slant of his toenails before concluding that he was walking normally. All the mothers in their quiet Connecticut town praised his obsessive care, his mother had said, boastfully; and Chester had thrived, strong-boned, lean, healthy.

"Shilly-Shally," Chester called Dr. Shelley privately, and the name seemed to fit him, for he had a manner that suggested he was willing to change a diagnosis to please his patients.

"What can we do for you today?" he always greeted Chester, as if he were contemplating selling Chester a cup of coffee and a sandwich, and asking for his choice of bread and cold cuts. At the end of each office visit, Dr. Shelley routinely inquired how many days off from work Chester required and often absentmindedly asked about his children.

Dr. Shelley had Chester's patient record open on his desk when Chester entered. His voice was its usual vague drone.

"Mr. Brookfield. Sit down. What can we do for you today? Ah, I see you want a vasectomy. How old are you? Thirty-five. Not a bad idea to have one at this age—most convenient all around. It's a minor operation, we do it right here in the office. You won't need anything but a local anesthetic. Thirty minutes is about what it takes. We'll need you to sign these forms, simple consent forms, you know, a legal requirement."

"You're doing it right now?" Chester's stomach churned. The tremors began in his upper thighs and traveled down to his calves. He crossed his legs to conceal the shaking.

"Oh, no. Make an appointment for next week with the nurse. She'll have to weigh you and take your blood pressure. It's only a preliminary check-up."

Chester closed his eyes. Then, placing his feet firmly on the ground, he asked, "Is there, ah, is the vasectomy final?"

"I thought you knew what you are getting into." The doctor's voice was surprisingly annoyed.

Chester looked away, ashamed at his cowardice. "Yeah, yeah. I thought . . . there may be a problem, you know, that it may not work."

"You don't have to be concerned about impregnating after the operation. It's completely effective." Dr. Shelley ushered him out with a mild smile, and patted him on the shoulder. "A minor operation. You won't feel a thing."

Chester was a head taller than Dr. Shelley, but he was so grateful for the pat that he wanted to put his head on the doctor's shoulder and bawl.

All week he went to bed hanging on to the memory of Dr. Shelley's smile. He closed his eyes and tried to see the slight pale lips stretching before him. Sometimes it worked and he fell asleep comforted. There was no tension in the smile—it suggested a slackening of the air around it, like a slumping, a caving in. The anxiety Chester carried with him during the day relaxed as he concentrated on the thin papery shape of a smile that said, "You won't feel a thing."

He was so relaxed that he left Meryl alone, although he realized she was getting into deep waters with her youth project.

She had received letters and calls of complaint about the outlines of her plan—to clear the overgrown trails and weed the loosestrife strangling the wetland vegetation at one end of the lake. She was busy writing a speech for the Grassroots and Parktops annual benefit dinner defending her plans to extend the youth work mission into the next decade.

The house was full of her books, Xeroxes, note cards, yellow legal pads, and back issues of conservation journals. Chester had to clear a space each morning on the kitchen table before he could have his herbal tea, and he carefully moved books and papers off of the bathroom counter before he had his shower. Meryl worked late each day and stayed up with the television tuned to a news program each night while she wrote her speech.

One evening, as she was taking off her coat by the door, he tried to tell her that the vasectomy had been scheduled for Friday morning.

"Umm, what did you say?"

"I'm seeing Shilly-Shally on Friday."

"Are you going for another test?"

"No, the vasectomy."

"Oh, wonderful!" She dropped her coat on the entrance mat and ran to peck him on the chin. "We'll have to celebrate."

"You think this is a victory?"

"We won't celebrate then. We'll just go out for dinner." She took her smile off her face and Chester was sorry he had been so short.

"I guess it's something to celebrate. Defeat of the spermatozoa plague."

She giggled and kissed him on the chin again. "After the benefit dinner. On Sunday. I'm only halfway through the speech." She was already going through her briefcase and pulling out a fresh stack of Xeroxed records.

Bitch, Chester thought. But he didn't say it. "Have you had dinner?"

"I had a pastrami at four." She headed to the living room and turned on the seven o'clock news.

Chester laughed. He was expecting she would be grateful and they would go to the movies and make out. Perhaps he could still make it for the 7:30 show.

He stood by the stairs watching Meryl arranging the shiny Xeroxes in piles on the coffee table. Her curls reminded him of his baby photos. His mother had told him he had beautiful bright red curls till he was four when they straightened out and darkened. "That's when you became difficult," she would add.

He never took her accusation seriously. For as long as he could remember he had not had a quarrel with his parents. He knew he'd had a sister who died at six months. His mother talked about her again last Thanksgiving. There was a name, SIDS, Sudden Infant Death Syndrome, for what killed her. They used to call it crib death, and the rash of publicity on recent medical studies on the subject seemed to have given this ghost of a baby sister a fresh life to his parents.

Her frail existence had haunted his childhood, made it sober, so that he was by all accounts "a good boy." When his mother looked longingly at communion frocks while she was shopping for his straight-legged trousers, size slender, he had known what was passing through her mind, and the tiny infant grew in his imagination into a doll-sized Thumbelina who would never make it to the prince's ball, unlike the Thumbelina that his mother loved singing about along with her favorite Danny Kaye record. He knew it was because his sister was dead that his parents loved him so intensely and gave him the best of everything, and he tried to make up for their loss by being a good child.

But it was hard to know what "good" was, outside of their presence. All his life, everything he thought or did or wanted immediately became good for them; he never had to grow up, his mother said, because he never ever did anything wrong.

Meryl was the first person to say he was selfish. She had named his faults more clearly than he could have acknowledged them, and the miracle was that she still wanted him. His gratitude came from not having to be good for her. She had accepted him—his unsteady job prospects, his squirreling away of odd artifacts, even his hazy desire to do good in the world, to save the world by being good, an impulse which, she pointed out to him, often resulted in discomfort and confusion rather than clarity and resolution. Considering her own clear goals he knew he couldn't afford to drift.

Meryl was frowning as she copied information onto her note cards. Chester wondered how she could seem sexy one moment and comically unsexed the next. With her angular jawline, she presented the profile of a cartoon figure aiming at a can of spinach. He usually responded to her moods, liking her best when the light of battle was in her eyes, and also when she was silly and her face twisted with merriment. Now, while she worked, the energetic contours of her face drooped so that she had the craggy croppings of a pugilist.

Chester never wondered that together they didn't want children. There was that strange moment a year before they married when Meryl seemed in danger of being sentimental, but if so it had been the only sign of conventionality on her part. He figured she now enjoyed planning too much to want a child. She planned even while she showered, an act Chester had always associated with singing, but that Meryl approached silently because she did her best thinking in the shower.

Chester had admitted it was foolhardy for anyone who liked things to work according to plan to have a child. "Well, would you be willing to stay home and do the child care then?" she had asked, when he conceded this point. No, he'd answered; indeed, he was content to follow through on their early decision. But he wasn't quite sure he wanted to be in a position where he could never have a child. When Meryl had pointed out how inconsistent his position was, he could only agree with her.

Looking at Meryl, who was now writing in her clear looping hand on a yellow pad, Chester felt sad that they would never have a child.

In fact, this was the question he asked Dr. Shelley, after he returned from the bathroom where he had eased a jockstrap over his scrotum, recognizably the same except for a bandage taped at the incision. "Can I ever have a child?"

Shelley gave him a look so aggrieved Chester wished he could just go home instead. "You didn't read the pamphlet last week."

Chester was afraid to tell him he had never received a pamphlet. Shelley continued to stare as if Chester had insulted him or brought a lawsuit against him, with the same countenance of regretful contempt the older boys used to wear when Chester missed a fly ball or when his can of water spilled and put out the fire they had spent the last hour starting. Chester knew he was being foolish.

"I'm sorry. I mislaid the pamphlet. I was wondering if the operation is reversible."

"There's some evidence it may be." Dr. Shelley's soft neutral tone had taken a professional edge sharp enough to make the nurse put her head in through the door. He waved her away and smiled carefully. "By the way, you may still have some sperm left in the vas. I hope you will take the usual precautions at least for the next few occasions. Make an appointment for a semen check next week."

Chester wanted to ask more. He stayed in his seat although there was an uncomfortable tingle between his legs.

"You may find yourself having some discomfort for a day or two." Shelley's smile was far away. "There should be no actual physical pain, but I'll give you some painkillers just in case. How about a week off from work?"

Chester had never accepted the doctor's generous offers before, but, daunted by the thought of standing bandaged and violated, perhaps still sore from the scalpel, before his scores of wholesome fresh female students, this time he agreed.

Three

It was almost noon and the Friday flow of women shopping on Central Avenue was heavy. Behind the wheel the air was pleasantly warm and summer musty. Large cardboard eggs and pasteups of pink and yellow rabbits filled the windows of the bakery and the pharmacy, while the New England Men's Store had mannequins sporting raffish boaters and pink shirts.

The lights by the traffic islands were slow changing, and Chester turned on his AM radio to the only classical station it carried. Strains of Handel wobbled tenderly in the enclosed bubble of the car as he navigated around the lights. Then the music faded and a voice-over began, gravely and eloquently. "Do you think American civilization has turned decadent? Then you haven't visited the gracious Colonial House Restaurant, where the classics of American living are presented in a soothing ambiance that includes chamber music and the very finest French wines. Discover for yourself the hospitable warmth of the sorrel soup or the magnificent mussels meunière. . . ."

He was barely listening, but his stomach gave a loud growl and he remembered irritably that he hadn't had any breakfast.

He did not want to go home yet. Meryl had finally finished writing her speech, and the detritus of her research no longer clogged the furniture and open spaces, but he was too depressed to sit indoors waiting for her to come home from work.

Chester had never liked the house, a fake Tudor that concealed an ordinary two-story box with square rooms laid out to form a larger square. There were no elements of surprise in its standard-sized window frames, no unexpected corners or hidden closets. The staircase went straight up. The attic was merely a crawl space, and the basement was a brightly lit large room with a new Everlasting furnace and some oil stains on an otherwise dull green-painted cement floor. The mock Tudor front, all black and white plaster with timber-boards made of some kind of composite Masonite, was its one interesting feature, and the house seemed to invite curiosity only to repel it with its absolute tract-house orthodoxy.

As Meryl proudly claimed, it was an easy house to maintain. Curtain rods, light fixtures, tiles, window glass, shower heads, and roof gutters were all extraordinarily standard in size, and the straight corridors and square corners did not attract dust balls, fuzz, lost pennies, or ballpoint caps, all of which had been much in evidence in Chester's old apartment on the Upper West Side with its sagging wood floors and sticking window frames, every surface rendered uneven through generations of painting by passing tenants.

Chester had filled the rooms of the house with objects collected during his Peace Corps term in Malaysia and his six months of fieldwork in Bali. Purple-stained woven grass mats from an interior village hung on one wall. Candlestands, watering cans, and oven reflectors fashioned from tin kerosene cans by Chinese tinsmiths in Seremban jostled for space with bronze Shiva statues and blackened stubby clay images of the lingam from South Indian shops and temples in Kuala Lumpur. A carved wood peacock with electric blue and lurid orange eyes painted on its plumage, which he had picked up at the Thieves' Market in Singapore, stood in the unused fireplace.

He flattered himself that each piece in his collection was an important statement of cultural adaptability or achievement. At the age of forty his mother had begun to collect what she called Old American pieces. Shaker chairs and dressers, tattered quilts from farmers' wives who would no longer use them in their own homes, and massive pewter plates that contained so much lead that they would have poisoned any diner who ate off them. Chester hated her things, and he hated the way she treated them, as if they had the heft of Western objects of worship—polished, dusted, kept away from touch and light, dead possessions of reverence.

He thought of his own collection as things of everyday usefulness, made to be dented, chipped, frayed, addressed in prayer; having no value except as the owners discovered it for themselves; lucky things that lit up the ordinary world with meaning. Reed baskets, coconut shell ladles and dippers, beadwork and shell necklaces—they had all seemed significant in his apartment in Morningside Heights amid the tacky dishevelment of bursting garbage bags, squashed soda cans, sodden newspapers, and pilling jackets. But when he had arranged them in the clean square rooms of suburban Westchester, they turned into ludicrous, cheap decorator pieces from the nearest discount store.

He had known for a long time that he should get rid of them. They were so obviously filled with sentimental value that he cringed when visitors asked about them. But since Meryl had taken the new position at Parks three years ago, she did not notice the house much. Chester had let the work go because he hadn't found anything to replace them.

Still mulling over his distaste for the house, Chester found himself driving the car along the familiar route home. He parked the small yellow 1967 Volkswagen on the street and moved at a lurching clip into the house.

The tingle in his crotch had developed into a small burn almost like pain. He went into the kitchen, swallowed two of the painkillers Shelley had given him, and drank a palmful of water from the faucet.

He decided he would call Trisha and take her up on her offer of lunch. His hands shook as he flipped through the Rolodex for her number. It was under Jack's name. Chester wondered if he should change his mind. His jitters were like those of a criminal breaking into a house where he meant to kill someone.

Aloud he said, "Damn. It's only Trisha," and felt heat. As the phone rang on the other end, he straightened up and smiled as if she were walking into the kitchen now. At the fourth ring he thought he should hang up, but someone said hello in a breathy tone and he grimaced.

It was only as he was pulling the car into the driveway one street down from his home that he thought of the tape and jockstrap. The pills had gone to his head rapidly and the space above his sinuses was expanded and filled with light. He was sorry now that he had called her. After all, he could have gone to the college and holed up in his office. Or driven to Columbia to call on Jason Kingston.

Trisha had the forlorn air of a housewife greeting a sales-man at the door. Her sulky droop mingled with a bashful eager-ness when Chester mumbled in response to her chatter.

"Nice to have you so neighborly," she cooed as she stirred the instant coffee. Acting like Chester was the Welcome Wagon lady whom she had to impress, she offered tuna fish on rye.

They ate in the formal dining room, furnished in shining fruitwood Mediterranean and dominated by an enormous arrangement of dried and silk flowers—gray baby's breath, white lilies, yellow celosias, pearly milkweed pods, tangerine bit-tersweet, all precariously balanced on a log of driftwood in the middle of the table. "These are for Jack's sales meetings when he's home," she said, waving a hand at the massed arrange-ment. "Me, I love flowers," she nodded toward the purple, white, and yellow crocus clustered around the patio outside the windows, "so I can't bear to pick them. I'd rather live with fake flowers than pick living ones."

Chester finished his sandwich in a couple of minutes while she nibbled on the edge of hers. In the living room, he drained a second cup of undrinkable coffee and listened to her talk about her children.

"Barbara and Wendy are in the church play together. It's so sweet to watch them rehearse. Fortunately Barbara has more lines, she's playing the part of St. John's mother. She'd never forgive Wendy if Wendy had a larger role. They are only two years apart, so it's very important for Barbara to know she's the boss."

The girls were in an Easter play, and Chester was surprised to hear the Standishes were Presbyterians who sent their daughters to a private school with a Christian curriculum. Jack was an elder in their church, but with his new job as a lobbyist for the food processing industry, he was away so often in Washington that he was considering dropping out of his church responsibilities.

The room seemed full of absent members. Trisha, timid in gray slacks and cream shirt, almost neutered in the midst of deep-pile wall-to-wall carpeting, sat chatting beside the heavy framed studio photographs of the four of them, smiling forward at Chester. Surrounding Chester beamed portraits of the two girls as infants, toddlers, and chubby charmers, riding ponies at a fair and posing with grandparents.

But his head was beginning to balloon, and apologetically he got up to leave. She got up also and abruptly banged her head on his chest as if in flight from something. Their kiss was smeary and clumsy.

Her lips were chapped, and her breath stank a little of tuna and mayonnaise. She applied more pressure to his lips, but whatever passion Chester had had was gone.

"I can't," he said. "It's the wrong time."

She cocked her head and smiled cheekily. It was almost the Trisha of the party. "Men say that too?"

Chester lied. "I have an appointment at Columbia at three."

"You mean you really called to have lunch?"

"I wanted to see you again." He didn't know if he was still lying, but she gave a grateful smile.

"I thought you came because of what happened at the party." Her arms suddenly twined around his neck. "Shall we see each other again?"

"Yes." He let himself be kissed. This time he felt her loneliness. She drooped by the front door, her light shirt blending with its cream paint and her pale face patchy as if suddenly middle-aged, and he was tender waving good-bye at the wheel.

Chester pushed open his black-painted front door hurriedly. The halo surrounding his head had solidified into an ice ring that dripped cold moisture onto his brow and threw prisms of rainbow colors before his eyes. He was almost hallucinating, but the Day-Glo flying objects disappeared around the corners of his vision as he tried to focus on them.

He swallowed another couple of the painkillers and headed upstairs for bed. This time the ice ring broke, but it re-formed as a clammy skin-suit in which he shivered uncontrollably for minutes. He threw the goosedown quilt over the skin-suit and pulled his legs in, a convict in blue-and-white striped ticking. His boots were frozen solid inside.

After a while it was warmer and his feet began to ache. He dozed off and woke up with a terrible furry sensation in his mouth. The cold had settled in his stomach and lay there like quicksilver—heavy, metallic, liquid, and unsteady. His stomach heaved and the mercury ball pushed up to the back of his throat.

Frantically he untangled his body, the hanging arms, leaden hips, crippled legs encased in massive leather, and scrambled to the bathroom. He had just time to reach the sink before it poured out, the thick glistening sour vomit.

He spat out the rest of the stuff sticking to his teeth, turned on both cold and hot water faucets fully, and splashed off the residual foam on his lips. He scrubbed his lips with soap but the stench of partially digested tuna fish and rye bread rose from the sink like a pall of alcoholic mash.

He closed the bathroom door to cut off the stink and lay limp, face down on the quilt.

This can't be what death is, he thought. The ice wrapped him tight again but he was too tired to maneuver the quilt over his body.

It's just a bellyache, he thought. Ice in the belly. Ice in bed.

Sleep. If he could sleep, the ice storm would pass. He'd get warm, warm in those toasty pile, footed bunny sleeping suits that his mother used to zip him into, airtight, one-piece, snuggling skin-to-flannel, safe.

The wind howled through the husk of his body. He tried to pluck at the quilt beneath him, but his fingers barely stirred; they seemed to have lost their mobility. Another storm of ice and his mind also seemed to rattle, together with his wasted frame heaped on the thicket of sheets.

Death is worse, he thought. Thirty-five. I'm not about to die.

He was amused by his morbidity, and in his amusement he managed to roll over, gathering the quilt around him as he did so, until he was lying sandwiched in a makeshift sleeping bag.

Gradually the intense iciness let up. He wriggled his head under the cover until only the top of his thin nose and his eyes and hair were exposed. He clamped his useless hands between his thighs and fell asleep, as the afternoon outside made dark circles around the first patches of early narcissi leaning their white-yellow gold-streaked heads into the wind.

Four

The house was dark as Meryl cut off the engine in the driveway, but she didn't think anything of it until she got up the stairs.

Then, pow—the smell!

She knew immediately that someone had thrown up; she couldn't miss the sour-sick smell of vomit trailing through the hallway. It smelled like someone also hadn't cleaned up.

"Chester!" she called, but there was no answer.

She went into the bedroom. He was sleeping all covered up so that all she saw when she turned on the light was his long hair. It was about time he had it cut, and she was going to ask him to go to the barber the next day before the benefit.

But he looked very bad now, his face pasty and his eyes switched off, like he really wasn't seeing her.

"What's the matter?"

"Don't know. Feel cold and tired."

"You threw up," she said. "Did you clean up?"

"Don't think so. Sorry."

She went to the bathroom. Luckily he seemed to have messed only the sink.

She turned on the faucet to run the stuff down the drain, but there were chunks that stuck. She finally had to use her fingers to clear the mess. She scrubbed her hands with bath soap, sponged the sides of the sink where the scum was sticking, threw the tacky sponge into the bathroom basket and put the basket outside the bedroom door to bring down into the kitchen.

Chester was still lying in bed, watching her, his cheeks a little pinker.

"How do you feel?" she asked.

"Better. A little rocky but less like death."

"What happened?" she wanted to know.

"Nothing. Came back from the vasectomy, took a couple of pills Shelley had given me, and threw up."

"Did you call him?"

"No."

Meryl couldn't believe it. It was too bad he was sick after the vasectomy. But she couldn't believe he hadn't called the doctor.

"Why didn't you? He should know what's going on."

She picked up the princess phone—it was right next to him—and punched for information. When she got the medical center, it was only an answering service. The receptionist said she'd call Dr. Shelley and he'd call back. Meryl told her it was an emergency.

She was suddenly sorry for Chester. Even though he frequently argued that men should do their share of population control, he had never been keen on the prospect of a vasectomy. Kate had pointed out in her most ironic voice that Chester's notion of human responsibility never seemed to include himself.

She sat by the bed and tried not to see the smear of saliva on the quilt. "How was the operation?"

"Fine. I could see him moving his arms but he had me covered with a damn tent from the waist down and I didn't know what the hell he was doing. I didn't feel the surgery. It was weird. I couldn't believe he was cutting my balls up."

"He didn't do that, it's . . ."

"I know. He explained as he was snipping and suturing and what have you. Would have made more sense if he'd explained before instead of during."

She hated the whine in his voice. Chester's parents had raised him to believe that the world owed him something. Well,

Meryl thought, the world owes no one anything, not an explanation, not sympathy. We do it all.

She leaned forward and kissed him on the lips, holding her breath in case he hadn't washed his mouth. His lips smelled soapy. He slumped back on the bed, old-mannish, and croaked, "Have a bad headache." He had his grumpy distracted stare, so she knew he was all right.

The phone rang. It was Dr. Shelley. Meryl told him what was wrong with Chester but he wanted to speak to him anyway.

"Mrs. Brookfield," he said, and she had to listen hard because his voice was tinny and slow, "he can't possibly have these effects from the operation. They may be physically proximate, but there is no connection between the vas and abdomen."

Chester had a hangdog face as he talked to the doctor. "I didn't do anything after the surgery. No, just a tuna fish sandwich. I took some of the pills you gave me. Four. About two, three hours apart. No, no wine or beer. Yes, two cups of coffee."

He listened for a while, twitching his lips and nose, then sighed. "Yes, I'm sorry. It was stupid of me."

He hung up and looked glumly at her. "It's all my fault of course. I took too many of those painkiller pills. And they aren't supposed to be mixed with alcohol or coffee. I had two cups of coffee. Probably shouldn't be mixed with sex, either."

"You never drink coffee, Chester. It upsets your stomach, remember?"

He winced. "Don't remind me. I went to a burger stand for lunch." He held up his hands—enormous serving-platter hands—and spanned his fingers round his forehead. He pushed his head up, let it sag again, and said under his nose, "Couldn't stand the smell of meat and ordered tuna instead. Maybe the tuna was poisoned."

It was seven already. She wouldn't get to the speech tonight. "What did Shelley say about you?"

"Besides calling me a yoyo who can't read directions? He says I should stay off solid food for a while. But ginger ale and clear foods like Jell-O are fine. Soft food. Should take it easy till I feel better. Even I know that."

"We don't have Jell-O. How about cheesecake?" She was hungry too.

Fridays were hard days in the parks, getting ready for the weekend. That was when your everyday nice grandmother took the kids to dig up the rhododendrons and pee in the baseball diamonds. What people considered pleasure was plain pillage and plunder. What did they want with park bench lumber and those ghastly chicken wire trash baskets? It was like commanding a losing army, planning the cleanup for Saturdays and Sundays. There were enough half-eaten hot-dog rolls to feed all of India, and the candy wrappers alone, not to mention newspapers, cigarette packs, and condom covers, could wallpaper the Pentagon.

"Actually, Jell-O and ginger ale sound good." Chester had a wistful lift to his mouth that he showed whenever he wanted something out of her.

She was really tired, but she said, "All right. Skivvy's is open late. I'll get myself a sandwich there at the same time. Want anything else?"

He shook his head, then said, "Rice pudding?"

Skivvy's was about two miles out past the public golf course, toward the Italian side of town. Meryl didn't like going there much because it was a hangout for the D'Anzio men. D'Anzio was a large pre-fab construction company over on the other side of the train station. Their factory used to be a municipal waterworks, but when the county stopped taking water from the river it became commercial property, and the pre-fab factory had been doing business there for the last twenty years or so. A worker waiting in line at Skivvy's for his lunch hero once told her the men had demonstrated against the peace hippies in 1968.

It was almost 7:30 when she got there. The place was blazing with lights but the parking lot was empty. It was dark there, so she turned the car around and parked in front of the building. It wasn't legal, but at this hour it didn't matter. She locked all the doors. Chester called her paranoid, but the town wasn't as safe as he thought.

When she got through the door she was glad that she had locked the car. A bunch of teenagers were drinking beer between the refrigerated cases and the snack shelves. They were worse than the construction men, although they didn't leer. She could tell from the way they shook their legs and bummed cigarettes from each other that they were looking for trouble. No money and nowhere to go.

She squeezed between them to get to the ginger ale. They hardly looked at her. Oouf! A cloud of blue smoke hung in the corner and she squeezed out at the other end.

She didn't understand why these kids didn't turn her on. Kate swore they were the best, but Meryl thought she might as well do it with a bull, all thumping protoplasm and semen.

She looked for Jell-O in the packaged food section. Nothing but boxes of Oreos and peanut butter cookies. The next aisle was the candy. She chose a couple of bars in case Chester got to sleep early and she could stay up late.

The man at the sandwich counter was the new owner. At least, he'd been behind the cash register for the last year and lately Meryl hadn't seen the burly Italian guy who had served for years before. The first time the Korean served her in Skivvy's—she thought he was Korean, since he was as short as she was and his head had a blocky cut like all the Korean grocers on the West Side—she had felt weird, like the city had suddenly intruded up-county.

Dan, who had helped them find their home right by the parkway and only two miles from his own condo, had first introduced Meryl to Skivvy's. Dan had been afraid that for sure the new owner would change the store, put in eels and dried mushrooms. But he hadn't changed a single item. There were still twenty types of gum and forty soda brands. Even the sandwiches were the same, maybe fresher and better—ham, bologna, and egg salad. He couldn't say "egg salad"—"eggie sarat," he muttered—but it was still the best egg salad Meryl had eaten. No wonder the customers came back.

She'd never heard him complain about the empty beer bottles and cans, the cigarette stubs ground on the floor. The customers peeled their gum and dropped the wrappers right in front of him as they waited for their change. He didn't look at anyone, just punched the register and counted the coins and bills. Meryl wondered if he'd have also remained silent in his own country.

She asked for rice pudding and an egg salad sandwich.

Chester had said the owner was Filipino because the rice pudding tasted like the fancy Spanish-style stuff he'd had in the Philippines. But Meryl had told Chester he was nuts. A Filipino would have spoken better English—after all, the Philippines had been an American colony.

Meryl gave the correct change and he counted it carefully, then looked at her as if he knew she'd been thinking about him all this time.

Meryl wondered if he would be thought good-looking in his own country. The thing with real aliens, according to Dan, was he didn't know what was ugly or what was beautiful about each of them, even if he did see them all over New York City. They just looked different. Meryl disagreed. There was usually something that showed her who was handsome and who was plain. She just knew the Skivvy's owner was plain, with those pressed-in cheeks and yellowish clay-colored skin.

He was the first alien storekeeper in their town, Dan had insisted, even after Chester had scoffed at his use of the word. "Asian, Asian," Chester repeated stubbornly. "You know, the kind of people we anthropologists depend on to be kind to us." Meryl had refused to join in their argument. But from the dinner last Saturday, she thought, it looked like Chester was right. Paul had said his company was planning to bring over more top engineers from Asia. There would be no stopping more from coming, and then even Dan wouldn't be calling them aliens anymore.

She turned her eyes away so he wouldn't see her staring, and she went quickly through the doors and into the car.

Chester had showered by the time she got back. His hair was wet and stuck out in little points below his neck and he smelled as if he'd scrubbed himself for a good ten minutes. There were purple patches under his eyes and he was reading in bed.

"I'm not feeling so hot," he said when she came in. He was reading Jason's newest book, which he'd agreed to review for some journal. She wondered if it was the book that was getting him down.

She brought in a plate for her sandwich and a spoon for his rice pudding and they ate in the bedroom.

"Why don't you go to sleep early?" she told him. He was slowly licking each spoonful of rice pudding as if he were eating an ice-cream cone.

"Don't think I can make it for the benefit dinner tomorrow." He gave her an apologetic smile and scraped the carton for the remaining pudding. "My stomach feels weak, like it ODed on tuna fish."

She didn't want to show that she was happy about this. "Maybe you'll feel better tomorrow."

What was she going to say to Lee and Vernon Chatswick when she got to the cocktail reception they were giving before the dinner? They had wanted the commissioner and were disappointed that she had been asked to represent Parks instead. She'd have to tell them Chester had come down with a stomach virus.

"Can't take the risk of throwing up during your speech."

She knew it was a joke but she didn't like it. "Do you think your falling sick has something to do with my speech?"

"Jesus, Meryl! If it has nothing to do with the vasectomy, what can it possibly have to do with your speech?"

"Perhaps it's a way of getting attention."

"Listen, keep your neurotic blather for Dr. Jenkins. He's paid to understand it."

"I'm talking about you. Don't get defensive." She sat on the bed beside him.

He gave her the empty carton and the spoon fell off onto the quilt. She picked it up and rubbed the smudge with her napkin. "I take it back. You stay home tomorrow. I'll make chicken soup and you can finish reading Jason's book." He'd been trying to read it for the last six months.

"Sorry."

She could always count on Chester to calm down quickly. Kate had said this was because Chester never cared much about anything; but it was Doris, smitten with him, whom Meryl had believed. "Deep," she'd murmured after he left one night, "gorgeously deep!"

Meryl often thought of Doris, even though they had lost touch right after the wedding. Perhaps it wasn't so peculiar that she and Kate were still friends but she had not bothered to write or call Doris, who had moved to teach at one of the expensive schools just south of Philadelphia.

Doris had called the taxi and taken her to the clinic, held her hand through the curetting, and comforted her when, unaccountably, she had wept after they had returned to the safety of their apartment. "It's all right, it's all right," she remembered Doris repeating, like a boring mantra. And of course it had been all right.

She had not confessed to anyone her fear of the procedure, the humiliation of the interview with the nurse, and that final ridiculous moment of lying on the cold surgical table, the paper under her slippery and scrapy, knees cocked and everything wide apart. No anesthesia, no name to the doctor, nothing she wanted to remember. And, just as Doris had told her, nothing hurt, not even for a moment.

She and Chester had married a year later. By then Doris was completing a master's in education and had moved out, and Meryl had grown closer to Kate, who had decided to keep the apartment after the wedding.

Kate was now on her fourth or fifth relationship, and each, she claimed, was an improvement on the former. Perhaps she would marry someday, perhaps not.

The only argument they had had that left Meryl angry with her was over the topic of marriage.

"It's just not that important, Meryl!"

She hated it when Kate used her supercilious voice. Kate had been the only student at Barnard to beat Meryl's grade-point average. Of course, that had something to do with Chester; her grades had taken a steep dive the semester she got pregnant. But by then she didn't mind coming in second to Kate. She had Chester, with his long hair falling over his eyes, his long body beside her in bed. Even the sight of his long tapering fingers tapping to the music in the afternoon concerts at the quad roused her, stirred her body so that she couldn't wait for night to come again. Marriage to Chester had seemed simply the most natural thing for her.

But Kate had seen it as her desire to overcome her mother's bad marriage. "It's a setup. You're afraid of being your mother, abandoned in—where is it now? Salt Lake City? Chester appeals to you because he doesn't appear to be the type to abandon a woman. He's safe. You know he depends on you. Like a fish on a line. You think it's lust, but if he weren't secured, you wouldn't be hankering after him."

Meryl was furious at Kate's cheap psychologizing, but Kate had gone on to complete her training with both the Sullivanian and Jungian groups and now offered only occasional sardonic comments.

For a few months, two years ago, Meryl had tried to get Kate together with Dan, but they had not liked each other's jokes. "Dan reminds you of your father," Kate had said accusingly, "lapsed Catholic, alcoholic, irresponsible, and in trouble. No way I'm going to become your mother, even if you are my best friend!"

This week, Kate was in London for a theater series with Edmund—Edmund who always stared if you called him *Ed*—whom she had been dating seriously for the last year. Ever since Edmund appeared, it was harder to reach Kate, even on the phone. Soon, Meryl thought anxiously, Kate may go the way of Doris. Then it would be only Chester and herself against the world.

Chester, Meryl knew, thought her friends like Dan shallow. What continued to amaze her was that he did not think her so. She had to remind herself that despite his complaints he could not do without her. She was his bedrock, he said often enough, his geological bed in which he was fossilized; and she had to be grateful for his puns, more difficult to come by, he added, than Hallmark cards.

Meryl stroked Chester's hair before leaving him, relieved. She'd been dreading having him at the dinner. He was not an organization person, she had explained to Kate, and he didn't always agree with what she did.

She had finished revising the speech, but she wanted to make it familiar. She'd like to speak at the benefit as if every word were coming out for the first time, round and complete and natural.

The trouble with women was their voices either didn't sound professional enough, like her Aunt Cicely on the phone, or they droned along like the junior high school principal during the awards day roll call.

It was a good speech, but she had to say it right or they'd miss the point. She wasn't going to worry about impressing people. She'd just have to remember to smile a lot in between paragraphs.

If it worked, if they liked the speech, the commissioner would eventually have to come through with the deputy commissioner position. That was the least he owed her. Dan had told her that on personnel matters Meyers was old-fashioned—he didn't like the human resources department and preferred volunteer little old ladies with tennis shoes and two publications on herb gardening and pests. Meryl had registered last September for a master's program on land resources and management. Maybe Meyers hadn't heard about it yet. She'd send him a memo and a copy of the speech on Monday.

She didn't know what it was about the job that kept her zinging. She couldn't wait to get back to the office every Monday. She guessed it was the first good job she'd had, where she didn't have to jump for another person.

It was like having her own room for the first time. She had never thought it was important to live alone. It was fun sharing the apartment with Doris and Kate, and then when Chester moved to 116th Street she thought it was important to straighten him out.

Everyone thought she'd be upset when Meyers gave her the old office near the greenhouse. But she showed them. It wasn't location but brains that counted. She loved the big old walnut rolltop desk and the green-and-red lead glass windows by the side. It was like moving into the nineteenth century.

Now everyone wanted her office because the *Times* had described it as belonging to a different era. She knew action made the center of power. She wouldn't have minded if Meyers had sent her to a cubbyhole; she would have made it into a powerhouse.

Professor Quinby used to scrawl on the chalkboard before every American literature class, "Do what you love." Thoreau had written that, she remembered.

The Barnard women had thought he was bananas, funny Quinby with his gray goatee and white bow tie. A poet, he'd published three books, but he never talked about them.

Meryl didn't recall the titles now. One was *A Steamboat to Pompeii* or some such place, maybe Stromboli. She didn't think she had looked up the other books.

"Do what you love." Thank you very much, Quinby, she thought.

When she got to bed it was midnight and Chester was hunkered face down into the pillow with the curtains open and the three-quarter moon flooding the room like a searchlight.

She closed the curtains and crawled between the sheets.

Her mother used to say sleeping with the moon in one's face made people insane. She was an Irish eccentric, given to weeping and melancholy, especially whenever Meryl mentioned her errant father. He had abandoned them when Meryl was ten, no one knew for what reason. The last time she saw him she was about thirteen, and he had come back to their rented house in Dutchess County to pick up his high school trombone. He was on his way to a better job in San Diego, he said, ordering supplies for the U.S. Navy, and he would send her a California postcard. But even that never arrived.

Meryl didn't believe in much after that. She never believed her mother's tales about her father's insanity or about the moonlight, but still she couldn't sleep when there was light in her face.

Chester could simply stuff his face into a pillow and sleep. There must be a mechanism that kept him from suffocating. Whatever it was, she was always the one to draw the curtains.

Five

Meryl was groggy getting up on Sunday. Usually she liked Sundays, when they looked like a pair of castaways, Chester in his flapping striped pajamas, a patient who'd just escaped from a maximum-security psychiatric hospital, and she in navy blue tattered robe and scruffy slippers, the bag lady who sat at the corner of Fifth and Fifty-seventh, the Bonwit Teller lady, as Kate called her.

It was the only morning in the week that they shared, and they always sat in the dining room with a pot of tea and a pot of coffee and read the *Times*. That was when she told Chester about Parks and he told her where she was doing things wrong.

Today it was almost eight when she woke. Chester was still sleeping. He'd been sleeping a lot since Friday and complaining about being tired.

He came into the kitchen and stood by her shoulder as she was pushing the eggs around with a wooden spoon. She scrambled eggs the way her mother taught her, thick custardy lumps that she could heap on toast without getting the bread soggy. Chester had been crazy for them when she first moved in with him. He'd ask for them for lunch and dinner.

She couldn't wait for the eggs to set, so she ate a slice of cinnamon raisin bread while she was turning over the curds.

"How many eggs?" he asked.

"Six."

Meryl was thinking about last night and the hundred people at the dinner. It was amazing how quickly people ate, even when the food wasn't good.

She was glad she had been scheduled to speak after dinner. Her mother always said people were better behaved after they'd been fed. She thought the eating would take two hours, but coffee and ice cream were served within an hour and then Vernon Chatswick stood up and introduced her.

"Make eight eggs?"

It was nauseating how much food Chester could put away. He should either be slowing down or putting it on, but nothing showed on him.

Doris had been crazy over his body; it was so tall and lean among the foreign students who hung around them that year. She could have killed Meryl the first time she saw him coming out of the bathroom in his Jockey shorts. Doris knew what the score was then.

Life isn't fair, Meryl had told her.

"Too late. Get me your plate." She divided the eggs, piled them in a mound on the plates and took the bread out of the toaster.

"There's something in the *Times* on you."

"No! What page?" She was nervous and didn't want to believe it.

"Third page of the "Metro" section."

The eggs were getting cold, but she wasn't hungry anymore. She got up and read over his shoulder.

"A Future for the Parks." The byline was Bertha Tandy. She knew it was Bertha, but she checked anyway. Bertha had been at the dinner.

"Sock it to them," she'd whispered, giving Meryl the eye.

Big Bertha. Funny, Meryl had never marked Bertha for an important future when she trailed Meryl everywhere in her senior year, just a fat freshman with a crush. Bertha had a pretty face even then, shaped like a valentine with a cat's green-yellow eyes. But the guys didn't like her, all they could see were her cathedral hips and the loneliness dragging down her mouth.

"Why don't they like me, huh? Why don't they?" She followed Meryl through the Columbia quad shooting pangs of hunger at the biggest studs and nagging like a peeping chick. "What's wrong with me? How come he didn't return my call? I like him so much. You think I should do it in a pick-up truck?"

The blond Argentinean grad student had a good time with her, his big American mama, but Bertha told Meryl it was love.

Meryl never thought Bertha would amount to much, and here she was, a feature writer for the *Times*.

She had hoped Bertha would give her a good write-up as soon as she saw her last night, but wow, the Sunday *Times*. What did it matter if it was only Big Bertha, who could never keep a man? The rest of the world knew her as the *Times*.

Chester gave her one of his oblique looks. "You really made it big this time, Meryl. Listen. 'Mrs. Brookfield argued for a rational development of the parks that will take into account the environmental and aesthetic concerns of the conservationists as well as the urgent requirements of urban recreation.'"

"That's a pretty good summary."

"How about this? 'Parks are the city's last green line of defense, and the city, through its spokesman, Meryl Brookfield, has finally outlined a survivor's future for tree lovers, bird-watchers and ballplayers alike.'"

"I hope the commissioner reads it."

"Think he's going to like it?"

"He'd better. The *Times* did."

Chester had finished his eggs and was eating hers. "How come you're so concerned about the future of all those ballplayers and not your own?"

"What d'you mean?"

"I mean what kind of future are we going to have?"

Meryl was still reading Bertha's feature and not paying him much mind.

"I don't know if the vasectomy was a good idea. I mean, aren't kids the future?"

She couldn't believe it. She stared at him. His nose quivered and he jammed his hands into his pajama pockets so they tore even more at the corners.

"Didn't you tell me that there are already too many children in the world?"

She could hear the birds squeaking outside. It was a dazzler outdoors, the kind of day when thousands of kids came out with their baseball bats and started bashing the Japanese dogwoods. Italians, Poles, Puerto Ricans, Jamaicans, Trinidadians: it didn't matter what shape or color. Lots of humans just didn't like trees. And everyone wanted to walk on the grass and have his pooch go on it.

Chester didn't say anything, just pushed his lips together in his mulish way.

"Aren't you always preaching about starving babies in Asia and how the cultural structures are going to collapse because . . ."

"Damn it, Meryl. America isn't Asia."

"What about your Spaceship Earth concept? D'you mean it's okay for Americans to have kids but wrong for Indians?"

"I'm not talking about a litter of them."

"I like that. You're a sow if you have six, but okay if you have two."

"One, Meryl, one."

It was too much. It was just like Chester. He'd say something and have her go along and go along. Then he'd change his mind and, wham, that was it! He didn't know what he wanted until he found out what she wanted, and then he didn't want that.

"Look what you've done!" she cried. She'd crumpled the papers and the feature article was balled up and torn.

"What, what?" Chester jumped up, then sat down again. "It's only the paper for crying out loud."

"It's my article."

He started to laugh.

Her hands were shaking as she tried to smooth the page and piece it together. She clenched her teeth. She couldn't help herself. "It's too late. It's too late for you, anyway."

Chester stopped laughing but she didn't look at him.

She got up, threw the *Times* into the garbage container, and went to the bathroom.

Six

Chester fished the *Times* out of the garbage container. There was a brown smear where the pages had been mashed into a banana peel; otherwise it was clean.

He unwrinkled the torn page, cut out the Parks article, found a roll of transparent tape and gently fitted together the three torn edges. He left the article, tape shining like slimy tracks across its square, on the kitchen table and went out of the house.

Except for not talking to him, Meryl had spent the morning on her normal Sunday routine. She steeped herself in a bubble bath, shampooed her hair, daubed her face with Elizabeth Arden's Purifying Clay Mask, cuticled her finger nails, and was now watching an interview with a state senator on television.

Chester waited for her to say she was sorry. He knew he had been unreasonable, but he felt she had been cruel and should apologize.

He folded himself into the Volkswagen reluctantly—he didn't want Meryl to think he was running away from an argument. But he knew he was running away, if only to Skivvy's for rice pudding.

The street was empty, and for the first time he wondered why there were no children playing in the yards. He drove slowly down the block but could see no one through his neighbors' glass windows, which were full of reflected shrubbery and sky. He wondered if he should tell Meryl about his child.

"There must be other men like me," he thought.

Since Friday's reaction to the painkillers he had been troubled by tremors of nausea, and his stomach twitched uncomfortably as he talked to himself.

"The world is full of bastards. One night here, one night there. How to count the children you may have fathered?"

He was surprised at the grief he felt. It gripped his body in a tight shell and seemed to lock his thoughts in a crazy rhythm that exhausted him.

He steered the car up the ramp onto the parkway. A gray Datsun swerved to the left lane to make room for him, but he continued to edge along the shoulder and did not accelerate into the free lane.

He heard a honking and suddenly a brown Oldsmobile shot from behind to his left. Chester swung the steering wheel to avoid hitting the Oldsmobile.

Briefly he glimpsed a contorted male face and an upright finger, then the Volkswagen went into a spin. For a second he thought the car would turn over, but it came to a stop with one wheel on a boulder and the two back wheels stuck fast in the black churned dirt beside the road. The Datsun and the Oldsmobile were already out of sight.

To Chester the accident was implausible. He sat in the car with the engine still running, his heart racing and a high singing in his ears. His seat was tilted and lifted upwards as if he had tried to clamber up the boulder with his car for a ringside view. More cars passed by, looking like speeding stunt acts through his angled windscreen.

He felt quite content to stay in his seat. After the first fear he was almost pleased to find himself in a situation where he didn't have to decide what to do next but could ponder what it was that was making him so miserable.

The state police were there in ten minutes.

The older man who knocked at the car door looked suspiciously at Chester as he climbed down from his suspended roost.

"Been drinking?" he asked as he thumped the door shut.

The Volks shook and rattled as if all its rusty bolts were giving way. The younger man checked the license and registration and took down Chester's account while his partner radioed for a tow truck.

Chester watched the soft spread of the belly around the grizzled officer as he was talking into the crackling box and wondered if the soft flesh would have turned to muscle had he caught a drunk instead.

He didn't wait for the tow truck but accepted the offer of a ride home. The yellow Volks, his contribution to a more sustainable planet thirteen years ago, would never drive again, he knew. The crazy alignment of the wheels could never be made straight.

Whatever the reason, he was not concerned about losing the car.

Sitting behind the bulky blue-clothed shoulders and listening to the officers' casual drawl, Chester thought he was in the worst trouble of his life. He saw again the upright finger stuck contemptuously in the air and knew he could not yet tell Meryl about the child, for telling would also mean explaining its existence, and his silence, indifference, and sudden concern.

The officers didn't drop him up the street but pulled right up into his driveway. The younger officer sidled out of the passenger seat, opened the door for Chester before he could move from his hunched curled-in position, and knocked on the front door as Chester was thanking the driver.

He almost expected to be marched indoors, but the officer turned away as soon as Meryl opened the door to avoid her startled gaze, surely to avoid having to explain his presence, and the police car backed out and sped away like a rehearsed chase scene in a movie.

"What happened?"

When he opened his mouth to explain, Meryl interrupted, "I was on the phone," and went inside again.

Stubbornly he stayed by the open door, flicking his finger at the dried black shell of an insect entangled in an old web between the fake wood molding.

"I put Dan on hold," Meryl said, appearing at the door again, as he surreptitiously wiped his fingers, sticky with the web, on his pants.

"Some jerk cut me off and I crashed the car."

"Oh no." Her face pinked up and she stepped outside and looked at her own maroon Chevy.

"It's gone. The wheel alignment's shot."

"You're okay?"

"Yeah." He left his long arms hanging by his sides and let her hug him. Her hair was wiry. It smelled of shampoo and tickled his nose. She pressed her face into his chest and her warm breath felt moist and young.

"Poor Chester. I'll make some tea." She held his hand and led him into the kitchen. "Dan's still on the line."

The receiver rested on the kitchen table like a third party.

"What does he want?"

"Actually he wants to talk to you."

He picked up the receiver, still warm from her holding it.

"Hello," he said and imagined Dan's large white face in front of him teetering between a leer and a wrinkle of pain.

"Chester." The voice was loud and clear; it sounded surprised.

"I just got home. Can we talk later?"

"Sure."

He listened to the click and was aware he was jealous of whatever it was Meryl and Dan were sharing together before the officer knocked on the door.

The newspaper clipping was exactly where he had left it. He turned to look at her as she stood by the sink washing the breakfast dishes and he felt a great sorrow for her. Her back was arched stiffly as if to prepare for a blow and her luminous hair, bowed over the flow of water, glowed with the light from the window.

She should be a mother, he thought. All that glorious flesh and her laboring, without its due, without a reprieve.

He touched her shoulder, taut and round under the blue woolen jersey, and stared into her shiny eyes when she turned her head around.

"Chester, do you hate my success?"

Her question was brisk, and her body leaned away from him as she pushed her hands, clutching at a slippery plate, further into the soapy water.

For a moment he didn't understand her; then he retreated to the table and sat across from the clipping. He watched as she rinsed the plate and carefully placed it upright on the drying rack.

"We have to talk about it." Her lower lip pushed out like a barrier over the upturned chin, and she wore the peering expression of reasonableness that had only become noticeable since she'd pronounced her therapy a success.

"You serious?" He pulled the neatly cut paper before him and traced the smooth slick tracks of tape with a finger.

"You get sick just before the benefit dinner, then you wreck the car. You've been sulking for the last few days."

"Have you been talking to Dan about me?" He saw he had surprised her.

Uncomfortable, she shifted her chin. "That has nothing to do with what I'm saying. Why don't you want me to do well? I'm just beginning to make an impression on Parks policy. Soon I'll get my promotion and will really be able to turn things around."

"Did Dan tell you I was jealous or did you tell him?" He thought of the two exchanging observations on him, Dan's sly voice booming in her ear and her own impatient description of his behavior, sharing with Dan the intimacy of her suspicions. "What do you have with him, anyway?"

"Come on, we're talking about your being jealous of me, not about Dan." She blinked and folded her arms, standing him off.

"No. You tell me what Dan has between his legs that I don't." He liked it now that her mouth was slackening in distress. Her eyes had a gloom that made her appear uncertain and soft.

"That's not fair. I never . . ."

"Look, if you can believe I'm jealous over a speech that got into the *Times* you can believe I'm jealous of Dan."

"You're tricking me again." Meryl's voice was rising steadily. "You're always setting up traps." Her arms were down and Chester knew she was itching to bang her fist on the table.

Then she did something that amazed him. She walked away from him, picked up the kitchen towel, and slowly wiped the pan she had left sitting in the sink.

"Why don't you grow up, Chester?" she asked in her polite company voice. "Everything that happens to you is what you do to yourself. That accident—you wanted it. That's why you went out. And you never drink coffee; it makes you sick. Why would you suddenly drink two cups of coffee after taking all those pills? You keep doing things and pretending that they aren't happening. Things don't just happen. You do them. That's called responsibility."

"I thought I was being responsible when I had the vasectomy."

"You called Dr. Shelley. You went to his office. Don't put the guilt on me." Her voice quickened and she turned to face him challengingly.

"Guilt went out with the sixties." He was tired and wasn't sure what they were quarreling about anymore. He only knew they weren't talking about the same subject. "I really don't care where you get your kicks. Be the Parks commissioner if that's what you want. I'm just beginning to ask what it is I'm missing."

"For as long as I've known you, Chester, you've never known what you want."

He believed her. Of course he was jealous of her. She, at least, knew what she wanted and went all out to get it.

When they were dating, he knew she wanted him. She said it every time she put her arm through his when Doris was in the room. When she insisted on doing his laundry, she was saying to him, "I want you this much." It made him feel good.

He had gone off to Bali on a six-month fellowship because his mother didn't think he should get married so soon, and for the first few months, he had almost believed he wasn't ready for her.

Jolting on the hard soil packed by centuries of other feet, stones rolling underfoot, the rhythm so different from walking in the city, every step a difference in level, slipping sideways, a shallow depression, a rise, then a pothole, feeling the differences in his gait as he adjusted to the bare earth rolling in all directions under his feet, he had felt very close to his body.

He observed, first with curiosity and then with a strange expansion of affection in his chest, the gait of his companions, the impossibly agile men and women, small, no more than five feet if that, swaying, moving their bare callused feet with toes spread wide and gripping the earth easily, a suggestion of the dancer in the swing of the hip that carried them forward.

This time he saw the remarkable and undeniable similarity between himself and the Balinese as among cousins, without a quiver of distaste, admiring instead their dancers' grace as they moved through the uneven paths with heads held high as if towards the high inland mountains that had blazed rock and ash in the memories of their stories.

He was busy with interviews, the Malay he'd picked up in Kuala Lumpur finally coming in useful. He photographed the ceremonies, the dances, the plays, spent time fishing with Buda and Mat in the incredibly gentle clean salty sea. The clearness of the water against his skin was like a shock of pleasure in which he was immersed over and over again effortlessly.

But her letters arrived twice a week without a break. Toward the end he got caught up in their urgency—the rapid-fire images of Columbia, her exams, the cold weather clamping down on the Hudson, the sharp-etched brown and gray of Broadway. He had hurried through the final village interviews, rented a bicycle to get down to the beach where the tourist hotels were, spent the evenings organizing and packing his materials, and flown away from Bali with relief.

Seven

Meryl had the lowest opinion of Jason—an overfed kid, she taunted Chester whenever his name came up.

But Chester had steered by Jason's star ever since he'd returned home to Connecticut from Malaysia, confused and knocking at loose ends, then found his way to Columbia. There, Jason's course on ethnocentrism and Asian culture had allowed him to distance himself from the violent repugnance that had inexplicably filled him as soon as he arrived that steamy August and found himself among neighbors who talked and walked and ate with knives and forks just like he did.

For a month, among the stately white-painted colonials of his hometown, he sweltered in a heat wave more debilitating than what he had experienced in the tropical enclosures of Malaysia. But he could not talk to his parents about his time in Malaysia coherently because of the tone that crept into his descriptions. He had worried over his tone even as images of Abdullah's and Samad's beaming faces smiling good-bye at the airport dodged in and out of his conversations. He put away the two Marks and Spencer sweaters his students at the Vocational High School had given him on his last day. All he could remember was their schoolboy pallor, the zany accent of their English as they shyly sang, "For he's a jolly good fellow."

He had had enough of difference for a lifetime, he thought, and when his father pressed him for stories he shrank inside and tried to muffle the memory of all those multihued skins, the black, brown, and yellow and the creamy-white of the Eurasians.

His mother thought his mumbling evasions were because he missed his friends—perhaps, although she feared and never raised the subject, a native woman.

But his father suspected his surliness, the way he left the boxes of souvenirs unpacked, refused to send the dozens of rolls of film for developing, and would not organize his slides for one private showing for them. "Didn't have a good time, did you?" he said after the first week. But that wasn't true either.

Jason knew the reason. That is, he knew about differences, about how beyond a certain point the individual could not adapt out of his particular culture. He knew that an individual was not all there was; that a man was a product of other men; and that a man was capable of doing and feeling things essential to his group although accidental to his being.

It was a relief sitting through Jason's lectures. The oppressive sensation he had suffered as he struggled to reconcile himself to living with Abdullah's and Samad's soft wrist motions, the odd-shaped noses sitting on his Eurasian friends' almost Caucasian faces, and the unsettling smells of Indian sweat, Chinese soya sauce, and Malay spices—an oppressiveness he had not dared express for fear of being condemned as superior, gradually dissolved during Jason's delicate explication of the laws of difference. To be white, to know one was white, to find anything else peculiar and uncomfortable, was no sin— it became, in fact, the basis for curiosity and inquiry, one's fate.

This truth made it easier for him to walk down Broadway, past toppled garbage cans and loud salsa music. It made it easier for him to stop by the black peddlers hawking African beads and batiks and copies of *The Autobiography of Malcolm X* on the sidewalks, to buy a shell necklace for Meryl. Ignoring the roisterous, clashing voices and colors outside the unwalled boundary of the campus for the books that taught him to study people rather than get mixed up with them, Chester was able also to carry this truth with him during his six-month stay in Bali. It made him comfortable in a way he had not been in

Malaysia. He was there to study difference, not overcome it, and he could finally relax with the natives, knowing guiltlessly that he was not one of them.

Monday was always one of Jason's days at home. He had been a fixture at Columbia for a long time. Having studied with Ruth Benedict as an undergraduate, he had returned to teach after four years in India studying the hill tribes in Tamil Nadu—a personal triumph. Jason had penetrated a field then exclusively and jealously guarded by Britain and established an unswervingly loyal fellowship of students, past and present, who followed him through his weekly schedule.

Thus, it was commonly known that Wednesdays and Fridays Professor Kingston lectured to overflowing halls of students who crowded his classes for his low-key, engaging rambles over Asian history, politics, philosophies, and personalities. Mondays and Tuesdays he held court in his apartment with coffee and tea brewing and the newest group of Asian students, visiting dignitaries, and young anthropologists milling about his four large rooms. The rooms looked as if they were still being arranged for an exhibition of ethnic artifacts, with stacks of spears leaning against corners, brass cooking pots knocking against grass baskets, stone talismans falling off bookshelves, and intricate beadwork unraveling over punched-in armchairs and sofas. Thursday, he told his department secretary, was his day for doctors, dentists, banks, and publishers; and all his friends knew his weekends were for his most recent mistress, usually one of many adventurous women who had given themselves to studies of Bhutanese translations, Tibetan painting, Burmese Buddhism, or Japanese masks.

After his classic volume, *Culture and Cultivation*, appeared in the late fifties, Jason had not felt the need to do more fieldwork, but his reputation as the prototypical field anthropologist persisted, and he had launched more researchers into remote societies and opened more isolated tribes to the energies of graduate students than Chester could track. It was Jason who got the fellowship for Chester to do fieldwork in Bali, and for the last seven years Chester had faithfully joined Jason's court at least twice a month.

Among the yards of books lining Jason's rooms was
Chester's monograph, dedicated, as many of the books there
were, to Jason. Chester was bemused by Jason, who, in the time
he had followed him, had gone from maturity to adolescence without missing a beat.

Today Jason was wearing a vaguely dashiki-looking shirt, a curl-
ing mass of graying chest hair sprouting from its large open
neckline. The shirt was maroon and stained with pipe ash and
coffee.

Squatting by the coffee table on haunches ripe as melons,
Andrea, Jason's newest mistress, was cutting Dunkin Donuts
into halves.

Chester received a two-arm hug from Jason, who, for all
his girth, still towered over Chester and talked into his hair.

Chester would have liked to confess to Jason today, but there
were at least ten other visitors in the apartment. The young
Malaysian students, one from Alor Star and the other from
Kuching, nibbled silently on their doughnut halves, while Bob
Restoff, just back from teaching at Tribhuvan University in
Katmandu, was describing the German renovations of
Nepalese sites to some of Jason's graduate students.

At 4 P.M., Jason went to the kitchen to break open the jug
of cheap California Chablis, a Monday and Tuesday ritual that
had created an afternoon-drinking, migraine-suffering sub-
group among a generation of American and Asian anthropologists.

Chester took the requisite glass, then left it concealed behind
a potted sword plant with the conviction that the wine
would be offered to the great snaky spikes when discovered.
In the kitchen he found a chipped pottery mug indented with
awkward shapes that appeared as if they could be vines and
fruits. Sheila, Jason's mistress two years ago, had filled the
apartment with brown and cobalt jars, mugs, and ashtrays.
Chester had liked her quirky touches and hoped she would
stay on with Jason, but she gave up pottery and moved to the
East Side when she found a job at Ming Galleries, the repro-
duction porcelain store started by Ambassador Turpin's wife
after their return from Japan. Filling the mug with the jasmine

tea that Andrea had left steeping in a pot by the stove, he went to look for Jason.

"What do you think of my returning to Southeast Asia?"

"Where?" Jason asked, seizing the wine jug and pouring a stream into a jelly glass, one of Andrea's more favored contributions among the dishware she had brought to the apartment. He poured with a free hand, and wine splashed on the wood floor. Wiping the puddle with a generous handful of toweling—all the young women who moved down the trough of his appetites, he boasted, were princesses but slatternly, while he, for all the clutter of things and people he collected around him, was methodically clean—he grinned with approval.

"I was in Malaysia, 1968 to '69. Thought I might go back to the region, perhaps to Singapore, to see what's happening with urban cultural development."

"Peace Corps teaching, right?" Jason swallowed the Chablis like grape juice, in gulps, and waved the jug before filling his jelly glass again. "What were you teaching? I forgot."

"Woodworking."

Jason's splutter of laughter was genuine.

Chester was annoyed. "Shop, damn it. I was supposed to teach woodworking, but after the first two months they made me into an English teacher."

"Of course. Governments don't import the Peace Corps to equalize classes. Teaching English, that's a capitalist venture."

"I wasn't a capitalist. It was hard work cramming two hundred kids to pass a British exam in English."

"But that's the point. Did you ask why they needed a British exam in the English language? More pertinently, did you teach your students to ask that question?" For all his joviality, Jason was beginning to be interested in his own questions. "As a cultural anthropologist you know that kind of interference is suspect."

"I wasn't an anthropologist then. Besides, I really preferred teaching woodworking, only no one wanted to learn it; something to do with class standing, just as it is here. Malays, Eurasians, Chinese, Tamils, Pakistanis, Sikhs, Indonesians— there was a parcel of them for a small country. I knew

Americans shouldn't have been there, adding to the mess, like we were doing in Vietnam, but it was confusing, figuring out what was interference and what wasn't. I didn't know what those people would have had in common if it weren't for that kind of British educational structure, even though I knew it was a colonial hang-up."

"They would have had another kind of education in common, as you put it." Jason's jowly face was handsomely alert, and Chester became conscious that he also had gulped his tea and was flushing.

He slowed his speech and pitched it to a casual drawl. "They do have another educational system now. English has been wiped out and Bahasa Malaysia made the language of possession."

"All this in a few years? Anything like the language riots in India? No, I would have read about it. Case in point for a successful reinstatement of native culture after the expulsion of colonialism. Well, here's a possible proposal for the Benedict Research Foundation. I take it that's why you're discussing Malaysia with me."

The warmth in Chester's cheeks was like shame. "Jeez, Jason, I'm not pushing you to find me a fellowship."

"No, of course." Jason chuckled and seized Chester's head in a massive forearm lock, then released him suddenly. "More wine?"

As Chester waved the bottle away, Jason's forehead unwrinkled in a noble gesture, and he spoke in his professorial voice: "You never expressed a research interest in Malaysia before. Always thought it strange an anthropologist would stay in a different culture and not want to study it in some way."

"I told you, I wasn't an anthropologist then. Besides, I'm considering Singapore."

"Doesn't matter. Same region, same mind, same person."

"No. Not the same mind, therefore not the same person." Chester wondered if he was speaking too violently; he was afraid he would tell Jason everything. "I was very young then, looking for adventure—you know, fun, tropical paradise." His voice cracked and he coughed.

"Found something else instead."

"Yes."

"Don't tell me. That was the time of the troubles."

"May thirteenth."

"I see. Anything happen to anyone you knew?"

"Not really. Actually, everything happened. Everyone I knew went kind of crazy, like a psychosis. People just cracked open. The nicest people . . ."

"Are you including yourself?"

Chester's throat tightened. Again he remembered Jason's power, his ability to strike at just the right angle to expose the human under the layers of grass costuming. He laughed shallowly. "You don't give a guy a chance, do you?"

"You don't want that. Out with it. What happened to you? Why do you want to return after all these years? What is it, ten years? Having a bad time with Meryl? She's a knockout. Would like a piece myself but afraid she'd never approve of me." He gave his foolish Saint Bernard grin to show he meant no harm and put his heavy sweaty arm over Chester's shoulder.

"I got a girl pregnant. It was just a one-night affair, though she was sweet and all that. She was married. I never gave it a thought, but she had the baby."

"Ah, an American baby."

"Well, I gathered that was the case. The husband divorced her after the birth."

"And she's putting the screws on you to get them into the United States."

"No, nothing like that. I haven't heard from her in all these years."

The fear that she would write, would claim a relationship with him, had dragged into everything in the first few months home, affected his eating, sleeping, being with his family.

He dreaded the mail. Each time his mother gave him a bunch of letters, he grew clammy at the sight of the red-and-blue-edged airmail letters. They always turned out to be from his students or his housemates, stilted letters about school holidays, exams, and camping trips that all sounded alike. He never replied, until only Abdullah and Paroo continued to write, Abdullah with funny blunt little paragraphs on political shenanigans; and then only Paroo, seldom raising Li An's name again after the delicate description of her baby and Henry's scandal, still faithfully writing two or three letters a year, filling him in on acquaintances as if he had never made new friends on his own without Chester.

By then Chester knew that Li An wouldn't write to him. He was no longer afraid of a letter from her, of an accusation or even of a reminder of their friendship. She would never write, and he quickly forgot—so quickly and thoroughly, until only now, with his vasectomy.

Jason stood looking at him, arms folded akimbo all this time.

"You know, I get older . . ."

"Tell me another one."

He tried again. "It's curiosity. I want to see what the child's like."

"So ask for a photograph."

"You're making it difficult for me."

"I'm making it?"

"All right, all right. I'm crazy. I want to see my child."

"You don't even know he's yours."

"I don't know if it's a son."

"Less reason for this sudden madness if it's a girl. Male progeny can be said to assert a special demand on the line of descent, but females have no special claim."

"It's my life, not a field study."

"You're whining, Chester. I'm not being unsympathetic, but you haven't shown an interest in this child for—what, ten, eleven years, am I right? The mother hasn't bothered to inform you of its existence, and you haven't taken the time to inquire. What makes you think you're wanted on the scene? Or more to the point, what makes you think you wouldn't be doing something harmful, intruding into a picture you've chosen to opt out of all this time?"

"You're right, Professor Kingston." Chester kept his voice low and ironic. Jason's accusation that he was whining hurt him, and he felt the grievance nosing in his voice box.

"But you're going to do it anyway?"

Chester nodded and dodged another of Jason's ferocious hugs.

"That's my boy! Why not? I've never understood this foolishness with children. It seems to me children only succeed in making one feel old. I never feel old except when there's some crying brat around. And I've never met a happy father, they're as rare as happy husbands. Children should be like mistresses—lovable, loving, with a contract not to renew unless desired. But our culture doesn't take as kindly to that idea for children as it does for mistresses. Hence, my childless, and happy, position."

Jason appeared quite drunk by this point and was slowly lowering himself onto the legless sofa. Chester held out his hand to help him down the final six inches, and he sat in a muddle of knees and purple dashiki, a giant fat flower against the pale green Indian paisley that covered the seat, with the empty jug in the heart of it.

"I'll get you more wine from the kitchen."

Jason gave up the jug and rested his gray head against the busy cushion. "We'll get you the Benedict Fellowship. There's a lot of good work you can do with your special background. Like measuring stress levels after the May troubles." He began to mumble, and Chester backed away cautiously.

Much later, carefully driving his new secondhand Volks, knowing that the house would be empty when he arrived and that much later, it being her night at the seminar, Meryl would not want dinner because she would have eaten in the Village, Chester felt good about telling Jason everything.

Eleven years, he was certain, couldn't have changed the region that much.

The change was in him. He was ready now to meet Li An and her child. His child, it was almost certain, if the years bore out what he had always suspected, ever since that last night he had seen her standing across from Ellen and Abdullah and Henry, struggling to tell him.

As for Meryl, she would be so busy writing her master's dissertation she would hardly notice his absence.

He ground his teeth at both his annoyance and his relief at this notion.

Book Three

LANDING
〜

SINGAPORE

1981

Chester did not remember the afternoon air as heavy and closed, with the density of warm wet wool. In his involuntary memories of Malaysia, he had recalled the rush of air in his hair, rustling pleasure, motorbike rides leaning into a wind, even through the thick traffic on Batu Road. The smells of cloves, jasmine, and human ordure. Glimpses of crimson and gold Benares silk cloths in the dusky fronts of shophouses. But he was in Singapore, because Paroo had landed in Singapore six years ago, the same city, Paroo's letter had noted then, to which Li An had moved with her child and her best friend, Ellen.

Singapore in 1981, unlike the Kuala Lumpur of 1969, was no exotic tropic. Tall glassy buildings, steel road dividers, pounding lorries and blue taxis—it was an Anglo-Chinese detour, a metamorphic metropolis of old British imperial might and new Chinese puritanical capital. It was a city for sociologists advising on policies to determine what kind of people should compose the city rather than anthropologists curious about the ways in which people shaped a city. He tried to imagine the Peace Corps volunteers who would be needed in the Housing Development Board flats to teach American enterprise and democratic ideals. No, Samad corrected him, the Americans in Singapore today were more likely to be junior executives in the new American Express office.

The polished white Mercedes in which Samad had picked him up from Changi Airport also suggested a different relationship between them.

Tactfully, Samad had found him a one-room apartment on Gilstead Road. "Wah! Staying here five months, ah?" he had advised Chester over the telephone. "Surely cannot afford five-star hotel like Raffles. Even Bencoolen Street also too much. My friend Chester, if you trust me, I find you nice flat with many orang puteh just like you. You feel at home immediately."

Leaning back on the white leather upholstery, Chester understood that Samad, now CEO and vice president of three companies, as his card announced, was trying to save his feelings from the reversal in their positions.

But he did not feel at home in his service apartment building among the transient Americans and Germans, oilmen on break from the Shell refineries in Brunei, lounging with their Thai and Indonesian girlfriends, whose English was restricted to hellos and good-byes. By seven the next morning he was walking down Gilstead toward Orchard Road, searching for an American breakfast in an air-conditioned restaurant.

Heat rose from the sidewalks and compact gardens in a pervasive vapor. It filled his pores, stuck in his Jockey shorts, and pressed on his face the sensation of a thick Turkish towel in a sauna. Dirty white-and-gray tigerish cats crouched in the drains, their mouths slick with the garbage they had torn from pink plastic food packages scattered around the cans outside the Spastic Children's School.

It was late July. Those yellow-green furry fruit on the tall thick tree, he remembered, were rambutans. He had eaten sacks of them in Kuala Lumpur, when Abdullah had brought them back from his kampung one season. Or perhaps they had come from Samad's village. Now he watched the sleek magpies snatch at the fruit, fluttering their black-and-white wings and squabbling over the pale shreds that splattered on the driveways where they had dropped them. Black ants encrusted the leftovers. He saw the cats and magpies as long-term residents, and felt his newness in Singapore.

Lengthening his stride, he hurried for a taxi. "The Marco

Polo Coffeeshop." Samad had taken him there for dinner last
night, and he remembered the fountain jets in front of the hotel,
promising reprieve from the sun.

Later he found his way to the university, where, among bull-
dozers and cranes roaring and whining on stripped hillsides,
he managed to track down a series of clerks in a series of offices
and to make his research project understood. The letters from
Kingston and from the Social Science Research Council
bearing the logos of Columbia University and the Social
Anthropology Association achieved an effect that was near
miraculous. Doors in the library, smelling of paint and fresh
books, opened to him; plastic cards were produced and telephone calls made. A university lecturer appeared and introduced himself as a graduate of Columbia. Chester was invited
to a department tea that afternoon, and asked to give a seminar during his stay. He wondered at the deference shown him.
He had left Malaysia as a longhaired student, and returned
to Singapore an esteemed professor.

But no one seemed able to tell him where Li An was.

"Ah yes," Samad said, chuckling, when he called the second
day, "I am trying for you, Chester. But must be patient, you
know. Girlfriends not so easy to get back. Okay, okay, not like
girlfriend. I know you got wife now. But like us Muslims, one
wife not always the case, yes or not? I call her for you first."

Chester wondered why Samad didn't offer to give him her
telephone number. Social rituals, the protocol of power. He
could not be patient with his own answers.

On the third day, Chester called Paroo, tracking down his
telephone number at St. Paul's Junior College, the address noted
in his last letter.

"So, so, so Chester!" Paroo's voice over the line was as rapid
and enthusiastic as it had been almost twelve years ago. "I know
we sure meet again. True friendship never dies, I say to my family. How many years we never see each other! Why don't you
write you're coming? How long are you staying? You must come
and meet my missus and daughter. Yes, not like old times.
Everyone, I think, is now living in Singapore, you know. Even
Abdullah and Samad, VIP CEOs. Abdullah also United

Malay National Organization ministry secretary before joining OKM—Overseas Koranic Majulis—big-time travel company bring Muslims to hajj in Mecca. Both are living in
Singapore—but both also have big big houses in Malaysia.
Sometimes I take makan with them for old times' sake. I visit
them on Malay New Year—Hari Raya Puasa—every year. Now
the gang is complete!"

Paroo's house in Serangoon Gardens had small hot rooms.
Next to the rattan cane lounge a statue of the elephant-
headed Ganesha, wreathed with sandalwood carved blossoms, puffed out its belly and beamed below its giant trunk
and gleaming tusks. Rani, kohl-rimmed eyes cast down,
greeted him shyly, and six-year-old Surani hid behind her
mother's green-silver skirt, a tiny dark maiden like a princess
of the evening.

Chester waited until Rani had served the hot sweet tea, until
she had whisked away the plates of curries and thin-sliced cucum-
bers and tomatoes—"Salad, I remember you always like
salad," Paroo had said—and the saucers of oily sour lime and
sweet mango pickles were gone. He kept the question short
and casual, so casual that Paroo didn't hear it, and he had to
raise his voice, repeating, making it more emphatic than he
had intended. "Do you ever meet Lee Ann? Whatever has happened to her?"

Paroo, of course, knew all about Li An. "I meet her quite
often. Oh, how often? Often, often. Maybe twice, three
times a year. Just to have lunch you know, talk about old days.
Not too much about old days, because it is still sad to remember. You remember Gina? Very sad." He sighed, rattled his teacup
anxiously, put it down again without taking a sip, then
smiled, forgetting Gina. "I know all about Li An's daughter
also. Her name is Suyin. More pretty than my Surani. Now
you know where I get my idea for Surani's name, only don't
tell my missus—she is sure to be jealous."

He looked at Chester with disapproval. "How come you never
helped Li An when she became pregnant? Everyone knows
Suyin is your daughter. Abdullah, Samad, also the husband.
Man, big shock for him, you know, suddenly he finds an
American baby. People said Eurasian, but I know baby is not

Eurasian, not Portuguese, but American champor-champor, yes or not? I see the baby in the hospital, looks like you, got your hair, dip down on forehead. For sure, not Chinese."

"Lee Ann never told me."

"Cannot be! Maybe you never heard. How can you not know something like that? But never mind, all that is old story. Li An is now here in Singapore, doing well, I think. She's happy, got money, got condo, got car, got big-time job. Only one thing she doesn't have is a husband." Paroo grinned.

"Can you arrange for me to meet her?" Chester tried to keep his gaze steady.

"What for?" The grin reshaped itself. "Okay, lah. Don't say I don't return favors. One year when I try to get Surani into an American university, I will ask for a favor also. But Li An is a very busy woman. I try for best date, maybe next week, maybe later."

Lying on the too-soft mattress that night, Chester conjured Meryl's countenance out of the warm tropical dark. He would write her soon, he promised himself. She had been too busy with the reorganization of the Parks bureaucracy to pay much attention when he left on the fellowship, and he had not tried calling her since he landed in Singapore. No matter how hard he tried, he could not change the irritated air that crumpled his countenance. He fell asleep concentrating on the power of the name *Suyin*.

Two

School reunions were a Western practice. Li An had read about them in the *International Herald Tribune* and in thinly disguised autobiographical accounts in American women's magazines: the fretting over clothes and jewelry, eagerness to preen before ancient rivals now rotund and drab, the happy shocks as sight adjusted to missing hair, overflowing flesh, and crows-feet. She had not considered attending one, although her British colonial school was only six hundred miles away in Penang, and, with the new air routes, closer by many hours than before.

A resident of Singapore for the past nine years, she had become accustomed to being merely a spectator in the city. Singaporeans talked to her about family events, weddings, Chinese New Year dinners, the Sunday sermons, and their thirtieth school reunions with relish and blandness. It was their culture, their world, their lives, and she listened with skillful attention, grateful to be included in the conversation, although slightly inattentive about the details, the lists of dull characters, and the stories never as funny as the speaker had found them. So she was surprised when, in the middle of a meeting to decide on a strategy for packaging the stock portfolio in new graphics, she received a call from Gwen, saying, "I've booked a table and told everyone you are coming to the school reunion. We are celebrating the Penang Free School Centennial in the Kuala Lumpur Presidential Club. Now, with the new flights, everyone who has left Penang has no excuse not to attend."

Still, her first response was unsurprising. "I can't go. I will have to rush back for a consultation on Monday, and my body just can't take all the travel."

"What travel?" Gwen's voice over the phone was brusque and impatient. "Excuse me, it's only forty-five minutes by plane to Kuala Lumpur! Come on! Don't you want to see all your old boyfriends? Besides, Mrs. Leong says she'll be coming to the dinner just to see you again."

"Who else will be at the table?"

"I'm not sure. You must come, you know."

She didn't know. After all, for nine years she had successfully avoided Kuala Lumpur, its smoky afternoon haze, the foul snorting lorries and women wrapped in black purdah like walking corpses. She remembered the heat and her confusion from the months when she had carried Suyin, blotting her fear and grief with the vision of the baby, hanging from its umbilical branch, unsexed, complexion shrouded in a sac shot through with crimson pulsing webs. It was the web she wove to save her life.

Suyin had not wanted to come out; the branch would not break, and the doctor had had to cut it down.

Henry had recognized immediately that the baby was not his. "She's beautiful," he said when Li An woke up from the anesthesia after the cesarean. His eyes were wet. Then he left.

The lawyer came next morning. She never saw Henry again, although he did not disown the baby. She refused the alimony as soon as she could pay their way, but Suyin kept his name. Yeh Suyin.

Second Mrs. Yeh had picked the name months before she was born. "Carry low, I know she must be a girl!" She had not abandoned them even after the divorce was final. "Keep the father's name," she counseled, as the papers were mailed back and forth. "Girls with father's name are more safe. Later, she can also marry. Later, she can change to her husband's name." Even then she was worrying about Suyin's place, fatherless, perhaps husbandless.

"She's Henry's baby," Second Mrs. Yeh crooned to the infant, her visits unchecked by Henry's absence. Humming her song, she rubbed olive oil onto the carapace where the skull bones had not closed, the light brown hair twisting over the tender spot where only skin protected the brain. "Ah Pah's granddaughter," she breathed over the membrane, fingers stroking the green oil into the scalp. Li An closed her eyes, exhausted from guilt, and saw the oil seep through the hair, staining the fine chestnut wisps a darker brown, seeping in atomic molecules through the skull. Invisible, unerasable. Second Mrs. Yeh's granddaughter.

But even after moving to Singapore, where a woman could be husbandless, a child must have a father's name. Meeting people with Suyin for the first time was always difficult. "Adopted?" "Luk-krung, mixed . . . ?" the strangers asked, taking in the curly reddish hair, the green eyes and peony pink cheeks, the fair gold skin so light the capillaries showed through like a tracing under a veil.

Suyin had come home from school laughing one afternoon when she was six. "Con lai! Mom, I am a con lai!"

Li An took her out of the missionary school where the principal had called her a con lai, mistaking her for a Vietnamese Amerasian—a bui doi, child of the dust. Despite the expensive tuition and extravagant fees for books, athletics, music, drama, and other compulsory options, she had placed Suyin in the American school, where there were a number of Amerasian children, and no one would call her a con lai, a mixed animal.

Today Li An combed her daughter's thick brown hair and curbed the curls in a braid, where it hung like a chain from her sharp widow's peak, a chain for a mother to steady herself.

"Good-bye," she said. "Auntie Ellen will be home by two to help you with your homework."

"I don't need any help." Suyin was eleven and already superior. Last week she had informed her mother that Li An was unhappy because she did not have a boyfriend. "So old, still no man. All my friends' mothers have boyfriends. Why can't you find one?" Was that what she was hoping Li An would return with from Kuala Lumpur, as her large olive green eyes appraised her mother's helpless shrug? Perhaps all she was thinking of was the cuttlefish Li An had promised her from the Petaling market in Kuala Lumpur.

In return, Li An teased her. "Can't leave you alone. The government will throw me in prison for child neglect."

Suyin's lips curled, and she turned her elegantly combed head away slowly. "There you go again! I hate it!"

Her voice was high-pitched, the tones of a songbird Li An couldn't take seriously.

"Hate what?"

"The way you never listen. You smile at everything I say. It's never of any importance to you."

"But I always listen to you," Li An laughed. The thought of her daughter's voice, sharp as a bird's beak, alone was enough to break through her selfishness. She listened to its murmuring rise and fall as Suyin, who could talk without stopping for as long as someone listened, chattered to Grandma Yeh. She listened as a communicant to a mass, an accompanist to a diva, a reader to a library of books. Suyin's treble, she thought defensively, overrode every other sensation: films, books, the hours of concentration at the computer, hunger and sleep, loneliness, anger, and men. She yanked the braid gently. "I smile because of the sound of your voice, so I am listening."

"But you don't listen to my words."

It was getting too complicated. Li An got up to leave. "Grandma's in the kitchen. She's got pandan cake and milk for you." She picked up her suitcase.

"I'm not a baby, I'm not a baby!" Suyin chanted as the door closed behind her mother.

Beng, a balding bachelor already stooped with routine and malice, was losing his hair. Chan was still tall and dark, reserved and careful. What was he afraid of, after all these years as a successful doctor, she wondered. Alex Yeo, Gwen whispered, was now a multimillionaire; cement was money where everyone was building as fast as they could. Like Singapore, Kuala Lumpur had become a stony paradise. Concrete shelters—bungalows and two-storied terraces, flats and projecting

condominiums—everything gated, walled, and fenced, a crazy
territorial imperative where the sun and rain blasted everything into a green fungus frenzy. Alex Yeo was shaking
everyone's hand, a success story proud of his beginnings, but
not too proud to acknowledge his awestruck schoolmates. He
had not grown flabby.

"Remember Li An?" Gwen asked when he approached.

The smile shifted, returned, broadened. "Ah yes, where have
you been all these years? Only in Singapore? How come you
never come back Malaysia?" He stuck out his hand.

He knew, of course. Nine years was not a long enough time
to forget.

"Lots of Malaysians leave. Australia, Canada, UK. We're
all over the world. Some of us can't succeed in Malaysia."

"Tough, it's tough here. Got to have luck." The handshake
was quick. He had seen Tun Datuk Hussein, the managing director of the National Bank.

She remembered Hussein had been the football hero the year
that Alex ran the Free School Youth Council. Football was not
supposed to lead to greatness. Nor was being a Malay then. Hardly
anyone ever used the term "Malay" anymore. Bumiputras,
the sons of the soil, were everywhere in Kuala Lumpur now, ruling, like Hussein, in penthouse offices of company presidents,
directors, chancellors, ministers, chairmen, and chief executives. She watched the men, who were faintly sweating, white
shirts crumpling around their waists, as they circulated, glasses of soda and beer in hand like drawn revolvers.

Surprising her, Gwen appeared. "Eh, buck up, okay? I
didn't know he was going to be here."

"Who?" She swiveled and caught Beng's bespectacled
gaze like a leech on her face. She stared at the miniature fluorescent lights flaring from his glasses, thick as jam jars, and
brushed the warmth off her cheeks. Gwen's hand was sticky
cool on her arm as Li An took in the clatter that rose like the
heat. Something moved over her eyes, a reddish wave that she
hoped would not glitter with tears.

Henry was still pale, although now with gray in his dark
hair, his thin figure presenting the image of a complete
Chinese mandarin. She knew his narrow shoulders, hairless

chest concealed in the light-colored pressed shirt, the frame slight as a woman's. Too distant for her to see his expression, he was leaning toward a woman who was obviously pregnant, her skin ruddy with the flush of late pregnancy, weight, and maternity wines. Grandma Yeh had told her that Henry had remarried.

"His wife is Gaik Choo," Gwen said, "Choo Loy's daughter, you know, the Penang Tower Hotel owner? She graduated from Penang Free School five years after us. That's why he's here."

"How should I know?" Li An was aware she was hissing. Gwen had betrayed her. She should not have come; she did not belong in Malaysia, just as Suyin did not belong to Henry. But still she stared at him, even as she felt Beng's gaze crawl on her eyes. "Do something about Beng," she whispered, turning her body away.

"Hey, that's your ex, you know, your ex!" he crowed, loud enough for Gwen to notice.

"Food, food time. Get up, queue for makan!" Gwen urged him toward the buffet.

Henry was moving toward the line at the far end of the hall. Li An allowed the beer to linger, cooling her gums, her throat that was suddenly aching. She remembered the ache as a familiar sensation. When it first occurred, she thought the tightness was from the loss of Chester, a tightness that she discovered could be relieved by Suyin's toothless tugs on her swollen nipples. She had watched the infant's water-wrinkled fists clench and unclench. She bent to the humming as the mouth puckered, a blind mole paddling through tunnels, pulling and pulling at the grotesquely puffed-up breasts, hmmm, hmmm. This blind singing had brought her down to earth, so that Chester faded, a figure in a distant story, and the life with Suyin became her whole life.

Why then had she refused to think about Henry? Henry who had wanted to save her from poverty, carelessness, and loneliness—from Chester.

Henry's wife, large and red, was eating vigorously. He was on another line at the dessert table. He appeared the very same husband, patient, indulgent. What had been the matter with her, she thought with a painful confusion, that she had not wanted indulgence? Could she not have been this woman, seated, eating, the baby within and the man with her together composing the magical triad by which families spun into existence?

There had been no time for regrets then. Too swiftly she was pregnant, she was a mother, then she was alone. And later, there were the jobs she had taken in Kuala Lumpur. English tuition in the evenings while Grandma Yeh slept with Suyin, the pale worm of the infant body fleshing out month by month in the hollow of barren arms. Copyediting for Longmans, a short successful period as creative director at Bates, and after the move to Singapore, a series of freelance and part-time positions while searching for the right school for Suyin. Interviews with principals, trying to explain Suyin's Chinese name and her rust-brown mane, the absent father and her delicate pink face. Taking Suyin out of classes where girls—they were always girls—pointed at the widow's peak and sang, "Chap-cheng-chap-cheng-kwei."

"Mixed-up devil," Grandma Yeh explained to Suyin. "Girls call you mixed-up devil because they are jealous, they want your green eyes, your brown curls. You are fairer than Princess Margaret, who is prettier than the Queen of England."

Li An's table partners were returning with plates, curried and soy-soaked meats running over rice and noodles, and saucers of pink and green layered cakes and white coconut-sprinkled tapioca. Food spread over all the spaces free of elbows and napkins and pilsner glasses. Gwen brought a plate spewed with scallion and curls of chilies. "So you will be more thirsty and drink more beer," she said anxiously.

Chan and Beng talked about shares, Australia, the prices of condominiums.

"Everyone is getting rich," Alex announced, the gold-and-silver Rolex on his wrist spinning neon colors as he pushed his fork into his mouth.

The lights went out. Henry would never see her now, she reassured herself. Blue and red spotlights ran up and down the open center of the ballroom, and the blast of thumping drums, trumpets, and cymbals silenced the talk of money.

Dancers with naked legs, smooth bare backs, and glistening mounded flesh poured into the lights.

"The dance company is called 'Paper Roses.' All transvestites," Gwen whispered. "So beautiful, yah!"

The dancers shook their tight round buns, threw up their legs, furs, feathers, sequins flying into the faces of the sheepish men trying not to stare, not to give away their excitement. "Too bad, they are only men!" Chan said reprovingly.

The music changed. The costumes changed. More breasts, more legs, more sweet curving shoulders and slithery backs. Li An saw their Adam's apples powdered to dimness, the jaws and shadows softened with pink foundation. A spectacle for correct couples like Henry and his wife.

She could have been that half of the couple, carefully tended, draped in brassy gold chains, fingers heavy with egg-sized sapphires. All over Singapore she saw women with Chinese husbands like Henry, driving in sleek Mercedes and carrying Gucci bags to hold their purchases.

"Why don't you want money, ah?" Grandma Yeh asked when she had quit the job at Bates, which paid so well. That was not accurate. She wanted security, but on her terms. Could those terms have included someone like Henry?

She tapped Gwen's elbow. It was time to leave, while the lights were out and the men were prancing.

Three

With a powerhouse like BioSynergy—or BioSyn, as it was better known—a weekly bulletin was not simply a news-sheet, it was a hot document studied by investors, shareholders, and the Monetary Authority of Singapore for clues to the company's health and future.

Ang Swee, the executive chief, had compared *BioSyn-Sign*—Li An had come up with the title three years ago, a creative feat that helped win her the job of editor in chief—to the fortune almanacs so popular with certain classes of Singaporeans. "You see these almanacs?" he asked. "Cheap print, mass production, but they provide the key to matching actions, images, numbers, and meanings. You dream of a car crash. That's the number eleven, meaning a big strike soon. A crash like a strike, two ones amounting to a big win. You see a horse any place, whether it is an ornament on a car hood or Tang porcelain in a shop window, and then suddenly you think of pigeons? Look up the section on flying horses and you learn that four is the number for you. In any combination you pick, four is sure to appear among the winning numbers. A death next door or an unexpected visit from a male cousin from a distant town can signal either good or bad forces, but, depending on which month it is, the almanac can give you different correspondences."

"Studying these almanacs," he continued humorously, "does not ensure that gamblers always pick the winning horses at the Singapore Turf Club, for they have to understand what the hidden meanings signify in order to calculate the correct sequence of numbers. And, as in any enterprise, there is always the element of luck, the propitious moment. Taking good care of your ancestors is also necessary in creating auspicious conditions." He jerked his sparse eyebrows in play.

"It doesn't matter that BioSynergy is a wholly research-oriented company, staffed by some of the best-trained scientists that money and top facilities can attract," he explained to David King, visiting executive officer from Birmingham, at an interview Li An was supposed to report but could not use. "We Singaporeans invest our Sing-dollars cautiously, and every good omen and sign is needed to keep us loyal to the company."

BioSyn-Sign's double naming had come to mean the doubling of the value of shares. But the newsletter remained a prickly venture for the company: an indispensable tool for investor confidence, it also risked losing this confidence with a misjudgment in content.

"Remember," Ang Swee warned her, "the company's shareholders are both extremely literal and extremely sensitive to hidden meanings. They've called incessantly to check on the intentions of your figures of speech. No Singaporean believes that there is such a thing as unintentionality in language, especially once your language becomes fixed in print!"

When she shared her impatience at carrying such financial responsibility with her title of communications vice director, Abdullah, then special assistant to the Ministry of Information in Malaysia, laughed. "Semua nasib! Everything is luck! Nasib. Singaporeans and Malaysians, all of us are fortune-tellers. If we don't believe in future fortune, how to stay satisfied?"

"But isn't it strange that our satisfaction depends on dissatisfaction with our present condition? Why can't we enjoy today and not be driven by superstition?"

"What is the difference between your Singaporean, thinking the year of the rooster is a good time for buying stocks, and you and your poetry reading, eh, Li An? You were also looking at signs for meaning—only your reading got no money reward, maybe it did not even make you happy. What is the purpose of all the literature they're still teaching in the university? Malay literature, Chinese literature, English literature—no practical use. Better to teach communications, public relations, like you are doing now."

Again she thought with a pang of envy that Abdullah's two years at Harvard as a Nieman Journalism Fellow had really changed him. He was even more confident than when he had been writing for the new paper years ago. Moreover, she had to admit, he had grown much sharper. It was harder for her to believe she was right and he wrong.

"Well, Abdullah, minister-to-be," she said lightly, unsure if she would flatter or irritate him with this prediction, "maybe that's the nasib for poetry. As you say, no purpose, no fortune. Except to make people like me unhappy."

She remembered this conversation when Paroo called late on Thursday, just as she was making the final decisions on layouts for the bulletin. She was doing the proofreading herself before dropping the copy off at the typesetter—the only way, she had found, to control the quality of the bulletin and forestall reader recriminations from the unintended meanings that might rise from innocent typographical errors. Usually she fended off Paroo's calls by having her secretary take a message, but at seven-thirty even Mrs. Lam had gone home.

"Oh, Paroo, listen, I'm just in the middle of getting the bulletin ready for the typesetter. I really don't have the time. Can you call back tomorrow?" she garbled in one breath.

"Li An, Li An, no lah, great news, only listen! Chester is here!"

She looked around the glaring arena of the reading lamp. Its brittle lighting picked up every black print and squiggle marked by the freshly sharpened pencils that Mrs. Devan, her assistant, had left beside the copy.

When Li An first came to BioSynergy, she was determined not to bring her messy private life into the office. In Kuala Lumpur she had felt the ostracism of friends as a horrible abuse. She had determined never to meet them again, the childhood intimate who had called her evil, the colleagues who had greeted her with distant eyes, those who had gossiped and those who had reported on them to her. No one on her staff had ever seen a photograph of Suyin. Paroo's voice ended that safe remoteness.

"Paroo, wait . . . I . . ."

"Li An, he is looking good. Only just now we said good-night. He called me two days ago. Lucky for me exam time is over, so I can spend some time with old friends. Chester is still the same, not fat not thin, only not so much hair . . ."

"Paroo, I have to finish my work first. I'll call you after I get home."

He had been in Singapore long enough to understand. Work had to be done before anything else could proceed.

She took an extra hour, checking the copy over and over. Scenes she hadn't known she remembered intruded. That past, like Ah Pah's death, had remained invisible to everyone who knew her now, shut down by the news blackout of twelve years ago, by censorship still unlifted despite the young and old historians.

In dark Petaling Jaya on the night of May 13, with Chester's arm around her waist and the warm length of his body by her side, feeling his pressure on her hip, she had invested the keen sensation with promise, a tenderness she'd believed real, surely more real than the killings and fires in Kuala Lumpur.

But almost immediately she had felt him turn blank, withdrawing, withholding, a deliberate nothing. He had set out to show her, wordlessly, that there had been no tender-ness, no promise. That moment—the sweetness of a body which she had revered—had signified nothing. In the author-ity of such nothingness, how could she continue to believe in its meaning?

Thousands of miles away, Chester had unwittingly continued to school her in the lessons of growing up. She no longer read significance, merely the acts. No ideas but in things, the poet William Carlos Williams had said. That had been the hard-est poem for her to learn, to embrace the empty depth in the glittering surface of things.

But learning it had allowed her to acknowledge the impor-tance of the bulletin as appearance—immaculate layout, letter-perfect editing, careful content control. A company organ, a mouthpiece, slick, glib, superficial, glossy—she knew the criticism the bulletin received from journalists and traders alike, but she didn't mind it. Anything less or more than that and there would be chaos. Investors selling short, government agencies doing audits, new regulations thrown at the company, hotshot researchers threatening to resign for calmer waters in Tokyo and Geneva.

She had seen the damage the first editor created when he published a faintly critical review of the company's carefully guarded DNA research. The author, a visiting Nobel Prize winner working for the Rockefeller Foundation, had flattered the editor by giving him permission to use the review, which had appeared first in a prestigious science journal. Chanh, an American-trained Cambodian, had argued that an article by a Nobel Prize–winning scientist would bring the bulletin notice and credibility, but he didn't know about the Singapore reflex. "No news is better than any criticism!" he complained bitterly, when the company's shares sank to half points overnight, and he was fired.

Li An didn't defend him. "Totally stupid," she confided to Ellen. "Only human nature, and he didn't know it. The Singapore reflex is simply an advanced version of the desire to be superior. Not a bad thing to have, after all—there is a superiority inherent in the reflex. One does not achieve superiority by aiming at inferior objects!"

She made certain that *BioSyn-Sign*, while it never published anything but what was factual and true, always presented the company in its most positive light.

"You think too much," Ellen said, not for the first time. "Everything here is about face. How to save face, how not to lose face. Even if you conquer the world and lose face, you lose everything."

Ellen never worried about saving face herself. She presented herself to everyone exactly the way she wanted. What you see is what you get, she said to everyone without a trace of laughter. Li An knew that this was because Ellen was unshakably confident of her own superiority.

LANDING

From her height, like a minor goddess, she bossed Li An, rearranging all their lives. "Oh, for God's sake, get out of Kuala Lumpur!" she had commanded after Suyin's first birthday. It took Li An another year to leave, after Ellen landed a position as a senior economics teacher in a junior college in Singapore. Through her Weston Allen connections, Ellen had later found Li An the job as a part-time copy editor in the communications department in BioSynergy. "See, an economics degree was a better choice than English," she boasted, as she helped Li An hunt for a flat in Marine Way. "Money makes the world go round."

"But you are helping me out of love!" Li An smiled, squinting at the traffic, her hair frizzy at ten on a Sunday morning when she would normally still be asleep.

"Where love?" Ellen snorted. "How can women love each other? I only do this for old friend's sake. Otherwise I will feel too guilty for words."

Suyin, only two, Ellen's godchild, whom Ellen had carried home to her bungalow from the hospital after Henry had refused to take Li An and the baby home, sat between them in the front seat.

Now she was eleven, and Auntie Ellen was still her second parent.

Except now there was Chester. Li An wondered, should she call Ellen for advice?

It was almost nine. Suyin would have finished dinner, her homework, and piano practice. Grandma Yeh could not stay up past ten. It was time to be home.

Again she felt her breasts ache with ghostly milk. It was uncanny, the bond she shared with her daughter—physical, transmitted through the nerve endings of nipples, even years after the last pull of infant lips. Years after she had picked up the fat-covered newborn, its eyes closed in curved slits, and cried with fear and pleasure that she would never again be unburdened or alone. Like a fruit blooming on her body, that union still prickled her breasts in odd moments.

Suyin's face was pale in the blue light of the television. "Why so late?"

181

"Did you get a phone call?"

"From Auntie Ellen?"

She felt her breath ease. "Yes, of course."

"You know Auntie Ellen calls every night. She wanted to know why so late you're not home."

"Thursday is . . ."

"Copy night!"

Li An smiled, and began the nightly rituals they both depended on. "Finished homework?" "Brushed teeth?" "Bath?" "To bed, to bed!"

With Grandma Yeh asleep, it was just the two of them, and the long-worn game of pajamas, tucking in sheets, smoothing hair, lights off, lilting the nightly lullaby, "Good night, good night, love you, sleep tight, love you."

It was always hard to let Suyin go for the night. Li An's time with Suyin was like the knitting Grandma Yeh had taken up after Ah Pah's death. Pick up, purl and knit, purl and knit, needles flashing; unwinding carefully chosen yarn in her favorite colors of pink, yellow, and green; knitting cables and finished seams; casting off to begin yet another chain. She and Suyin were the needles, their days the fibers of knitting and purling. Each night was a way to learn to say good-bye without letting go. This was what she did to endure, the way Grandma Yeh had endured Ah Pah's death through her mad knitting of sweaters and shawls, blankets and scarves, crazy handicraft too hot for Singapore. Blaming Chester for her unhappiness, Li An had wrapped Suyin to herself. And now, years later, what would his arrival mean to them all?

She lifted the receiver and dialed Paroo's number with terror.

"Li An? Never mind, it's not so late. But my wife already sleeping, so please wait. I get the telephone in the kitchen."

The telephone lay inert in her hand.

"Hello, hello? Okay, Li An, yes, so Chester wants to meet you. What for? Friendship what! Now older, he is different, man! All right, all right, we're all different. Like me—I find it also not so good to live in the old days. We must make a new life; we cannot stay all the time in the past, yes or not? You remember my wife, Rani? She can never take the place of old love, but my daughter Surani, she is like a new world. She makes me so happy."

"But where is he?"

"In Singapore, of course. Doing fieldwork, research. Chester now is big shot professor—so funny, eh? Remember he began Peace Corps teaching woodworking in Brickfields? You forgot? So, I say maybe you and I and he can meet, take tea in Raffles Hotel. We show off Singapore still got British class, eh?"

"We're in the middle of special productions . . ."

"Yes, always busy. I tell him, Li An she has changed, she is businesslike now. No more poetry, no more literature. She's trying to make a buck. Singapore is go, go, go. Everyone is trying to make a buck. I tell him I will enjoy putting you together for a reunion. . . ."

The danger was imminent like a burglar outside her door. "Later, Paroo. After the graphics are completed. I'll call you." She tried to think of disasters at work, but dropped the attempt, Ang Swee's finger wagging in her head.

"Aiii, but what can I tell Chester? He is very hot to meet you, I think maybe still interested, eh, Li An?" Paroo chuckled. "No, no, sorry lah. I don't mean to be naughty." His voice grew pleading. "For old times' sake, yes, just once you must meet him. I also will be there, like chaperon—no funny business. Okay, okay, I wait for you to call. Don't forget."

She called Ellen immediately, the bossy voice in her ear a lifeline.

"Yah, so late!"

Fatigue hovered in front of Li An's eyes, a curtain of hatches and crosses. Godmother, godmother, make me a wish. What was she wishing for? She was too old for wishes, for genies and magic lamps, beliefs in secret gardens; too grown-up even for hope. Her fingers had figured out computers, cropping, montage, paste-ups, layouts, spreadsheets, indices. Lotus was a program, utilities essential. She had adopted a new language of symbols. She wanted to fall asleep. She wanted a different simplicity.

"Don't be stupid. Why do you have to see him? I bet he wants to meet Suyin. These men, they think they can come back any time and claim everything." Ellen always said aloud what Li An was afraid to hear.

Li An let Ellen's voice break against her, "No, no, no!" But she knew she would disobey. She had never listened to Ellen when it came to Chester.

Four

Paroo was late. The clouds had begun thickening about eleven. By noon the sun was nowhere in sight. Chester waited outside the Institute of Southeast Asian Studies library as Paroo had told him to, hoping that the trees stirring did not signal a downpour. Of course he was completely unprepared. No one traveled around the world with an umbrella, except maybe the British.

The young Malay assistant came out of the library to ask him if he was Professor Brookfield. Paroo had sent a message that they should meet at the New Asia Hotel instead. He smiled as he gave Chester the message. "Bad day walking, sir," he said. "Rain surely coming soon."

Clouds were churning in massive black cumuli as Chester hurried to find a taxi. The wind kicked up the long brilliant grass in the wasteland that bordered the road by the newly constructed institute. Lallang, Samad had told him. The lallang looked like paddy, but without any grain. Like some people, Samad had added, who grow on the land, but give nothing back. Strange how Chester remembered such small details about Samad. The mark of an anthropologist, Jason had written in his letter of recommendation—seldom misses an observation that counts.

Brown leaves, yellow and purple petals, and large twigs sprang up from the pavement. The wind was now bending the tops of tropical giants; thick branches, spilling over with staghorn ferns, leafy epiphytes, and the dangling roots of strangle

figs, creaked above him. Coolness gushed, drawn down from
the turbulent sky. Chester stretched his stride with the sensation that he was slowly flying. A crack sounded like a
muffled bomb, followed by a series of rumbles, hallucinato-
ry, amplified in the deserted scene, which was suddenly as dark
as nightfall. Drops splashed, each one separate, then together faster and faster. Chester sprinted the last few yards and
stood under a bus shelter to wait for a taxi, his shirt stuck, wet,
smelling of sweat. Damn!

Two buses went by, faces pressed to the water-streaked windows, passengers wondering at his patience. It was almost twelve-
thirty. Where was the New Asia Hotel? Paroo had not told
him, and he'd figured the taxi drivers would know. Would Li
An wait? The light blue taxis sped past, sprays of brown
puddles careering beside. His outstretched arm was soaked,
stubborn; Chester felt himself a penitent. Yes, he wanted to
see her, although the reason was obscure to him. After all these
years, he remembered only the face, that small smile when she
said good-bye. "Be good," he had said. That was what everyone was saying then. It did not mean anything. He could not
mean anything to her.

What he wanted now was to see her. No, not her alone, but
also the child. Paroo had confirmed what he had wondered
about—a daughter. There was a sickly echo somewhere in his
body at the sound and thought of the word. The word lodged
in his head. *Daughter.* A newly dangerous word. It had meant
little to him before, merely a word he had learned with
thousands of other words. Not the way *ladder* had meant something when he had to buy one to clean the leaves out of the
gutters the first year after he and Meryl had bought the
house. Wood? Aluminum? Five feet, ten feet, eighteen feet?
Medium-weight? Balanced? Choices to make, a weight to pick
up, heft home, and make space for, a place for his foot that
was strong enough to bear his weight. But *daughter* echoed somewhere in a cavity. Was this word something he could share
with Meryl?

The receptionist looked up as he walked in, shaking the
drops from his hair.

"Halloo . . ." Paroo was reading a tourist brochure. "Big storm, I think you cannot come."

Chester did not like the dejection in Paroo's face. The hotel armchairs were upholstered in a pretty green-and-blue jungle pattern with coral-red parrots. He pretended not to notice the empty seats, as a hollow in his stomach rose to disturb him.

"We wait," Paroo said, studying Chester's frown. "So much thunder and lightning, maybe Li An will be late."

Outside the large glass doors rain was whipping down so thick it looked as if the island was under a waterfall. Thunder mumbled under the humming air-conditioning. The air indoors was clammy chill. Chester hitched up his trouser cuffs, which were sagging with water, and examined the wet socks wrapped around his ankles. He said nothing. Paroo coughed and kept his eyes on the brochure.

They turned at the whoosh of air as the automatic doors opened. Two rain-stained sunburned tourists stumbled, laughing, to the desk. Sulking, Chester ignored their banter, audibly intimate and arrogant. "Keys, please! A hot tub, darling?" "Who would've thought . . ." "We'll ask for Tiger beers." "No, it's champagne or nothing."

By 1:30 P.M. the yawning desk clerk had disappeared. Paroo returned from the washroom to say, "Okay, I also must go back to work. Saturday also I must do extracurricular. Two-thirty I get my chaps to debate, prepare for big October meet. Only two more months, then important interschool competition."

"What about Lee Ann?"

"I call her tonight. Raining, maybe she will not come. Always like that in Singapore, lah. I know you Americans are John Wayne type, real tough. Rain, snow, bullets also never stop you. But Li An is an Asian woman. You must understand. Asian women are all soft, frighten at a little bit rain and thunder. I'm sorry you're disappointed, Chester, but remember how many years you never come. You cannot expect her simply forgive you."

It was Abdullah who brought Chester to her office, a couple of days after he took Chester for an early morning drive around Singapore.

"I like getting up early," he had said, when Chester finally reached him in Kuala Lumpur. "When I get back from
Denpasar, I will call you from my Singapore home. I enjoy driving, and this way we can talk about your troubles."

Chester had not expected Abdullah to change so much in
a dozen years. The voice had deepened, and the American accent
was more pronounced. But despite the changes he appeared
as delighted as Samad had been with Chester's arrival. It was
simply a matter of his catching up with them.

"Remember Samad always liked American cowboys?"
Abdullah laughed. "Wah, now he is a very tough operator.
Government man, one successful bureaucrat. Business man,
even better. Top of the class. Samad makes money like
nobody's business. But I tell you a secret. He still has a soft
heart, never forgets a friend. Business is business, friendship
is friendship, but Samad is a gentleman all round."

Abdullah's Mercedes was an exact replica of Samad's,
down to the tooled leather trim and white leather seats.

"No, I didn't look you up in New York. You know, Chester,
I cannot understand why you never claimed your daughter.
We Malays, we love our children. We will kill for them. So
I cannot understand a man who does not know what it is to
love like a father." Abdullah's English had become New
England; two years at Harvard had done what almost twen-
ty years of British education had failed to do.

"She never told me."

"I cannot believe that! Li An is not a fool."

"I never knew her well. She . . ."

"Come, Samad was there on May thirteenth. You knew each
other very well."

"Abdullah, one night does not mean . . ."

"In Islam, we do not count the nights. Our bodies break
the law, not the numbers of nights. For khalwat to be com-
mitted, one touch of the hand is enough. The fire of the body
burns even at one touch!"

"Well, I was the fool then for not thinking of the burn. It
never occurred to me . . ."

"The child, man, the child! She is beautiful. That is the
way with Eurasians. Allah is merciful. These children will

always have problems, so beauty is the gift to sweeten their path. I was officer-in-charge five years ago when the boat people were landing in Kelantan. Kasehan lah! So pitiful! The pirates, they killed so many. They raped even the old grandmothers. Our people are not so evil, so we took pity on the Vietnamese. But then thousands came, tens of thousands, like sand crabs. You Americans promise them the golden mountain, but you want them to stay in Malaysia. When we try to send them away, your newspapers carry bad stories about us. But they are not our problem. They are an American problem! There I met some of the bui doi, children of the dust. Beautiful children! Golden skin, golden hair, face like orang puteh, soul like Asian. But no one wants them. Even the Vietnamese don't want their own. They are not just dust but dirt, American dirt you leave behind in Asia."

Chester had heard this criticism of America before and refused to respond. He needed Abdullah to find Li An. He kept his eyes fixed on the golden shower trees on the median, every single tree the exact height and width of the others. Aloud, he wondered if they had been cloned for such regularity to prevail. Bali, especially Kuta Beach where he had interviewed the hotel boys and maids, had been more cluttered than this city coastline. On one side of the highway the green-blue sea glittered like crinkled Thai silk, and the benches and walkways between uniformly pruned bushes were deserted on a Tuesday morning.

"I tell you what, Chester," Abdullah said, glancing at Chester's sneakers and duffel, "I have meetings all day and tomorrow, and Friday I must fly back to Kuala Lumpur for the opening of the new masjid. We show the fundamentalists that we can make money and also be good Muslims at the same time!"

"I guess the Americans had a go at that once. We called it Puritanism."

"American civilization is over, finished, habis-lah! In Boston I saw all the old houses on Beacon Hill. Everything in America is like that, everything is history, past. In Malaysia and Singapore, you don't see us worry about history, old houses, old forts, and cemeteries. All that is British colonialism.

Here everything must be new, best quality, best for the future. We make a new identity, a new Asian civilization."

"Is that what your company does—making a new Asian civilization?" Chester kept his voice light.

"Yes, that is true. We are helping with an important project. You know, we Muslims spend big money on pilgrimages to Mecca. Some spend all their life savings. They sell their house, farm, even their pension, to go to Mecca, and they come back with nothing left! Big headache, man. My company arranges Mecca pilgrimages, and helps save the hajis. We make sure they come back and have something in Malaysia. We let them know life is not over after the hajj, but is just beginning."

Clearing his throat, Chester managed to unstick his voice. "And so can you help me? I am on a kind of pilgrimage in Singapore!" The car's air-conditioning whirred and blew on his cheeks, which were warm with embarrassment.

"That was what I wanted to say. Lots of meetings this week, but I arrange for you to meet Li An on Thursday. She's afraid to meet you. You know why. But she will do it. She owes me a favor."

Five

Nuisance!" Auntie Ellen said.

She was talking to the key sticking in the door, but Suyin pretended she meant her. "Better you don't come and get me from school, I am such a nuisance."

"Now, Suyin, don't be difficult."

She knew Auntie Ellen and Mom had been talking about her again; they both began using the same word on her a few weeks ago. "Difficult" was Auntie Ellen's favorite word this month. Last month it was "Too much!" and "So, when are you going to grow up?" A few months ago, she was talking about "adolescence," "cohorts," and "self-esteem." She was the principal of the Cantonment Girls School, and Suyin wished she wouldn't talk like that to her at home. But Auntie Ellen was just like the way she dressed, really dark blue and straight up and down, like a police officer!

She was tired of calling her Auntie Ellen. But Mom insisted. "She's older, you have to show respect."

She was tired also of calling her mother Mom. "Li," she said last night. It was ten, about the time her mother would begin fussing over her going to bed. Sometimes Suyin didn't mind her lecturing, it went on like an automatic switch, sort of comforting. Ten o'clock, bedtime. You have to blah blah blah. But last night her mother had forgotten to begin the lecture. She was folding and putting away her jeans, a silly quiet look on her face that Suyin didn't like. Her mother folded everything, even her dirty laundry, although the maid who came in to keep Grandma company every day was just going to throw them all into the washing machine the next morning.

Her mother was so startled that she stopped folding.

"Li An." Suyin felt good saying it. Revenge for all the times her name had been made fun of. So-ying-yang. Sue-ing you.

This year her mother had moved her to a new school for secondary one. "You must begin to learn Mandarin! American School is not going to prepare you for the university in Singapore."

She said things like that, as if Suyin didn't know she was a Singaporean. She didn't care that Suyin cried. "This is Singapore," she kept repeating, as if Suyin didn't know where she was.

Her first week in Cho Kang, the boys were so crude. "Sweet Yin," they teased. "Sweetie Yin, lah!"

And the girls were worse. "Si-in Yeh, Sin Yeh, Sin-Ner!" Ee Chai and Ah Hong called her, pretending they could not pronounce her name properly. "No father, lah, so sinful. Can see got white father, mah!" she heard someone say clearly on the first day of class. But she lifted her nose as if there was a bad smell. Don't hear, don't know. Besides, as Grandma Yeh told her, let them be jealous. She was always going to be the prettiest girl in school.

Auntie Ellen said she'd better not get too vain. "Vain women spell trouble."

What trouble could Auntie Ellen mean? Auntie Ellen could never get into trouble. Work, then pick her up from school, take care of her, watch TV, eat, then go home. The next day, work, take care of her, etcetera.

Her mother said she could not have managed with her job if Auntie Ellen were not sharing the childcare with her. As if she was a package they passed back and forth to each other everyday.

Suyin loved Grandma the best. She never made a big thing about childcare, like Mom and Auntie Ellen. Cod-liver oil, Evening Primrose pills, and fluoride drops—those were her mother's idea. No ballet classes, her calves will grow too muscular—Auntie Ellen's. Orthodontist, front teeth crooked—Mom. No bicycle riding, can get run down—Auntie Ellen. "How come you can drive a car and live all by yourself, Auntie Ellen, if the world is so dangerous?" Suyin asked. Auntie Ellen's mouth drooped. She didn't like Suyin to talk back to her, but she would never scold Suyin herself.

"She's just being difficult," her mother said.

Suyin must have been eight when she first understood she should not ask about her father. "Your father is my son," Grandma had told her over and over again. "You are my granddaughter." Suyin knew he was living in Kuala Lumpur, because Grandma sometimes talked about Henry in Kuala Lumpur. It was the only man she ever talked about, so Suyin knew Henry was Grandma's son and her father.

Suyin remembered when she first knew Grandma was lying. One Sunday night, after her mother had turned off the light and closed the bedroom door, Suyin had closed her eyes. She didn't want to go to school the next day because the girls were always teasing her about her hair and eyes. "Eee, green like stone, brown like rusty, eee, who your father?" they yelled. Then, in the back of her eyes, Suyin saw that Grandma's son Henry must also have black hair and eyes like Grandma. But her father must have had green eyes and reddish hair like hers. Suyin could see him under her eyelids. He was suddenly a presence, a real man whom she knew had been alive once. He was a ghost floating in her body, rising in the green flecks in her eyes, which, no matter how hard she stared at them in the mirror, remained stained green like old mossy stones. He glittered in the red shining hairs that were scattered throughout the dark—red hairs like the mark of Cain, Mrs. Andrews at the American School had told her. Her father was big, he must have been terrible to make everyone so silent about him, and he was dead. That must have been a relief to her mother and Grandma, and maybe even to Auntie Ellen.

But he had left part of himself in her. That was why she was so tall—taller than her classmates—and why her hair was rusty and came to a funny point in the middle of her forehead. Her mother called it a widow's peak. He must have died before Suyin was born. What she worried about was why no one talked about him. For Grandma to tell a lie about him, he probably did something very bad, like selling drugs, and was hanged, or got murdered by gangsters.

Grandma was a good Christian and read her Bible every day, but she never attended any church. She said Christians didn't have to go to church; Christ would save her when the last trumpet called. Not like the devil worshippers who fed the hungry ghosts on the seventh month, she said. Suyin had asked her about the red-and-white tent that went up on the other side of the Cho Kang School playground.

"What is the stage for, Grandma? And the strings of lights and plastic banners? My Mandarin isn't good enough to read the words. Mrs. Tan says we should not play near the fence and we should not look at the offerings. Curiosity kills the cat, she says. What kinds of offerings are they? Why can't I look?"

"Father, forgive them, for they know not what they do," Grandma replied.

Grandma said that a lot. Every time they watched the news and reports of wars, killings, massacres, or bombs blared out, she prayed out loud: "Father, forgive them." But this time Suyin felt strange hearing Grandma pray. Father, father, father. Suyin knew she meant God, but she was tired of hearing the word. Why was Grandma always talking about fathers when they had no father in the house, only women? Grandma, Mom, and Auntie Ellen. Grandma's father was also dead, up in heaven. How could he forgive anything?

Auntie Ellen told Suyin. "Ayah! Eleven years old and still don't know about the seventh month? You know, the Chinese believe eating is everything. Even after death— ghosts, too, must eat. The lucky spirits have children and grandchildren to take care of their needs. Their families offer chicken, brandy, all kinds of paper effigies: Mercedes cars, bungalows, servants. Today, also television sets, VCRs, American Express cards. Anything we have, the dead also want. But some are not so lucky. Those without children roam the world on the seventh month of the year looking for offerings. If not appeased, they bring chaos and suffering on humans. The wayang, the stage show, is like charity to the underworld.

Chinese business and home owners make offerings to those poor ghosts who have no one to feed them as insurance against misfortune."

Then Auntie Ellen gave her a suspicious stare. "Why are you so interested? You don't have to do ancestor worship!"

"But why, Auntie Ellen? Why don't I have any ancestors?"

She frowned, the same furrow cracking her forehead as when she had one of her bad gastric attacks. "Of course you do. You have Grandma Yeh and your mother. Ancestors do not only mean your forefathers." She frowned even more deeply, showing the scowl she got when she was about to yell at a bad driver. "Ancestors are those who give birth to you."

"But Grandma and Mom are both alive. Don't I have anyone dead?"

"Silly girl. Dead is gone, vamoose, vanished. No one has anyone dead—they are all buried!"

"I mean, like the ghosts I'm supposed to feed. Why don't we have spirits to give offerings to?"

"What do you want with ghosts and spirits and ancestor worship? We are modern, Suyin. One hundred years ago, even twenty years ago, women were tied to ridiculous rules and customs—cannot do this, cannot do that. Your mother and father were always controlling your life. Now we have the right to live our lives exactly the way we want to."

Auntie Ellen began stroking Suyin's hair, which Suyin hated. But Auntie looked hurt whenever she moved away, so she stayed quiet, because she had a few more questions to ask.

"Well, Mom controls my life. Is my father a ghost?"

The hand stopped stroking. It rested like a heavy mop on her head, damp and hot.

"What a question for a young girl to ask!" Auntie Ellen was a terrible liar. Her voice squeaked, so everyone could tell she was putting on an act.

"What's wrong with the question?"

"You're being fresh again! Fresh girl!"

"Piiish!" Suyin blew a breeze into Auntie's face. The short gray hairs on her forehead rose and fell.

It was the wrong thing to do; Auntie Ellen laughed and got away. She went to the kitchen to make Ovaltine for Suyin's afternoon drink, switching on her favorite television program when she came back. Nothing was allowed to interrupt Auntie Ellen's Cantonese show.

Auntie Ellen might as well have moved in with them. "Cannot have three women and a girl all in the same house," Grandma had advised. "It will not look good." So Auntie Ellen picked Suyin up from school, supervised her homework, and then went home, many evenings only after Li An got home from work.

"She's her godmother, and as much Suyin's mother as I am," Li An told her teachers. Suyin didn't think she was such a lucky girl to have two mothers—three, if Grandma was counted.

"Why can't I come home by myself?" Suyin nagged. "I don't need Auntie Ellen. I'm old enough to baby-sit myself!" She didn't like doing her homework to Cantonese opera and canned laughter. Hahahahaha. Crash, bang, cymbals, high-pitched *eeeee* through the nose.

"Listen, Suyin, Cantonese shows are Auntie Ellen's only traditional thing. Otherwise she is as young as you are," her mother said. That made Suyin laugh. Auntie Ellen was a poky spinster who had never been a young girl.

"What did you say?" her mother asked.

"Li An."

"I like you calling me Mom. You're the only person in the world who can call me that, and I'd miss it a lot if you stopped." She was trying her mushy act on Suyin, giving her that open-eyed smile.

"Li An." It made Suyin feel powerful to call her mother by her name. As if she had become simply another person, a stranger or a classmate—no one important. "Li An."

"If you must." Her mother, head down, lips straight, no smile, picked up the clothes all folded and neatly squared off. Her tough act, Auntie Ellen called it. "I'm leaving these in the laundry room for Ah Soh. Your blue jeans are hanging in the closet."

"But I like them folded. I don't like them ironed." Suyin hated the way everything was done for her. She didn't like her room clean. She didn't like ironed jeans; they looked so fake. Three mothers were too many. Grandma prayed for her soul, Auntie Ellen supervised her studies, and her mother kept her ironed.

"Mom," she said, "can I go away for the school holidays?" Suyin saw an island with just herself and seashells and turtles, coconuts to drink, and cans of sardines for food. "Just for a day, or two."

Then she saw her mother's face droop. She began to cry, just like that, as though Suyin wasn't there to see the tears. Suyin never thought her mother would cry over something she'd say. Her mother's nose turned all pink and tears fell on her dirty clothes. Suyin expected her to say something, but she cried and cried like a monsoon. Suyin had seen her mother yell over the telephone when her bulletin was late and scream when a gecko dripped its tail in her teacup. She'd seen her with pink-red eyes, but she'd never seen her weep.

"Mom," she said, "Mom, I'm sorry."

That was why she couldn't ask her mother about her father. She just knew she would cry if she asked that question.

Six

I t was like when he went scuba diving for the first time, off
the quiet western reefs in Bali. One minute he was in a
world of air, with a sky as blue as in calendar covers, absorbed
by the slip-slap-slap of the waves against the boat hull; the
next minute, he was in water, green-and-gray light shimmering
through in blurred refraction, then becoming grayer and
grayer, with his heart thumping steadily against the glug-glug
of his breathing, and the constant gurgling of water reminding him that he was where he shouldn't be. He wasn't a
fish, a ray propelling backwards fast like a popped cork, a curious green-headed coral stinger investigating this loosely
floating protoplasmic mass. He was an oxygen-eater, a crea-
ture of terra firma, whose blood approximated the salty density of the ocean, but who was nonetheless fated to drown in
salt H_2O if the oxygen tank strapped to his back emptied too
quickly, broke loose, or failed.

In the same way, Chester thought, he had been a man for
years—married, propertied, tax-paying, all the social rituals
fulfilled, basking in the sunshine of Meryl's attention, his students' awe, women's glances, the talk of colleagues. He had
been a man for as long as he had had the Volkswagen,
stashed away in his parents' garage while he was in the Peace
Corps in Malaysia; as long as he had had his driver's license,
leading the way to kegs of beer at Brewley's. But now, this very
moment, finding himself diving into a new element, more

dangerous than being a man—being a father—he breathed shallowly, nervously.

The air-conditioning in Li An's office was very cold. From the basement garage, sticky with clinging humidity, through the vestibule, into the elevator where the polished mirrored walls showed his face sweaty and his chin and throat bluish shadowed, up without a stop to the twenty-fifth floor, past the gold-lettered sign for BioSyn on the frosted glass door, Chester had traveled from summer to winter in under five minutes.

It took barely a second to recognize her—the short nose, eyes like bright raisins. Her hair was shorter, sleeker. She looked like she had been through a fashion course. She had on pink-colored lipstick and makeup of some kind—brown and darker brown. Her dress was white linen. Funny how he had always remembered her in crumpled dungarees and T-shirt. It hadn't occurred to him she would change.

She looked the way Meryl had wanted to look when she went on that shopping spree last year after her promotion. It must be an international phenomenon, this women's fashion— some kind of world feminist movement that had them all in pressed jackets and skirts. And stockings! But then of course with that frigid air-conditioning she would have to wear stockings. He wondered if she took them off before heading to that parking basement, as hot as the original equator. But that's the kind of thought he was not supposed to have.

Her secretary showed him in. The two women looked at each other as if they had agreed on something. Li An didn't look friendly. He didn't know what he was expecting: a handshake, a hug? "Hello, Chester," she said coolly. That couldn't be all.

She was standing behind an imposing desk, an expanse of polished blond wood, egg-shaped. Behind her were lots of blown-up magazine covers in Plexiglas frames. On the floor was industrial ash-gray carpeting, not the ugly speckled kind of carpeting in his college office. As suddenly as he had recognized her, she appeared unrecognizable, a stranger. She gestured to the chair in front of the desk.

When he hesitated he saw the broody expression fall on her face. That he recognized. Her cigarette melancholy. His eyes scanned the room—no ashtrays.

He looked for photographs or other signs of the girl. Abdullah had told him her full name when he dropped Chester off by the garage. Suyin Yeh. A very Chinese name. He didn't think he could say it right.

Singapore used to be British. It had been full of English words when he stopped over in 1969: Raffles Hotel, Stamford and Mountbatten Roads, Clark Quay, Elizabeth Walk, Newton Circus, Somerset and Orchard, City Hall and the Cricket Club. The Chinese were everywhere, but they had English names also. Wilson, Janet, Harry, Robert, Thomas, Susan, Irene, James, even odd English names like Anson and Clifton, Deirdre and Verena. Anglo-Chinese was the norm. British subjects, Chinese ancestry, for over a hundred years.

Nineteen sixty-nine was the beginning of the debate on a Singapore identity. Even in his rush to return to America, Chester could see how conscious they were of questions about how Western they should be, how Asian, how modernized. But he wouldn't have bet they would choose Chinese-Chinese to be the norm.

Everywhere now there was a push for Chinese identity. Mandarin was spoken over the taxi radios; the primary school children chattered in Mandarin; even the English-language newspaper encouraged Mandarin reading. A recidivism of identity? Or another historical invention, as bold as the invention of Germany or of Italy? A late twentieth-century desperate experiment, something so original that there was yet no name for such a political creation? Or a return to original source, to something ancient called race?

Whatever it was, he couldn't imagine Li An a part of it. She was too English educated. He remembered her anger when he dared to laugh at her precious British poetry, which she had showed him in her home in Petaling Jaya. Even Meryl's Barnard literature courses had dropped most of those writers.

The papers neatly stacked on her desk, the rows of sharpened pencils lined up like surgical tools—they did not go with his memory of her.

"How've you been?" He felt slow. He had expected more from her greeting. They had been the best of friends. Well, he had not written, but then neither had she. How was he supposed to know about the child without her telling him? She had never been the type to be silent. At least not until after that crazy night on May 13. But no one spoke much about that night. Not Abdullah or Samad, not the United States embassy, which sent a message that the Peace Corps volunteers were advised to refrain from intervening in internal matters in their host country. It was a mistake all around.

"Now, Chester, are you really interested in my answer?" At least Li An's voice remained as British as ever.

He ignored her question. "It's been a long time. Eleven, almost twelve years. Some would say that's a long time."

"Twelve is an auspicious number, and not just for Asia. It forms the astrological cycle, the structure of the mandala, the number of disciples for the Christ figure, the months in the year, the cognates in the I Ching . . ." She was twisting one of those yellow pencils.

Her nails were polished pink. She'd had scraggly bitten nails when she was riding her motorbike. He had often felt an odd tenderness at the sight of them, he remembered, for the chewed cuticles had made him think of the family story of the infant sister who had fallen asleep one night and never woken up. Bitten close to the fingertips, her nails had fascinated him, suggesting something voracious and self-defeating, some inward-turning energetic passivity unrelated to her usual verbal confidence, her swift moving body and quick gestures.

The sensation he felt now at the sight of her fingers turning the long thin pencil in smooth rhythm, the perfect nails shining like smooth matched pebbles, confused him. His feeling was less tender, more defensive. She appeared to him also to have grown a polished patina of success. He felt the need to lie, to dissemble, until he could recognize her again.

"Yeah, it's hard to know what to say after so many years. How have you been? You look well." The words came out like a lecture, practiced, easy. He was aware that they had remained standing. The pauses between their words seemed artificial, forcing him to look around, as if curious, when all he wanted was to stare at her, figure her out, find a way back to their first happy friendship.

The phone rang. She was on the line for a long time, while she scanned papers, schedules, photographs.

Taking a seat on the purple-brown sofa facing the wall of glass, he looked out at the windows of the high-rise office buildings that seemed to float across the way. There was an unselfconsciousness about the uncurtained transparency: work taking place for all to view, business as usual, no privacy needed.

She must have changed to be comfortable in such a space.

He felt the comic irony of his visit. For the past twelve years, he had imagined, even feared, the image of Li An as abandoned.

When Meryl had dragged him to the Met to listen to Pavarotti in Puccini's *Madama Butterfly*, he had been overcome by the obscenity of the pathos. The soprano in her tarted-up kimono, cradling a plastic baby to her bellowing bosom, was only an orientalist vision, he explained to Meryl as they drove home to their fake Tudor in Westchester. This was the West's degradation of Asia, the imago of what had gone wrong in Vietnam. Asia was independent of the West, had been independent for centuries, did not need America to know itself.

He told Meryl about the brown men and women walking barefoot and pigeon-toed along the brown bunds of the flooded rice fields in Bali, to whom the Australian and German backpackers were amusing guests, unheeded. It was only when we took too much heed of the other, when we allowed our visions of them into our dreams, our politics, our desires, that horrible stories got concocted. Fantasies of their desire for us, our desire for them, grew, until the young Hmongs in their new American homes died of fear of images coming alive from their television screen, and the arias of an Asian woman dying over a careless American man sickened him, he explained.

But what did the opera have to do with tourism in Bali or Southeast Asian refugees, Meryl wanted to know. She could not see that a Japanese woman's suicide over a jerk like

Pinkerton was in any way related to the Pentagon or to the boat people. It was a stretch, something academics invented for lack of more significant work.

Of course, he thought, shifting his feet, balancing a foot on a knee, Meryl was right, as always. He need not have worried about Li An.

"I'm sorry," Li An said now. "Thursday is the busiest day. That's when the bulletin goes to the printer." Her briskness irked him. It reminded him that he did not belong there.

"When you said you wanted to be a writer, I didn't think you would be a business writer!"

She gave him a smile that declared nothing.

"Paroo waited with me last week. He wanted to come with me today, but he has extracurricular classes."

"Yes, Paroo hasn't changed, has he? He still wants to be part of what happens."

Chester took the opening. "Abdullah has changed, however, don't you think? I never thought he would have a Harvard accent. Whereas Samad has become as prominent in Malay politics as I predicted."

"Bumi politics," she said, smiling again. "Malay is out of favor; it sounds too racist. Bumi is political, not racial."

"I suppose I am completely ignorant of developments in Malaysia. In fact, I lecture on Indonesian sociology, never on Malaysia." He was speaking lightly.

"I wonder why." Her voice was almost a murmur, disinterested. She looked up as the secretary opened the door, and spoke more loudly. "Is it time for Chun's presentation?"

He would not let her off. "Wait a minute, Lee Ann. Do you think you would have time to have dinner with me?" He was aware that he had embarrassed her in front of the secretary. The slight awkwardness of her hand as she waved the woman away suggested something unspoken.

She waited until the door closed again. "Chester." It was the first time she had looked at him directly. Again, her fingers turned a pencil. He remembered that she had reached just so for a cigarette whenever she was thinking hard. "Why are you in Singapore?"

"I'm here to do research, a funded project. I'm looking at

cultural transformations when populations move from rural to urban, and from industrial to technological bases, and what communication networks accompany shifts in kinship structures, if traditional belief systems . . ."

"No, really, why are you in Singapore? Why do you wish to meet me for dinner?" She stopped twirling the pencil and leaned forward over the pale yellow wood. He noticed, glancing down, that her reflection showed beneath her, as in a tilted mirror— hair and eyes receding above, chin prominently central.

The lecture he had prepared for her would not start. "There's nothing unnatural in checking on an old friend, surely? We were good friends in Kuala Lumpur," he added, appealing to memory, the place. Something in the reflection shifted on the wood.

"Do you know I'm divorced?" She became matter-of-fact, and pushed back against the chocolate leather chair.

He racked his mind for the correct answer. He was being tested. "Umm, yes. Paroo told me." Only the truth. She had already known his answer.

"And did Paroo tell you I have a daughter?" This time it was she who looked away, out the sun-glazed expanse of window. Anyone looking in would think him a client or a job applicant.

He nodded, silent.

"Everyone believes she's your daughter." Her voice was casual, and he was afraid she could hear the thump in his chest.

A mist materialized over his eyes. He had wondered for months how to talk about it. He need not have worried. Li An was clearly not going to be coy. "Is she mine?"

When he saw her eyes brighten, he knew immediately that she had trapped him. "No, of course not. She's my daughter."

"I mean, who's her father?"

"Her name is Suyin Yeh. On her birth certificate her father is Henry Yeh."

The polar air was blowing straight into his face. His throat swelled and thickened. She was obstructing him, he knew it, insisting on her way in the same way that Meryl had. "Is he her father?" he asked, his voice ragged with phlegm.

"He has not met her. Except once. At least, she has not met him."

Round and round the yellow pencil turned. He was tired. The frigid air-conditioning, coming after the clinging swampy heat of the city, had left him enervated; he was aware he had no words at hand. He watched the color twirling in her small hands, which looked capable of anything.

"Will you let me meet her?"

The pencil stopped. She gave an impatient shake of her shoulders. "Remember Ellen? Henry walked out of the maternity ward, but when Ellen found me crying she swore at me. No tears. All my strength was to go into nursing the baby. Ellen's Suyin's second mother. She doesn't want Suyin to meet you."

"I won't talk about rights. As you say, she's your daughter. But hasn't she the right to know, to meet me, if, if . . ." He struggled to finish his thought.

She frowned, showing a straight furrow between the brows that was new to him. "Does a child know her rights? Besides, I make all the decisions for her." The phone rang again. "It's the secretary reminding me of Mr. Chun," she said, a sudden smile showing a younger Li An to him. "You'll have to leave."

"Well, what do you think? Be fair. You were always fair. I have come partly to see you and to see what the rumor is about. I can't leave without seeing her!" He knew his voice had sharpened, even as he was rising to his feet.

Her hand sheltered her eyes from him. Her lips were pursed, a librarian's pout. He feared her opposition.

"I'll talk to Ellen about it."

"No, talk to Suyin. She's the one who should decide. You would have said so once." But he had to be contented with the frown, with the secretary's efficient opening and closing of the door.

Seven

Suyin was in a school play. She was playing Madam White Snake. "You don't know the story of Madam White Snake?" she had asked Ellen in genuine horror. "How can a school principal not know?"

"I'll have to read up on it," Ellen grimaced. "Never studied Chinese, you know. In the old days we studied French."

"And English literature," Li An added, looking up from a new graphic design journal that had just arrived in the mail. It was all dragons, knights, and dungeons, just like in the old children's storybooks—although this time the journal came from San Jose, California, not England. "Or Greek. Westerners have their own version of Madam White Snake. Her name is Medusa. At your age I didn't know whether I liked Medusa or not. It was a change to find a woman who could freeze a warrior in his tracks and hold him for eternity."

"Stone. She changed the soldiers into stone," Ellen corrected her.

"It was those snakes, hundreds of hissing loving reptiles coiled around her head, that freaked out the men. They wanted to cut her head off because she had snakes in her head."

"On her head," Ellen interrupted.

"Hissing, spitting venom, fangs curved." Li An danced around the kitchen, waving her fingers above her head.

Suyin wished her mother wouldn't act so childish. It was only a game, but why couldn't her mother play real games like

Monopoly or badminton instead of stupid made-up games that embarrassed her?

"It was one way to keep the men out of her face!" Ellen laughed as Li An leapt, hissing, arms raised, a queen cobra weaving her hooded head in a ritualistic trance.

"But her eyes, yesssssss, her eyessssss, they were the real danger. Because as the men dodged the venom, the whirling twirling long slippery serpents, they would suddenly see her eyes—so large, so intelligent, so sad, so different from those venomous creatures. Ssssoooo dangerous. Intelligence. Woman. Put the two together—how incredible, how awful. Wham! Stone."

"You never act your age, Mom," Suyin complained. "Grotty old fairy tales! Who cares about them?"

"But some fairy tales are beautiful!" Li An would not stop dancing. "Like the firebird to the Russians and Feng Huang, the sacred bird, to the Chinese!" She fluttered her arms and pirouetted. "You see, I do know some Chinese myths. Feng Huang, of five mystical colors, twelve tail feathers, part swan, part unicorn, part dragon, part tortoise . . ."

"No point to these stories!" Ellen interrupted.

" . . . part snake. Universal phoenix, symbol of rejuvenation, from the same root as *juvenile*. To the Arab, bird that immolates itself, burns down, down to a heap of ash, and then is reborn. To the Greek, bird of brilliant feathers, rising from the darkness each morning, yes . . ." Li An sprang up from a crouch, then stopped.

Suyin, much more concerned with her role as Madam White Snake, had already turned to her Mandarin schoolbook. Her Mandarin was bad. Still, she was lucky; with her green-brown eyes, reddish hair, and dramatic height, the Chinese language teacher had insisted on putting her on stage for Chinese drama night. But in a speechless part!

Dressed in white tights and tee, sequined and spangled, she was to wriggle on stage. Female, snaky, hissing, nonhuman, non-Chinese-speaking freak of Cho Kang Secondary School, Li An thought. A sweet kind supernatural reptile falling in love with a scholar and transforming itself into a woman to meet him, Mrs. Weng told Li An. The teacher had explained that Madam White Snake was breaking the laws of propriety and of ascribed positions by changing into a human. Suyin's slinky silence was supposed to represent a divine spirit, not her failed Mandarin.

Li An discussed the Chinese language teacher's assignment earnestly with Ellen. Should she file a complaint? How often could she complain? It would be the twentieth time or so in three different schools. Was she being overly sensitive? Suyin's school records were already filled with Li An's letters and formal replies from various principals, boards, and ministries. What would hurt Suyin more—to write a letter to the principal, to speak to Mrs. Weng, or to pretend the role assigned to her meant nothing malicious? How would Suyin's classmates react to a complaint, to her costume, to her mute wriggles?

Finally, Li An did nothing. "Don't fight Suyin's battles for her," Ellen had said. "She will always be treated as different!"

Li An recalled Ellen's words as she listened to Ellen's passionate denouncement of her meeting with Chester.

"I give up!" Ellen said, dropping with a bounce on Li An's bed. "You will do exactly what you like, so what's the point of my talking?"

She wanted to deny it, to plead Ellen's place in her life. "I do listen to you."

"Aiyah!" Ellen's exclamation spread, a small explosion, silencing Li An.

She concentrated on hanging her freshly pressed suits in the closet. She felt more confusion than shame at Ellen's incredulity, for they both knew that in the most important matters Ellen had not been the significant player. Ellen was happy to be needed; her usefulness was a great part of Li An's love for her. But there was another Li An, a not-so-secret self, to whom Ellen, wonderful, sacrificing, generous Ellen, was less relevant. Li An knew herself to be withholding, withheld, from everyone except Suyin.

For the first few years with her daughter, Li An had lost herself and forgotten grievances. Nothing was so important that it could not wait till after Suyin was minded. Sensations flowed and filled the cavities in Li An's body: her infant's mass, the baby hair texture, fine as cocoon threads, the odor of baby—a milky powdered sweetness, perfume of the newly born, her blessed existence. Li An was surfeited by those moments, which shaped that compact space encompassing Suyin and herself, and which sufficed, she felt, forever.

But of course, forever was an unnatural state. Motherhood was only a passing condition, like love and its heat, and at eleven Suyin resisted soothing. She did not want to be hugged.

"So you are simply going to let him take her away?" Ellen picked up a pillow and turned it over and over.

"No." Carefully Li An brushed off a faint chalk mark that the cleaners had left on a dark gray jacket.

"Then why allow her to meet him? She never has to know."

Li An avoided looking at Ellen's hands as they thrashed wildly at the pillow. "Am I to keep her in ignorance all her life?"

"I don't like that word *ignorance*. It isn't like that. He's not important. He's been nobody to her. What's wrong with keeping it that way?"

"But isn't it for her to decide?"

"Are you out of your mind!" The pillow flew out of Ellen's hands, a missile of foam. "Suyin's still a child. She can't decide what skirt to wear on Saturday, not to mention whether she wants this man for a father."

"It's not 'this man.' It's Chester. You used to like him. He looks and sounds the same. You could meet him with Suyin." Li An kept her voice low, feeling for the steadiness of business writing, the clear agenda of the memorandum.

"Don't want!" Ellen jumped out of the bed with a violence that surprised her. "You're not afraid!" Her voice was an accusation. "You think your daughter is going to love you no matter what happens. You never tell her anything about your sacrifices, your hard work, how you slogged to give her all she has. Now she will simply meet this romantic man, her American father, who walks in so late, and she will never come back to us!"

Li An's mouth trembled. She wasn't sure if she was going to smile or frown. "You have very little faith in Suyin. Love can't be hoarded, you know, like rice and sugar. We generate it, it's an energy, and it has to be used up to be any good. I don't mind if Suyin learns to love Chester, I think she has been hurt by not knowing, you know . . ."

"Yes, what? That she's illegitimate? That you've never told her the truth? That her father didn't love her enough for the first eleven years to even make an effort to find out about her existence? How cheap can you get?" Ellen's voice cracked, and she buried her face in a second pillow.

Li An was astonished at the anger suddenly in the air. She pulled the closet doors closed, picked up the pillow from the dressing table where it had landed, and smoothed the green-striped cotton where Ellen had clenched it so fiercely.

It wasn't that Li An didn't want to scream. But she had screamed enough that Monday, sitting in the Petaling Jaya bungalow garden, when Chester left for America.

His flight had been at 3:00 P.M. Everyone was going to Subang Airport for a good-bye party. She had been invited, along with his woodworking students who had never learned to make a stable table, the pale Chinese Malaysians who trust-ed him to help them pass the General Paper, Paroo, not so sad anymore once Chester had taken him up, and Samad, Abdullah, and some other Malay men who played guitars and whom he had taught to sing "This Land Is Your Land." Other Peace Corps volunteers would be there, those staying on for another year, intertwining fingers with their Malaysian girlfriends, giggling and terrified at the sight of Chester get-ting on the huge Boeing airplane, flying away, back to America.

She had lied about a German test that could not be missed, her life being tied to Henry's fellowship. But she had waited out in the burning shadeless backyard, sitting by the spiny spider lilies and sparse yellowing allamanda, head cocked to the vast blue dome, waiting for a glimpse perhaps of Chester disappearing in a trail of vapor. She could not imag-ine him gone from Kuala Lumpur, from the days in her life. No, never, never again the smile for her, never again to have his body inhabiting the same space.

At 3:15, she thought she saw a line of smoke, the metallic glitter of a passing jet, and screamed so loudly that Letchmi came flying out of the back door, crying, "Missy, Missy, you hurt, you hurt?" When she shook her head and pointed dumbly at the snail chewing on a spider lily leaf, delicate horns poised above its whorled shell, Letchmi laughed and stepped on it, the soft crunch and squelch under the rubber thongs seeming to pierce Li An's chest in a pang of guilt sharper than anything she had felt toward Henry. She had screamed again, this time with tears, and Letchmi had taken her back into the shelter of the kitchen and made her a cup of tea. "Sorry, Missy," she'd murmured over and over again, "Sorry, Missy, don' kill snail, don' kill snail, sorry, lah!"

That was the last squeamishness. Letchmi had reported her fit of crying to Henry, and after that afternoon, Mrs. Yeh had taken over her pregnancy: no Frankfurt trip for her in her delicate situation, and a new bungalow large enough for mother-in-law, Henry, Li An, and the new grandchild to come, with no snails in the garden to set her off in hysterics.

And after the silent scandal of Suyin's birth and Henry's departure from the hospital alone, Ellen had stepped in. Grandma Yeh, accompanied by her nurse, visited Li An and Suyin at Ellen's house nearly every day, until eventually all four of them had moved to Singapore, moving south for big city tolerance and anonymity.

No more screams, Li An had promised herself as she packed the bundles of notes on seventeenth-century Britain, on lyric and blank verse, Wordsworth, Coleridge, Yeats, Eliot, Auden—all the Romantics and Modernists noted in cramped handwriting on lined paper—and the note cards on Chaucer's *Canterbury Tales*, Shakespeare's *Hamlet* and *King Lear*, more writing than she wanted to read again. Weeks and months of writing and studying, years of her life, were swaddled with plastic string. Astonishing Ellen, Li An had left them all to yellow in the sun out by the gate for the paper collector's next pickup. She could not explain why her books of poetry seemed suddenly too noisy with feelings. She could only throw them out.

And life had quieted down, slowed to the rhythm of Grandma Yeh's knitting needles, clicking like heartbeats, and Suyin's light breathing, susurrus magic for a love-besotted mother.

Watching Chester walk out of her office earlier, she had remembered the pain of that Monday afternoon. Monday afternoon—a time to be always occupied, a slot in her schedule to be filled with interviews, price-quotation conferences, meetings with Ang Swee and his committee to review last week's figures, brainstorming sessions with the *BioSyn-Sign* photographers and public relations people. Li An's Monday afternoon attacks were noted in the company.

"Man, she's in high gear on Monday! All weekend no action, then Monday comes and watch out, all teeth!" Keno, the Japanese-Malaysian vice president, had pursued her for six months, then dropped the chase after a Monday afternoon meeting, when she had awed the entire board of directors with the graphics for a report on the company's international performance.

"Too much," he had said, explaining to Li An his loss of interest. "Cannot keep up. How can you do all that on Monday afternoon!"

She pressed a forefinger deep into her right temple, ringing with migraine, and smiled, like the flowing unbroken Kuan Yin that Grandma Yeh had allowed her to keep.

Li An had felt a scream start up when Paroo called, his jubilant tone echoing through the tinny soundbox of the telephone earpiece, "Chester's here!" When she had agreed to meet them at the New Asia Hotel, the storm that had broken out that afternoon was like the scream she had uttered years ago. She would not leave her large dry office for Chester, not with the jumpy thunder and cascading rain reminding her of how her body had twisted in pain for months after he left.

She had thought these were memories, husks emptied of senses, but knowing he was somewhere on the island, her body had drifted away from her, tugged by phantom sensations and yearnings.

No, she would not give Chester the satisfaction of a scream. Let Ellen throw the tantrums.

•

So, calmly, she had come to decide that Suyin could meet Chester. Tracing the vivid widow's peak with a gentle finger, humming wordlessly, she set to brushing Suyin's hair, a ritual so old to her daughter that Suyin could not remember a time without the caress of brush on scalp sweeping her languorously to sleep.

"Suyin, I want you to meet an old friend of mine."

"Hmmm . . . "

"Chester Brookfield. From America."

This was something new. Suyin's eyes fluttered, but drowsiness weighed them down again.

"Maybe sometime this week, after school, Auntie Ellen will take you to meet him at the Café Delon."

The brush worked its way, up and down, up and down. Suyin's breathing slowed, her body, already bent in fetal curve, toppled onto the pillow. "America" flickered in her consciousness, a spark of strangeness, then she was asleep.

Eight

Auntie Ellen was in a bad mood. Her face was cross, like in the cartoons when Nancy was angry with Sluggo, and she wore a big mouth like an upside-down watermelon slice. Except Auntie Ellen's mouth got narrower and thinner, more like a scythe. It meant, Watch out! I don't care who you are, get out of my way! Li An had said she would've been promoted to schools supervisor a long time ago, if she didn't have such a bad temper. But Auntie Ellen only laughed. "I cannot even supervise you and Suyin! It's hard enough to take care of twenty-five teachers, how to supervise hundreds?"

Suyin wouldn't talk to Auntie Ellen after she threw out her *Seventeen* magazines. "All rubbish! Lipstick and brassieres, boyfriends, perfume! You're too young to rot your mind with decadent values!" Suyin thought all school principals spoke like her Auntie Ellen. Bam! Bam! Bam!

Why must she have a principal for an auntie? Her mother said, "She loves you. Attention is love, Suyin. She and Grandma Yeh are your closest relatives. We've got to stick together, no matter what!"

Suyin wouldn't answer. Even an aunt had no right to throw out her stuff without her permission. Auntie Ellen was always reminding her that she was only a child. But a child also had rights. And she knew secrets.

She knew Auntie Ellen did not want to take her to Café Delon.

She humphed when she took Suyin down to her car, humphed as she drove down Buona Vista Road and waited behind an empty bus that was pulling into the bus lane, and humphed as she was picking through the parking coupons. Usually she would smile victoriously when there was plenty of parking space and she found a spot under a tree. She had come straight from her Tai Chi class to drive Suyin to the cafe on Holland Road.

"Just an excuse," she said, frowning as she stuck the parking coupons upright on the dashboard. "She's never had a deadline on Sunday. Why this Sunday? Hmmm!"

"Why must I meet Mom's friend?"

Auntie Ellen was very bad at lying. She displayed all her teeth every time she was faking.

Suyin teased her, "False smile, false smile!"

"Aiyah, cannot help it," Ellen said. "Like a hyena, I must laugh and bare fangs. Best thing is to be direct. But, in my job, must be DIP-PLO-MA-TICK! Look at the spelling lesson: the principal is your P-A-L. So I show teeth. Look, no bite!"

She showed all her teeth this time. "Hummph!"

"Is he someone important?"

"We'll see."

They were walking under the awning of some shops. Auntie Ellen was wearing her sunglasses and almost stumbled over a bamboo stool; she put out a hand and it just missed a stack of twig baskets. A whole raft of rolled-up pandan mats shook as she held on to the plastic cord that roped in the rattan goods—plaited elephants, hampers, doll furniture sets, trunks, plant hangers—and the shopkeeper in his white singlet came hurrying out, yelling, "Hey, hey!"

Auntie Ellen pretended not to hear and kept on walking. "I haven't seen him in almost twelve years. Don't know if he is bald or not, same or not."

She, of course, was ageless, or so she joked. "School principals are gold," she often boasted. "Never tarnish, always currency. In Singapore education, only gold will do. Pure merit never ages."

Suyin recognized him immediately—the tall, uncomfortable-looking white man, the ang moh standing guard by the only unoccupied table in the cafe. Her mother used to like Café Delon until it got popular. Now the small tables were stuffed with ang moh and their pretty girlfriends, the marble tabletops all covered with funny porcelain ashtrays shaped like bathtubs, toilet bowls, or encyclopedias, and different shaped glasses of cappuccino and Italian fizzes. She was sure it was her mother who had suggested Café Delon. He was looking quite pathetic alone, holding the table for them.

Suyin had already figured he was someone who knew her father.

Last night, her mother had been distracted. "Auntie Ellen will be bad tempered," she warned. "Just ignore her. Say hello nicely to Chester. He's not a ghoul, no matter what Auntie Ellen says, okay?"

Suyin didn't ask her any questions. Her mother had that pinky look in her eyes that meant she had been crying.

The ang moh was staring rudely at her.

"Chester!" Auntie Ellen's voice boomed.

All the girlfriends turned to look. They were like models— bobbed hair, purple lipstick and eye shadow, black short skirts, and tight tees. Who said Asian girls had no breasts? Her mother wouldn't let her dress like that.

Well, he wasn't bald. She felt tingly when she saw that his hair came down to a V in the center, just like hers. Did he marry her mother? Were they divorced?

He acted as though he was going to hug Auntie Ellen, but Auntie Ellen stuck out her hand instead.

"Ellen, you look just the same!" Suyin watched his face to see what it looked like when he was lying. But it was too new for her to tell.

"Can't say the same for you. Where's your long hair?" Auntie Ellen sat next to him and pushed out the chair beside her for Suyin.

"I'm a professor now; my students have the long hair." He stretched his legs away from the table. Suyin hoped the waiter would notice them and not trip.

She watched him carefully. He didn't look like a father, only like an ang moh—very red in the face from sunburn. She couldn't tell what she was feeling. Both big and small.

Curious. Like Alice in Wonderland. Curiouser and curiouser.

They were reading the menu, acting like everyone else, except Auntie Ellen kept her sunglasses on, although the cafe was dim.

"What would you like?" "Anything interesting?" "Are you hungry?" "Too early for lunch." "Something cold." "Yes, very hot all the time in Singapore." "The cold melon fizz sounds good."

He was saying something to her, but Auntie Ellen answered before she could hear it. "Suyin will have the vanilla ice cream."

At least once a week, even after her mother had forbidden it, Auntie Ellen bought Suyin her favorite vanilla ice cream from Cold Storage. "She gets cavities because of her bad Chinese genes, not because of ice cream," she had argued. So this time Suyin couldn't be angry with Auntie Ellen for being bossy. Besides, she couldn't speak.

"Funny, that's my favorite flavor also." He had a crooked smile, one side more up than the other. Suyin could see he was quite old because the skin around his eyes had lines, like hatching, when he smiled.

"You are still good at talking." Auntie Ellen was probably glaring at him behind her shades, her voice was so Mrs. Grim Principal.

He continued smiling at Suyin. "Tools of the trade. I'm starting a new study on the ways the English language is being resourced in Singapore and Malaysia."

"Resourced?"

"How it is used, deployed, exploited, operated, tapped. What aspects of the language have been most institutionalized."

"You should talk to Mom! She is the editor of a terrific magazine." Suyin's voice was just a little bit shrill.

"A bulletin, Suyin. Not a popular magazine."

"She writes and interviews and does graphics and layouts . . ."

"She has staff to do the work."

"Her magazine has won a prize . . ."

"It's the most highly respected in-house business journal in Singapore." Over the top of her sunglasses, Auntie Ellen gave Suyin her crafty look, which meant to shut up, and the waiter came to take their orders.

Suyin held on to the menu and pretended to read it even after the waiter left.

"You sound very proud of your mother." She looked up to see if he was flashing all his teeth.

"We are all very proud of her." Auntie Ellen's voice was still grim.

"So, what does your name mean?" This time, he bent his head toward Suyin.

She giggled nervously. "The Chinese meaning or what my classmates say?"

Auntie Ellen stared. Suyin had never talked to her about what the other children said at Cho Kang.

"What do they say?"

"Sue-ing You, So-yin-yang, Si-in-Yeh, Sinner Yeh!"

Auntie Ellen's mouth turned down, just like a punctured tire with all the air hissing out. Suyin looked up quickly to catch his expression. Strange, an ang moh face was so different, she could not tell if he was lying the way she could with Auntie Ellen. He also had green stone eyes like hers. They must be kind. She knew her eyes were kind, no matter what names Ah Hong and her gang called her. She was glad she had told him about the name-calling. He didn't look like he'd cry like her mother would have.

The vanilla ice cream was huge. It filled a glass dish shaped like a shoe, and the ice cream was supposed to have a vanilla bean hidden somewhere in the toe of the shoe. Suyin dug at the ice cream with the long spoon, and peeped at him while they were talking. New York. All women's college. She wondered if his students had a crush on him. Ellen not married. Too busy for men. Li An also alone. Very successful. Has a nice mock Tudor house. What type? White plaster and black wooden beams, like old English. Met Paroo; very happy. Hasn't seen Paroo in years. Different paths.

Then they began talking about Auntie Ellen's job. Educational system in Singapore. Mother-tongue policy. Mandarin-based. Students sometimes culturally biased.

Auntie Ellen was talking faster and faster. Too young to know better. Excellent school system. Best preparation for competitive world. Principal—she should know!

Bigger world outside should be seen. She can come for a holiday, no problem. Visit Museum of Natural History, Botanical Gardens. A short stay would also be fine. As short or long as she wishes. No pressure. His voice was low.

Auntie Ellen must be at least one foot shorter, but also one foot louder! Even paying close attention, Suyin had to listen hard to hear him. Auntie Ellen kept interrupting—well, no, no, cannot, cannot, too young, what's the use, no point, what for, confusing her—until Suyin was all confused.

Finally Auntie Ellen said, "I'll tell Li An." Then she looked over her shoulder to see if the waiter could hear. "But I tell you, Chester, you are a real nuisance. Suyin is a wonderful girl, no thanks to you, and I'm not sure if all this means more mischief or good for her and Li An."

Suyin supposed being quiet had some advantages. She doubted they would have said so much in front of her if she had interrupted with questions.

They shook hands when they left. He wouldn't let Auntie Ellen pay the bill, and she drove Suyin home with her lips pressed tight and without a single humph.

Nine

Chester had expected a little girl, but Suyin was already taller than her mother. Perhaps that wasn't surprising, since he had been one of the tallest boys in his high school.

He had thought she would have been immediately recognizable, like his sister would have been had she survived infancy. Fair and pink, gold-red hair, straight high nose, and finely etched lips. "A rosebud," Mother had said to a visiting neighbor a long time ago, when he was about five.

He had never forgotten the word, because Mother hardly ever spoke about her. The doubled sound, *rosebud*, lingered as a mysterious effect. He had not known what a rosebud looked like when he first heard her say it. Then it took on the folded shape of a pink flower when, a few months later, he accompanied her to a florist and the woman at the shop asked, "Do you want some roses?"

His mother had replied, "Oh, aren't they the sweetest rosebuds?" gesturing to the leafless stems from which single creased heads of infant roses sprang. But she bought the spicy scented freesias instead, burying her nose among the blooms hanging like orange bells from stalks just bursting out of spring bulbs.

Closed in, meshed petals, crimson bleeding into black: dark red rosebuds were Meryl's favorite flowers. Each time she carried some home from the Chilean florist on First Avenue he felt a pang, as he had at the moment of the first sounding of the word, for what had stood between him and only-childhood—not even a remembered ghost of a sister, but an image of a flower. Disappointment stirred at this memory.

"Suyin," the child announced herself prosaically. Her color was all Asian—brown and ochre mixed, like a tropical clay, no leaden gray or chalk. She was sun-colored brown, pecan-shelled, and her hair appeared dark, Chinese, in the low-lit cafe. He saw that she needed braces; her large teeth crowding in a small mouth would need expensive orthodontic repair to straighten the haphazard angles.

Her eyes would not meet his. He found them small at first, but once she gazed at him fully he saw that they were round, with broad whites and shiny green-hazel irises the color of his.

The pulse in his chest hurt like after too much exercise. He had not felt so much hurt even after the last argument with Meryl. This time, the hurt was with himself.

Through the cafe noise, he said things about the food, about his English language use research. It was like talking above the engine sounds of planes landing on every side. A roar inside his body echoed outside in the bass voices of the white men in the cafe. He heard a French accent, some Californian, tones like German or Norwegian, lots of British—flat and broad vowels, the high-pitched nervy jingly paces of women. The women were all speaking English. "Yes, lah. So Susan say what for." "True-loh, my boss don't give me day off." "My mother like chocolate, meh. We buy Col' Storage."

Chester watched Suyin scoop the ice cream, shiny stuff dripping off the small bowl of the spoon. She was a dainty eater and took a long time finishing it.

By then he was talking recklessly, not understanding why he was asking if she would be interested in a visit to New York. He would have to call Meryl if Suyin accepted. For once he did not know what Meryl would say. He was walking a plank, blindfolded, crossing over to some place he could not see. Nothing would be the same, and his plans, whatever plans he had had with Meryl, were changing even now.

He had not wanted to change on returning home in August 1969. The Peace Corps term in Malaysia, cut short, was

finally over, like a too-long movie—fascinating in the first few
hours, dreadful with smoke and blood in its conclusion. He
had wanted reality, the bland clean shampooed middle-class
reality that bright energetic Meryl promised. No puddles of
darkness, no dark skins, no nasal curses, no sharp unidenti-
fiable smells. Vanilla ice cream.

He stroked his thighs thinking of Meryl.

The noise in his head subsided. He was able to pay the waiter without, as he'd feared, fumbling for change.

"Auntie Ellen is waiting outside," Suyin told him.

He shook Ellen's unfriendly hand. In the white-hot sunshine he saw red-gold hairs shining on Suyin's arms, and her
dark hair gleamed with russet streaks.

He knew it was shame he was feeling, shame that was like
a different kind of love—the first time he had loved so
shamefully—as he watched his daughter walk away.

Ten

It was Li An's idea to have a family vacation.

"Yuck! With Auntie Ellen and Grandma Yeh? I don't want to go!"

Suyin used to be an obedient child. Li An had worried that she never talked to her about school or friends. "I don't have any!" Suyin had said when Li An asked her last year, although Li An knew it wasn't true. Her teacher had reported she was a popular student.

Now she'd become loud and assertive. Li An almost wished she hadn't grown up.

"What do I call him?" she had asked Li An the first time Chester was taking her to a movie alone.

"Call him Chester." She knew Suyin was asking her a different kind of question. Just as she had let Henry discover Suyin for himself eleven years ago, she now let Suyin discover Chester. If Suyin had asked her directly she might have told her.

Perhaps Li An was more Chinese than she knew. Writing about stocks and shares was easy. It was all that murky everyday stuff—relationships, feelings, what's there and not there, love, guilt—that she left unspoken.

Later that evening, she didn't ask Suyin what she and Chester had talked about, what they did, what she thought about finding her father at the age of eleven. Let Chester carry the weight of their relationship!

•

All right, Port Dickson was not everyone's idea of a holiday, but it was nicer than St. John's Island, and they could all go without much fuss because none of them had given up their Malaysian passports.

"I'll get around to it," Li An had told Ang Swee when he pushed for her to become a Singapore national. National identity was the kind of information that seemed important when exchange securities were discussed, he said, and the shareholders were concerned about where her loyalties lay as editor in chief of *BioSyn-Sign*.

"Aren't you still an Australian citizen?" she asked.

"Catty, catty!" he mocked. "But Australian has more cachet than Malaysian, you know." Ang Swee never worried about being superior. He simply enjoyed the condition. He was good with the board of directors; he knew their every social-climbing impulse, and he beat them at it.

Most Friday nights he came by the office in a tuxedo with a red or white cummerbund, his hair slicked down with perfumed hair grease, on his way to some charity function or art gallery opening. BioSyn's own mambo bandleader, Li An teased him. He liked men more than women, and some kinds of women more than others, but that was the kind of information that didn't count on the balance sheets.

Thinking of Ang Swee and then of Chester, Li An remembered Auden's poem. "Lay your sleeping head, my love, human on my faithless arm." None of the British lecturers at University of Malaya had taught her about Auden's lover, Chester, when she was studying contemporary poetry. All that time she had believed Auden's beautiful words were about men with women. While Chester was in Kuala Lumpur, she had read Auden's poem over and over again, imagining faithless Auden was speaking to her, that her Chester and Auden were one male voice, one male body, betraying her desire. Later, when she read Auden's letters to his lover, she was startled by the coincidence in the names, then amazed that she could have believed the feelings in Auden's poem to have been speaking for her.

Discovering how remote the poem was from her situation may have been the first time she saw how she had betrayed

Henry, whose love she had not valued. In Malaysia it was husbands, not lovers, who were vulnerable to betrayal.

And Chester, that name she had found so profoundly American? After reading the letters, she imagined Auden's Chester to be a small, nervous, envious alcoholic. Auden and Chester were lovers. Her Chester was only a passing body. Or she was only a passing body to him, a handgrip, a spasm, an unmemorable memory. If she had not read Auden's poetry, perhaps that was all Chester would have been for her also.

Now, Suyin formed the only chain between them.

Li An had Suyin despite everything that made her impossible. She had believed a baby was born to her parents, not of her parents. She had not expected that Henry would not love the child. Had she, morning-sick and then heavily pregnant, been slightly crazy? She had deluded herself that it made no difference, and Henry need never know. It had been easier to slide with the days and months, until on February 13, 1970, exactly nine months to the day, if one was counting—an improbability, the gynecologist had said, to have a first baby exactly nine months after conception, when they usually waited and waited, refusing the world—six months after she had last seen Chester, the water broke, and although the baby did not want to come out, there she was, cut loose, with those long fringed green eyes, almost blue at first.

What if she had been born with dark brown eyes like Henry's instead? Would Henry have allowed himself to love her? Green un-Chinese eyes, no Yeh of mine. He did not have to say it; when he came up to her hospital bed, she saw immediately that he had been crying. She had watched him cry quietly for the first time at Ah Pah's funeral. This time he must have cried at another death. She must have hurt him so badly that he never wanted to see her again.

"Dadah kills!" The antidrug posters were plastered over the concrete pillars behind which the border guards stood talking. The causeway immigration police were even more hostile than usual this Saturday. The two guards went through their bags as if searching for smuggled swimsuits and towels.

Ellen had said they should bring along tins of ham. "Hello, oink, oink!" That would get them through without stressful pawing. But Li An wouldn't do it. After all, she respected Muslims, like Abdullah and Samad. Nasty immigration officers were simply nasty, she argued; it didn't have anything to do with being Muslim.

"Mom, are they looking for something?" Suyin wrinkled her nose when they dug right down to the bottom of her duffel.

"Yes, heroin, cocaine, amphetamines, opium, marijuana, dadah! Avon lipstick, Breck shampoo, Maidenform bra, Elizabeth Arden compact, Cadbury chocolates, *Newsweek* . . ."

Li An elbowed Ellen in the ribs to shut her up. But the officers had heard her mocking voice and shook out the car mats, determined to find something. Then they lost interest and wandered off to the car behind, until one remembered to wave them on.

"Terima kaseh! Thank you!" Li An said loudly, as Ellen put the car into gear and stepped on the accelerator.

"Ah, always so rush!" Grandma Yeh muttered in the backseat, skeins of wool rolling off her lap. Suyin had reminded her that she got carsick each time she tried knitting on a trip, but Grandma Yeh would not leave her work behind.

"Nothing to do in Port Dickson," she declared, "only look at waves and people in swimsuits. Cannot swim, and not good to walk in sun. So I must have my knitting!"

"But sand, sand, sand . . ." Suyin had pointed out.

Li An didn't worry that Grandma Yeh would have a hard time keeping sand out of her woollies. She was meticulous in everything, including keeping wool separate from sand.

In Suyin's world atlas, Port Dickson and Singapore appeared barely a fingertip apart. The Esso road map was more accurate, showing new winding lines—first-class roadways—nailed down to towns: Muar, Ayer Keroh, Melaka.

Finding a toilet for Grandma Yeh was difficult. She was sixty-one, not old by modern standards, but as a recluse who was rarely more than a few steps away from her bathroom, she had grown to be barely toilet trained. The few times she traveled with them, they calculated distances by toilet need and access. They could not stop at the urine-drenched pits in the petrol kiosks. Instead they called ahead for coffee shops in the air-conditioned hotels for Western tourists. Suyin accompanied Grandma to the fresh dry restrooms of the Merlin Hotel, Emperor Heights, and the Riviera, while Li An and Ellen ordered coffee.

It was almost sunset by the time they arrived at the Casuarinas Resort. When Henry had first taken Li An to the Casuarinas, it had only wooden cabins and a small swimming pool. Now the resort had cottages with thick pagoda-style attap roofs, carved lintels, and batik curtains drawn over wall-sized sliding doors; the giant swimming pool shimmered like an upturned blue bowl in which near-naked captive mermaids stroked through the water with languorous arms.

They had two interconnecting bedrooms with twin beds in each. When they discussed who should sleep where, Grandma Yeh would not share with Ellen.

"Aiyah, must we have air-conditioning?" Ellen was looking for the sunblock when the hum started up.

"It's Grandma Yeh. You know she's suspicious of Malaysian air."

"Singapore is better?"

Ellen and Grandma Yeh were friendly only in relation to Suyin. The two cooperated to make sure she never missed having a family.

Li An didn't argue. "Let's get down to the pool."

Suyin carried a hotel beach chair for Grandma Yeh from beside the pool to under the casuarinas. The trees were as tall as Li An remembered, their low sweeping branches green and piney fragrant, and the earth around them covered with brown needles. She had brought thongs to walk under the casuarinas.

"Really, Mom!" Suyin said when Li An hugged the patchy trunk, the rough bark grating against her arms.

Grandma Yeh settled into the chair. Purl and chain, purl and chain. She looked as restful as anyone's grandma.

Li An got into the pool, where Ellen was already doing her laps. Ellen swam vigorously, brown arms like flashing chopsticks devouring the distances—back and forth, back and forth, a frothing beast upsetting the equilibrium of the evening. Everyone else had packed off for tea or to get away from this sudden churning torpedo.

In the shallow end, Li An watched the orange-red sunshine slip over her body like liquid color. Suyin wandered to the beach, an empty jam jar in hand, to pick up the miniature whorled shells for which Port Dickson was noted.

Ellen's white swim cap bobbed beside Li An. "Have you told Suyin anything about Chester?" Her voice burbled with water.

"She knows."

"But have you told her?" She ducked her head into the shimmering pool, then raised it alert for Li An's answer.

"No."

Splashing her arms, she blew a jet of bubbles. "Now, why does that not surprise me?"

"Because you know I am a coward." Li An looked away from the pool. So much glittering light!

"Not true. You can be a tough lady." She stood up beside Li An, the water slapping at her chest. "But you can't be tough with Chester. Or Suyin."

"You know I haven't spent any time with Chester." Li An was anxious about Suyin walking alone on the beach. But she was also anxious about leaving Ellen with the wrong impression.

"It's what you feel that counts, isn't it? I don't know why he should matter to you after all these years. After all, he's married; he seems to have gone on with his life. Now he wants to meet his daughter, but you aren't in the picture, right?"

Water was dripping from her hair under the cap into her eyes. Ellen never swam with goggles.

Li An squinted at the beach, searching for Suyin. At five foot five and a half, she should have been easily visible. Was she wearing the Chinese straw hat Ellen had bought in the Riviera lobby that afternoon? It was the Australians who liked the conical peasant hats, too coolie for Malaysians. Suyin had wanted one immediately. She had no idea of Chinese sentiment.

"If I were you . . ." Ellen said, then paused.

Li An looked for the tall hat. It was moving up the beach

toward the casuarinas. Suyin must have gotten tired of pick-ing shells.

"If I were you, I would talk seriously to Suyin. Tell her about the May thirteenth riots. The trauma. How much you love her and how Chester is simply a minor player in her life. Of course it's good he is finally taking an interest in her existence, but he's leaving after his research is over. You don't want her to be upset when he goes, do you?"

The watery sunshine was beginning to lull Li An. Her body tilted, rocking, half afloat.

No one had ever told her why or how she was conceived, whether in passion or duty. Was it on a daily bed, smelling of bedbugs and long dried sweat? Or was it on the grass in the park, late at night, after the football players, peanut vendors, and other murmuring couples had left, when the heavy trop-ical dew was condensing like a protective mist over their inven-tive bodies? The beginning of her life was wrapped in silence, in sacred ignorance, as was everyone's she knew.

She wanted Suyin to be no different from other children, her birth no freakish accident to be explained. Suyin would arrive at her father's significance by herself, and if she were to be hurt by him, she would make a meaning for herself out of that hurt.

Li An's hair floated around her and air bubbles gurgled in her ears as she lay back. The water felt cool and warm all at the same time.

"If Suyin were my daughter," Ellen said, "I wouldn't be so relaxed. I would jaga, guard her happiness like, like . . ."

Ellen stopped talking.

Li An remembered Suyin in her white snake costume. It had hurt her to watch the play. The parents laughed as Suyin slith-ered on stage just as Mrs. Weng had taught her. "Crawl on your elbows, left, then right, and squirm from your waist down!"

Suyin had practiced on the living room floor. "See, my elbows are dusty, Mom! On the stage more dirtier. So black I must wash in the smelly toilet sink after rehearsal!"

She had quickly discovered that wriggling her body got her attention from the boys. In Singapore Suyin would never be Chinese. She would never be the lead actress, and she would learn to enjoy the eyes of the boys as her body moved, sinu-ously exaggerated.

The sky was burning orange bruised with purple. Li An closed her eyes. Soon it would be sprinkled with spots, a dusk that was never totally black. The surge of the waves whooshed dully yards away, and Suyin's cries seemed like the calls of seabirds above the water's rhythm.

Eleven

If Suyin had stayed with Grandma like she wanted her to, Grandma might have been all right.

"Get another chair and sit with me." Grandma had been arranging the green and yellow balls so the skeins would pull up together smoothly once the needles began jabbing sideways and in and out.

Suyin usually liked sitting with Grandma, who was so peaceful, not like Auntie Ellen or her mother, who could never stop moving. But she never wanted to sit close to Grandma when she was knitting. She was afraid one of the long needles would jab her someday, and Grandma would be so engrossed she wouldn't notice the blood bleeding all over her. Jab, jab.

"No," Suyin said, "I want to look for shells."

Grandma stopped fussing with the wool to stare at her. Suyin knew she was being rude. Boh tuah, boh suay, Auntie Ellen would have said, neither big nor small, not knowing her place, which was the smallest in the family. It seemed funny to hear Auntie Ellen say it now, because Suyin was already taller than any of them.

She should have gone back to sit with Grandma. Grandma was pathetic the way she needed someone around all the time for company. Her mother said Grandma had had a fright a long time ago, before Suyin was born—some hooligans had broken into her house and killed Grandpa Yeh—and she had never been able to be alone since. So Grandma needed a maid when Suyin was in school, otherwise she worried no end.

Suyin was careful not to get out of sight. She stayed right by the water where she knew her grandmother could see her, even if she wasn't looking at Grandma herself. She could not think when Grandma was clicking her needles, clicking like those beetles that her classmates had found in the old library books—click, click, click, click—deathwatch beetles, they were called, the teacher told them.

Suyin kept right on picking up the pink and purple shells. The nicest biggest ones always seemed to have hermit crabs still in them. Click, click, click. She could hear Grandma's needles as she dropped the shells into the jam jar. After a while the clicks were making her crazy. She shook out all the shells and left those with the hermits on the water's edge. She couldn't see bringing dead hermit crabs back to Singapore. She picked through the rest. Most were not pretty—colorless, broken, or so tiny they weren't worth keeping. But the sand felt good on her bottom after those hours in the car keeping her mouth shut about Auntie Ellen's wild driving.

Although she had complained when her mother suggested coming to Port Dickson, she admitted she'd had a good time on the way. So many timber lorries and speeding taxis on the road! "Mad, Mad!" Auntie Ellen kept muttering every few minutes. Grandma fell asleep, so Suyin looked outside and had some very good ideas for her class play.

Mrs. Weng had said that even if she couldn't act she had good dramatic sense and maybe she could try writing a play instead. But there were so many things to include! Costumes, short speech, long speech, characters' names, staging, must have love interest, action cannot be too crazy, exits and entrances. Really, finally, what to say.

First, Suyin had wanted to write about school bullies, to make fun of Ee Chai and Ah Hong, who always had bad things to say about her. But after meeting Chester, she stopped hating them; Chester said they were just narrow-minded mean kids.

"Chester wants me to go to New York," she had told her mother last week. Suyin didn't know what to expect. Recently her mother would snap at nothing; sometimes she was laughing when Suyin would be crying.

Her mother was silent; she just kept stirring the Ovaltine for her.

"Do we have the money?" Suyin added.

Money, her mother had told her, was why they were in Singapore instead of Malaysia. "All I want is a room somewhere," her mom would sing in a horrible flat key, then add, "Singapore is home!"

"Singapore is money and home," Suyin had reminded her the last time she sang it.

But Li An ignored her and continued singing, "Far awaiiii from the cauld night aiiii." Her mother wasn't funny even when she tried.

Suyin didn't believe her mother when she talked about money anymore because she had seen a bank statement for Grandma Yeh that had seven figures in it. That was over a million dollars. Even in Malaysian ringgit, she knew it meant they could live anywhere they wanted to—in Malaysia if her mother wanted it, because she made all the decisions for them.

There must be some other reason why they were in Singapore. It was because they were all women, four women and no man. Grandma had said they lived in Singapore because they were safe there, but Suyin knew her mother and Auntie Ellen were afraid of nothing.

Suyin took the cup of Ovaltine from her mother and asked politely, "If we have the money, can I go?"

"There are savings for your university fees, and Grandma Yeh's medical bills are getting higher . . ."

She didn't want her mother to keep lying, so she turned on the television set, and for once her mother didn't tell her to listen to her instead of watching TV. All mothers control their daughters, Auntie Ellen had told her. But Suyin had three mothers, with Grandma and Auntie Ellen always backing her mother.

On the way to the rides in Sentosa last Saturday, Chester had told her about his wife, Meryl. She was a big shot in New York City. Why was it that American men married big-shot women, but in Singapore men were afraid of women like her mother and Auntie Ellen? New York was much larger than Singapore. It even had a Chinatown, Chester said, although she wouldn't be interested in visiting it. It couldn't be as big as People's Park. But she could stay with Chester and Meryl for two weeks, during the school holidays; Chester said Meryl had invited her, and wanted to show her where she worked and everything. He sounded really excited about her going with him.

Suyin noticed that the sun was sliding like a giant yolk into the sea, and suddenly she realized that she couldn't hear the needles clicking and that she was alone on the beach. All the other children had gone back to the hotel for dinner.

She looked for Grandma. She was still sitting on the beach chair under the shade of the casuarinas, but the shade was now so large that Suyin could see only her dark shape. Perhaps Grandma had fallen asleep, she thought guiltily, knowing how she hated to be alone. Then she remembered that Grandma could never fall asleep when she was alone, and she ran toward the trees, frightened.

It was her mother who told her that Grandma was dead, although she looked like she was simply shutting her eyes from the glare of the sunset. Suyin stayed behind with Auntie Ellen while her mother went with Grandma in the ambulance. It felt like a play, only she had not written it—her mother climbing up the back of the ambulance, and Grandma on the stretcher with a sheet covering her face—she would never write a play like that.

Auntie Ellen had gathered Grandma's balls of wool; they were full of sand and brown casuarina needles. Suyin had dropped her jar and shells on the beach, but it was too dark to look for them, and they had to pack. They were driving home first thing tomorrow, and Grandma's body would follow them in a lorry.

"If I had stayed with her like she wanted me to, Grandma would have been all right," she cried when her mother returned from the hospital.

Her mother had this white color in her face; shock, Auntie Ellen called it, although it seemed like a determined and faraway look. She had to make a police report, call Singapore for funeral arrangements, contact lawyers and Grandma's relatives in Kuala Lumpur, write the obituary to appear in the *Straits Times*, reorganize her staff meeting for Monday. She didn't comfort Suyin.

The doctor had said Grandma had an aneurysm; that was when a blood vessel burst in your brain. Suyin wondered if Grandma's fears had been adding up, bit by bit, in her head, as she herself was wandering on the sand. She had taken her tall funny peasant hat off to bend down and pick up a periwinkle shell. For a moment her grandmother couldn't see her, and the blood must have whooshed crazily in her head. Then Suyin straightened up, and she sighed and began knitting again. But the sun was dropping lower into the water. She looked up and it was both bright and dark. She forgot how tall Suyin had grown since last year, and saw instead that all the children had left the beach. That's when her fears exploded, and the blood burst out of her artery like water from a broken pipe.

Auntie Ellen helped Suyin get ready for bed while her mother made phone calls.

"You'll be getting Grandma Yeh's assets when you become eighteen," Auntie Ellen whispered as she brushed Suyin's hair. "Then you can leave Singapore if you wish."

She was getting drowsy as the brush eased through her hair, up then down, up then down, and she remembered her mother singing her lullabies. She saw Chester like a windup toy flying in the wild tornado to America. He was growing smaller and smaller, and her eyes closed.

Twelve

No one knew how Ellen felt. She also didn't know what she was feeling. She had no answer when her mother, her tough hands tugging at a thorny mimosa, asked, "Aiyah, thirty-six years old already, so old—why you still want to live alone?"

Her mother knew more than she would say. She no longer bought Ellen perfume, silk blouses, anything in the color red. She no longer talked about her friends' eligible sons, about sending Ellen for a holiday to China or Taiwan where Auntie Tai Sim had friends—older bachelors looking for a wife. She did not ask whether Ellen was meeting any nice people— she always meant men—or whether she had seen her old school-mate Gek Neo's newest baby, or heard that another school friend had gotten divorced but managed to remarry.

She continued to look at Ellen inquisitively but with an air of resignation that should have upset Ellen. It no longer upset her because she had become resigned herself. And why should she have been upset at the inevitable?

Ellen thought back on the nuns at the Sacred Heart Convent who had taught her Bible classes, home economics, drawing and painting, music and folk dancing. All were les-sons for a gentle lady who did not have to go out into the world to work for a living. Lessons in home economics from white women who had never kept a house, whose pocket money came directly from God. Or the Pope. As good convent girls, she and her classmates could never make the distinction.

"Those good nuns are my models," she told her mother. "They were contented to be teachers rather than wives, to be mothers to other people's children. As I am now."

At this, her mother blew the air out of her nose loudly. Ellen was ashamed to hear it, because she recognized that snort as hers. She had learned the trick from her mother and could not unlearn it, which embarrassed her, for she had tried very hard—and had mostly succeeded—to leave her mother behind in Malaysia. This trick with air and nose, however, she could not lose.

Her father did not talk to her about her personal life. Women's business, he said. Instead he talked to her mother about it, her mother told her. She did not say, see what you are putting me through! She never accused Ellen of being a bad daughter, an unnatural daughter. They were relieved she had become so stable, staid even, and they were a little afraid of her authoritarian manner, although she told them this was an act she had needed to learn in order to be an effective principal.

But then they had no opportunity to become comfortable with the ways she had changed, for she came home only twice a year, for New Year and Ching Ming. Her mother preferred Ellen's visits on Ching Ming, when she could talk to her more frankly as they cleaned the ancestral grave sites. Every year her mother remembered to bring some old toothbrushes to brush the dirt off the inscriptions on the gravestones, and asked Ellen to pack the cups and dishes for the ancestral offerings. The paint had long disappeared, but the granite had remained uneroded and the Chinese ideograms as incisively carved into the hard stone.

They had been clearing the wild brush from this ground for many years. Ellen remembered being carried as a small child from the narrow road where they parked their car and across overgrown and uneven trails to this family plot; here she was allowed to burn the joss and gold paper as her part of the annual adventure.

Now she started the joss as quickly as she could to keep the mosquitoes away. She was afraid of getting dengue fever and dying, but her mother thought only of the dead.

Yet her mother never talked about them. Their names were inscribed in Chinese characters Ellen couldn't read, and she had never heard their names announced. As a child she had been curious about the real persons buried under her feet, but it had seemed a sacrilege to ask for human names when Mother was worshiping ancestral ghosts. Now she was no longer curious. She was satisfied to know them only as past relations. Grandfather, Grandmother, Great Grandmother, Great Grandfather.

Her mother seemed happy here. As she busied herself grooming the mounds and stones, she appeared to be simply doing the kind of housework that occupied her daily. Energetically she cleared the debris, pulled at the tough tangled roots of the lallang, and clipped the thorny mimosas down to the ground. Next year the weeds would all come back, tall and thick, hiding the stones so they would have to hunt for their plot again.

Ellen worried that one day Mother would not be able to locate the graves. What would she do then? It would be like a disaster movie, except that instead of an approaching meteor or wall of fire, it would be the collapse of Mother's entire world. No more ancestors, no spirits, no family ties. No past, no future.

Her mother talked to her constantly as they arranged the gold paper squares before setting them alight. By now Ellen had learned to fan out the papers so that the gold showed face up. Stacking them in pyramids ensured a good flow of oxygen, and the papers flamed up steadily and rapidly. When the pyramids were constructed right, she didn't have to poke at the semi-charred remains to try to get them to burn down evenly. Mother got nervous if the papers did not all crisp down to a straightforward heap of ash. She worried that the gold they were airmailing to the spirit house of the ancestors would be insufficient for the rest of the year. Grandmother, Grandfather, all their dead, would be poor and hungry, and for the living members of the family, the year ahead would be equally poor and miserable.

Suyin had asked Ellen about the Hungry Ghosts Festival and wanted to know why she did not have her own hungry ghosts to feed. What could she tell her? Ellen's mother was an anachronism. When was hunger ever appeased by smoke? She couldn't tell Suyin about her mother's beliefs, the annual family observations with Hennessy brandy and boiled chicken set out under an open afternoon sky in a treeless land pockmarked by hundreds of standing stones. Suyin deserved a better education.

Ellen told her mother that she treated Suyin as her niece. She brought home photographs of her, and her mother had an album filled with them: Suyin as a baby in Grandma Yeh's arms, wearing diapers and sitting on a rocking horse, dressed in her first school uniform.

In the past few years, Mother had stopped pasting them neatly onto glued squares on the pages. Instead, she stuffed the photographs haphazardly in between the pages, so they fell out when Ellen picked up the album and she had to cram them back in. She had found the album on the bottom shelf of the television table, covered with a collection of months-old Sunday newspaper television schedules. Her mother, of course, did not view Suyin as any relation; Suyin, she had once said accusingly, was merely Ellen's excuse for not marrying and not having her own children.

Her mother was wrong there. Suyin was Ellen's responsibility. Secretly—or perhaps not so secretly—Ellen believed that she was her responsibility more than Li An's. Li An had her special claim as Suyin's mother. But it was Ellen who had taken the infant home from the hospital and given her her first bath.

An aunt had many responsibilities and no claims. Ellen didn't resent her position; in fact, she was grateful to Li An for handing her this responsibility—yes, this excuse—for having the life she did. Mother told her she was wasting her life, but she was living it the way she wanted to. And taking care of Suyin filled up the little of her that was left after her work, her teachers, her students and their parents, the meetings, and the papers to be read and signed. Her mother would never believe that she was contented, just as Ellen could not understand how her mother could be contented with her life, keeping house for her father. Ellen's work was her house, and there were no spirits to appease in it except hers.

She looked around at the other grave sites. Each year there were fewer cars parked by the road, fewer people wandering on the trails carrying their baskets of paper and food offerings. Father had walked some plots away, tidying the ground above the Chan family, all five of them killed in a car accident when Ellen was ten. Father continued to write to their closest relations, now in Canada. "Usually it is bad luck to disturb the graves of those who are not your family," Mother had told her. "But Ah Pah is taking the place of the next oldest brother. Better to have a substitute than to have nobody."

Did Mother ever wonder if Ellen would return home to groom her grave, to stay and talk and eat with her once she was gone?

"The Temple Association is hiring a caretaker. He will cut the lallang, also make offerings for the families who cannot come back on Ching Ming," Mother announced as she tugged at a stubborn root. "Aiyah! So many chidren now go far away and never return. Your brothers all in America and UK. Lucky for us, you only in Singapore!"

She looked at Ellen inquiringly, but Ellen refused to respond.

"A proud old maid! Sombong!" her husband said reprovingly each time after Ellen had returned to Singapore, but Mother was more loyal to her daughter.

Ellen tried to ignore the gray smoke that was now floating all around her. Her eyes stung and her lungs burned with the hot air.

She could not talk to her parents, but it seemed as if she could not stop talking to Li An, even when she knew Li An was tired of her nagging. Li An was the sister she'd never had. She had been told that sisters were often different from each other. Sometimes Ellen was impatient with Li An for being a dreamer still, even after going through the school of hard knocks. When Chester suddenly turned up, she was afraid Li An would fall apart again. She was relieved that Li An would only talk to him over the telephone, and even then she wanted Ellen to be in the room during the call. Ellen knew cowardice and dreaming were not very different from each other, but she preferred Li An as a coward. She presented fewer problems then.

Grandma Yeh had worried that Ellen would want to share the flat with them. What a thought! Sharing a few hours each day with them, sharing the responsibility of Suyin, was enough. Gina had been another story. But she didn't have to try to understand Gina anymore, or herself with Gina. It was all past, and the present was plenty to keep her occupied.

Standing up from her kneeling position, she watched as the paper pyramids burned lower and lower. Soon they could pour the brandy onto the earth, and pack away the cups and dishes, and she could drive away again, alone, leaving memory and guilt behind her.

Thirteen

Chester hadn't imagined Li An as anything but the woman she had been in Kuala Lumpur. He had successfully avoided thinking about her even when he was in Bali, just a few hundred miles from Kuala Lumpur. The slender brown women around Denpasar had reminded him of her, but he had deliberately recalled sexy Meryl instead, rereading her letters that arrived regularly, the Barnard logo on the envelopes like a seal of approval from America. He could never have imagined Li An as this cool and distant figure, staying always behind her egg-shaped blond desk, saying no, no, and no.

Still, he argued, she could have let him say good-bye to Suyin. What was the harm in that?

For a brief while, it had seemed to him that Li An approved of him. Well, if not of him, then of Suyin getting to know him. She had not objected when he asked to take Suyin to the zoo for that second Saturday. They had discussed the excursion over the telephone. He could hear Ellen's deeper voice as well over the telephone line, a contrapuntal chord in the background.

"Why don't you come also?" he had offered. "That is, if you have the time?" He did not want her to be indifferent to him. This successful Li An with her twenty-fifth-story office was, after all, Suyin's mother. He wanted to get to know her all over again, a new woman in the fresh new Asian city, who was too busy to meet him, too successful to remember their friendship.

Yet there was the daughter between them, an astonishingly full human, with her unexpected inflections of voice and body, her surprising, delightful, separate existence—yet still a link, breathtakingly perfect by simply being no longer missing. Suyin could lead him to the Li An he had known, resident somewhere still in Li An's self-containment. He was confident this Li An would talk to him, if only he could arrange for them to meet.

But she had had company clients to meet for lunch that Saturday, and it was Ellen who walked Suyin down to the condominium lobby when Chester rang the bell.

He had recognized Ellen from the first awkward moment in the crowded ice-cold cafe. Years older, she was still attractive, but it was clear she would never marry. Her practical hair, too short to catch a man's eye, too long to be chic, declared this. She wore brown plaid pants, a tailored shirt stylishly tucked in, leather flats. She could almost pass for an American female executive, or one of the women teachers who filled the offices at Seven Graces College, role models for those students who refused to hang on the arms of the men who wandered through the halls on weekends looking for pickups. Independent, assertive, perky. Almost, he thought with a pang, like Meryl. Except Meryl cared about clothes and men, perhaps even for more men than just him.

He had studied Ellen while Suyin was slowly slurping her ice cream. What was the difference between a woman who married and one who never would? Was there a briskness about Ellen that suggested she was not to be detained by the peculiar anxiety of women waiting for male attention? An absence of chemically transmitted sexual ions normally induced by male presence or even the fantasy of male presence?

Ellen was not feigning an unconsciousness of his body. She was fully reactive to his attempts to draw Suyin into his humor. She was vigilant, but she was invulnerable.

He had thought she preferred Li An to him when they had been together in Kuala Lumpur. Saturday, as she stood in the lobby, her straight-backed image multiply reflecting on the polished terrazzo floors and pillars, he knew she did.

"Bring her back before six. She has study time then."
The voice was as unyielding as her back.

Chester did not wonder that Ellen had taken on the
role of the other parent with Suyin, but he wondered if it
was something Suyin or Li An found remarkable. He knew
he had no right to object to her tone, so resentful of him,
but he did, he did! He disliked her jealous protectiveness,
her speaking for Suyin, her answering for Li An sponta-
neously and uncritically, as if she possessed them, were
them. It wasn't natural.

He was as brusque with her, taking Suyin by the arm
immediately, hurrying her away from the lobby as if from a
boarding school, toward freedom, without saying good-bye.

When they arrived at the zoo, Suyin, fresh in red-checked
Bermuda shorts and tee, he sweating despite the white polo
shirt that the salesman at Robinsons had guaranteed would
keep him cool, it was the golden-haired langur monkeys
that fascinated her most. Chattering excitedly, the mothers
crouched high up on the artificial branches, little furry
infant bundles carelessly carried in their arms. Suyin watched
for a long time as the babies were snatched from one langur
to another. A female with hanging dugs groomed a silent infant
close to the wire mesh, while another paced nearby waiting
for the baby to be surrendered. To the back, young half-
grown langurs raced up and down the molded plastic trunks,
which had been painted to match the giant rain trees growing beside their enclosures.

Chester was content to stand in the afternoon sun even as
his nose, sticking out from under the shade of his safari hat,
burned and blistered. Suyin drew close to the green mesh that
formed the enclosure, her eyes on the infant. Its eyes were shut,
even as the female's fingers tugged through its fur.

"What is she eating?"

He examined the animal closely for the first time. "Probably
some nit on the fur. Free protein."

She didn't make a face as he had expected. "Is she the
grandmother?"

"Do you think monkeys recognize their relatives?"

"Why not? Don't they?"

He was silent. Primatology was not a subject he had paid attention to.

"Don't they?" she persisted. "After all, they are also our relatives. Look, her hands are just like mine!"

"Which? The baby's or the grandmother's?"

"See, you think she is the grandmother also. Grandma, Grandma!" She waved her fingers, but the animal had already raced up a pole screeching, the infant langur dangling on one arm, as the other monkey approached the mesh wire.

"And that must be the mother," he said teasingly. "She's looking quite upset that she has missed out on the supper of free nits. Maybe she wants some from you."

She gave him a superior look and moved closer to the mesh.

"Don't!" He pushed her away even as the langur lunged forward toward her outstretched fingers. "Let's move away from here."

Her lips pursed, she hesitated, glanced back at the langur, which was even now chattering rapidly as it clambered over the mesh. Its nearness must have persuaded her, and she moved toward the reptile house, Chester firmly gripping her elbow, without a complaint.

He was thinking of that moment of hesitation when he called Meryl to tell her Suyin's visit was off. "Her grandmother died last week, and her mother thinks she should stay in Singapore for the six-month mourning period."

"But it's just as well that she can't make it to New York, isn't it? It would have been a bit of a mess, don't you think? How would we have kept her occupied? How would you explain her to your parents?"

Meryl's voice sounded eager with relief over the telephone line. She had surprised him when he had first called to tell her about Suyin. There had been the moment of silence he had prepared himself for. It seemed like the air between the black receiver and his ear had turned leaden, a dead weight through which no voice came, only a rattling whistle that communicated how many thousands of miles away Meryl was, breathing long-distance into the voiceless telephone. "Meryl?" he repeated, unable to add more.

But Meryl had been conciliatory. When her voice came back, it quivered. "Is that why you were quarreling with me? That you had this black mark in your past you couldn't tell me about?"

No, he wanted to say, it isn't as simple as "a black mark." Instead he said, "She looks a little like me. Tall, green eyes. I'd like you to meet her."

"And her mother?"

"Lee Ann?" He could not tell what Meryl was asking.

"I mean, what about her?"

"Oh, well, she's just barely polite to me, I guess. We've met only once. She's a successful businesswoman, nothing like the student I knew. I told you it was an accident, a night when there was a military curfew and riots and hundreds killed. It wasn't like we were having an affair."

Her breath whistled in his ear.

"Then I met you, and it was like the past wasn't important. I never thought much about whether the baby was mine. I figured she didn't write, so that one night couldn't have meant that much to her either."

"Poor Chester," Meryl's voice had turned soft and forgiving. "You should have told me about her. It was way before you met me. I would have married you anyway!"

He had felt a profound gratitude for her rationality. Over a series of calls he discussed bringing Suyin home to meet her. Yes, she agreed, of course she would be willing to meet her, even have her stay with them for some time this summer. But, she warned, it would have to be for a short visit. She worried over what kind of relationship she could have with Suyin. An adoptive mother? No, they were not considering adopting her. She supposed it would have to be more like a stepmother, except Chester hadn't married the mother, so that wasn't right either. "A foster mother," she finally decided.

"She could call you Auntie," Chester said.

"What do you mean, Auntie? That's what Singapore children call women in their extended families? Am I supposed to be some kind of extended family for her?"

It was difficult for Meryl to imagine what she was going to do with Suyin for the two weeks in New York. She expected Chester would have to schedule activities for them.

"What does she call you?" Meryl wanted to know. "Chester? She doesn't know you're her father? You don't know if she knows?" She thought it all sounded murkier and murkier. Her mother would call it malarkey. But yes, of course, she understood he would have to do the right thing, if Suyin was his child.

Chester let the *if* blur in the static, tangled in the thousands of miles of phone lines between Singapore and New York. It was too difficult to explain the situation over the phone, he decided. He stroked his wet palms on his pants and listened.

She wished Chester had told her what had been bothering him all that time before he had taken off for Singapore so precipitously. His news was painful, but together they would be able to come up with some solution to the problem.

Listening, Chester knew he would have to spend even more time talking to Meryl about Suyin. He knew Meryl would like her. She could make Suyin her project, teach her to be as independent and strong as herself. She could take her to her Parks office some days and show her what she did. Women liked doing that kind of thing for younger girls.

As for him, he had plans to take Suyin to the Museum of Natural History, the Metropolitan Museum of Art, and the carousel in Central Park. He would introduce her to real bagels, pastrami on rye at Wolf's. She was going to try all the things he loved as a child—Carvel and Dairy Queen ice cream, fresh corn, ball games, the Knicks. He was going to take her to his office at Seven Graces College and introduce her to the secretary, Mrs. Offen, as his daughter. He had thought about how he would laugh at Mrs. Offen's expression. He had imagined the startled look in her slightly bulging eyes, her dignified air damaged by avid curiosity.

The oddest thing about the time he had spent with Suyin was how natural it all felt, even as everything about her was new to him. He found himself watching her, watching her so intently that he often forgot to watch himself watching her. That consciousness of the voyeur, the science of eavesdropping and snooping that he had picked up in Bali and tried to teach his students, disappeared when he was with her. He was only conscious then of wanting her to be happy for the moment: the moment of peeling open the wrapping off the ice cream cone, extravagantly named Treasure Mountain; of hugging the largest toy koala bear in the store, now unexpectedly hers. He was rewarded by her giggles at these moments—a series of them, arriving with the largest popcorn buckets in the cinema, and brought on predictably by the jokes and joke books he lavished on her each time they met.

Moments, moments: they were never enough. He wondered if there was something sick about the way his chest filled with warmth when she ran down the stairs to meet him on Saturday mornings. But it was tender desire that filled him, to surround her with everything that was good and generous, to have her grow up, as his sister would have done had she lived, as he had, a Brookfield. He had never understood this hopefulness of the flesh before. It made him a better person, he thought, and Meryl would not, could not refuse Suyin when she saw how much he hoped for her.

"I know her grandmother's death has been traumatic for all of them," he had said to Abdullah at their last meeting, "and that may be a reason for stopping her visit to New York. But I cannot understand why Lee Ann would not let me have a proper good-bye." They were waiting for Samad at the Cairns City Club, where Abdullah's membership permitted them ice-cold drafts of microbrew beer.

Abdullah signed for them as "tonics." "Cannot tell, lah, Chester, what kind of information one day your enemies will use against you," he smiled as he signed the bill. "It is the same with your life. What you do one day, like this simple thing, signing a chit, years later someone will put in front of your nose and make you eat. Only then you find out the power of your act. You act without thinking, and that is when it has the most power to destroy you."

"Too late to tell me that now," Chester muttered. Then he repeated more loudly, "Why wouldn't Lee Ann let me say good-bye properly? She could be present at the meeting. That's not too much to ask."

"Of course you are lying," Abdullah said pleasantly. "You are asking Li An to give her daughter to you."

Chester swallowed his beer silently. It helped check his rising anger.

"That's the way with colonialists," Abdullah continued cheerfully. "You white people, Americans, believe you can claim all kinds of things that don't belong to you. Land, plants, tin mines, even other people. You want to possess, but you do not care for what you take. Perhaps in your own country you love and care for what you have, but sometimes I think not even in your own country."

"All right, I admit we white colonialists have a rotten history. But that doesn't help me say good-bye to Suyin. I'm not sure what Lee Ann is afraid of in a simple meeting with me."

"Chester, Chester," Abdullah said soothingly. "See, you cannot even say Li An's name correctly. You have made it an American name. That is what she is afraid of, that you will make her daughter an American daughter."

Ignoring Abdullah's comments, Chester talked to Samad determinedly about his English language project. Samad was driving him to Changi Airport in three days for his flight, via San Francisco, to New York, and he still had not packed the materials he had gathered from the university language archives. He needed to find appropriate packing cases for his files.

But Abdullah stubbornly kept raising Li An's name. "Do you remember, Chester, that you laughed at Li An because she believed in the importance of English literature? Now you are studying the place of English communication in Singapore's social development. Li An was right. The national language is the soul of our country, but English is the language of money for Malaysia and Singapore. The goal of Malaysia is to make money. So English is also the destiny of our country."

Aggrieved, Chester wondered if he had been wrong to consider Abdullah and Samad as his past. He had seen himself, although a separate character for the past dozen years, as one of their company. But Li An had remained in their circle while he had merely disappeared. Now, they remembered him through her aura, and he had no history for them in Malaysia except as it had been intertwined in her life. He suspected they were no longer interested in him except as he was interested in her. The rest of the evening was a dismal pantomime of listening to their business and political exchanges. No more a cultural debate as he had remembered it, their talk was a matter of stocks and company start-ups, honors received at the last annual royal investiture. Their wives and children, he noticed, were never a topic to be shared with him.

In three days he was getting on the plane alone to fly to New York. But he was already planning his return to Singapore. He would write up his research, get it published in the issue of the *Journal of Anthropology of Communications* that Kingston was editing, get another grant and fly back to Singapore, this time with Meryl. He would come for a longer stay—six months. This time he would write to Li An to prepare her.

He listened to Abdullah and Samad talking about language and money and politics, and he knew that Li An would eventually let Suyin come to New York. It was not so much to ask, and he could wait.

Fourteen

Grandma Yeh had given Suyin her jade pendant; she called it a special amulet, a talisman. Suyin liked its pear shape. Grandma said it was a peach—the peach of longevity that grew in the Garden of Immortality and that Kuan Yin hid from the other gods to share with humans because she pitied them.

Humans, Grandma said, were much to be pitied. The old statues in the Har Paw Villa showed our terrible sufferings: incurable sores, toothaches, starvation, sword and fire, wild animals and wild men, amputations, madness, demons. She said there were more than a thousand thousand ways to suffer, but even then humans suffered most from a shortened life. Until Kuan Yin stole the peaches of long life for them.

She was sorry she had laughed at Grandma's story. Every girl in school had one of these jade pendants, and everyone seemed to have had her mom or grandma tell her a grotty story to go with the jade.

Her mother had made her apologize to Grandma, but Grandma wasn't mad at her. In fact, she said she was smarter than all the other girls because she knew it was only a made-up story. It was really Jesus Christ who helped them. Only, Grandma used words like *salvation* and *heavenly father*. This time Suyin didn't laugh because her mom was keeping her eye on her.

Suyin wondered if Grandma was with Jesus in Heaven or with Kuan Yin in the Garden of Immortality. She didn't like to think of her as dead. Maybe that was why Grandma had given her the pendant—as a talisman for remembering.

Every time Suyin saw the jades hanging from the necks of all the Cho Kang girls she thought of them as millstones of memory. They looked so light—green and cream and white and translucent, curved and delicate. But her mom said that true jade was one of the hardest stones and could be cut only by another jade.

Jade reminded her of her mom and Auntie Ellen; they looked like small skinny women, but she knew how tough they were. Wearing Grandma's amulet was like wearing her memory and the memory of her mother and Auntie Ellen; it was like wearing the memory of women.

She almost wished Grandma hadn't given her the pendant. Now she was like all the girls in Cho Kang, and maybe like all the Chinese girls in Singapore. Sometimes she thought memory was only another grotty story, like Grandma's story about Kuan Yin and the peach of longevity.

Her mother and Auntie Ellen never forgot she was just a child. Or perhaps they forgot that she was still a child, because they were always telling her what to do, what to expect, what to be prepared for, how she had to be strong.

She just wanted to be a kid; she wanted to feel safe. She wanted to think life was easy, that she could be happy and have fun. Not all this about how life was work and studies and passing exams and struggle and fear and making the right choices because one wrong choice could mean disaster. Maybe all that was true, but she didn't want to hear it every day.

Chester was the only one who never talked that way to her. Sometimes Suyin thought he was a Martian because he talked all the time about having fun. What fun she'd have learning the subway system in New York, how college was so much fun because she'd get to choose the college that was right for her and she could take whatever courses she liked, that she'd have fun trying out all the thirty-one flavors at the Baskin-Robbins near his home because Baskin-Robbins had only twelve flavors in Singapore.

Maybe that's what fathers did—have fun. But somehow Suyin didn't think that was so in Singapore. Even at school games she could see how glum they were. They smiled only when their children won. And they never smiled at her, because she wasn't Chinese.

Mom didn't want to talk to her about what was really important. Like why she knew Chester was her father and why no one said he was. And like why Henry, whom she had met for the first time at the church service for Grandma, now said he was her father. Suyin wished Grandma was still with them and could explain it to her, even if she told another unbelievable story.

It wasn't that Suyin disliked Henry. Grandma had talked often enough and always nicely of him. Only Suyin didn't have to be smart to know there was something confusing about having no father all her life, and then suddenly having two.

When she asked her mother who Henry really was, she said he was like her adopted father. But Suyin wanted to know adopted by whom, because she didn't adopt him.

Think of him as your protective male figure, Auntie Ellen said. In the afternoons, after he brought her home from school, he had begun explaining complicated ideas to Suyin, like wills, shares, dividends, commissions, interest rates, rentals, credit, and debt. He said that Grandma had left everything to her, so that he and she were now business partners, and her mom said she could trust Henry implicitly.

She liked the sound of the word *implicitly*. She told Auntie Ellen that that was what Henry was, not a protective male figure but an implicit figure.

I trust you implicitly, she said to him when he came the second time with all kinds of papers for her to read, and she could see he was shocked. He turned white like he was in pain, and then he took her hand and held it to his cheek!

He said he'd come to see her at least once a month when he was meeting his accountant or lawyer in Singapore. Then he'd pick her up at Cho Kang after school and take her home and spend some time helping her with her homework—especially algebra!—until her mother left her office. Suyin didn't think he liked her mother, but he said he loved Suyin and he wished he had met her while her grandmother was still alive.

Her mother had been mysterious about Chester, but Suyin thought she was even more mysterious about Henry. This was because she had admitted that Henry was Suyin's father, but still she said nothing to Suyin about the matter. That first week after Grandma's funeral, she had signed a school form giving Henry permission to pick Suyin up after class. She had written "Father" on the form, in the line that asked "RELATION," and Henry had come by inexplicably every afternoon to drive her home, just like some of the other students' fathers.

He didn't take her to movies or toy stores like Chester did. Instead he drove her straight home and sat with her until she completed her homework. Then he took out piles of papers and read her passages, stopping to explain to her what they meant. There were company papers with heavy embossed signatures, some with ribbons attached. There were thick glossy brochures that showed buildings and offices. She was too young to sign anything on her own, he said; he was the executor of Grandma's estate and could sign any document for her, but he wanted her, Suyin, Grandma's beloved granddaughter, his own daughter, to understand what he was doing and why. He wanted her to co-sign whenever possible.

Suyin blinked at his explanation. "Executor" sounded unpleasant. "Is that like being an executioner?" she asked, and he laughed nervously.

"No, no. That's like being a caretaker. Someone to keep an eye on the estate so when you grow up you will be even more well-off than you are now."

"Estate? Is that like having a block of HDB flats?"

"No, not like it. A lot of it is invisible. You have shares in many companies and businesses. Your grandfather left a lot of his shares to your grandmother. She never sold them, and they have grown larger and larger in value. She made me her business partner and now her will has made you my partner." He smiled. He seemed to enjoy teaching her about his work.

Henry left promptly at five. "It's the traffic jams," he said, looking at his watch. "I want to avoid being stuck on the highway to my brother's house."

Suyin lifted her head from the mug of Ovaltine she was drinking. Was Henry's brother her uncle? Grandma's death seemed to have opened the door to a weird parallel world in which all kinds of relatives were possible. Chap cheng kwei, chap cheng kwei—mixed breed devil, she had finally learned, was what her classmates had called her from her first day in school. Perhaps that was what it was to be a chap cheng kwei, to have all these strange relatives whose existence she had never known, living in Kuala Lumpur, in Singapore, in America. Here, there, and everywhere.

Mom never questioned her about her afternoons with Henry when she came home from work. Just like Henry did not talk about Mom or Auntie Ellen or Chester.

Perhaps, Suyin thought, he did not know about Chester or Auntie Ellen either. For the week, Auntie Ellen had absented herself in the afternoons and came by only in the evenings to chat with Mom over tea. And Chester just as mysteriously seemed to have disappeared from Singapore. No one raised his name; there was no phone call to take her out on a Saturday, although he had promised a concert when she returned from Port Dickson.

Mom had framed some of Grandma's photographs after the funeral, and the new pewter frames seemed to glow in the corners of the living room. Suyin knew she owed Henry to Grandma. He was Grandma's last present to her. No one called her "Sin-ner" again in Cho Kang, not after they had seen him come for her. "My father's waiting," she told Mrs. Cheung loudly when she wanted Suyin to stay behind to help wash down the white-board, and everyone was so surprised they watched her walk out without the usual protests whenever someone tried that trick.

Henry was small and balding; his hair was thinning at the top and fine wisps traced along his forehead, nothing like her own sharp V cracking her face into halves. He kissed her on the cheek every evening when he said good-bye—a formal and shy kiss, a new daddy; and on the last day, a Friday, he brought chocolates, a big two-pound box, wrapped in red cellophane and tied with gold and green ribbons, like the boxes of chocolates that decorated the Orchard Road store windows at Christmas.

255

"Oh, oh, I can't open it until I have Mom's permission!" she said, her grin a mix of anxiety and delight.

"I give you permission." His smile was also anxious, but it grew wider as he tore the ribbons and cellophane packing apart. Li An walked in on this scene of gluttony, the two of them crunching their third chocolate truffle over some property deeds.

No one had remembered to warn Henry that Fridays were Li An's short days. *BioSyn-Sign* having gone to press on Friday morning, Fridays meant an easy day of clearing her desk of old materials and the beginning of the migraines that would overtake her by the weekend. Home by three, she spent Fridays tidying Suyin's laundry and room. She set aside these afternoons to be mother, afternoons when pleasurable rituals slowed her pulse and the pressure in her skull gave way, almost with an audible twang of a broken bowstring, and her yawns grew wider and wider as the dull ache took on its penetrative edge.

Today her rush through the front door was checked by the sight of Henry, his mouth open for the truffle, looking toward the door, and turning pale, his pallor as distinct as her own intake of breath.

"He gave me permission, Mom!" Suyin's mouth, full of chocolate, chewed desperately even as she pushed the box further away.

"No, never mind me. It's fine. It's a treat. What a large box! Did you say thank you?"

Guiltily, they all stared at the box, still brimming with shiny squares and wedges.

"No, finish your work with Suyin," Li An protested when Henry got up to leave. "I'm going into the kitchen to make myself a cup of tea."

But he was stiff, refused the tea she offered, would not eat any more chocolates, even after Li An disappeared into the kitchen. His daddyness vanished. The deeds were perused like so many supermarket flyers. "I'll be back next month," he kissed Suyin on her sad cheek. "I'll call your mother before coming to see you. And I'll have more papers for you to co-sign."

He had already told her he had to return to Kuala Lumpur on Saturday. Prepared for his leaving, still Suyin wondered at the pain he left with her. It had taken only a few afternoons for her to believe in him. Knowing now that he would always avoid Mom made no difference. Her belief was as certain as finding a new planet. He had promised he would return, every month, like a planet coming back into her orbit. She simply had to have her telescope out and ready.

Chester, however, had left without saying good-bye. Her mother told her this one Sunday night when she was brushing her hair. It was still strange not to have Grandma at home, and her mother was brushing her hair slowly as if to make up for the time Grandma would have spent with her.

She thought Suyin couldn't understand important stuff, but Suyin knew how her mother's mind worked. Her mother believed that if she told her difficult things when she was sleepy, it would be easier for her to accept them. Her mother thought her brain stopped when she fell asleep.

"He may be back on another research project," she said, which Suyin translated into the warning that she might never see him again.

"I don't care." Her eyes were closing but at the same time they felt like they were swelling with tears. She knew her mother was wrong. Chester was coming back to Singapore. But she would no longer be eleven years old when he returned. She might not even be who she was, now that Henry had taken Grandma's place, now that no one in Cho Kang called her "Sin-ner."

"Suyin Yeh." She turned the sound of her name in her mouth soundlessly. It slipped easily, like a cream-centered chocolate, down her throat, spreading a rich sensation of warmth in her chest.

Auntie Ellen had said she could decide whatever she wanted to once she was eighteen. That was less than seven years away. Her mother couldn't be brushing her hair all her life.

When she turned eighteen, Henry would still be her father, and then she could find out about her other father. Soon, Mom and Auntie Ellen told her, very soon, she would be eighteen and a woman like them.

Fifteen

In the last two weeks, everything had been excruciatingly important, every detail potentially dangerous and to be overcome by her most focused attention. Li An could not spare the time for even a cursory consideration of Chester's request for another meeting with Suyin—Suyin who now refused to sleep without her mother present in the house. Suyin, Li An was determined, would be saved the pain of another departure.

She had asked Chester not to attend the funeral. After all, she explained to Ellen, who had not asked, he had never met Grandma Yeh. In all the time she had lived with them, Grandma Yeh had never asked who Suyin's father might be. Li An sometimes had the queer feeling that Grandma Yeh fully believed Henry was Suyin's father. She seemed to have been unaware of any oddness in the circumstances of Suyin's birth, as if it had been only natural for Suyin to look as she did, un-Chinese and mixed. Chester had no place in Grandma's imagination, and she would not have welcomed him at her funeral.

Through her grief—the shocking acknowledgment late at night of all that Grandma Yeh had meant for her and Suyin, and the almost paralytic selfish fear at the loss of her constancy in their lives—Li An knew she had to continue as the editor in chief of *BioSyn-Sign*. Although the obituary informed the world about her loss, she could not carry the news of it with her into the office, where any slip in the shares would have been interpreted as a contamination.

Only a generation ago, a death in the family would have meant that she would not be welcomed back into the office for at least a month, until rituals and time had purified the taint of ill fortune. She would not have been permitted to step over the threshold of another house, for death was a contagion, a stagnant water that the survivors carried like dumb vessels and that they could spill onto the healthy and fortunate.

She could almost believe this, for tears, raw and plenty, lay close near her eyes. But she remained dry-eyed in the office. The newsletter depended on her editorial eye, and like her copyediting pencils, she kept herself sharpened to a point at work. *BioSyn-Sign* appeared when it was supposed to, mailed out on the usual date, delivered to the CEO's desk exactly on the usual morning and at the usual time. The major news was that the threatened recession in Germany had grown less threatening at the second quarter report of a steady growth in East-West trade. But a more major news item was quietly reported in the monthly snippets: Singapore and Israel had signed an understanding of mutual cooperation in the development of military aircraft.

This time Ang Swee called to congratulate her on the tweaking of the company logo, a matter of some tense negotiation with the board of directors, who agreed it was time for something new but who did not want to unsettle anything when the company was doing well. He had warned her casually during a brief update, "Change and security, very tricky to have both at the same time, eh, Li An? But that is the Asian way, you know. Not like Americans. Americans never fear because they have so much land, so many opportunities, they can throw away and still be safe. For Americans, change is no change because so little risk. America is the lucky country. But we are not so lucky. We must always be sure that our change means more security. We never change for change sake but for added security, added advantage."

She knew he was telling her to be careful about what kind of new logo she would produce for the newsletter. Transforming the two Ss to suggest the shapes of the dragon and the phoenix was a simple matter of computer graphics, and a reader had to be observant to make out their shapes.

But once the eye saw the sinuous figures it could never not see them again. The logo suggested something European and medieval, yet it was clearly Chinese in origin, and Li An knew she could count on every board member to understand the dragon's harmonic meanings and the phoenix's regenerative energies, from the failure of human aspiration to its destined reincarnation as something more wonderful. Like Singapore itself, self-sprung from the ashes of a shabby colonized city, looked down upon even by the British who claimed to govern it, and then again from its ashes as a partner in the nation-state called Malaysia. Every stockholder would understand the symbols and would approve of the history they were retelling.

Her private story, of course, was not for telling in the company, and she did not request a personal day off, although she knew Ang Swee would not have questioned it.

If she could only be as clear-eyed about her private life, Li An thought impatiently, as she debated how she was to call Henry about the funeral arrangements. She had no idea how much contact Henry had had with Grandma Yeh. For the first few months after their move to Singapore, Henry had written to Grandma Yeh to transfer deeds and accounts to her and to send boxes of curtains and bedding and dishes. The Kuan Yin statue with the red flowing jade hair came in one such box addressed to Grandma Yeh, but he had never sent anything to Li An. It was always the lawyers who wrote to her and whose offers of a settlement she had refused.

Never, she had said to Ellen, who had yelled at her for her stubbornness, her pride and stupidity. Never. She would never take any money from Henry. She had felt his abandonment as a betrayal, refused to understand how he could have held Chester's role in fathering the baby as cause for rejecting Suyin. Yes, she agreed, she was being unreasonable; Henry was only like other men, but Suyin with her green eyes and red-tinted hair, in all her baby beauty, could be any man's daughter. She would have become Henry's lovely daughter had he been willing to love her.

Would she inform Henry about the funeral? Was he expected to attend as Grandma Yeh's stepson, although an estranged stepson? In the end, she let the lawyers call, and to her surprise he came for the funeral.

He did not come, however, to the night watch at the Singapore Casket Company. She and Ellen kept vigil on their foldout chairs. Companionably, they counted the bouquets of orchids that came from the expense accounts of Bio-Syn's board members and from the directors and editors of rival companies, and watched the air-conditioning stir the white-and-yellow plumeria and fern wreaths sent by Ellen's school-teachers. Grandma Yeh was stiff and slightly yellow. Only her face, fair and reserved, and her prim folded hands were exposed where she lay on the cream-colored satin coffin bed. Still unbelieving, Suyin had not nagged to sit with them but remained in the flat with the maid.

On Sunday, after the coffin had been sent to the crematorium, they went to the small Anglo-Chinese church to which Grandma Yeh had mailed her Christmas donations. No one in the congregation had ever actually met Grandma Yeh, but the pastor was familiar with her large handwriting and signature on the cards that accompanied her generous annual checks, and had agreed to hold a special ceremony of remembrance for her after the Sunday prayers.

Too early, they waited as the congregation filed past the pastor, who was shaking hands, patting backs, murmuring Sabbath greetings. Soon the pews were empty. Then, as if a bell had rung, the teachers from Ellen's school arrived, and Li An's three office staff members, and Ang Swee, and someone from the printing company, and then Henry, alone.

Li An held on to Suyin's hand as if to a life buoy. Henry sat alone and stood up alone to say the Lord's Prayer. She could hear his voice, low and confident. He had had a daughter, she knew, just a few months ago—his first child. She saw him across the distance of the aisle and thought how she had never understood him because she had never loved him enough. But she also saw that that was not of her doing. She had never known what it was to love enough—it was either too little or too much with her—and she held tighter to Suyin's hand as the pastor prayed for Grandma Yeh's meager sins to be forgiven her.

To her surprise again, Henry did not leave immediately but came up to say good-bye. She watched him watching Suyin, who opened her eyes wide when he took her hand and said, "I'm Henry, your father," and for the first time, Li An's tears appeared where everyone could see them.

Chester's departure was not unbearable. He had called often, each call more urgent than the rest. He was calling for Suyin, not for her, Li An reminded herself each time the receptionist said in her lilting English, "Mis-ter Ches-ter Brook-field, Mrs. Yeh."

She could have refused his calls, but something sad in her made her take them all. "It's too soon," she repeated. "Suyin isn't ready for more stress. You may think of her visit as a holiday, but it will be emotionally difficult."

She knew she was being wise, a good mother, yet at the same time, she wondered at her relief that she was right and he wrong. "There's nothing to be gained from another meeting. Of course I will tell her you are leaving. Of course if you wish to meet her again, if you come back to Singapore . . ."

She knew her sadness was also for Suyin, for whom Chester's love was already too late. Her daughter would have to count her blessings among women, for she had failed in one of the most important duties of a mother, which was to find a father for her child.

And yet, Suyin was meeting Henry every afternoon after school. She was calling him Father, and he seemed willing to take on the responsibility that Grandma Yeh had so much wished for; no, more—he seemed to have a tenderness for her.

It must have been an impulsive gesture on his part, Li An decided. Only a few months ago he had picked up a squalling baby and must have felt the heavy tick of a father's heart for the first time, and so it must have been easy to look at the tall skinny girl and say to her, also, "I am your father." This was what Grandma Yeh, his father's wife, had wanted him to say all these years, and with her death, he could finally say it.

Li An saw that her tears at the funeral had disturbed him. It would always be difficult for him to meet her. But Suyin was his father's wife's granddaughter, and, as Grandma Yeh told everyone, she was therefore Henry's daughter. Suyin was a backward family bond; but Henry, being now a good Chinese father, would not refuse that bond.

"So he has gone." Ellen's statement was also a question. She had knocked on the door late on Sunday to retrieve her date book, she explained, left by mistake on the kitchen table. They had not been able to talk about Chester or Henry or about anything significant since Grandma Yeh's death, for Suyin had been constantly present whenever Li An was home.

"Well, has he gone?" Ellen repeated. Too much, she feared, had been happening for her peace of mind. She had waited for Li An to get out of her doldrums, but she worried that the change in her, toward pensive melancholy—caused, she was certain, by Chester's reappearance—was permanent.

But Chester could not stay in Singapore forever. He would have to return to his real life in America, just as he did in 1969, and then they would be able to get on comfortably with their lives. Ellen did not have to tell Li An, standing by the door as if startled by her visit, all this. Li An knew her well enough to know that her abrupt question carried all these thoughts and more.

"Henry or Chester?"

"I know Henry left last week."

"This afternoon."

"Good. Soon Suyin will forget all the nonsense he has been putting in her head." She frowned at Li An's silence. "Don't you agree?"

"I'm not sure what ideas you mean precisely."

"Precisely, precisely," Ellen mimicked mockingly. "Suyin has talked to you about going away to New York."

"Well, no. We have talked about a two-week holiday with Chester."

"An eleven-year-old girl and a middle-aged American man."

"Ellen," she said warningly, her cheeks hot.

"All right, all I am saying is that you might as well tell the whole world that Chester is Suyin's father."

"To the whole world, Suyin's father is Henry."

"No, you know what I mean. You have her all confused. One father in Kuala Lumpur, one father in New York. It was better when she did not know about either of them. Now she has all these places, all these fathers who never wanted her to begin with. Why take them back into her life? What can she gain from such fathers?"

"It's Suyin who has to answer these questions, and there is no way on earth, godmother," Li An spoke slowly, retreating into the room, "that you or I can stop her from answering them the way she wants to."

They looked at each other perplexedly. Henry and Chester had left yet again, but they knew it was Suyin's leaving they were preparing themselves for.

"Well," Ellen said uncertainly, "perhaps you don't wish to stop her."

"No."

"You don't wish to stop these questions yourself."

"Whatever it is, I cannot stop myself."

"Well," Ellen began again, "I can stop myself."

Li An stood, silent, leaning against the bookshelf. In the face of such deep silence, Ellen, her face fallen, marched into the kitchen and went out again, her mouth drawn down for the night.

As the door closed, Li An listened to hear if their voices had wakened Suyin. No, Suyin was asleep, like her migraine, for once somnolent on a Sunday night. Imagining the slow regularity of her daughter's breathing, she followed the unwinding chain of her life: marriage, love, whatever she shared with Henry or Chester, might have ended, but the traces had not disappeared. Nothing she lived through was ever finally over. This thought struck her with a conviction that was oddly comforting.

She opened her old copy of *The Oxford Book of Modern Verse* that lay on the chair. She had taken the book from the shelf, from between some back issues of design magazines. When Ellen came through the door, Li An had hurriedly turned the book over, as if it were a piece of pornography she did not want to be found with. Already worn when she bought it from a secondhand bookshop, it was the only book she had kept with her from her student days. She had not picked it up since she left the university, not looked at the poems by Housman, Yeats, Hopkins, those poets the British lecturers had tested her on.

Wryly, she read aloud Hopkins's "The Leaden Echo and the Golden Echo." If she could recall the rhythm of Hopkins's crooked lines, sprung from who knows what hidden sources of his language, she would know she had not lost the past entirely. But her voice, echoing without a listener, it seemed to her, was ragged.

She remembered instead her anger at Chester when he had laughed at the poems. But Henry had also laughed with him. She had not thought this important then. Together, their mocking laughter, even now, subtly, was caught in the labyrinth of her inner ear; one of the many complicated memories that had set them apart from her. She knew it was not their laughter that mattered now or then.

She settled down to read the poems again, pulled in by a music of feelings that had remained set in print, even as the pages had yellowed and turned brittle. A muse of feelings she thought she had forgotten, more than words, more than poetry, returning to the spaces inside her body its silent and eloquent touch. For the moment, standing again before Suyin's bedroom door and listening to the golden echoes in her daughter's breathing, she did not ask for more.

AFTERWORD

~

Joss and Gold, Shirley Geok-lin Lim's first novel, is characterized by sensibilities that have distinguished her work as a poet, fiction writer, scholar, and autobiographer. Crafted and complex in style, engaging and thought-provoking in substance, the novel explores the possibilities for individual fulfillment in love, work, and family in a world in which the postfeminist, postcolonial, and multicultural have left indelible marks. In the process, it interrogates stereotypes of Asian women and their identities, and provides a provocative alternative to the Madame Butterfly myth.

Begun in 1979, *Joss and Gold* took over twenty years to complete. Its protracted status as a work in progress, and the revisions and rewriting that it must have undergone, indicate both an author whose competing commitments as an academic, a writer, activist, wife, and mother have interrupted the project, and one whose patience and tenacity have allowed the negotiation and development of narrative vision over time. The growing body of not only academic and scholarly works, but also creative and autobiographical writings by Lim suggests that the writing of *Joss and Gold* has been preceded as well as attended by the author's production of other writings and experience of lives lived. Lim's first book of poetry, *Crossing the Peninsula and Other Poems* (1980), won the 1980 Commonwealth Poetry Prize for the best first collection published in the British Commonwealth. Four collections of new and selected poems have followed: *No Man's Grove* (1985), *Modern Secrets* (1989), *Monsoon History* (1994), and *What the Fortune Teller Didn't Say* (1998). Lim's short fiction first appeared in *Another Country and Other Stories* (1982). Four stories were added to the first collection's fifteen in *Life's Mysteries: The Best of Shirley Lim* (1995), and five to the edition published in the United States as *Two Dreams: New and Selected Stories* (1997). The autobiographical *Among the White Moon Faces: An Asian American Memoir of Homelands* (1996), published in Singapore as *Among the White Moon Faces: Memoirs of a Nyonya Feminist*, won an American Book Award in 1996. With *Joss and Gold* finally published, Lim is working on a new collection of poems, *Passports*.

Three countries share the narrative territory of this international, cross-cultural novel, reflective of a world where air travel has made distant countries and their disparate cultures mere days apart (a characteristic made even more salient now by postcolonial globalization): Malaysia ("Book One: Crossing"), the United States ("Book Two: Circling"), Singapore ("Book Three: Landing"). Not coincidentally, all are countries where the author has lived. Malacca-born Lim grew up in Malaysia and studied English at the University of Malaya, leaving in 1969 to pursue graduate studies in the United States, where she eventually settled and, in 1980, became an American citizen. Though she has spent the greater part of her working life in the United States, Lim, now professor of English and women's studies (and former chair of women's studies) at the University of California, Santa Barbara, has siblings and relatives in Malaysia and Singapore, countries to which she regularly returns. Lim has held visiting academic appointments in Singapore and as chair professor of English at the University of Hong Kong (in 1999 through 2001).

We first meet Li An, Lim's protagonist, as a recent graduate of the University of Malaya and newly employed there as a tutor in English literature. The social and political backdrop is a multiracial, young, and developing country where issues of race, religion, identity, and nationalism are in ferment. In the lively exchanges of Li An and her Malay, Chinese, and Indian friends, the Malaysian chapters provide vignettes of evocative detail. Set against the Malaysians' debate and banter, Princeton-educated Chester Brookfield, a Peace Corps volunteer, is an outsider/sojourner. This tall and long-haired American puts the tomboyish Li An, already married to a diffident and dependable biogeneticist, Henry Yeh, a modern version of the Chinese mandarin, on the defensive. Li An's interest in Chester is largely founded on his exotic difference: unlike the relatively reserved English academics she has encountered in more formal surroundings, he is the transparently outspoken, loud-voiced, questioning American. Skeptical of the relevance or value of English literature except as a conduit for the promotion of British culture in a country which should have little use for it or its language, Chester is critically observant of the persistence of a colonial mentality despite political independence. Chester's accentuated Americanness is the probable result of a reaction to alien surroundings, or culture shock. Even as he learns to adapt to the country and makes friends, this woodworking-turned-English teacher finds himself comparing Malaysian history with American and the residuals of British colonialism with American democracy, to the detriment of the host country. Confused and alienated, he returns home before the end of his service.

After securing independence from Britain in 1957, Malaya had formed the Federation of Malaysia with Sabah, Sarawak, and Singapore in 1963 (Singapore however, left the Federation in 1965 to become a republic). Nineteen sixty-nine, the year in which the novel's first section is set, is invariably associated in Malaysian history with the racial riots of Kuala Lumpur, the federal capital, which started on 13 May. The riots followed general elections which saw opposition parties supported mainly by ethnically Chinese Malaysians make significant inroads into the political ground held by the Malay-led ruling alliance of distinct Malay, Chinese, and Indian parties. The events of 13 May 1969 confirmed the hegemony of race in Malaysian life and the tensions inherent in a multiracial and multi-religious country.

Lim's Malaysian chapters are alive with discussions of postcolonial issues such as identity formation, multiracialism, and what constitutes a "Malaysian." (Issues pertaining to the evolution of a national identity continue to be discussed and debated in Malaysia, and separately in Singapore.) But the real tensions in interracial relations are immediately demonstrated in the tragedy of 13 May 1969, when a mob breaks into Li An's father-in-law's house, destroys its contents, and kills him. (By coincidence, the writing of this afterword in March 2001 has been preceded by the outbreak of racial clashes—the first since 1969—between Malays and Indians living in several squatter settlements outside Kuala Lumpur. Six died and forty-eight were seriously wounded.)

No less dramatically, Lim also shows how the stubborn pressures of race are played out in the tragedy of Paroo, an Indian student, and Gina, who comes from a traditional Chinese family. In despair over a relationship hopelessly fraught with disapproval from both families, the two attempt to take their lives, and Gina dies.

The curfew imposed on May 13 to restore order forces Li An to spend the night in the house Chester shares with his Malay friends. As a result of this circumstantial encounter, Suyin, child of a single night's passion, is conceived and born to Li An, who is three months pregnant when an unknowing and uninformed Chester returns to America, where "Circling," the middle section of *Joss and Gold,* is set. It is eleven years later, in 1980, and Chester and Meryl Brookfield are settled in one of America's most affluent middle-class suburbs, Westchester County, New York. This second book surveys and delves into the social and marital life of Chester, now an academic teaching sociology and anthropology at a private college, and Meryl, his dynamic and ambitious Barnard-educated wife. Before their marriage, Meryl, still a student, had an abortion, with Chester's knowledge. Childless by choice, Meryl, wishing to guarantee continued freedom from conception and to have Chester share in the exercise of sexual responsibility, persuades him to have a vasectomy.

The panic Chester experienced when a Malaysian friend wrote to say that Li An's child is his had been momentary. Long-distance paternity was too remote a fact to become a distracting preoccupation. Now that he is unlikely to father a child, Chester becomes acutely curious about fatherhood. The conscious longing for paternity which the surgery catalyses furnishes Chester with the motive for returning to Southeast Asia, specifically to Singapore, ostensibly to conduct anthropological research, but really to locate Li An and her/his daughter.

Despite differences in culture and distances in geography, the two women in Chester's life are more alike than different. Both have had limited experience of fathers, and whatever exposure to fathers they have had has been less than affirmative. Li An's died when she was three; Meryl's left when she was ten. Both are emotionally detached from their mothers, who have remarried. And both are goal-oriented professional women. Meryl chooses career development over maternity, with its embrace of unpredictable children; Li An has found security on her own terms for herself and her daughter. Why does she become a mother, knowing—with what trepidation, one may surmise—that the baby is not Henry's, and that the Amerasian infant presumably would be visual proof of her guilt? Though Lim does not explicitly answer this question, it may be that Li An's own emotional need for a baby far outweighs her estimate of the consequences for her marriage and her daughter.

But why, as Suyin's godmother, Ellen, bluntly asks, does Chester seek the recovery of an accidental paternity which for twelve years has not affected him—and which the mother has never attempted to communicate to him? Despite the considerable lapse of time, Chester, prompted by self-interest rather than any chivalrous desire to own up to the past, returns to the region where his "Asian" past will bestow upon him fatherhood, an experience his American present and future deny. Ironically, this selfish and hitherto childless man becomes a supplicant before his ex-lover—now a putative benefactress, and a mother, divorcee, single parent, and successful career woman. Where previously Li An's "subject" status as a refugee in Chester's house empowered her American protector, the positions are reversed as they meet, in the novel's third and final section, on Li An's turf and on her terms.

It is apparent that in Lim's exploration of the changing identities of Asian women, stereotypes are challenged and displaced. Li An is no Madame Butterfly, abandoned by her western lover. Nor is she, as Chester's old teacher, Jason Kingston, has suggested, a typical would-be immigrant Asian woman who would use her child to compel from the father entry into the United States. She is too proud, independent, and successful for such a strategy. There is nothing Li An wants from Chester, or owes him. Rather, as a dutiful mother, she owes *her* daughter the right to meet and know her father. This pretty green-eyed, brown-haired Amerasian, whom Henry rejected after she was born and with whom Li An escaped to

Singapore for "big city tolerance and anonymity," has been raised by three women—her godmother, Grandma Yeh (Henry's father's second wife, who has accompanied Li An to Singapore), and her own mother. She now finds herself for the first time, at eleven, with not one but two fathers. The sudden death of the childless Grandma Yeh at Port Dickson's beach while on holiday in Malaysia makes Suyin beneficiary of her estate, and Henry her executor—at the same time that Chester is visiting Singapore for "research."

The presence of her ex-husband and ex-lover in Singapore, her sanctuary, forces upon Li An a reexamination not only of her past, but also of her relationship with her hitherto father-less daughter. It forces upon Suyin the possibility of owning a father (even two!) with Henry's presence at the funeral of Grandma Yeh and his assertion that he is her father, and Chester's appearance in Singapore and his unspoken invitation to regard him as one. While Li An has made a reputation for herself in the "stony paradise" of Singapore as the editor of a respected business bulletin and—except for one school reunion in Kuala Lumpur—has distanced herself from her Malaysian past, Suyin has lived under the protection of a tri-umvirate of women "who cooperated to make sure she never missed having a family"—even a father (227). In reopening the twelve years that Li An, now thirty-five, has intention-ally silenced, Henry and Chester, one Malaysian, the other American, create new possibilities for mother and daughter.

There is the prospect of security and respectability offered by Henry. Already, Suyin can see how his appearance at school as her acknowledged father puts an immediate end to the malicious insinuations and taunting about paternity she has long endured. He has become a familiar presence, visit-ing her and helping her with schoolwork. There is the prospect of the widening of her horizons, of spending time in New York with her unacknowledged, if intuitively known, bio-logical father. For Li An, too, an acknowledging rather than evading of her past—which turned a mistake into a scandal, then a necessary responsibility—may allow her to make peace with that past and open possibilities for the future.

As Li An herself has found her way from Penang to Kuala

Lumpur to Singapore, first to escape an uncaring stepfather and an indifferent mother, then to escape others' knowledge or speculation about Suyin's foreign father, so too is her daughter, on the brink of becoming a teenager, offered corresponding opportunities. The partial and intermittent presence of men in the novel as a whole, which suggests their uncompleted roles as husbands, lovers, or fathers, is complemented by acknowledgment of the need, as the third book, "Landing," suggests, for a father—too late for the mother, but perhaps not too late for the daughter. Knowing that he can never father a child with Meryl, for whom maternity is an option to be declined, Chester learns to be a father to the child he accidentally conceived and circumstantially recovered. Henry, who has just become a father from a second marriage, and whose surname Suyin bears, is now willing to substantiate that name in deed.

"Nothing she lived through was ever finally over. This thought struck her with a conviction that was oddly comforting" (265). Li An's reexamination of her Malaysian past in the concluding section of *Joss and Gold* is played out against a city-state driven more by economics and rationality than sentiment or sentimentality. Yet whatever its limitations and material priorities, Singapore has offered Li An and her chosen family of women an alternative life of security. Chester observes the "polished patina of success" on Li An, an independent woman whom adversity has taught strength (202). Unknown to him, there is something remaining of the old Li An—lover of English poetry—still. Though diminished, that literary past—exemplified by the *Oxford Book of Modern Verse* she has brought with her to Singapore—has not been relinquished. Indeed, Li An's encounters with the past she has been determined to bury returns her to the world of feelings and the music of words that so engaged her as a young woman in Malaysia.

Joss and Gold is a work of fiction, but like all works of this genre, it bears its individual stamp of truth and reality. In interweaving what is historically real with the imagined, in bringing the past into the present and future, and in combining the unpredictable with the ordered, Lim has brought to this

crafted work the resources and experience of a sensibility alive
to the humanly imperfect and surprising ways in which characters pursue, and are pursued by, that narrative—life.

Leong Liew Geok
National University of Singapore
March 2001

CPSIA information can be obtained
at www.ICGtesting.com
Printed in the USA
LVHW091056210220
647568LV00001B/7